Seeking Justice

Angela K. Crandall

Angelada books

ISBN-13: 978-0692073247

ISBN-10:0692073248

Kindle edition

ASIN:B07DSWZTPB

First Edition

Cover design by Angela K. Crandall

Special thanks to:

Friends and readers who helped me choose the book cover from my mock-ups for this novel. My husband for listening to me yell at my computer and everyone who made this book a reality.

Other books by this author:

Myth

Spirit Guide

Chapter 1

(Friday, April 9th)

(Starla)

I couldn't stop tossing and turning in my bed. It had been a week since the hearing took place. I kicked the covers off of myself, then sat up. Megan was probably snoring logs. She had no problem sleeping with the lights on. Me, I needed complete darkness. I'd considered shutting off the lights, but Mom complained I shouldn't take the chance. Suddenly pain filled my chest as emotions rose up from my throat. Tears formed threatening to fall from my eyes. No, I wouldn't cry. At least that horrible paper for Jones was completed. I'd passed math with a 2.5 barely making it. I guess it's a good thing I wasn't planning on being a doctor, scientist, or whatever. Lit, had been easy in comparison, a 4.0. Both of my parents were proud of me. Thank goodness they'd let me accelerate my classes. Maybe I could write for a Newspaper someday.

"Starla?"

I turned my head towards the voice, slid off of my bed and tiptoed to the door. Bit by bit I pushed it open and peered out into the hall. Megan stood in the entrance leading to her room wearing her pajama's. "Did you hear someone call my name?" I asked her.

"No, but that is weird. I thought I heard Nayla calling me? Can't sleep?"

"Nah, not at all. I'm waiting for my grade from Jones. Did Dad say anything about him to you? Trigger seemed to think he would help us. Jones was pretty freaked when he suggested it."

Megan shrugged leaning against her door.

"What time is it anyway?" I asked.

"Almost time to get up. Six a.m. to be exact. Do you want to go downstairs? We can make Mom and Dad breakfast. Either that or you could try going back to bed."

"Nah," I replied.

"What about that voice? Do you believe it was Nayla? I know she's planning to return home soon," Megan commented.

"It's possible. We're facing many dilemma's and questions left unanswered. Trigger's trapped, but somehow on occasions manages to visit us. Do you expect we'll have to free him before he assists us with the next mission? Any thoughts on coming with us?"

"Yes, I'm not sure mom's prepared. I'm not even in high school yet. It's kind of young to be starting Buffy missions," she smirked.

I choked as my eyes began to fill with tears, then reversed the waterfalls.

"Am I making you sentimental, Sis?"

"Don't, let's go make breakfast. Later I'm going to see Cal out at the cabin. Nayla's meeting us there."

"Alright, let me get dressed. See you downstairs in fifteen? Some of us still have classes," she reminded me.

"Okay," I answered, turning away from her.

"Starla?"

The voices, again? What was this? I stepped forward further into the hallway looking for any signs of life or shadows. I stopped then closed my eyes. "I am not going crazy. It's just stress from everything that's happened," I whispered.

"You're not going crazy. It's Amare. We need to talk."

A fluid figure resembling a fox sat in the entryway to my room. Cautiously I moved toward it. I'd only seen Amare a few times. I couldn't tell if it was her as she didn't appear to have any markings that differed from any other foxes.

"I know, I'm rather plain," she said. Then turned and trotted into my room. I followed, shutting the door behind me.

"Is anything wrong? I told Megan I'd meet her downstairs soon."

"Be careful. I've tried to keep my distance these past few weeks. It was important to allow you to explore your heritage without interruption. At this time, it's necessary I step in to guide you. Trigger's already contacted me. I've spoken with Nayla. You're meeting today?"

"Yes, later with Cal. I need to get everybody together soon. Molly and Jenson must meet her. I have to speak with Maine. That's Moll's sort of girlfriend. Star plans on working with her concerning the study of Wicca."

"Have you used the cards at all?" asked Amare.

"The Tarot?"

"Yes, that," she replied.

"Only once with mom. I'd planned on pulling them out to do a reading for Megan. Why?"

"If you're able, do a self-reading. Ask a question regarding Trigger, the clan, anything on your mind."

"Um, is that all?" I asked.

"I'll be around," she said, turning to go. Wisps of vapor rose from her body. Then she was gone.

3

"Did all spirit guides disappear in a similar matter? Wisps of vapor, evaporation, eh? I hurried over to the chair near my dresser grabbing the clothes off of it. Jeans, and my long sleeve green thick shirt. It was supposed to be in the forties today, heat wave!

I took my purse off of the chair near the door and tucked my cell phone into the pocket of my jeans. Then rushed out of my room, stopping at the top of the stairs. Already the smell of food wafted into my nose. Bacon! I grabbed the railing, then rushed down them, turned past the front entrance and entered the kitchen. Megan was at the table setting down bacon and a plate full of toast.

"Where were you? You said you'd help with breakfast."

"I know, I'm sorry. Amare came, my spirit-guide. She had a few updates," I answered, hanging my purse on the kitchen chair. Then realized she was wearing the new blue sweater mom had bought her.

Megan gave me a puzzled look.

"I know you're not familiar with her. Did you make coffee?"

"Yeah, even though I won't touch the stuff. Mom and Dad are still sleeping. I'm sure they'll be up shortly."

I headed over to the coffee maker, while Megan set the juice and creamer on the table. She pulled out a chair and sat down. After pouring my coffee, I joined her.

"How are you holding up? Is Dad taking you to school today? I could drive you if you want. Mom wouldn't mind. If I remember, she is off today."

"I'm alright. The kids at school think it's strange that I'm constantly examining my shadow. I know it can't hurt me. Still, a part of me keeps expecting it to detach itself from my body. Then come after me as if it's a horror film."

I smiled, then took a few sips of my coffee. Ugh! I grabbed the cream, added it, then the sugar. "And Chaz? Anything new there?"

"He's been pretty helpful saying whatever it is I'm worried about will pass. Keeps telling me he'll protect me. He's cute, but no superpowers." She grabbed a piece of bacon stuffing it into her mouth.

"Hey, girls. I see you made breakfast," said Dan. He stood in the entryway stretching and yawning.

"Could I drive Megan to school today? I need to visit Cal. Please?"

"I don't see why not," he answered, lowering his arms to his sides. Then moved towards the coffee pot.

I turned back to Megan. "I've been saving a bit of money aside from Denny's. I went to the bank the other day."

"What for?" asked Dan.

I looked up at my father. "I almost have enough to buy a decent used car. You and mom talked about me getting one."

My Dad picked up his coffee cup he'd filled. Then pulled out a seat next to Megan and began to fill up a plate. "Right, we did. I'll help you pick one out. Of course, it's ultimately your choice. I want to make sure you get something safe. Especially if..."

"What Dad? What is it?"

5

"I spoke with Mrs. Fretner. She doesn't think it's a good idea for Molly to be on her own. You know how she is so overprotective."

"So," I said, putting down my piece of toast and picked up my coffee to sip.

"I thought you both could share the apartment I'm trying to find occupants for. Then you'd be free to live underneath your own rules. I'm not trying to push you out. I just think it's time."

I set down the coffee I'd been sipping. "Molly and I aren't fighting, but..."

"But?"

"She's not exactly happy with me right now. I had to convince her that Maine will be kept safe even though, they're on the outs. It's confusing."

"Consider it, talk to Molly when you see her. Could you pick Megan up after school? If Nayla gives you trouble..."

"It's fine. Megan, I should get you to school. And Dad, thanks. You know, for saying you'd help me find a good used car." I pushed back my chair, grabbed my plate, and coffee cup then stood up to head to the sink. Once there, I placed them in it and turned around. Megan reached for her backpack on the floor as Fritz meandered out of the laundry room in search of scraps. He gave a short bark. I laughed, then patted him on the head, his dog food was on the counter. I took it and poured some into his bowl. Afterward, placing it back where it belonged.

"Come on Sis. I got your coat and purse, for you when you were feeding Fritz."

"Thanks," I said, taking them from her. I put on my coat and slung my purse over my shoulder while I headed for the door.

"You girls be safe! I'll see you tonight at dinner. Call if you'll be late, and take my car!" He threw the keys to me.

"Thanks, because?" I asked, catching them.

"I gave you permission, so use my car."

6

"Okay, bye Dad." I shot him a mischievous grin, shutting the door as Megan hurried out onto the stoop.

"Come on. I don't want to be late."

"You won't. I'll get you there on time," I answered, glancing at Fern shoveling the slushy snow. I waved at her as Megan brushed past me. Fern nodded, and I proceeded to jog to the car where Megan stood waiting. When I got there, I bent down unlocked the door, then climbed in sitting down to buckle up. Afterward, reaching over to unlock and open the passenger side door.

"What will you do while I'm in school all day?" asked Megan taking a seat. She slammed the door shut rather loudly.

"Cal and I are going to thrash out plans for the first half of the operation. Come up with ways to destroy The Shadows," I answered starting up the car.

"Could I help?"

"Well, you'll have to keep it top secret," I said, tossing my purse in the back seat. "Nobody and I mean no one can know what we're plotting." I scanned the complex for traffic before pulling out of the lot. The middle school was two blocks from the college I reminded myself drumming my fingers on the steering wheel.

"No problem. You do know how to get to Springville middle school, don't you?" Megan added, raising an eyebrow.

"I can handle it. If not you're my co-pilot."

"First of all, I'm not twelve anymore. Secondly, I'll start brainstorming at lunch. That is if Chaz doesn't ask me to sit with him."

"Alrighty then," I answered, turning the car towards our destination.

Chapter 2

I'd successfully dropped Megan off at school. Carol and Tasha had been there to greet her. Once she and her friends had taken off into the building, I'd called Cal on her cell to make sure she was home. We hadn't discussed a time to meet Nayla today. Could she trot over? It would be easier than driving to Hunters park I thought as I passed a few coffee joints but didn't stop. Willpower, Minder would have a pot on anyway if she was home. Pulling up to the log cabin, I saw her outside tinkering with her bike. I put the car in park, pulled the keys out of the ignition and hopped out.

"Hey there! How are you?" I asked, walking up to her.

"Good, this bike though. I've had a bit of trouble with the starter. I'm replacing it, almost done. Cal's inside. She said Nayla's on her way."

I snickered, "Cool."

"What are ya laughing about?"

"I was hoping she'd trek it out here. That way I wouldn't have to drive to Hunter's Park later. That's all," I said, stretching while I walked up the steps to the cabin.

"We're all connected. I keep telling Cal that. She thinks I'm nuts." Minder stood up, then wiped her paws off on an old torn cloth. "I'm just going to take this bike back into the shed for now. Let yourself inside. Cal's in the shower. You'd think she was prepping for a date. Then again, that skunk sure did scare her!"

"She got sprayed! When?" I asked, holding on to the door handle getting ready to go inside.

"Yesterday, we were out for a walk. Eva had come over to see her. Nuria's been staying at Rascals. Um, but you don't know that."

"Okay, mum's the word," I said. Then twisted back to the door, pulling it open. Skunk, I sure hope she got the smell out or at least covered it up a bit with perfume. Poor Cal!

The inside of the cabin was chilly. Minder must have opened the windows to air out the smell. Not a lot had changed. Cal's school books sat on the living room table. I pushed aside a few jackets lying on the couch to sit down. The smell wasn't too bad. It seemed like the fresh spring air had found its way here finally. I heard the door to Nuria's secret room slide open. Cal emerged out of it as she dried her wet hair with a towel.

"Sorry about the smell. I guess I'll need to be more careful. Yesterday on a walk I stepped off of the trail into a bush. I'd been watching an owl, tracking him using my binoculars. I got rather involved in his flying, and tree hopping," she said, laying her towel on a chair.

"Yeah, Minder told me. I'm sure it sucked for you, but it is funny. Ah, so um Nayla should be here any minute. How are you?" I asked.

"Alright," she answered, sitting down next to me. "Um, did Nayla give you a week off too?"

"She did. I caught up on college stuff. Jenson and I managed to go out for pizza. Molly hasn't contacted me since the meeting. I've thought about calling her. I know I should," I replied, turning my head to look out the back window. A fawn stopped to nibble on some grass. Cal placed her hand on my shoulder, and I turned back to her.

"Hey, why don't you take me to meet them? You can use me as an excuse. I didn't get a chance to say hi at the hearing."

"Sure, I have to get a hold of Maine anyway. I don't have her number."

"The girl who's practicing Wicca? You and Molly, need to smooth that over," she replied. Then stood up from the couch as the front door swung open. Nayla trotted into the living room while Minder closed the door behind them. I watched her head to the back of the room towards the coffee pot.

"Ladies, I hope you've enjoyed your time off. I wish I could offer you more. Starla, Dan told me you'd finished the semester. Thursday was your last day?"

"Yes," I answered, then stood up from the sofa. "How are Lance and Shellena? Are they keeping the Bandits in line? What's the plan of action?" I asked.

"Sit down. I'll explain a few things," Nayla replied.

Cal and I situated ourselves back on the couch while Nayla sat on her hind legs in front of the coffee table. I wasn't sure what to expect Would she disappear, before the mission?

"Your process of becoming a guardian is near completion. There's one more test I want to give you before I go. Shellena and Lance are going to help with this for your protection, should something go wrong."

"What is it? Does my mom know?" I asked.

"She'd certainly freak out. She can't know, trust me. If we pull this off, you and Cal will be able to protect yourselves from these shadows. Afterward, we should be capable of determining their weakness. We have to uncover what drives them before we go to Grandville."

"So what's the plan exactly?" asked Cal sitting on the edge of the couch.

"Remember when you both linked you emitted an electric current that pushed Tri and me away. You might be able to repel The Shadows. We need to find out. The only problem is they have no physical form."

"Okay, what then? They'll still exist. If they can enter our physical bodies what other powers do they possess? Starla and I might be able to keep them at bay, away from ourselves, but what about everyone else joining us?" questioned Cal.

Nayla began her pacing. I glanced back at Minder preparing coffee for us. She filled a small bowl of water and placed it on the table for Nayla; she didn't drink coffee.

"Nayla, for goodness sakes, stop that pacing. I've got coffee on for the girls and me. Perhaps you'd like some water?" she asked, pointing to the bowl.

"I suppose, girls," said Nayla, raising her eyebrows.

Cal and I stood up and moseyed over to the table to sit down. Minder had made my coffee as I liked it. She turned to a cupboard, taking out a box of cookies. She put them on the table as she sat down. I grabbed a few out of the box, then passed them to Cal.

"Nayla. Now, Shellena and Lance have been observing the phantoms. They've taken notes. Tri is part of us again. We shouldn't keep this from her," Minder stated.

"I agree. My mom should be there," I added between nibbles of cookie and coffee sips.

Nayla took a few long drinks of the water set before her before replying. I watched her lick the excess water from her whiskers. She cleared her throat.

"Starla, I'm a fox, so I can't use the phone. I'd hate to buzz your mom via her fox print. It freaked her out last time. I'll have Ranger, Mike contact Dan, regarding this. I'd rather get in touch with her directly, but for now."

"That will work. In the meantime, what do you want Cal and me to do?" I asked.

"I'll permit you to meditate to contact Trigger. Please, by all means, take a crack at it. I haven't heard a peep since the hearing. I'm growing concerned. Also, connect with your friends. Molly needs to practice healing. I'd like Maine on board, and Jenson will need to meet with Lance. Oh, you should consider going to the gym to update yourself on self-defense. It's never too soon to renew your abilities outside of magic." Nayla hopped off of the chair. "I have to depart. Cavin and I need to mull over how and if we'll reveal to Jinx, what he did to Du-Vance. If I need you, I'll buzz you."

Nayla trotted to the door, lifted her paw up, and turned the doorknob letting herself out.

We sat in silence while I palmed my cell phone in my pocket. Should I call Jenson? I pulled it out flipping it open. It was only ten-fifteen. Would Minder let Cal out of her sight for once? Had she left Nuria's, or even been outside the clan territory since she'd been back?

"Hey, do you want more coffee? Or can I take this?" asked Minder interrupting my thoughts.

I looked up at Minder as she started to clear the table. "Yeah, sure," I said setting my cell on the table. A chilly wind flowed into the room, from an open window in the living area. I wrapped my arms around myself trying to get warm. I should have worn a heavier jacket.

"Are you going to call someone?" Cal asked, staring at the phone.

"I should get a hold of Jenson, then Molly and Maine. If they're not busy, you could come with me. I have to pick Megan up at three from the middle school. I could swing back here then, drop you off. What do you say, Minder? Will you let her out of her prison cell?" I joked.

Minder turned around from the makeshift sink she'd been using to wash out coffee cups. Then came to sit with us again at the table. Saying nothing, she perked her wolf-like ears up listening. After several minutes had passed, she responded to me.

"The sun's shining, the snows melting, and I haven't seen any shadows lurking about the forest. My wolf senses tell me the Trinity is out and about. A few of them are hunting, as I heard wolf feet, either that or a pact from these parts. I have to let go sometime. It might as well be now," she smirked. "Oh, and if you get a chance, set up a time to meet with Lance in the fitness center hut. Both of you, I don't think it would be a good idea to mix amongst humans. Maybe I'm paranoid."

"No, just cautious. Thanks," I replied, standing up. I grabbed my phone and dialed Jenson's number. It rang, but no one answered. He was probably with Owl. I ended the call, then dialed Molly. She picked up on the first ring.

13

"Hey, I'm at Cal's. Can we come over for a bit? I'm trying to get everyone back on track. I know we haven't talked since the trial. You're not still upset with me. Are you?" I asked, watching as Cal raced to Minder. She hugged her. Then grabbed her coat off of the sofa in the living room.

"No, I've had other things going on. Did you turn in your paper for Jones?"

"Yeah, but no grade yet. We met with Nayla today. She said she'd like you to work on healing. Cal and I've been ordered to improve our self-defense skills. Maine is she around?"

"No, she's at some Wicca group right now. Mom and Dad started counseling. Come over, bring Cal, we'll talk more then."

"All right, but don't cringe when we walk in the door. Cal got sprayed by a skunk. The smell isn't too bad. She took a bath in tomato juice."

"Will do, drive safe, and I'll see you soon," Molly replied. I ended the call. Afterward, stuffing the phone back into my pocket.

"Do I really, smell okay? I don't want to make a bad first impression," said Cal, holding open the front door.

"Cal, don't worry so much. We can sit outside on the porch at her house if you want," I joked as we left. Minder gave us a slight wave, then closed the door.

Chapter 3

I squinted to see the road ahead of us as the sunlight flickered through the gaps between the trees. Where was my super fox sight? I leaned towards the windshield and when that didn't help sat up a bit straighter in the driver's seat. Eventually, the brightness subsided.

"What happened to Denny's? Are you still there?" asked Cal from the passenger's seat.

"I didn't quit, but I'm taking some time off. I don't know if Don, my manager knows what's happening or not. Only that Dad told him we had family business to take care of. Any word from your Dad?"

Cal pulled her legs up onto the seat and moved them closer to her. She leaned forward, placing her head on her knees.

"Did something happen to him?" I asked, turning right onto the main road leading into town.

"My mom told me he left us. I didn't want to bring it up. Nuria says I should talk about it," she mumbled. Cal released her hold on her legs, placing them back on the floor of the car. "I know I'm not little anymore. The last time I saw him, I was. The day before I got lost in the woods... I mean taken. Maybe he found it too difficult to say goodbye. It's hurtful and wrong. I'm his flesh and blood even if he can't accept what my mother and I are."

I took my right hand off of the steering wheel and lightly patted her on the back. I wasn't sure how to comfort her otherwise.

"I'll be Okay. The mission will take my mind off of family troubles. Besides, I'm out of the cabin, on an adventure, meeting new people. Best of all, I'm free. Almost, anyway."

I smiled at my friend, remembering what Megan had said after the trial. I'd have to involve her in training, take her to the gym with us.

"Everything okay with you?" asked Cal.

"Yeah, I'm contemplating whether I can convince mom to allow Megan to train with us."

"She's terribly overprotective. Look at Minder though, with me. She isn't even my mother. Although I believe she has taken over the role."

"Do you ever see Eva?" I asked, pulling into Molly's driveway.

"Yeah, most of the time she's home given that Nuria's been spending a lot of her time at Rascals. Love will do that to you. You look as if you have it together with Jenson."

"Well, I still live at home under my parent's rules. Besides, I'm not entirely fearless when it comes to taking our relationship further. I want to, but let's face it. We've only been dating for a month and a half. I'm not a fast girl. Jenson makes my heart beat, gives me butterfly tingles. That's a sure thing," I confessed, parking the car. Then reached into the back seat to get my purse I'd left there. We weren't in the woods anymore.

Molly opened the front door, motioning for us to come inside. I could tell she hadn't had time to do much with her hair. It was in braids and pinned in the back. She'd been keeping up with the hippie style she now loved. She wore bell bottoms and a hippie sweater. It was probably straight out of her mom's closet.

"I called Jenson. He was out with Owl, but they'll be here shortly," she said, shutting it. "Do you want anything to drink? We have soda."

"What kind?" asked Cal as she examined the staircase leading up to the bedrooms. They were pretty cool.

"Orange, cola, and grape. Here, let me take your coats first." Cal awkwardly removed her handmade sweater coat and gave it to Molly.

"Starla?" she asked, holding Cal's coat.

I removed my jacket, handing it to her. After she'd hung them up on a nearby coat rack we followed her through the hall, and the living area into the kitchen.

"So, Soda?" she asked.

"I'll take grape of course. Cal?" I asked as I pulled out a seat at the table.

"Orange would be great! Ah, Do I smell okay?"

Molly walked over to the refrigerator. Then took out two orange sodas and one grape before replying. "Not bad for having been hit by a skunk," she answered, bringing them over to us. She pulled out a chair and sat down.

"I didn't even know it was right in front of me! I'd been scoping out this Horned Owl. Of course, I wasn't expecting to run into an animal. Minder wouldn't even come near me till I showered. I've showered three times, no four since yesterday!"

"That must have been awful. I'm not too woodsy," Molly remarked.

"True, but you've made several visits to Hunters Park with me," I reminded her.

"Best friends make sacrifices. It's been a learning experience. One, I am happy I've fallen into."

"Ah, Dad, he mentioned your mom is still reluctant to let you move into the apartment. Would you at least consider moving in with me? Tell her that if Maine comes over, she'll sleep in the living room," I suggested.

Cal's mouth dropped open. She popped the top of her can of Orange soda, took a long drink and set it down.

"You Okay, Cal?" I asked.

"Yeah, I thought that someday it would be us sharing a place. I know it's childish. We've been apart for a long time."

"It just means we have a lot of catching up to do. Right, Molly?" I asked, raising an eyebrow.

"That's right. Starla was saying a few weeks ago how devastated she was that you weren't able to attend the college dance with us. We were walking out of the beauty salon at the time."

"If you move into your new place before the Smackdown. I want to help decorate it. Um, I'm not sure how I'll measure up on the hip factor. I'd lend a hand though," said Cal.

"That's if my mom agrees to it," Molly admitted. She picked up her can of Orange soda to take a drink when several loud knocks echoed from the hall into the kitchen. She stopped and set the can back on the table. "That must be the guys. I'll go, let them in."

"Alright, we'll wait here. Do you want me to grab them soda's?" I asked.

"I'll get them on the way back in," she answered, sliding her chair back and stood up. I turned to Cal as she left.

"Do you have any plans once you've finished classes? I'm only curious if you've given it any thought?"

"Currently I'm focused on defeating The Shadows. Lance is supposed to be preparing the Bandits. Eva. My mom suggested I ought to assist Star in training the new kits. It sounds rewarding. There's also college if I so choose. I considered leaving again, but not right away."

"Yeah, it's probably best for now. At least until things settle," I answered, glancing at the doorway. Jenson and Owl looked exhausted. What was Rascal putting them through?

"Hey," said Jenson. He leaned into the kitchen with a silly grin on his face. I watched him run his hands through his brown hair, and they dropped to his sides causally.

"Hey, yourself. What's up?" I asked.

"After working on plans for the Spring art market, Rascal took us to the gym to train. We worked with Kali sticks. Afterward, he showed us a defense skill from Tao. It's called 'Kun Tao Bear Style.' You put your hands up to your head to protect it and kick your feet out at the person. I'm not sure how useful they will be against shadows. It seemed irrelevant; magic is our best resource.

Owl came up behind him and hit him on the shoulder. "No, but we did get our buts kicked. Didn't we bro! "

Jenson chuckled, "Somewhat, if you call it that."

Molly walked around the two standing in the doorway to the refrigerator. She pulled out two orange drinks and handed them each one. They meandered to the table, then sat down with us. It was the first time we'd all been in a room together since the trial. Everyone was staring straight at me.

"Cal and I met with Nayla today. She thinks we might be able to repel The Shadows. When we link, we give off an electric pulse propelling our enemies away from us. It doesn't kill them but sends em back by at least ten feet."

"They do not possess a solid form so it's difficult to believe it would affect them," Molly clarified.

"Well, Nayla wants us to take a crack at it. She didn't say when. One advantage of our ability might be the noise and or vibration created. What we'll need is a spotter. Someone with the skill to create a false distraction. A hologram, of sorts. I'm not sure it's possible. I've only seen it done in films," I admitted.

"The problem, we're facing is it would have to be something The Shadows desire. Something they want more than us," said Cal.

"How do we figure it out without pissing them off? That is unless their goal is to deliver us to the scientists," Jenson suggested.

"We can't let that happen. I'll get in touch with Maine. I'm not sure if she's learned anything fresh in such a short time. It's worth a shot. Starla, would Star be willing to meet with us?" asked Molly.

"It's a possibility. We'll need to set up a gathering. In the meantime, I'll try to do a tarot reading and attempt to connect with Trigger." I stood up getting ready to leave.

"Where are you going?" asked Jenson.

I walked up to him, then placed my arm on his shoulder. "Cal and I need to pick up Megan from school. If you want to stop by the apartment later, we'll continue this discussion," I added. Then pulled him close to me, leaning into him I gently kissed his lips. Slowly I turned back to my friends. "Molly, Owl, if you want to drop in."

"It's good, you both need time alone, but soon," said Molly.

Chapter 4

I slammed the car door shut, buckled up and started the engine. Cal put on her seat belt as I reached for the defrost button and turned it on full blast. It had begun to snow while we'd been visiting with the gang.

"Are you warm enough?"

"It is chilly, but the car will heat up," Cal reassured me.

"This morning it was almost forty degrees. Now it's back down to twenty. I'm trying to recall when my Dad said he wanted us home. We've got to contact Star regarding Maine. Fudge! I forgot to ask Molly for her digits again. I slumped back into the comfy car seat.

"You could go in there and ask."

I shook my head no. The windshield was nearly clear of ice. I hit the wipers making it worse. Then turned them off and waited for them to clear. Cal reached for the stereo turning it on as I pulled out of the driveway.

"Oldies?"

"Yep, it's Dad's favorite station. He's not into Alica Keys or Usher. I like this station, even if it's not from our era," I said settling into small talk. Cher sang about gypsies, tramps, and thieves while we passed several homes, including Jenson's. After a block or two, I turned onto the street where the middle school was. I parked along the side in the loading zone. Why did they call it that? No one was stocking up on children, or school supplies.

"Nice school. Does Megan like it?" asked Cal glancing at the large building. It had two stone lions in the front. They were pretty impressive.

"I guess, she's not fond of homework. Math is her favorite subject. I'd rather write a book report." I heard the bell ring from the top of the tower.

"That's their signal? How many schools have a bell tower?"

I shrugged. "It's old architecture."

The doors to the school opened and several students filtered outside most of them heading to parents cars or walking home.

"Have you had any new recollections concerning the scientists?" I asked Cal while I looked outside trying to spot Megan.

Cal fidgeted in her seat. "Somewhat. Nuria calls them nightmares. It's only recently, ever since the hearing. I can't seem to make out the faces. I only see blurs. There were two women both with dark hair. One's is black and the other maybe brown. The man's hair is red. I'm sure there's four of them all together. Another guy, but I can't say for sure. I can only confirm the one who has ties to the entity. It's the man with the red hair. I'm pretty sure."

"I thought you never had any contact with them? If the Bandits were planning an elimination why were they at the camp?"

"I know, it doesn't make sense. Unless I'm experiencing visions."

Megan appeared in front of Cal's passenger door. I leaned over her to roll the window down. It was stuck, so Cal pushed the door open.

"Are you coming home?" I asked.

"About that, Tasha wants me to go hang out. Hey, Cal. It's good to see you. Anything new?" asked Megan.

"Lots, but you seem like you've got plans," Cal answered.

"I called Dad, and he said it's fine. Tasha's mom will bring me home later." Megan pushed her backpack up further on her shoulder to keep it from falling.

"Okay, suit yourself. It gives Cal and me the opportunity to go visit Star."

Megan's eyes fell to the ground. She looked back up at me. "Sorry, I know I said I'd be there for clan stuff. I'll come to the next assembly."

"Okay, I'll tell Star you said hi. We've got prep work, before the journey. Although Trigger hasn't contacted me yet." I shivered, the cold air drifted into the car. "Now shut the door. I'll see you tonight. All right?"

"Okay, but don't diss me!" She slammed the door, then strutted off.

"Sisters, let me call my Dad, then we'll stop by the cabin before we go see Star. Is that okay?"

"Sounds like a plan."

Minder moved around in the back seat. She'd decided to tag along with us. When I'd asked about Nuria, Minder told me she'd left for Rascal's earlier in the evening. I pulled into the parking lot at Hunter's Park. Mike was milling about picking up a few beer cans. It looked like someone had a party. I parked the car, then got out. Minder and Cal trailed behind me.

"Hey, what happened? I thought there was no drinking allowed," I frowned. Afterward, pushing my keys into the pocket of my jeans.

"Tell that to the kids from out of town. How are you? I suppose you're on your way to see Cavin?" he asked, pulling his coat tightly around himself. The wind had picked up a bit.

"We're meeting with Star. Is Eva around?"

"I have no clue. Jones came by this morning on his run. Stopped by headquarters to let me know about the mess, said he would have helped had he not been in a hurry. He's discussing backup options to aid in the operation. He's got a few people interested and was on his way to talk about it with Cavin."

I nodded to him, "This last week I was out of the loop. No one contacted me."

"Nayla administered individual guidelines. Why? Have you seen her recently?"

"Yeah, she stopped by to debate some things with the girls this morning," Minder interrupted.

"Well, she must be ready to get everyone on track. I've got to finish up here I'll see you later."

Ranger, Mike turned around. Then continued picking up cans. Cal and Minder moved ahead, and I followed them to the clearing leading to the huts.

"Hey, Starla. Over here!"

Shellena and Lance stood next to a tall mound of snow. As I stepped closer, to them, I could see it was a snow-fox.

"Are you two, actually having fun? What is this? I thought we weren't to bring any attention to ourselves?" asked Minder.

Lance shrugged, "Kaya has a meeting planned for the kits in the dining hall later. It's a small party for Bitsy. Nothing fancy. She's graduated from survival training."

"It's a nice touch. Is Star around?"

"She and Eva are in the kitchen working on the goodies for the party. You might catch them if you hurry."

"Thanks," I said. Cal nodded to them.

"Girls, you can stay for the party if you like. How's Dan?"

"Good, he's relaxed into being home. But I'm anxious to talk to Trigger. We need to find out how to get him un-tethered. We can't go after the scientists til we do. In order, to do that we have to rid ourselves of these shadows. The sun goddess won't stay forever," I reminded them.

"Is that Maine girl going to help?"

"That's why I'm seeing Star. Maine could use a guide. She's studying Wicca. Since Star is a Shamen, I thought she could give her some advice."

"Sure, kid!"

"Lance!" Shellena shouted, waving him to her.

"It's fine," I answered, walking up to the hut. Minder grabbed the door handle, pulled it open and let Cal and me in.

"It doesn't look right. Where are we?" I asked.

"Star made some magical modifications in case of intruders. She's taking precautions in case the scientists invade before we can go after them. Follow me."

We took a right, then a left, down two long halls. They were familiar, but the photos had been taken down. In their place were pictures of flowers, fields, and one of an old farmhouse with a meadow behind it.

"Where's the door?" asked Cal.

Minder nodded to her as we stopped at a bare wall. She pressed a small area in the partition that receded a tad, then pushed harder. Automatically it swung open, revealing the dining hall. Kaya, Star, and Eva were setting large bowls of pink punch on tables. They looked up and came over to greet us.

"It's so good to see you. Nayla spoke with you both I presume?" asked Eva.

"Yes, Mom," Cal answered. "I miss you. Minder and Nuria are great teachers, but they're not my mothers."

"I understand, I've certain obligations. Star, and I will attend the gatherings you'll be present for. I'll try to slip away tomorrow night. We'll go out to dinner at any place you'd like."

Cal relaxed, then reached out to hug Eva, who accepted her embrace.

"Now, what can we help you with?" asked Star.

"Would you assist me? I need to contact Maine. I'd like to bring her here. Or we could meet elsewhere. She might be able to calm Jinx before revealing the truth. Prepare him for the shock. Keeping it hidden for too long will only lengthen the issues we might encounter. Plus, the material Rascal is teaching Jenson and Owl. I don't see how it's going to be useful against these shadows. Maine could help with that. Unless you'd like me to learn some magic spells on my own," I suggested.

"Come sit. I'll bring out a bite to eat. How about carrots and hummus. I have cheese and dry crackers somewhere," Kaya commented, heading to the kitchen.

We pulled out chairs and sat down as Star poured our punch.

"I'm glad you came to me. Maine is essential. I understand at the hearing Molly didn't want her to be any part of this. It's scary, but she'll come around. Nayla talked to you concerning Molly brushing-up on her healing powers?"

"Yes, and about Cal and me attempting to repel The Shadows," I answered.

"Good, we're on track. Jones met with Cavin this morning. They discussed some semi-mortals like himself, joining us. They'll be present during your experiment with The Shadows. Power beyond belief. Jones describes them that way. He claims they're much better suited to defend us."

"Why not have them solve our issues if they're so great," Cal commented. She picked up her punch and took a sip.

"It drains them. Simple. Lance cannot spit out fireballs without needing to recharge. They may be amazing, but refueling is usually, needed no matter how strong one is." Star reminded us.

I nodded, "Shellena and Lance, freaked out once when I broke out my fox bark. Maybe it would affect The Shadows the same. Of course, Lance and Shellena would be right down on the floor with them," I admitted.

"It's an option. I'll make sure Nayla is aware. Contact me when you know, Maine's availability. I'm willing to meet as soon as possible. Find out how far she's delved into the craft. If I detect any hint of black magic..."

"She's not into that. Molly wouldn't hang out with anyone who abused power," I cut in.

"True, but she is an innocent and can be compelled. There's no reason not to be cautious," Star pressed.

The door to the kitchen swung shut, and Kaya walked over to the table. She set down the tray of assorted crackers, cheese, carrots, and hummus. Cal and I helped ourselves.

"What did I miss?" asked Kaya.

"Well, I am going to access Maine. I'll determine where she is at in her study of Wicca and whether she's a white or black witch. It's necessary to take safety measures."

"And this is happening when?" asked Kaya as she took a seat.

"As soon as Starla can set up a meeting for us."

"And the assessment of The Shadows?" asked Eva.

"That's up to Nayla. Starla, please get a hold of me no later than Sunday. The sun goddess will only hold us til Friday, April 16th. I'd like to be on the trail of the scientist well before then," Star replied.

"Sure thing. I'll meditate this evening to connect with Trigger. I should get home," I said, then stood remembering I was supposed to call my Dad.

"Cal, why don't you stay with us for a bit. I'll take you home later. If that is Okay with Minder," said Eva.

"Of course," Minder answered.

"Starla, be safe on your way out. Do you think you can manage?" asked Kaya.

I nodded, then pushed in my chair.

"I'll see you soon?" asked Cal.

"Yes, I'll call you when I find out what's going on with Maine. Molly, we'll be with me when I bring her," I added.

"Very well. Update, Tri, and Dan. I expect to see them as well," Star confirmed lifting an eyebrow.

"Yes, Ma'am," I said, saluting her. Then turned about face away from them and marched out the door military style. I could hear Cal chuckling. Then Kaya, and afterward Star, and Eva. I had to break the tension a bit.

Chapter 5

Cautiously I pulled into the parking lot of our complex. The snow had stopped, and it had begun to rain. I leaned back on the headrest for a minute. Then took a deep breath, unbuckled my safety belt, and pulled my legs up onto the seat. *Hadn't the Bandits said The Shadows came for them?* They wanted to control us, but their goal was to attack Sika's crew. I closed my eyes, put my hands in my lap, and concentrated. The hum of steady traffic gave me something to focus on. I wasn't comfortable enough to enter the wheat field. Gradually I projected the bulletproof box. Why had Nayla picked that image? I slowed my breathing attempting to lose the edginess. Then concentrated on Trigger in my mind, hoping to draw him to me. I sat there for a good fifteen minutes before opening my eyes.

The streetlights in the parking lot had turned themselves on. I felt for my purse around my midsection, took the keys out of the ignition and opened the car door. Stepping out, I noticed Jenson's red vehicle across the way. Perhaps that was why I hadn't received a phone call asking where I was. I shut the door behind me, and locked it, pocketing Dad's keys. As I walked towards our building, I pulled my cell out of my jean pocket, then flipped it open to see if I'd missed any calls. An unknown number popped up, *Maine?* I hit the call back button and placed the phone to my ear. After several rings, it went to voicemail. I left her a brief message, then stopped at the door to our apartment. Before taking out my keys, I reached for the door handle and found it unlocked. Swiftly I shimmied inside, then closed the door behind me.

"Hey, I'm home," I said, taking off my coat. I hung it on the rack along with my purse in the hall. The smell of fried rice and sweet and sour sauce drifted out of the kitchen into my nose. I turned around in the foyer, following the delicious scent.

"Starla, come eat! Jenson's here. I figured you got held up with Nayla or one of the clan members. Is everything Okay?" asked Dan.

"Yeah, it's fine. Have you contacted anyone about the operation? You mentioned getting those on board who worked Du-Vance's murder case," I said sauntering into the room. I pulled up a chair next to Jenson at the table and sat beside him. Mom was enjoying her Tofu Lowmein, no sign of Megan. She must still be out with Tasha.

"It's a no go. I thought they would be on board. According to my department head, this thing happens. People get frightened, they bail."

I nodded and took Jenson's hand in mine. He squeezed it, then let it go.

"Aren't you going to eat?" he asked me.

"It smells great, but I have news." My mother set down her fork she'd been using. I watched her take a long drink of water, then put the glass down.

"What did you find out from Nayla?" she asked.

"The goddess will not be able to protect us from The Shadows forever. You heard at the hearing. It will only last, two weeks. It means we must find a way to defeat them or keep them at bay using our clan's skills. Nayla believes Cal and I may be able to do this," I replied. Then waited for the big debate, my mother's protest, or her fear.

"Who's going to guard you as you're attempting this?" she asked, frowning. Then stabbed a piece of chicken with her fork.

"Shellena and Lance. Jones will be there too. I considered a distraction might aid us. Then remembered The Shadows were initially after the Bandits."

"I take it the plan is to try to repel them with the bond you and Cal hold. And if that doesn't work Nayla will have Shellena and Lance step in. In this situation, they would need to compel them to leave or attempt it anyway. We can only hope their power of submissions stronger than that of The Shadows."

Jenson moved his seat closer to mine.

"You're okay with this?" asked Dan.

Tri laughed nervously, "I'm a part of the clan now. There's a chance my psychic ability could identify what they fear. Nayla's right. If this works, it could offer us some security once the goddess is gone. It doesn't solve the predicament we're in, but it keeps them at bay. If we're traveling to Grandville soon, we must find their weakness. When we do if they pursue us, we'll be equipped to fight back."

I felt a weight lift off my shoulders, hearing my mother say that. I relaxed and helped myself to some fried rice with veggies. As I placed the container back in the middle of the table, my mother grabbed my hand.

"I'm here for you. Dad told me today; you might move in with Molly?"

I pulled my hand back setting it on my lap. Jenson sat up a little straighter in his seat.

"Yeah, if I can convince Molly to talk to her folks about it. It's convenient right by the college. Dad spoke to me about it this morning. I'd be closer to Hunter's Park too. I know you say you're on board with all this, are you?"

My Mom and Dad looked at one another. Mom blushed while dad got up clearing his dish from the table. My stomach grumbled. I picked up my fork and ate till I was full. The whole time Jenson kept quiet. What was with this boy? He always had something to say. I pushed my plate aside, then stood to take care of it.

"I got it. Why, don't you and Jenson go out for a bit," Dan suggested.

"Dad, I just got home. Where's Megan?" I asked.

"Ah, she's staying the night with Tasha. They're working on a book report. If not I'm sure they're hanging out with Chaz. I'm not too concerned. I spoke with her mother today," interrupted Tri.

"Oh," I answered.

"Starla, why don't we hang out upstairs. I brought my laptop if you want to watch a movie. Unless you'd like to rehash the rest of today's events with me," Jenson suggested.

"Both, I'd like to watch Buffy though. I almost have the whole series. I only need the last season. It came out recently. I would have bought it by now, but having a car would be better," I mused. Tri stood up and carried her plate over to the kitchen countertop. After setting it down, she gently placed her hand on my Dad's shoulder, then turned back to us.

"It's alright, go ahead," she said.

Jenson pushed the door to my room open. I reached in turning on the light. Then went over to the bookshelf and bent down to grab Season one of Buffy. It had been there a while. It wasn't as if I'd had time to catch up on a lot of television since I'd moved here. Plus, T.V.

Time even now as an adult was rare. If I moved out, I'd have to snag a used television and DVD player. My insides sang out with glee at the notion of such freedom. I stood up and gave Jenson a big smile. He'd set the laptop on the bed, turned it on, and it was ready to go.

"What? Get over here. We'll watch an episode," he answered, returning the grin.

I scurried over, handed him the box, and plopped down beside him. He pulled out the first DVD in the set, placed it in the disc drive, and shut it.

"Are you sure you can handle this?"

"It's late. I don't think we'll make it to the episode where Zander rejects Willow," I answered him. "It's soo sad! Then again Willow does meet Oz!"

"I thought you liked that Angel and Buffy are star-crossed lovers yet kind of together," he smirked, selecting episode one after the menu came up.

"Yes, but Zander is like a sad, adorable puppy dog. It's not easy to see him get hurt. And yes, I know it's only a show."

"Yes, but...."

"Jenson, snuggle and watch," I ordered.

We leaned back into the pillows on my bed. I inched closer until he placed his arm around me. Then lay my head against his chest. I sighed, allowing all thoughts of the clan to subside. Tomorrow I thought, drifting off as I stared at the computer screen.

Chapter 6

(Saturday, April 10th)

Prepare for your fears to arrive out of the darkness. When the light is no longer there, despair finds you. It takes hold of you, drawing you into infinite shadows. That voice? Where's it coming from? Where am I? I looked around only to find myself surrounded by a white mist. Step by step I moved forward. If there's no light how can Shadows exist? Shade and Sun work together to create them. It's why the goddess is shielding Hunter's Park. Where was I? Not in the field, on the edge of a road leading into Hunter's Park?

"Trigger? Are you here? Am I dreaming?" *I asked. Then turned in a circle like motion surveying the area. I wanted to see if there was anything but the haze before me. I had to be imagining this. What was the last thing I recalled? What had I been doing? I heard something running towards me. What the heck! I turned then stumbled backward in a frenzied motion. A tree stopped me from continuing my escape. I hit my back upon it and fell to the ground.*

"Starla, it's me." *Trigger stepped out from behind the tree.*

"Are you Okay? None of us have heard from you since the trial? How am I supposed to free you from entrapment? You told us that until that happens, we can't go to Grandville. Nayla wishes Cal and me, to use our connection to keep them at bay. It won't destroy them. I understand it's what needs to happen first?"

"Slow down, Nayla's idea is well thought out. It could work. However, the rest of your clan will need to prepare. As I was saying before I located you, these Shadows prey upon fear. Once they get inside you, they'll use nightmares against you. The group *must be psychologically strong to fight it. You must distinguish the illusions created to manipulate you. They can project your fear outside of you or put it in you. I'm not sure how the inside part works."*

"What about the scientists? Are they still in Grandville?"

"Yes," he answered, turning away.

"Do we battle The Shadows inside Hunters Park, then travel to Grandville?"

"It's one option, not the only one nevertheless...."

I stood up quickly intending to follow him. Unexpectedly, he pushed his feet into the dirt, struggling against an invisible pull. I watched as something dragged him away from me.

"Do what you think best! You're the guardian Starla! Go with your gut!"

Wham, I felt the floor beneath me then opened my eyes. I pushed myself up into a sitting position. Had I fallen asleep in bed with Jenson watching Buffy? Carefully, I stood up, turning to look. The laptop sat on the edge of my double bed. Thank goodness it hadn't fallen off with me! Jenson laid right smack in the middle of it. I leaned over and touched his arm.

"Jenson wake up!" I said, shaking him.

"Whoa... What is going on?" he asked. Appearing startled he rubbed his sleepy eyes.

"Last night we fell asleep together! Jenson, you've been here all night. I'm surprised my mother didn't check in on us. Heck, maybe she did," I answered, leaning against my nightstand.

Jenson sat up, stretching out his arms. Then returned them to his lap. A slight grin formed on his lips followed by a look of apprehension.

"Did did anything happen last night I need to know about?" he stammered.

"No," I said, blushing. At that moment I grabbed the pillow lying on the bed and flung it towards him as I walked over to my chest of drawers. I pulled open the top drawer and took out a pair of loose fitting jeans, after that a gray sweatshirt.

"I'm going to head downstairs, see what's for breakfast," he commented.

"You do that. I'll face the wrath of mom after my shower. I'll see you in fifteen," I replied.

The shower had felt fantastic! I sighed, remembering I'd missed most of Buffy last night. Meandering into the kitchen, I had no clue what time it was. I'd stuffed my cell in my jeans without even glancing at it.

"Hey, I'm glad to see you two are up," said my Dad. He set down his morning coffee he'd been sipping on the table.

"You're not upset," I asked as Jenson wordlessly ate his bacon beside him.

"No, these things happen. Anyway, your mother came to check on you. Said she had a bad feeling about something. When she saw you nestled together fully clothed, her concerns were laid to rest. Why don't you grab some coffee, take a seat?"

She must have turned off the computer last night. Unless, it had put, itself in sleep mode. I walked to the counter, grabbed a cup from the drain, and poured myself some coffee. I probably should fill Dad in on what happened this morning.

"There's cream and sugar on the table. I set you a plate next to Jenson," said Dad.

"Thanks," I answered, sitting down. After doctoring up my coffee, I cleared my throat.

"This morning I had a lucid dream where Trigger came to me. I found out more about these Shadows. They'll project our fears in order to manipulate us. It can be outside of us, or they place it in our minds. Trigger isn't sure how they push them within us. He said one choice is to stay here and fight them in Hunter's Park. The alternative is to travel to Grandville. Afterward, we'd eliminate The Shadows gaining access to infiltrate the Scientists."

"We'll have to make a decision soon," Dan replied.

"I'm positive Cavin, and the others will facilitate that. I'll need Nayla to set a date for our experiment."

"Agreed," he answered, wiping his face with a napkin. "Nayla spoke with me briefly yesterday when I stopped by to pay Ranger, Mike a visit. I hiked to the Park about an hour after you'd left to take Megan to school. Mom will want to be there. As far as Maine is concerned. I haven't done any investigating on her background. Have you spoken to Star?"

"Yes, and Molly. She's interested in meeting Maine. There's a lot to do, and it's rather overwhelming," I admitted.

"I bet, all Rascal has been implementing are fighting stances. How come you didn't tell me about Trigger when you first woke up?" asked Jenson.

"I was shocked I'd fallen asleep with you last night. I wasn't expecting to plunge to the floor. Then I got up to see my boyfriend sleeping in my bed. Nice surprise, but startling!"

"You fell on the floor?" asked Dad.

"Yeah, it woke me up out of a vivid dream. Trigger was pulled away from me by whatever's holding him hostage, in all likelihood a shadow."

"What's everyone jawing about?" My mom asked, peering into the kitchen.

"The clan, and Nayla's plan to repel The Shadows. Trigger says we need to be cautious. They'll use our fears against us," Dan blurted.

"When did you speak to Trigger?" Tri asked raising an eyebrow.

"Starla did this morning, followed by a rude awakening on her bedroom floor," he chuckled.

"I'm sorry to hear this vision got you so worked up. I imagine you were going to fill me in on this eventually?" Tri asked.

"Of course. I was worried, you'd be upset that Jenson fell asleep with me last night," I squeaked.

"That? I'm happy you're both comfortable here, you're adults. At a snail's pace, I realize this, but I still have rules here. Now, fill me in on everything," Tri replied.

Chapter 7

"It seems like your mom's done a 180 since this clan thing," said Jenson. We were sitting outside the apartment on the stoop. I'd already called Molly, hoping to get together with her and Maine.

"A smidgen," I replied, laying my head on his shoulder. My tarot cards tucked away safely in my purse. The snow had nearly disappeared overnight. "She's coming around, admitting I'm an adult. Year's ago, she'd have flipped finding me clothed with a boy in my room."

Jenson chuckled at that, "Should we get going? It's almost eleven O'clock. Maine and Molly should be at the park by now."

"Sure," I answered as he reached for my hand. I took it in mine, and we stood up together sloshing through the wet parking lot. The warm sun felt refreshing on my face. Glancing back, I spotted Fern outside shoveling away the slushy snow mess that covered her mini patio. She waved to me, and I waved back.

"Was that Fern?" asked Jenson.

"Yeah, it's good to be neighborly, keep them at bay. Ya know?"

"Of course," he said, stopping at his car. He opened the passenger's side door for me. I sat down, buckling up as he shut it. He got in and started the car.

"Are you ready, my lady?"

"As long as I can be the DJ for the whole ten minutes it takes to get there!"

He rolled his eyes, then pulled out of the parking area. I dialed in an eighties channel and sat back to unwind.

Jenson pulled into Hunter's Park while I slid my purse under the seat. It should be safe there. If we were going to the gym, it would get in the way. Why else would they want to meet here? So much for Megan training with us. I sighed, then sat up. Jenson turned into our regular parking spot.

"Hey, look! It's great to see the whole gang together. Minus Owl," I exclaimed. Cal, Molly, and Maine sat at a picnic table. It looked like they'd brought lunch. A basket sat on Maine's lap. I fumbled with my safety belt. Once it unlocked, I flung it backward, and it hit the window pane. I jerked aside slightly taken back. "Sorry about that."

"It's Okay, no damage done. I've done it before. Rascal wasn't happy when I did it, he had to replace the window," said Jenson.

"What were you trying to do?"

"Nothing, it was just old glass I guess," Jenson answered, pulling the keys out of the ignition. He put them on his belt loop, leaned over me, and pushed open the passenger door. "Are you all set? Maybe they brought food to grill. You never know," he shrugged.

"It's kind of cold for that, but it could be marvelous," I replied, grinning. Then got out of the car, careful not to slam the door. Jenson joined me taking my hand, and we sprinted towards the group. We stopped in front of the picnic table winded. I stood for a few minutes catching my breath.

"Yesterday, I met with Star. Kaya was there too. We discussed what must take place concerning The Shadows. Cal, is that why you're here? I recognize she sought in-depth information regarding you Maine." I said, nodding towards her.

"I filled them in," chirped Cal while she fidgeted with the ties on her hoodie. I was surprised she wasn't cold. It wasn't even 60 degrees out yet.

"Thanks, so why did you guys want to meet here?" Jenson asked.

"I thought it was a good day for a picnic. A bit chilly still, but Ranger, Mike set up this table for us. He hasn't put the others out yet. Then after maybe we could take a hike to the huts. Star and Kaya should be free today," Cal stated.

I looked at her, then at Maine and Molly. I shrugged at Jenson.

"I know how to use a phone book, and following yesterday's meeting I figured I'd take some initiative to bring everyone here," Cal quipped.

"Alright, but how are we going to grill? Do People usually bring their own? I don't see any at all. They're usually embedded in concrete," I argued.

Jenson started to laugh.

"What?" I asked.

"That they are, I plan on having them installed this year."

Was that Mike? I turned around to see him headed towards us in his park uniform.

"Lance and Shellena will be here soon. They have a gas grill for you to use. I wanted to chat with you about The Shadows. The Bandits seem to be behaving themselves for now." He acknowledged, sitting down at the table." Starla, and Jenson, why don't you take a seat? Kaya and Star are looking forward to meeting you, Maine. Since the Trial, we've been contemplating what to do about Jinx." Ranger, Mike scanned the perimeter of the park.

Jenson and I sat down then.

"I'm glad it's quiet today. It won't last long though. When summer hits, we'll have campers. The capacity of the park is 24 people."

"That's not many. Is it because the back lots protected?" asked Maine.

"Yes, and it's land the state doesn't want anyone hunting on. Thank goodness for that! If it got out that I was protecting a supernatural race." Mike stopped and shook his head, "Imagine if they shot Nayla. Nightmare. She's a rare fox. Cavin would never forgive me."

"Are you going to stay and eat with us?" asked Molly.

"Nah, but thanks for the offer. Starla, tell your Dad I said hi." He got up and waved goodbye as Shellena and Lance emerged from the forest.

"I can't believe Cavin doesn't think we're nuts out here cooking. After the trial, his seriousness, I thought we'd all be on lockdown," I said to Lance as he placed the hot dogs on the grill.

"That may be true. Yet, with the Sungoddess present, we're fairly secure. I've seen a few shadows surrounding the boundaries. You and Jenson Okay? They haven't come after you, have they?"

"No," I said, observing the others, mingling at the table. Lance placed a friendly hand on my back. Then after emptying the package of buns onto the grill with the other turned to face me.

"Kaya and Star have explained the preparation to us. An alarm bark might work. Just don't attempt it until after we know you can repel them via your link. If not, we won't be able to help you, when you're in trouble."

"Right," I answered.

"These will be done soon. I hope Cal informed Maine as to why she's here."

"Me too, she and Molly seem to be getting along alright," I said.

"They got into a spat recently?" asked Lance. He turned back to the grill, took off the hot buns, and put them on a plate. Then rotated the hot dogs.

"Yeah, Molly is old-fashioned, Maine not so much. On a positive note, it's brought out qualities in her that helped her to stand up for herself."

"You seem unsure," he commented.

"I am, but it's not my call. I trust Molly, so I try not to worry."

"Lance, have you got those dogs done yet! I've got the chips, potato salad, and macaroni ready. We need to sit down, thank the gods, and chow!" Shellena hollered, adjusting the sides dishes on the table.

"She's getting impatient, I see."

"Nothing unusual about that," Lance grumbled picking the tongs up off of the picnic table. He placed the hot dogs on the serving dish. Then sat down, and we bowed our heads in prayer.

"Goddess of light, and those surrounding us. Thank you for your wisdom, understanding, and protection. Please guide us while we prepare for our journey. Help us to seek assistance from one another, avoid arguments, and discover peace to overcome any adversary, amen."

"Well, said. Now can we eat?" Shellena muttered.

"Of course," he replied, handing her the plate of hot dogs.

"You guys crack me up," I chuckled. Then finished putting food on my plate. I took a few bites of my hot dog and noticed I hadn't anything to drink.

"I'm a bad hostess. I've got cans of soda somewhere in this basket." Maine reached in, rummaged around, and then took out several cans of grape soda handing us each one.

I popped the can open, then drank. "Thanks, now you know, why you're here, right?" I questioned.

"I filled her in," said Cal nudging Maine.

Molly blushed, then gazed at her. "You should have heard her. She about leaped out of her chair while we were on the phone with Cal."

"I can't help it. People are generally against the Wiccan practice. It isn't all dark, evil, and gloomy stuff. In addition to that I've gained Adventure, excitement, maybe even danger!"

"Oh, it will be dangerous. You may not be so excited when you see what we're up against," Lance added eyeballing me.

I stabbed my potato salad, added in some Mac N cheese, then stuffed it into my mouth. Yum! "Who made this? It's great!"

"Shellena did, Kaya made the potato salad," said Lance.

"Does everyone in the clan know how to cook?" asked Jenson.

"Nah, not everyone, most of us. Jenson, I need you and Owl to come to the fitness center with me. I heard you've been practicing some newfangled moves with Rascal. I'm not convinced it will do us any good."

"Me either. Starla's one step ahead of everybody. Trigger visited her this morning. One thing we'll need to master is overcoming our fears. The Shadows, use that to get inside you. Once they do that, they can tap into your body," said Jenson.

"Is that so?" asked Lance. He took a few large bites of his hot dog.

"It's how I interpreted Trigger's description. That's how they used Jinx. They froze him using what scared him the most. It made him vulnerable," I added.

"How was Jinx supposed to defend himself?" argued Maine.

"Instead of allowing the fear to paralyze him, he should have fought back. How I'm not certain. There's an episode in season one of Buffy where if you face your fear head-on. If you laugh at it and are not afraid of it, then it will disappear," I noted.

"Here we go again! You and Buffy. I know you love her and all, but it can't be that simple. If it is I'll hoot," said Lance.

Shellena hit him on the back hard.

"What! I'm only saying...."

"Yeah, but what if it works," Shellena grunted.

"It's alright." I pushed my plate aside. "If that doesn't work what about The Shadows fears? They must have them."

"If you and Cal can repel them, all we need is a spotter to shield one of us against an attack. We'll place this person in the line of fire to deflect the terror. If we could somehow mirror it back onto The Shadows, our fright might consume them. Use our fears against them, make them work for us."

"Reverse psychology?" I asked

"Fearology," joked Maine.

"Come on, let's wrap this up, and get to the huts. We could theorize all day. We're meeting Star and Kaya in the gym."

Chapter 8

Molly, Maine, and I traipsed through the forest. When I glimpsed back at Jenson, I noticed Shellena and Lance engaged in a deep conversation.

"So, has Nayla said anything to you about me gaining more control of my healing powers?" asked Molly.

"We haven't discussed it in depth. Have you considered practicing on a hurt animal or human?"

"Tell her about last week! It was a few days after the trial," Maine gushed.

"We were walking to her house, and I freaked out when out of nowhere I saw this tiny bird. He must have fallen out of his nest. It was trying to fly away, so I bent down to inspect it, and saw it's leg twisted."

"And?" I asked as we continued walking.

"I wasn't sure I should use my powers. If it was right, I didn't want it to die. Without thinking, I placed my hand on the injured leg, then took the strength from within myself and pushed it to the bird. I had to back up quick! It practically flew in my face. I suppose I scared it."

"Yeah, but it was rad! If I could do stuff like that using Wicca imagine the possibilities," said Maine.

I smiled at them. Jenson, Lance, and Shellena ran up to us. I grabbed Jenson's hand before he could whiz by me.

"Did you have a nice chat?"

"A plan of attack is more like it," Jenson replied.

"Did it have anything to do with the Bandits?" Molly asked.

"Not yet, they are the last instrument we'll access. If I'm correct, we won't utilize them til Grandville."

"Yes, but The Bandits might be a good way to draw them out. Do you sense we should fight The Shadows before leaving Hunter's Park?" I asked.

"Yes, they did come here after them first. Then us. The best choice is to fight in our territory. We'd have the advantage that's for sure. It may cause some conflicts with the neighbors in the surrounding area. Although Grandville contains residence also."

"So no matter what we're putting others lives at risk?" asked Maine.

"It appears that way," Lance answered.

"Is this it?" questioned Maine.

"Yes, it's just up here," he said, pointing. "We've got all kinds of equipment. I'm sure Star and Kaya set it up for us. Come along," said Lance.

When Lance opened the door to the hut, I expected to see an obstacle course. Instead, nothing had been brought out, nor moved. Star motioned for us to sit in the middle of the gym floor. Once seated, she addressed us.

"I'm glad you've arrived safely. There are several things we need to work on as a group, then as individuals. I'll pair a few of you up. Kaya and I are unsure of who you may be with on our journey. Today Cavin talked to us about rather we'll defeat The Shadows in our terrain or if it's best to attack in Grandville. We've had some disagreement over it. Jones assumes we should go to

Grandville while Cavin believes if we confront them here we'll have a straight shot to the scientists. I agree with Cavin. Kaya?"

"I do as well. Mostly due to the fact, our area would be left unguarded when the Sun goddess departs. If we fight them now, then we'll be free to explore Grandville without interruption while searching for the enemy."

"While that's a great observation Trigger told me it doesn't matter which we choose. If we're able to eliminate them, it's possible Trigger may be freed. If so then he'd be able to guide us to the Scientists. Thus benefiting us," I said.

Kaya nodded her head. "I see your point. Does anyone else hold strong perspectives on this proposal?"

Cal raised her hand as if she was in a school room.

"Go ahead, Cal."

"The best time to move forward will be during the experiment Nayla has planned. If it works as it's supposed to defeating them during it is a possibility. We should make the decision then and there only."

My friends and I nodded in agreement.

"I can't say I deviate there," said Star.

"Alright, let's move ahead to today's objective," said Kaya.

"Which is?" I asked.

"Maine, I want to work with you a bit on spells. Molly I'd like you to bond us. You are dating correct?" asked Star.

"Mmm hmm, yes."

"You'll make a good team. Molly has amazing internal strength. Come along."

They followed Star over to the far right corner of the gym. It had a small table with a few books on it. Kaya came and sat down beside the rest of us.

"We'll come together after they've mastered a few spells. It's important for Cal and Starla to practice repelling others. It will become a bit easier each time."

Where was Nayla? Didn't she want to be here for this? I stood up from my seat, stretched myself out, then looked at Cal then back at Kaya.

"Do we have to be in fox form for this? Because neither of us brought a change of clothes," I stated.

"It's not necessary. You'll remain in human form. Lance and Shellena, you're going to be the ones driven off. Jenson, you'll observe."

"Alrighty," Lance answered, saluting us.

Shellena stifled a laugh.

"We've got to remember what Nayla had us do! It's been a few weeks. Please give us a moment to recall it," I urged her.

"Very well then. I'll sit back, watch, and if need be, jump in," Kaya replied.

Cal and I sat facing one another. I placed my hands on my legs. I sure hoped this worked in human form.

"I'll draw you in with a current memory. Relax, it won't hurt. I'll try not to suffocate you," Cal said.

"You better not," I chided.

"Close your eyes, take a deep breath, and let go," Cal instructed me.

I did so, then cleared my mind to allow her thoughts to reach me. My brain felt fuzzy. Who was the guardian here? I sighed, rubbed my hands on my jeans, and tried to sense her soul's presence. Where was this recollection she was going to shove into me?

"Cal?" I mind-spoke to her.

"Shhh," she answered.

After a few seconds of static. Mentally, I wandered into projected memories. Cal meeting Fritz for the first time. Us, hanging out while she told me her father had disappeared, and a distorted image of myself grilling her about the Bandits. I felt myself gravitating towards her. This time, unlike the last offering myself up to unite. The warmth wasn't crushing. My skin tingled; adrenaline pumped throughout my body, we linked.

"Stand up, but do not break your focus," Kaya instructed.

In unison, we got up off the floor, mirroring one another.

"Good, you're controlling it. Nayla said, you buzzed, emitting vibrations without any ability to command who you repelled last time," Kaya added.

Shellena and Lance stared straight at us. Anger, flaring in unity.

"Now send out the pulse of vibrations!"

Electronic waves pulsated out of our bodies. The vibrations shook us. Still, we stood. It was in a way rhythmic creating an intrinsic beat.

"Stay close to one another. No touching or you'll shock yourselves!" demanded Kaya. She motioned them to attack us. Rapidly they ran into our vicinity. Wham! It threw them back as we held onto our center.

"Again!" she shouted.

Shellena and Lance by now a bit bruised rushed us. One furry arm breached the barrier. I couldn't tell whom it belonged to. Cal and I quickened the pulse as the vibrations grew stronger generating heat. It wasn't throwing them back.

"I'm on fire. My arm is on fire!" Shellena shouted, slamming it on the floor trying to put out the flame.

"Lance, grab a wet towel!" screamed Kaya.

Cal and I fell to our knees. My body shook out of control while the power of our connection subsided. Sweat dripped from my forehead. I wiped it off lifting my head up to see Lance race to the back of the room. He grabbed a cloth off a nearby shelf and ran it under the drinking fountain. Then dashed back towards us skidding to a stop next to her. He held the wet towel on Shellena's arm. Then slowly lifted it off.

"She's a bit singe, but she'll live," he said.

"Thank you, Lance. At least it didn't burn her skin," Kaya observed.

Cal sat beside me stunned. I looked over at Maine and Molly with Star in the far corner. Why hadn't Molly come over to heal Shellena? Hadn't they heard anything that had happened? I shook my head. At that instant, I turned to Jenson currently beside me. He placed his hand on the small of my back.

"If you can't repel them, let's hope you can burn them," he smirked.

Kaya grinned in approval. Shellena stood up, heading towards Cal and me.

"I didn't mean to hurt you. I was only trying to keep you at bay," I stuttered backing up several feet.

"I'm aware of that. Nayla told us you'd only practiced once. Now we know you're capable of giving off heat. Of course, we won't know if it is useful until you employ it on our enemies."

"That's if they don't fill us with fear first," I admitted. Then turned my face to stare at the floor. Why did I feel beaten? Cal and I had a new magical power. I should be grateful. Instead, I wasn't sure we'd pull this off.

"Listen, you've helped us capture the Bandits. You saved me, and I have faith we can defeat The Shadows. How many mysteries, did you crack back in L.A.?" questioned Cal.

"A few, but nothing this extreme. Nor did I crush any mythical creatures," I said, rolling my eyes.

"It may be true, but now it's different, and so are you," said Cal.

I nudged her with my elbow playfully and stood up.

"Come on, let's go see what Maine and Molly have been up to," she suggested.

Star had several notebooks open on the table. A few of them detailed spells used amid herbs. One of the journals near contained a list of herbs used for medicinal purposes.

"I was just going over this list with the girls. I'd like everyone to familiarize themselves with these. I've made copies for everyone," said Star gesturing to the sheets on the table.

I took one, scanning the contents of the page.

Healing Herbs

1.) PATCHOULI: Reverses spells, peacefully removes troublemakers. Use in clairvoyance, divination. Use to manifest & draw money.

2.) PLANTAIN***Blood detoxifier for the treatment of poison ivy, snakebite, bee stings, mosquito bites, etc. Apply juice of crushed leaves to bites & stings. Reapply often, drink the brew of leaves made into tea, eat & chew on fresh leaves.

3.) SANDALWOOD: Use a poultice for bruises & minor contusions, reduces fever. For use in clairvoyance & protection spells, purification, meditation. Burned in rituals, aids in Magickal work, stimulates, aids in healing spells.

4.) SAGE: Use as an antiperspirant, healing of wounds. Aids digestion relieves muscle and joint pain. Gargle to heal sores of the mouth & gums. Healing to colds & flu, reduces fever, preservative. For use in spells for wisdom, healing, money, protection, longevity, powerful fumitory for a ritual.

5.) SKULLCAP: Tranquilizer & anti-insomniatic. Sedative (mild to moderate) Eases nervous tension, drug & alcohol withdrawal symptoms, eases menstrual syndrome. Use for fidelity, commitment. Relieves anxiety and promotes relaxation & peaceful feelings.

"This is a small list. One I imagine, will be effective for our needs. I'm preparing a packet of these herbs and a list of spells for their use. Only use these herbs as instructed and sparingly," Star advised.

I rolled my shoulders back, then looked up, from the list at Star. "What about Mugwort? Doesn't it have something to do with protection and strength in traveling? It's a consecrate divination tool and is used to add or boost power in scrying," I added.

"It is. However, I would like to start out with the basics. The list here could be longer. In fact, I encourage Maine to look further into this on her own. Please be cautious of using any plant or herb you're not familiar using. If you've any questions, write them down. Keep a notebook," she suggested.

"Thank you," said Maine.

"Well, our religions are both earth-based. We do share a few similar elements," Star acknowledged.

"Molly, how do you feel about this. Being Christian and all?" I pondered.

"As long as it's used for the right reasons. God wouldn't want people to suffer. He created the earth after all."

"Coexist, love, let be," Star commented.

I let out a sigh of relief. Friends arguing over beliefs could kill a relationship. I folded the list into a square, then placed it in my pocket.

"So when is our next meeting? I'd like to get this show on the road," I joked.

"Nayla will expect everyone here tomorrow. She had a meeting today with Mango. They're preparing mirage tricks to throw off The Shadows. Jones will bring his semi-mortals. Starla, as you know, you and Cal will attempt to repel them. Do you suppose Megan could tag along? She could stand with Jones. I'd like her to observe this," said Star.

"Okay, I'll let her know. Mom and Dad, won't be thrilled, but I think they'll understand," I reasoned.

"We'll have a large army on our side. It's a test after all unless anything out of the ordinary occurs. That's why I have Jones and his crew in attendance. Mike's staying at his station. This time of year we always seem to have someone wander into these parts. We can't have that right now."

Kaya stepped up to Star and pulled her aside, whispering something in her ear. Star nodded to her and rejoined us.

"I've got to go. Cavin needs me at the dining hall. I'll inform him of this. Kaya will end the meeting. Molly and Maine, you need to work on trust, connection. I should have those packets to you by tomorrow. Starla meditate tonight, read your Tarot, seek guidance," Star instructed.

"Okay," I groaned.

"Be prepared. Jenson, call Owl. I'm not sure why he wasn't here today. Rascal may have him cleaning the house, or perhaps he's with the tribe. Kaya, please put my books away. I'll see you later," she said. Then trotted out of the room.

"Is that it?" I asked, turning to Lance and Shellena.

"It's enough for today. Cal, Minder is waiting at home for you. Kaya will escort you there."

I saw Cal ready to protest. Shellena held up her hand.

"Even though nothing has occurred, we've got to be cautious. Listen to my bro."

Lance nodded at Shellena then spoke, "Eva's planning a meal tonight at the dining hall. Jones will be there. I suspect he and I will formulate a defense for our travels to Grandville. I'll inform you when a decisions made regarding departure."

"I feel somewhat secluded. You've always included me in these things. What the heck is going on?" I argued.

Lance breathed in deeply, then let out a long sigh as Shellena turned to face me.

"Cavin doesn't want any casualties of war. Death. To ensure this, he's meeting with those closest to him. You'll be brought up to date at a later time."

Molly and Maine gathered a few notebooks, and items Star had given them as Jenson took my hand in his.

"You okay?"

"Miffed, but Yeah. Let's wait for Maine and Molly." I touched his arm, and he drew me into a tight hug while Cal wandered over beside us. She gazed at Kaya putting Star's books, in the tote and strolled over to us.

"We'll assemble at the Rangers at eleven a.m. tomorrow. I should know then where Nayla needs us. There will be a brief meeting before. Take care and be safe," Kaya instructed us.

Chapter 9

After Molly, spoke with Kaya we headed out of the gym. Maine ran in front of us and pushed open the door, holding it for everyone as we departed. Intense sunlight radiated out from behind the trees. I shielded my eyes from it afterward gazing at Jenson. He stopped beside the hut, then pulled his cell out of his pocket holding it up to show me. Owl, he mouthed. I nodded to him, then continued walking the path to the community area of the park. Maine and Molly strolled hand in hand next to me.

"So how come you didn't come to my rescue when I burned Shellena?" I asked, kicking the slushy ground as I walked. My shoes were getting drenched, and muddy.

"Star wanted our attention on Wicca and Shamanism. I'm positive she would've had us step in if things became grim. Lance handled it well. I do feel guilty. I should have offered to heal her burn. Sorry about that."

I peered at Jenson gabbing away on the phone. Then turned to Maine who had taken a book out of her tote. She was flipping through the pages.

"Are you looking for something?" asked Molly.

"Not anything particular. I'm noting what Star said. That Shamanism is usually used to enter altered states to interact with a spirit world. You know versus my Wiccan Religion. I'm looking at the training and initiation I'll need to go through," she replied.

"So this is regarding your studies, not Star's beliefs?" I asked.

"Yes, she gave me various tools I'll need to aid us. I'm to familiarize myself with these items. After I've mastered the skill to practice them; we'll take the next step. Both of us will assist in curing Jinx. He'll require a mourning period. That won't pass on its own," she answered.

Jenson jogged up to me and placed his arm around my shoulders. I, in turn, put my arm around his midsection.

"I filled Owl in on everything! He was at a tribe meeting. Nothing major, but he did say April 16th is the Spring Market. Hopefully, all of this is taken care of by then. I told him if not I wouldn't be in attendance. Then asked him if he planned on being here tomorrow."

"And?" I asked.

"He'll be here. Molly, Maine, what did I miss?"

"For one, Star being a Shaman is a practice, not a religion. They seek altered states of consciousness to interact with the spirit world. It's found in many religions, for example, Native Americans and Eskimo-groups. It's off the hook! Right?" Maine asked.

"I guess, is that what your book says?" Jenson asked eyeing it.

"Yes, Star put this together for me," she said, holding it up for us to see. "It helps me decipher the differences between the Wiccan Religion and Shamanism. In a way I'm exploring both," she admitted.

"Will it be a lengthy process?" I pondered as we entered the picnic area. I spotted Ranger, Mike outside of his station.

"Hmm, not sure reading this I'm surprised Star wants my help. It says 'that in her practice they believe they can heal one's soul. It says they can treat ailments and illness by mending the soul and or alleviate traumas affecting the spirit or soul thus restoring it to a balance of wholeness.' Man, what does Star need me for?"

"Perhaps she cannot do it on her own," Molly offered.

I shrugged, it was beyond my ability to comprehend in this instance. "I've got to get home. Mom and Dad need to be filled on this. That is if Jones hasn't contacted my father yet. Molly, have you heard anything about our grade in his class?" I asked.

"Nothing, I checked the online database last night. It looks like he's behind in some of his other classes too."

I shook my head at that. "You really shouldn't hack into the system. They might catch you!"

"It wasn't me," she answered, pointing to Maine. She grinned at Molly, then closed her book, placing it inside the bag. We were nearly to the parking lot. Jenson muffled his laughter as he nestled his face into the side of my jacket.

"I'll see you guys at eleven a.m. tomorrow. I'll bring Molly," said Maine. They gave us a quick wave, then traipsed to the pink car.

"Here we are, back at your place," said Jenson. He'd pulled up to the rear of the building close to the apartment. I could see our outside door that led to the kitchen. I'd either have to run around to get to the front or hope it was left unlocked.

"You're not coming in?" I asked, bending down to retrieve my purse from underneath the seat. I set it on my lap, then took off my safety belt.

"Nah, I've got to meet with Owl. He wants to discuss a few things regarding the tribe. It won't take long. You'll call me later? Let me know how things are?"

"Duh," I said, as I tugged on his shirt. Then leaned forward, letting my forehead touch his. I looked him directly in his eyes for a minute. Afterward, tenderly planting a kiss on his soft lips Then, as I turned to go his hand brushed my shoulder.

"I was pretty freaked back there. You know, when you burned Shellena? I just didn't want to say anything. Be the overprotective boyfriend," he acknowledged.

A sly grin spread a crossed my face while I opened the car door. "You know me; I can take care of myself." I slapped him playfully on his shoulder with my other hand.

"True," he agreed.

"It is nice to know you care. So, Um. Thanks. I'll call you. Promise." I placed my purse on my shoulder and shut the door. Then stood outside it for a few minutes laying my hand on the passenger side window. Jenson put his hand on mine through the glass, and I turned away.

While I hobbled to our back door, the wind blew fiercely against me. I pushed forward as the branches of the bare trees swayed against the gray sky. I hadn't bothered to look at my phone or a clock. It had to be around three. If Megan was home, maybe I could talk with her about the gathering. Now at the door, I grabbed the handle, twisted it, and pulled. The wind blew it outward almost smacking me, but before I could get inside Fritz came barreling at me. Quickly I moved out of the way and bent down to take hold of him. Instead of taking off, he snuggled up to my ankles. I turned to take one last look in the parking lot. It was quiet except for Fern hollering at Earl. I sighed to myself as I stood up. Then led Fritz inside, pushing the door shut as I went.

"Megan! Are you home?"

Fritz ran to his empty food bowl. Hadn't anyone fed the poor dog today? I noticed the dishes from this morning, still in the sink. Mom didn't work today. Oh, well. They could have decided to go to a movie. I didn't think Dad would let her drag him to the shopping mall. I waited for a bit, and when Megan didn't answer, I filled up Fritz's food bowl with the bag left on the counter.

"There you go boy," I said, setting it down. Then marched upstairs to see if maybe Megan was in her room with her headphones on.

Once up the stairs, I tiptoed passed my room. A light shone into the hallway. Yep, Megan was probably up be bopping to her tunes. She didn't like to be bothered during her music meditations. Who could blame her? It was like me during a Buffy marathon! The door was ajar, so I pushed it open and entered without consent. She had her school books sprawled out on the bed. Math homework! Ugh...

"Hey, take off your headphones." When she didn't respond but could see me, I gestured for her to remove them.

"I'm sort of in the middle of an important Linear equation lesson. What's up?"

"Clan stuff. Can you make some room for me? I have news if you can pull yourself away from your math assignment," I quipped. She picked up the book, placed her paper in it, and pushed it off to the side.

"Okay, but you've got to read my Tarot cards. You keep promising." She crossed her arms, scooted against the headboard, and sulked.

"That's a great idea! Only if it has to do with what your role might be in the clan. Kaya wants you there with us tomorrow. She said you could stand by Jones. He's semi-mortal. If he can't protect you, I'm sure Lance would bust out his ability to coerce them."

"That would be fabulous!"

I sat down on the other side of the bed. "Yeah, it would be. Let me remind you; you're not twelve anymore. How's Chaz?"

"Good, Tasha and I were debating if he's worthy of me. Is that arrogant?"

"Not if he's done something immoral. I'm not talking; he has to follow religious norms. As long as he's not into anything evil-creepy," I shivered.

"No, he's not into anything like that," she answered. Then got up, shut the window, and slouched into the seat below it.

"Good, so where are Mom and Dad?"

"They went out to see a film. There's this old cinema somewhere around here. You know Mom. They're probably drooling over an old black and white classic."

"Yeah, the best one of all was 'Hush Hush Sweet Charlotte.'"

"I was younger than you, and who couldn't sleep for a week!"

"I remember. Anyway, do you want me to read your cards or what? They should be right here in my purse." I sat on my knees, lifted my back half up, and bent down to unzip my bag. After fighting with the zipper, I pulled them out and handed them to her.

"So I shuffle?"

"Yes, you shuffle. Can I give you a short, sweet reading, or do you believe The Celtic Cross holds the answers to your placement?" I asked.

"Simple and sweet first, then if we have time The Celtic Cross. Mom and Dad won't be home for another hour."

"Okay, get back on the bed then. We'll need room to set the cards down. Mom won't care. She'd be more freaked about us requiring your presence tomorrow. Besides, they allowed you in a makeshift courtroom full of monsters."

"Yeah. What type of crazy parents do we have anyway?" She asked, settling back down beside me on the bed.

I pointed to the cards, "Shuffle."

"Okay, Okay. I've got this."

"Now cut the deck in half and put one on top of the other. After that choose three cards. One will represent your past, present, and last your future. Please lay them from right to left."

"Like so?"

"Yep, that's it. Now turn over the first card," I instructed.

"**Ace of Pentacles**? A flower with a moon like a globe star and unicorns. So what does it mean?"

I pulled the tiny booklet out of the empty container and leafed through it. "Birth, this is the past, it represents your youth. Days of playfulness, happiness, and naivety. You have security within our family unit. No need for any worries for financial matters."

"That doesn't say a lot, but makes sense," she scoffed. Then turned over the next card revealing **The five of swords**.

"Oh, my! This represents the present. A warrior, that's you. You'll overcome enemies with friends by your side. There will be more waiting to bring you down, but it doesn't appear that they will succeed."

"So I must have a genius superpower! If not these cards know how to lie."

"Mom said they're used only as a guide. We can't take it at face value. Lance and Shellena have our backs. Jones wouldn't let anything happen to you. He's known Dad since, forever," I stressed. I leaned over and gave her hand a reassuring squeeze. "Do you want to keep going?"

"Why not. There's only one card left." Hastily she turned it over.

"**The Devil**? Am I going to die!" Megan bolted off of the bed. Then ran out of her room down the stairs before I could tell her it wasn't as it seemed. The card was reversed, which made it more favorable. The description read that you were more able to conquer weakness including addiction. There was a light at the end of the tunnel. You will make it out alive. Unfortunately, this card is creepy. My fearless Sister now was not so brave. I picked up the cards as they were careful not to mess them up. I'd need to make a note of this reading.

Chapter 10

I lay on my bed listening for any sounds of movement downstairs. After Megan wigged out, I'd gathered my things and left to hide in my room like a wuss. Of course, when Mom and Dad came home, I realized I'd have to face them. Kaya and Star wouldn't be too pleased if I didn't notify them of tomorrow's meeting. As I stared at the ceiling contemplating getting up, I heard the front door swing open downstairs.

"Mom! I think something might be after me," Megan squealed. I tried not to laugh as I listened to her chatter echoing up to my room. It wasn't funny, just tough for me. I thought since Megan was in middle school, she could handle it. Their voices became whispers. I waited with anticipation til I heard the staircase to our upper-level squeak with each step my mother took. Then prepared myself to give her an explanation the second she barged through my bedroom door.

"What did you do to your sister?" Mom asked, pushing the door to my room a jar. She took a few steps into my room, glancing around as if I was hiding something then looked back at me. "As soon as I came home, she was spouting on the subject of how the devils out to get her. She said you read her cards. What kind of reading did you give her?" Tri demanded.

I sat up, "Mom, sit down with me, please? I was trying to help. Kaya and Star requested her presence tomorrow. There's this meeting at the Ranger's station. Then I'm supposed to practice repelling The Shadows. If they hadn't been so adamant about her being there, I'd have never done a reading for her."

"That's not the point," she said, taking a seat. "Your sister's scared to death. I should let her sleep with you tonight."

"I'm not sure that wouldn't make her feel any better. She went racing out of the room before I could give her any explanation for the card." I slid over to my nightstand and took the notebook off of it handing it to my mom. "Read it. It's not so terrible. In fact, The Devil's reversed. Not that it's any less frightening of a card I'll admit."

Mom took it from me to read it over. She nodded her head from time to time. Then set it down on the bed.

"I'll talk with her. What else should I know about this gathering?"

"Jones will be there. He's bringing his semi-mortal friends with him. I'm irked he hasn't got my grade up yet. I'd like to know if I should sign up for classes next semester."

"I'm sure you did fine. Did Kaya, or Star ask about my ability to read minds?"

"Nada, nothing," I said, waving my hand in the air. "Maybe you could find a way to creep into a shadow. Not sure if it would do us any good." I shuddered.

"If Jones has my back, it may not be a bad idea. I had to tune out Fern the other day. I could hear her outside complaining to herself about spring not coming fast enough. My ability does have its downfalls," she said, getting up from the bed.

"At least it wasn't anything intimate… her and Earl, gross. Anyway, I'll help with dinner. I'm famished. Has Dad spoken to his landlord yet?" I got up off of the bed, grabbed the notebook and stuck it in my back pocket.

"Not that I know of," Tri answered as I shuffled to my closet to search for a sweater, then pulled the door open.

I looked through quite a few before I pulled out a light green sweater. Then took off my gray sweatshirt flinging it on a nearby chair. I pulled it over my head and around my torso as I inched towards the door. "I'm super surprised the landlord hasn't rented the place out. I wish Molly would talk to her folks," I complained.

My mom smiled at me, "Come on, we'll make dinner. Your Dad will be home soon. Megan can help. That way I can talk to her about the cards."

I nodded lingering near the doorway. Mom swiftly walked past me into the hall as I shut off the light in my bedroom. "Good, you can convince her there's nothing to be afraid of," I managed, peeking down the hallway to Megan's room. The light was off. She'd probably left to watch television.

When I got into the kitchen mom was looking for something in the cupboards. She'd already pulled out items for fajitas. I stood against the counter with my notebook in hand.

"Starla, can you pass me the package of tortillas? They might be in the bread box on the counter. I could have sworn I bought some yesterday."

"Okay, where's Megan?" I asked. Then set my notebook aside and began to rummage around.

"In the living area, are you looking?"

"Yes. Dad's not working, is he? On a Saturday?" I asked, spotting the bread box in the right-hand corner of the counter.

"He is, some kind of paperwork," she stated, taking a mixing bowl out of the cupboard above the counter. "He can't give me details, secret stuff something to do with a robbery," she disclosed setting the bowl down. "That's basically it. If I remember correctly, your Sister loves Mexican food." Tri grabbed a package of fajita mix and poured it into the bowl. "I could hear the television blaring on my way in here."

"Did you tell her to turn it down?" I asked, setting the flour tortillas next to her.

"Yes, she glared at me. I told her we'd talk about what happened at dinner. She rolled her eyes at me, so I gave her my best mom stare."

"Good for you. I'll set the table. Later, I'll try to pull Megs away from the PBS special she's engaged in."

Mom smiled at me as she took a package of mixed vegetables out of the freezer. I watched her add them to the bowl before retrieving the plates. I placed them on our table, then put on silverware, and plastic glasses. Afterward turning to look at the clock. Five O'clock on the dot Dad should be home soon. I swung around to face my mom.

"I'll go get Megan. See if I can pull her away from the tube," I added, raising my eyebrows.

"You do that, and I'll finish up here," she said, pulling out the tofu. Ugh! Every now, and then mom made a vegetarian dish. The tofu was my least favorite.

"Okay, no tofu for me! So gross, I can't believe you like it!" I exclaimed as if I were two. Then hurried into the hall. Without warning, the front door opened, and my Dad stepped into the foyer.

"Hey, how was your day? Did anything exciting happen?"

I smirked, "Plenty. I met with Kaya and Star. There's a gathering at 11 a.m. tomorrow. We'll meet everyone at Ranger, Mike's station. Oh, and about the apartment. I don't imagine we can put it off much longer. You said you had to find someone. Now, I'm going to try to rouse Megan from her T.V. Coma. I've got to get her back on my side after frightening her with tarot cards."

"What!?"

"Mom will enlighten you." I smiled mischievously, then moved down the hall and took a left while he entered the kitchen.

"Hey, come on we're going to eat," I said, staring into the living room. Megan stayed glued to her seat, eyeing the television. Step by step I inched towards her on the sofa. Glancing at the set, it appeared to be a documentary on Judy Garland. One of our all-time favorites. I lightheartedly punched her in the arm.

"Stop, I'm trying to watch this," she said crossing her arms. "Plus, I'm still mad at you."

"Why be angry at me? I didn't ask the cards to fall the way they did. You didn't even give me a chance to explain it."

"Okay, then," she said, turning to me. "Tell me what's so great about getting the devil card?"

I took a deep breath, then let out a sigh before continuing. "It's not great. Despite that, it means you're capable of defeating weakness as well as overcoming obstacles. There's a light, and the unicorn gathers strength to bring you out of this stagnant phase. Maybe this means you'll discover your ability soon."

"Unicorn?"

"Yes, Mom's deck features them. Anyhow, I was hoping you'd assist us tomorrow. Jones will have your back. He's got some semi-mortals helping. Besides, I don't imagine Lance would let anything happen to you. Shellena, she's cool too," I said, standing up from the sofa.

"Yeah, I wish. I'd love to smash those shadows for you. I'm not convinced, I'm as fearless as you'd like. But I did promise to be there for you."

"Girls, dinner!" Tri hollered.

"We'd better get in there. Make sure you watch out for Tofu. I told her not to put any in mine! You'd better hope she remembered, you hate it too," I chuckled as my sister narrowed her eyes and stuck out her tongue in disgust.

Megan and I exchanged secret sister smiles. Part of me worried about her. How would she do during the experiment? Especially since she hadn't had, any experiences prior. The Bandits were contained throughout the hearing. Here these monsters would be out in the open. Still, I needed her there. I pulled out my chair and sat down while Megan took a seat next to me. I eyed the tofu sitting in a separate dish. Well, we were both saved! Tortillas sat on our plates ready to be filled with food. In front of me was a can of cola with a side dish of pinto beans beside it. I helped myself to a bit of everything except the tofu.

"Megan, how was your day?" Dan asked.

"Uneventful til Starla got home. I finished my homework, then listened to some music. Why?"

My Dad shrugged as he took a bite of his fajita. A small piece of lettuce hung out of his mouth. He popped it back in, then finished chewing. I cracked open my cola and took a sip.

"What about the cards? Your mother was telling me you freaked out. Now you seem fine. That was quick, too quick."

"I guess, nothing has happened yet. I shouldn't have gotten upset with Starla for how the cards fell," she said, looking at me. "I jumped to conclusions. Usually, that's her job." She pointed to me.

I stifled a nervous laugh. Then started in on my pintos beans with cheese. Yum! Even being a tad anxious I still had my appetite. Maybe underneath it all, I was hiding my fear. A part of me hoped I wouldn't freeze in the middle of connecting with Cal. I finished my beans, then set down my spoon.

"Dad, did you talk to Cavin, or anyone today?" I asked. Then wiped my hands on the napkin beside me.

"Only work," he said, looking up from his plate of food. "It isn't anything for you to fret about. They have someone in custody now. I can't say who. You wouldn't know them. Now, regarding the clan Cavin trusts Kaya and Star. I'm certain he'll be standing beside Jones and his semi-mortals during this conducted experiment. Don't you think?" he asked, turning to my mom.

"That's Cavin. He likes to be in charge, but Kaya puts him in his place."

My mom had barely touched her tofu. I could tell she was uneasy. Had she been hiding it from me? I pushed aside my empty plate.

"Aren't you hungry mom?" I asked.

She forced a smile. Then took my Dad's hand in hers.

"Don't tell me we're going to have another sibling. Is that it?" I asked.

"Nothing of the sort," Dad answered.

"It's cool that I'm going to the meeting? Jones, Lance, and Shellena have my back. I trust Starla. Don't you?" Megan remarked.

"Obviously, we do. It's The Shadows. If things do not go as planned, remember Eva has guardianship over both of you."

"Mom, Dad, your acting like your going to die. Do you know something we don't? What do you mean?" I pressed.

My mom rolled her shoulders to ease some tension, then pushed her chair back and stood up at the table. Dad followed suit. I got up to clear the table, confused at what was happening.

"We're only telling you, in case we die protecting you. It's improbable, but it would be unfair to assume it will work out as planned."

"Would Kaya and Cavin put us in that kind of situation? Why would they let me do this if I could die? Is it our only choice?" I questioned, picking up the dishes.

"If it wasn't then they wouldn't be putting Shellena and Lance at risk. If chaos strikes, I'm sure they'll use their power of manipulation to control The Shadows. It's not something they mess with frequently."

"True," I admitted, getting ready to put the dishes in the sink. Megan reached out and took them from me.

"I'll take care of em' Sis."

"Thanks, ah do you mind if I go meditate? I should call on Trigger, or Amare, get some advice on all this? I haven't been filled in on the calculations of this trial run. If I can't reach them, perhaps Nayla will visit me," I added, turning to go.

"Starla, about the apartment..."

"Yeah, Dad?" I asked, turning back to him.

"If you'd like. I'll give my landlord notice on Monday. Molly's folks will come around," he said.

"And if not?"

"Mom and I can spot you till you go back to Denny's," he replied.

"Alright, but just till then. What about furniture? We'd have to make time to get everything set up. Currently, we're in the middle of seeking justice. How's it going to work?"

"Your Dad will sign the lease. We won't worry about the rest until The Shadows are eliminated. And we've taken care of the scientists. I'll help Megan with the dishes."

"Um, thank you. It's as if I'm being given leave to adulthood."

My mom chuckled as she got up and turned, walking to the sink. Megan had by now begun washing the plates. I felt a tad guilty for not joining in.

"Dad, I presume this makes up for all the time we lost, sort of," I stated.

"Not a chance. Nothing will make up for that, but I'm here now. I'll see you at nine a.m. for breakfast? If not Hunter's Park. Don't be late."

"Is that it?" I asked, raising an eyebrow.

"Yes, now go. Meditate, call Jenson. Do your thing."

I nodded to him, turned, and headed to my room.

Chapter 11

I'd opened my bedroom window to let in the cool breeze. It felt refreshing in my stuffy bedroom. After the trial, No one had said anything about the Trinity, or Crusaders. It hadn't crossed my mind until now. My speculation was they had either vacated the premises due to The Shadows or Nayla had them guarding the park. I turned away from the window where I'd been standing, then froze. Across from where I stood in the right-hand corner of my room a dark outline of something floated. I couldn't make out its form. Was it a shadow? When I'd come up to my bedroom, the sun hadn't yet set. Now it was barely visible. I moved closer to my bed. On the other side of it was a small lamp. I dove for it, then clicked it on glancing back at the corner. Nothing. I let out a sigh of relief. Without Cal, I was pretty powerless. I had crazy visions, I could use memories against enemies, but I had none of The Shadows. I laid back on the bed, taking in slow deep breaths. Then tried to recall some of the spells we'd learned before we went to Thunderhead Bay. Something about banishment, protection then paralysis. Yes! Megan could learn how to use it. I'd forgotten about it. Jenson had half-frozen Owl. Perhaps we'd be saved after all. I jumped up off the bed and grabbed my purse I'd slung over the chair. During the test tomorrow it could come in handy. I rummaged around in it for my phone. Then flipped it open to dial Jenson's number. He picked up after the first ring.

"Hey, what's up?"

"Crazy! There was a shadow in my room. I flipped out, lost it, nothing I'd learned in the past or present helped me. I dove for the light, turned it on, then it vanished! I'd come up to my room to meditate!" I blurted, meandering back over to my bed and plopped down on it sitting with my legs crossed.

"Calm down, you're alright, alive, and breathing," he reassured me.

"Of course, I am. Hey, do you remember when we trained for Thunderhead bay? The spells for protection, banishment, and paralysis?"

"Yeah, that's right. I half froze Owl. Are you beating yourself up for not trying to freeze it yourself?"

"Well, I didn't try to hurt it. I could have done something," I moaned.

"No, you saved yourself and gained insight into the impending combat. I'd come over, but Sage has been bugging me to play a round of Candy Land with her."

"You should. I miss that kid. She hasn't spilled the beans?"

"About you being a fox? No, she just keeps asking when you'll visit. I told her we have secret spy missions. I tell her snippets of tales. She enjoys them, and it keeps her entertained," he replied.

I laughed. "Alright, then. I'll permit you to travel through a land of chocolate bars. Try landing on the shortcut near Rainbow Trail. Me, I'm sleeping with the lights on tonight."

"Will do. I'm picking Owl up at ten thirty. Do you want a ride?"

"I should meet you there. When I remembered the Paralysis spell, I thought Megan would be safer if she could wield it. I'm not sure she'll be able to learn in one night. Or if she'll be interested, after what happened," I added.

"And that was?"

"I read her cards. The last one for the future was the devil reversed. She lost it and ran out of her room, but I was able to discuss it with her. I'm not sure she's ready for this."

"Take it up with her at the gathering," he suggested.

"Okay, night Jenson, hugs."

"Night, and if anything tries to get you scream. Nayla will be there, your dad, mom, Megan. I would be, but I'm here."

"Yeah. Well, as soon as I get the apartment it could change," I answered. Then hung up the phone before he could reply. I sighed and placed it on the nightstand.

After tidying up my room, I went to check on Megan. I stood near her door; hesitant then pushed it open little by little. She appeared to be sleeping peacefully. There was nothing, lurking anywhere inside. I glanced at her stuffed teddy bear she'd thrown on the floor. My eyes wandered over to a pile of dirty clothes lying in a corner. She'd better pick those up. Mom would have a fit. Gradually I backed up into the hall, then turned around to head to my room listening for any sounds or movements. Zilch, nothing, nada.

"Starla Araina?"

I stopped, it sounded like Trigger. Was it? The corridor was empty. I stood waiting for something to emerge.

"Follow me."

No, no, no. I mentality spoke back to it.

"Yes."

Trigger, Nayla, where are you? Amare?

A sudden gust of air hit me in my midsection slamming me against the wall. The back of my head hit it, and I stumbled forward. Before landing on the floor face first, something caught me, but my bottom still hit the floor hard. Ouch! Whatever it was, it had a solid form. I tried to move my lips to speak. I managed to croak out "Was that a Shadow?"

"Starla Ariana, it was Trigger. He was trying to cross over."

I looked up at Nayla stunned to see her several inches from me.

"Did you mean to kick the wind out of me!" I shouted.

Nayla paced back and forth. "No, Shh! You'll wake your sister. Trigger was coming to watch over Megan. I'm taking over till dawn," she answered.

"Why is she in danger? What do you know?" I demanded.

"Cavin came to me this evening rambling on about a breakthrough. It occurred a few hours after you left."

"Did he find a way to obliterate The Shadows, is it her?" I asked, peeking in at Megan.

"We don't know yet."

"I saw one in my room, then rushed to turn on the light. As soon as I did, it vanished."

Nayla nudged my hand. "You should get some rest. I've been preparing you for this. The guardian's role is to protect the clan. If your sister is the Key..."

"Key, no. If this ends like Buffy..."

"What are you going on about child? This isn't a television show," she scolded me.

"Okay. I'll go. Keep Megan safe, and you better enlighten Tri and Dan in the morning," I scoffed. Then gave her an irritated look, but softly patted her on the head before turning to go.

Chapter 12

(Sunday, April 11th)

I ran my hands along the covers surrounding me, then reached up to rub the sleep from my eyes as I listened to the birds chirping outside. Sunshine streamed into my room from the window. I sat up and noticed the globe-light on my ceiling still lit. Then chuckled to myself remembering, what I'd told Jenson. Anything that had riled me up last night was long gone. My sleep had been dreamless. After Nayla told me she'd watch over Megan, I'd come back to my room and crawled into bed. I'm not sure how I'd fallen asleep after the adrenaline rush. I looked down at myself realizing I should change into clean clothes, maybe even shower. My hair felt so utterly gross! I was about to get up when the door to my room swung open. "Starla, why aren't you up yet? It's almost ten thirty," said Tri.

"Mom, why are you barging into my room?" I grumbled, tossing off the covers. I got up quickly, shoved the blankets back over my bed, then walked to my dresser. I turned away from her and started to take out outfits. I wasn't sure what to wear to this meeting. "You did talk to Nayla didn't you? I'm surprised I even got any sleep after last night," I pressed.

"I did," she said, leaning against the door frame.

"Well, then you're aware that Megan has some kind of gift. Nayla said something about a key. How can she know, when we don't even have a clue?" I asked, pulling out a pair of my favorite faded blue jeans.

"Cavin was incredibly vague with Nayla pertaining to how Megan plays a part in this. I'll let you get ready. If you shower, make it quick. Megan's downstairs eating breakfast. You can grab a banana and meet us at the car. We're taking Dad's."

"Okay," I said, taking out my undergarments, then found a pair of jeans crammed behind my purple hoodie. I snagged them both and pushed my drawer closed as mom left. I hadn't even told her about my idea's on how Sis could help out. Had Nayla spoken to Megan about any of this? I thought then turned to the bathroom. I pushed opened the door and shut it behind me. My cell rang, but I let it go. If it were Jenson or Owl, I'd see them at the meeting.

Anxiously I'd showered, dried off, and threw on my clothes. There was no need for makeup besides, when had I last even applied lip gloss? Oh yeah, the dance. The purple in my hair was gone. I'd enjoyed it while it lasted. Don hadn't made much of a fuss about it. Gah! The odd thing was I kind of missed Denny's. Even the kids, spilling juice or milk on the floor. It was some semblance of normality. I snatched the pile of dirty clothes off the ground, putting them in the hamper beside the door. Then exited the bathroom to snag my cell off the nightstand. Once I had it in my grasp, I fumbled with my purse I'd left hanging on the chair. I put it around my shoulders, then pushed my phone inside. There, I thought shutting off the light and then headed down the stairs to the kitchen. When I got there, Megan stood next to the countertop with a banana in her hand. "Why aren't you in the car with mom and Dad?" I asked.

"I wanted to wait for you. Nayla told me you came to check on me last night. After the trial, I told you I'd watch out for you. Now everyone is looking out for me," she stated.

I walked up to her and took the banana out of her hand, peeled it, and took a bite. It wasn't too bad, almost ripe. Then grabbed a bottle of orange juice someone had left on the countertop.

"I'm not sure what Cavin knows. Nayla said he'd had a breakthrough regarding your ability to assist the clan. She said something about a key. Before I found her in your room, I was thinking about the spells we'd used for Thunderhead Bay. Paralysis is one you might like to try. If you could freeze The Shadows, it would momentarily stop them from attacking us. Anyway, we'd better get out of here," I said meandering towards the back door. Megan rolled her eyes but followed me.

"Come on. They hate being late. Plus Jenson, Molly, and Maine will be there."

"I know," she replied, opening the door.

I shielded my eyes against the bright sunlight as we stepped out into the complex area.

"Where's Nayla?" I asked as she shut the door behind us.

"She left this morning after talking with mom, vanished. She never leaves the normal way. It's not safe."

"Nope, not with Earl and Fern around," I whispered in case they were near. We continued towards the parking lot. I stepped off of the curb heading to the car. Then felt Megan grab me. She dragged me back as a car pulled up to the curb I'd almost stepped off of.

"You'd better be more careful," Tri scolded, rolling down the car window. Dad was at the wheel as it was his car. Mom didn't like to drive much.

I nodded at him. Then grabbed the door handle and got in. Megan squeezed in beside me in the back seat. I remained silent the rest of the way to Hunter's Park.

"Here we are, I'm sure they're waiting for us," said Dan.

I unhooked my seatbelt, then turned to push open the car door holding my purse tightly to me. My mom got out of the vehicle, stretched out a bit, and then morphed. I watched as she ran towards Mike's station in fox form.

"Show off," I muttered as I got out. Then sighed, not truly certain what had triggered my lousy mood. I held the door open, but Megan had by now exited on the opposite side. She sprinted ahead following behind my mother. I closed the car door, took a deep breath, and exhaled examining the outskirts of the park. Only a few small piles of snow were left in patches. I could do this. Lance and Shellena would protect me. Jones, too. I needed to be strong for Megan. A chill traveled up my back causing me to shudder. Hopefully, for us, the key meant something else.

My Dad reached out, placing his hand on my shoulder. "Starla? Are you okay?"

"I'm frazzled," I replied, turning towards him. He let his hand fall to his side. I moved forward, then put my hand on the hood of the car. Was this how Buffy felt? She loved protecting her friends, and family, but at a price. I let my hand slide, across the hood as I walked to the picnic area. My Dad hurried to catch up with me.

"I get that. Things have come down on you extremely fast," he replied.

"It's alright, Dad. This whole being an adult thing. It brings a lot of anxiety, doesn't it?"

"It can, at times," he admitted.

"I suppose I never really grew up. Relying on you and Mom. After high school, most people go away to college. They move on."

"Not everyone, look at Molly, Jenson. Not everyone's parents have the funds to send them away. Some of us worry, your mother would have had to visit you every weekend," he joked as we drew closer to the station.

"And you if we'd never come here... Would you have ever come back?" I asked.

"It's hard to say and better not to play the what if game," he answered.

I nodded, not having the heart to create conflict between us.

Chapter 13

When Dad opened the door to let me in what I saw was overwhelming. Ranger Mike's station wasn't enormous. I don't imagine we could have fit another creature into the building. As you walk in, there's a small room with a viewing area of the park. I turned to the right and noticed Mike had set up a table in the conference room. Jenson, Owl, Maine, and Molly sat near Star and Jinx. I frowned. What exactly was he doing here? Would Star spill the beans before Maine, and Molly's training was complete? I hesitated, then smiled at Jenson and Owl. Those two had formed such a brotherly bond since they'd met. I glanced over at Shellena, Lance, and Minder all seated together. Cavin was at the head of the table in his usual place. Nayla sat on one side of him and Kaya on the other. Eva and Cal sat near Ranger, Mike. Jones stood off to the side with a girl and a guy I'd never seen before. The girl had bright red curls, and the man's hair was black. As we meandered into the room, Cavin nodded to us. My mother and Megan had saved us seats in the far left corner. Everyone talked amongst themselves, and I couldn't understand one conversation from the other. I sat down next to Megan, and my father by Tri. Cavin cleared his throat loudly.

"Now that everyone's here I'm calling this meeting to order! Listen carefully. The safety of the clan is at stake. The Bandits are currently being held in confinement. Starla, I understand you had a meeting yesterday with Star and Kaya. We're prepared to go ahead with the experimentation today. Keep in mind that anything could go wrong and probably will. Lance and Shellena, you're both primed to use manipulation if this happens?"

"Of course," they answered in sync.

"Alright. Before we do, I wanted to..."

Cavin stopped mid-sentence and gazed at Molly and Maine.

"It's only been a day. We haven't yet prepped for what could happen," Molly squeaked.

Cavin nodded, then looked at Star.

"We'll have to take our chances. That is if Star thinks it's time."

A shiver ran down my back. There wasn't one face at the table that didn't look concerned about what was about to be revealed. I hoped that Jinx wouldn't go racing out into the woods. Mango? Why wasn't she here? Was she watching the kits, if not who was?

Kaya laid a paw on Cavin's back. He took a deep breath, exhaled, and then looked at Jinx.

"I'm just going to come out and say this. It's something you shouldn't have to live with but will. Trigger saw a Shadow enter your body, Jinx."

"It wasn't a giant rabbit? It tried to attack me. I thought the scientists had modified my prey. After I charged, I tore it to shreds, that was the end of it. Are they after us? Have the scientists sent them too?" he asked, appearing bewildered.

It sounded as if Jinx had watched a late night horror film. I covered my mouth with my hands trying not to laugh. It wasn't humorous.

Star laid a comforting paw on Jinx's back.

"That's not the case. I wanted to inform you when Molly and Maine were proficiently skilled in aiding you. Trigger told us he saw you that night in the woods."

"The... The night Du-Vance was murdered?" he stammered.

"Yes, that night. It wasn't a rabbit you killed."

"No!!!! It can't be, couldn't be," he screamed shaking uncontrollably. "I didn't see him at all. I rushed off after tearing it to bits. I ate some of it. Awe I'm a cannibal!"

Jinx jumped up off of his seat. I thought he was going to hit the ceiling. Then sped toward the door while Shellena and Lance hurried to block it. He skidded in front of the exit, then moved from side to side trying to find a way to evade Shellena and Lance.

Star took out a pouch from beneath the table. She pulled out two small sized biscuits.

How would food help in a situation like this? I looked at my Dad who shrugged his shoulders at me. Star threw the biscuits to Lance, who caught them in mid-air.

"Jinx, you need to eat these. It will help calm you."

"It won't change what I've done! What have I done," he shouted tearing at his ears with his paws.

As Lance threw the biscuits on the floor towards him, Nayla bolted out of her seat zigzagging to him.

"Stop, Rascal wouldn't want you to be so hard on yourself," she pressed. Then nudged the biscuits on the floor to him.

Jinx stopped pulling at his ears in anger. He gave everyone a mournful glance and looked at the food on the ground.

"We're here for you. Eat, then rest," Nayla instructed.

Without a word I watched him scarf down the food.

"It will ease your emotional pain for now. Star made them using a small amount of Skullcap. One of you will need to Monitor him, the other needs to stay here," said Nayla.

"I'll go," Shellena offered.

"Okay. Minder, go with them," Star added.

Nayla trotted back to the table reclaiming her seat. Star nodded to her then spoke to Minder. "Make sure when he wakes you burn some sage. Molly and Maine, I hope you've gone over the list I gave you. Did you find any spells useful with the material on the list?"

Who was running the show? It seemed Star had taken over. I slouched back into my chair as Minder and Shellena helped Jinx exit the station. Cal appeared horrified by the ordeal. I caught her hiding her face in the crook of Eva's arm. I hoped she was up for this.

"Yes, but most of them deal with healing the body when it's physically damaged. Maine and I discussed Jinx's issue soon after we did some research on our own. First, we'll need to use a calming spell. He'll require consoling from a trusted friend. Once he's in the correct mindset, you should be capable of helping him find the part of his soul lost during the trauma. It takes time, a period of weeks depending on the severity of the distress," Molly informed us.

"Good, good. I need you both to put together an appropriate spell. I'll speak with Merit and Sera. They are the other two members of the Trinity. I'm not sure who Jinx is closest to inside his tiny circle," Star commented.

"Thank you," Cavin stated. "For now, we'll keep him comfortable. I spoke with Rascal briefly yesterday. He's hesitant to join us when we head out to Grandville. These shadows destroyed his boy. He's afraid of what he might do if he encounters the scientists face to face."

"What's the plan of action for today? Do you have something set up?" I asked out of the blue.

"Lance, why don't you take the lead. Tell everyone the layout for this mission," Cavin instructed.

"Before we begin the prayer to the sun goddess we'll take our stances. It will take place outside of the huts. The Crusaders will be joining us. I'll want Starla and Cal positioned in the middle of the forest. On the outside, we'll form a circle. In that loop, we'll have Amer, Jun, Nayla and myself. Sensi is sitting this one out. She's offered to tag along on our journey to Grandville. There her Owl capability will come in handy as we'll be traveling at night. We'll go over that more when the time comes. Outside of the circle, we will position Jones, Trax, and Sina. They're skilled at diverting attention away from Cal and Starla. The Shadows may try to breach the barrier Cal, and Starla construct. If we're lucky the heat, you produce when linked may affect them. We can't be sure until you try. Molly and Maine do not engage The Shadows. Maine if your able chant a protection spell. Molly, you'll heal if required."

"What about the rest of us? We haven't trained for this type of combat," Tri snapped.

My Dad tried to lay a tender hand on her shoulder. She shrugged it away. Owl and Jenson wore scowls on their faces.

"And what about Owl and I? Rascal's been training us with various moves. I might be able to half-freeze them if necessary. Starla suggested Megan might be able to assist with that. I'm not sure she could learn it say in 15 minutes," Jenson jeered.

I cleared my throat, then looked directly at Nayla. "What are we going to do about Megan? Is she the Key? What does it mean? Do you even know?" I prodded.

Nayla shook her head, then jumped from her seat onto the table. She sat in the middle of it glaring at me.

"It wasn't something I wanted to discuss currently. It was supposed to be kept between, you, Trigger, and I. Paralysis should imprint when Star or I place a paw on her head. After that, if she's the key, she'll absorb spells. It can only be performed via a Shamen or that of a tribe member with a god or goddesses permission." Nayla turned to face Megan. My sister for the moment was in awe. "Wait! Don't get too excited. You can only soak up so much at a time. If you're given a large amount all at once, it could kill you. It weakens your strength." She stopped talking and looked at me. "Like Lance and his fireballs. She has to be able to regenerate power. That is if she's the Key."

I nodded to Nayla. Then out of the corner of my eye saw Megan shudder in her seat. She started to stand.

"Oh, no you don't. We're in this together. You promised you'd be there for me." I said, giving her an evil stare. She sat back down immediately. The can of worms unleashed.

"Lance, can you please continue to tell us what we need to do. Star will imprint on Megan if Dan and Tri agree."

"Why do you suspect Megan has this gift? Who provided this top secret information? Why wasn't I informed of this? Dan, were you hiding this behind my back?" Tri accused glaring at him.

Whoa! I hadn't seen her this upset since he'd asked me to help with the Du-Vance case. The one she was okay with now. A part of me was happy for Megan. This would mean we could protect one another. Still, I was terrified. She'd be putting herself in danger for me.

"No, I had no clue! This is the earliest I've heard about it!" He shouted, and threw his hands up in the air. Then let them fall back onto his lap. I inched away from them both.

"Trigger came to me with a hunch. Called it a gut feeling, it could be nothing, but I figured it was worth a shot. The worst that could happen is Megan'll have to learn spells like everyone else. This would be an additional benefit," Nayla assured them.

Megan turned to my mother, " I'm as frightened as you are, but let me do this. I promised Starla I'd be there for her. She's my sister, you're my parents, and I too am a part of this clan. It's my turn to uncover my destiny. Starla has found hers. It can't hurt can it?"

"I suppose not. But it's upsetting to think someone knows more about your child than you do," Tri snapped.

Dan laid a hand on her back patting it lightly as Cal and Eva whispered back and forth amongst each other.

"Cal do you have something you'd like to share with us? How are your nightmares?" prodded Nayla.

Cal sat straight up in her seat. "Mom and I were discussing something else, for real. I wish I could tell you the nightmares have evolved into more details. No earth-shattering revelation has yet occurred out of them. I'm praying I don't have flashbacks when we face The Scientists at Grandville," she grumbled.

"Alright, that is that! Cavin, are there any other matters at hand?" inquired Nayla.

"No, but perhaps we should open the floor so others can express concerns before we take our positions," Cavin offered.

Jenson stood up, "Lance, you never answered my question. How can Owl and I help? I won't be left on the sidelines," he demanded.

"I'd like you both to back up Megan. That cannot be accomplished unless we get on with the imprinting. Dan, Tri, I'll need you to give Star consent to do so. It would be better if done outside near the huts. We'll meet there and later take a short break. I can feel the tension in this room. Kaya? You haven't spoken a word."

"I'm in observation mode. If Cavin doesn't mind, I'd like to go help Mango with the kits. Cavin, you know where the food I prepared is. Would you please make sure everyone gets some?"

"Of course, Nuria is already there. Nayla, please contact her by-mind-speak. Let her know we're on our way. She should have a picnic lunch set up. Then after we've regained our strength, we'll do this thing!"

"Cavin, where did you learn such slang?" asked Kaya.

"Mango and the kits are a bad influence I guess. Now everyone, take a deep breath and head out. Ranger, Mike. Thank you for letting us use your station today.

"It's the least I could do. I apologize for being unable to offer advice," Mike replied.

"Keep the visitors on the trails, warn them of bears, and under no circumstances, let them find us," Cavin demanded.

"As always," Mike answered.

Chapter 14

I know I should have offered up advice or thoughts before racing out of the station. I'd quickly handed Tri my purse to put in the car. I didn't need it, what I needed was some fresh air. A refrain from the turmoil. What had I been thinking? That the meeting would be speedy? We'd kick shadow butt and move forward? I stood outside in the middle of the park breathing the crisp air into my lungs. Everyone would be heading out soon. I had bailed while others lingered on a bit. Cavin wouldn't like it. After a few minutes of solace, the door to the station swung open. Molly walked outside as the door slammed shut nearly missing Lance. He grabbed it before it clocked him one in the face.

"Sorry," said Molly, looking back at him.

'It's okay, kid. I have to head out too. I'm going to help Nuria set up the picnic area and food. When everyone gets there, we'll chow. Then it's action time! See ya girls," he said, waving as he strutted off.

Molly wandered over to me.

"How are you holding up? Do you suppose Cal will come out and hike with us to the huts?"

"I'm not sure. I have to wait for Megan. Is Maine coming?"

"Yeah, she had a few questions for Star. She gave us our packets of herbs as promised. Rather a small amount, but I'll get more later. Maine said they're available at this herb store she's familiar with. Are you prepared for this?"

"After food, and a slight break... Yes!" I answered attempting to motivate myself.

Molly looked back as Maine, Jenson and Owl strolled out of the building. Jenson jogged up to me firmly taking my hand.

"Hi," I said, leaning my forehead against his.

"Hey," he answered, kissing me lightly on the lips. I pulled him closer, kissing him a bit deeper, then drew myself away.

"That was some kiss," Owl commented.

Maine whistled at us, while Molly blushed.

"Well, if it's the last time we get a chance for a smooch like that, then yes!" I exclaimed.

Jenson smiled at me holding both of his hands in mine. Megan must be lingering with my parents in tow. They probably had a dozen questions for Star before allowing her access to their daughter for clan purposes. I let go of his hands, then looked towards the station.

"I should get Megan. She's almost certainly struggling with wanting to save me, find herself and be with Chaz," I speculated.

Then took a few steps towards the building. I was roughly to the door when Tri, Dan, and Megan strolled outside with Ranger, Mike. Cavin stood just inside the station.

"Take care folks, Megan it was nice meeting you. Cavin will be on his way along with the others. Jones and I have some things to discuss," Mike stated.

"Starla would like to know about her grades." I overheard my mother say.

"I'm sure she can discuss it with him during the reprieve," he replied.

My mother nodded, and Dan placed his hand on her back as they and Megan walked away.

"What's up?" asked Maine.

"Grades, Mike wouldn't say anything. I've tried to put my anxiety in the back of my mind. Jone's class is what will decide my G.P.A. for this semester," I grumbled.

"And next?" asked Jenson.

"Not sure, I hope there is a next," I replied.

"Starla, you've always been dramatic," Megan snickered as she and my family gathered near us.

I shrugged it off, then turned to face my parents.

"We've given Star the okay to test out Megan's ability. We're going up ahead," said Dan nodding to me.

"Okay, so I'll see you and mom there?"

"Yep, play nice," said Tri.

"Don't I always? Right Sis," I joked eyeing her mischievously.

"Almost always, let's go. Jenson and Owl are here to protect me," she teased.

"We are, don't knock it," Owl blurted.

Cal raced up to me stopping near him out of breath.

"Cal. Are you coming?" he asked.

"Yeah, give me a second."

"Second's up," chirped Jenson.

I elbowed him, grinned, and then moved closer to Cal.

"Come on. We'll walk with Molly and Maine. I don't know about you, but I'm hungry," I admitted.

"Me too. The meeting was tense. I wasn't sure who was going to start throwing sparks from their eyes at any instant, or fireballs," Cal laughed.

I linked her arm in mine, then giggled. Gah, I was girly. Maine, Molly, Cal, and I trekked towards the path to the huts while Megan hung back with Owl and Jenson. They in all probability pictured themselves as her knight in shining armor.

I sat with my crew on an oversized blanket. Nuria had laid out the food on the picnic table. It looked divine! I turned to see Jones and his immortals seated with Amer and Jun. My mom and Dad decided to sit with Eva. On the hike over, all Owl and Jenson could talk about was how they'd defend Megan to the end. We'd ease dropped hiking ahead of them. Megan had shaken her head in annoyance. Then joined Molly, Maine and I to banter about her new found self. I warned her not to get overly excited until the ceremony was performed.

"Earth to Starla, are you there?" asked Molly.

"Yeah, sorry. I was off in my little world again pondering the mysteries of-of... I'm not sure what exactly. Anyway, I keep forgetting to ask you about your folks. How are they?"

"You should tell her! It's entertaining, also eye-opening," Maine confessed, grinning like a fool.

"Good or bad? Spill, then I must eat!" I gushed as my stomach growled.

"Mom decided after all of the fights about overspending, and other issues they'd go see our minister. She's new, plus I like her. She has a lot of new angles on Christianity. Dad's hesitant to how she interprets the Bible; he's so old school!"

"What Molly's trying to say is her dad isn't happy about it," Maine implied.

"And?" I pressed.

Molly face lit up, and she glanced at Maine. "She's okay with Maine and I. It's between God and me. It's a huge relief. Some people have left the church because of it. She says they can't progress."

"So true! What do you believe Jenson?"

"As an open-minded fool, I couldn't agree more. Now, do you want me to fix you a plate? Any of you? I'm feeling chivalrous today," he offered.

I laughed, "I'll get my own, thank you. Does anyone else want to take Jenson up on his offer?" I asked, then stood up and paused for effect. "No, okay then. Let's eat. Jenson, take screech with you."

"You haven't called me that in ages. Are we bringing it back like the eighties?" asked Owl.

"Sure, why not," I replied.

I picked up a plate to fill it with fruit, cheese, and crackers. Cal piled on the chips, dip, and veggies. Hmm, I glanced at Megan being selective about her choices. Was she unsure of what was to come? I eyed the large bowl of punch in the middle of the spread. After we filled up our plates, Molly poured us each a cup and handed them out to us. We drifted over to Shellena and Lance sitting next to Jones, and the newbies. They were to me anyway. Megan smiled at my professor and turned to me.

"That's your Myth teacher; he's cute!"

Jones blushed.

"He's right there," I whispered, glowering at her. Cal held her hands over her mouth, stifling a laugh. Shellena and Lance grinned at one another. She must have left Jinx in good hands. I'm positive Minder had it under control.

"It's okay to sit with you, right?" questioned Megan.

"Of course, I bet your sister came to harass me about her grades! Am I accurate?"

"Precisely," I replied, sitting down. Megan and Cal found spots on the grass near one another. Molly sat and juggled her plate on her knees as I waited for Lance and Shellena to say something, but they just continued devouring the food on their plates.

"While Shellena and Lance take advantage of the grub I'd like to make proper introductions. I should have introduced you at the meeting earlier. This is Trax, he's my right-hand man," he said, patting him on the shoulder. "Over here to my left is Sina. She's unpredictable, but that's what I love about her."

"Yeah, and it comes in handy against villains," she grinned, winking at me.

"Ah, so you're?" asked Maine.

"I fly both ways kid; I just try not to go in both directions at once. I'd hate to be split in two, but in a way, it's what I am." Sina appeared a tad sullen after her reveal to us. Jones gave her a quick side squeeze.

"We love you Sina. Now, about those grades. Starla, it was a nice attempt. You made a lot of good points about wolf spirits in tribes, how they affected Native's beliefs. You didn't find a way to tie it into your own life. I took a crack at the research myself, which I found some of it inconclusive. Due to this, I've given you a B-. It shouldn't hurt your G.P.A. too badly."

"Thanks," I mumbled annoyed but relieved.

"Molly, you covered your ground on the healers. It was cunning relating it to Wicca, and afterward how modern day medicine also uses plants for some commercialized drugs. I had to give you an A- since you forgot to cite a quote at the end of the paper," he explained.

"Thanks! See Starla, you passed. A B- isn't so bad," Molly clarified while I ate my cheese and crackers.

"I guess," I mumbled my mouth full of food.

"I did help her," Maine added.

"I'm thankful, examining the healing process through natural methods can be beneficial to our clan.

"Before they round us up to start the experiment tell me what being semi-immortal is like?" asked Megan.

"An immortal creature lives forever. I'm semi-mortal because I can be wounded but heal faster. And as long as I'm not hit directly in the heart, I'll survive most of the attacks my enemies deliver."

"Rad," she exclaimed, digging into her pile of chips.

"Eat up," said Lance.

"Are we getting ready right now?" asked Megan.

"In about five minutes. I'm going to go over a few things with your folks. Shellena, would you start collecting everyone's trash, make sure they've eaten. Then we'll begin."

"What am I, your slave?" Shellena remarked.

"No, but I could use your help, please?"

"Alright," she reluctantly agreed, standing up.

Megan emptied her plate full of food in less than three minutes. I hoped she didn't get a stomach ache from eating so fast.

"You don't have to hurry on my account," Shellena commented, taking Trax, and Sina plates from them.

Megan tipped her drink into her mouth finishing it in one gulp. Then crushed her cup as she stood.

"Where are you going?" I asked.

"To gather the trash, then find Star. She has to be around here somewhere," Megan pondered turning towards the other groups of clan dwellers on blankets. We were pretty spread out in our clicks.

"Okay, but make sure you stay close. Don't leave the area," I advised.

She glared at me, "Sis, I know. I'm not stupid Okaaay..."

"I recognize, I'm only being cautious, think about Chaz. You don't want to end up the victim of a shadow."

Megan huffed off after Shellena. I'm not sure why. Maybe she thought she knew where Star was. Then again, she was pretty stubborn. I wonder where she got it from.

I finished my food as Molly and Maine talked amongst themselves. When I glanced back up from my plate, Cal was gone. I scanned the area and noticed her with Eva. Nuria stood nearby. As I got up, Jenson and Owl strolled towards me.

"Hey," I said. My voice shook, and my shoulders joined in the chaos as I crossed my arms, rubbing them up and down. Jenson came up behind me, pulling me into a hug, and Owl placed his arms around me on the other side.

"Guys, I love you too, but you're smashing me. I can't breathe," I gasped. They let go so I could breathe again.

"Don't be nervous. We've all got your back," Jenson reminded me.

"Yeah, and Megan's," Owl added.

"I'm just a bundle of nerves. If violence and death are never the answer how come I want to kill these things!" I blurted, nervously scanning the forest.

"Anyone who tampers with those you love creates great emotions of anger. It's a survival instinct, animal, a part of us even when we fight to be civil," Trax acknowledged.

"Even if it makes sense, it's scary that our love for another can bring about abhorrence," I murmured staring at the ground.

"It is. Sorry I was so quiet." Trax stopped to clear his throat. " I needed to meditate to get into the right mindset for this.

"Okay, um so Jenson. I'm going to grab the blanket, the trash is taken care of, and we'll head to the middle area. That's where it's all happening." I bent down to pick up the blanket. As I did something, hit me on my side.

Nayla?

"No, Trigger, be safe. I'm here to protect Megan. Now, go on," he mind-spoke to me.

I nodded, even though no one else knew who I was nodding to and finished picking up the blanket. Jenson took my arm helping me up.

"Let's go everyone's getting into place. Look, Lance is in the middle delivering orders. Cavin, he's over on the sidelines. We've got to get geared up."

"Mm-hmm," I whispered, tucking my hair behind my ears. I had to be strong. Pull it together Starla, I told myself.

After all of the picnic items were taken inside. Cal and I took our place in the middle of our clan area. The rest of the group spread out as instructed. Star and Megan were off to the side. Jenson and Owl remained close behind her. Amer, Jun, Nayla, and Lance formed a circle around Cal and me. Tri stood aside near Dan with Jones, Sina, and Trax. My dad has no superpowers, but his ability for quick action. He hadn't done so well at Thunderhead Bay. I took in a deep breath and turned to Cal.

"We should change. It will make it easier to retreat if we're in fox form," I suggested.

She rolled her eyes at me, then looked at Nayla.

"Really? Wouldn't it make us more susceptible to them?" Cal asked.

"It doesn't matter what form you're in. Either way, we could go down. Star are you all set?"

She rolled her front shoulders back and stretched out her body. Then sat on her hind legs peering at the sky.

"I am. I'll begin by asking the Sun goddess permission. I'll need silence to proceed. When I've received the okay, I'll place my hand on Megan's head. Afterward, we'll see if it takes. If it's unsuccessful, it will be up to Tri and Dan if they wish her to stay for the duration of the operation. I'm sure Owl and Jenson will do their best to protect her, but there are no guarantees."

My body tensed as I heard those words spoken, *no guarantees*. No one objected to it. Everyone remained quiet. I kept my eyes on Star and Megan, as Cal took my hand squeezing it. Jenson gazed at me, then scanned the surrounding area.

"Megan, please close your eyes, concentrate on tranquility, clear your mind. If you're at ease, this will proceed smoothly."

"Okay," Megan whispered.

Goosebumps formed up and down my arms in anticipation. Cal let go of my sweaty palm and wiped her hands on her jeans.

"It will be fine, breath."

Trigger, I'd forgotten he was here, somewhere. I looked over to my right, then my left, but I didn't see him.

"Don't try to find me, just be here for them. Focus on the now."

I nodded to the air. Cal scrunched up her face at me; then Star cleared her throat.

"I call upon our protector, the goddess of the sun, Igaehindivo. There is one among us who may be the Key. An answer, to opening doors to possibilities of security. A sister, of the guardian. In this new found opportunity we may be able to extinguish The Shadows," Star admitted, bending her head low to honor the deity.

A gush of wind-swept throughout the forest, then promptly subsided.

"Do not take this consent lightly. It's to be used to protect, guard, and defend only in times of need."

"Yes, absolutely," Star replied, placing her paw on Megan's forehead. A light emerged out of her paw growing brighter, swirling around in a mist above her head before it entered. Megan jolted upright, opening her eyes and gasped for breath. She fell forward, digging her hands into the earth.

I rushed over to help her, but Star put her hand out to stop me. It was then I noticed my dad holding Mom back. He whispered something in her ear. I stood watching my sister try to catch her breath. Star placed her paw on her back, taking deep breaths herself, urging Megan to do the same.

"It's alright, taking that in knocked the wind right out of you."

When Megan's breathing returned to normal, Star took her paw off of her back, allowing her to stand.

"I'm a bit nauseous, and my head hurts. Is that common?" Megan questioned.

"It should subside," Star assured her, staring beyond the trees. "Minder will be here soon. We have to draw out The Shadows."

"Is she bringing The Bandits with her?" I asked.

"Two of them, Gavin and Gladiator. Sika's refusing to cooperate. He's not to be trusted. Therefore, I will not authorize access to an opportunity to endanger someone. I don't want anyone interacting with them. Minder's in charge. Do you hear me, I'm not asking!" Star demanded.

There were several mumbles of yes, and okay when Minder traipsed into the area. Gavin and Gladiator walked behind her in compliance. No shackles, chains, or cuffs. My jaw dropped open in surprise.

"We're here. They've been warned that any ill-behavior will be punished, and any immunity promised null and void. Star, please call back the goddess. Let's finish this!"

Cal took my hand in hers, both of them shook uncontrollably. Megan stayed beside Owl and Jenson. Everyone was currently at their posts. Minder stood with Gavin and Gladiator a few feet from Cal and me.

Star bowed down, placing her hands in prayer. "Goddess of the sun, Igaehindivo resume. We must eradicate this wickedness hovering above to progress. Once Trigger is free, he'll guide us to the scientists. Only then can we rid ourselves from years of affliction."

"This is not an easy undertaking. It's full of risks, and blood may be shed. Let your strongest warriors rise, put them at the forefront at Grandville. I've observed your scheme for this it's efficient. When you need me call out this 'Come back Sun, make us one!' Say it twice, and I will reappear. I shall retreat presently."

"Wait! What about me? Will I be able to use the Paralysis spell?" asked Megan.

"You'd better let her try it before I leave. The Shadows are near," said the goddess.

Star waved to Dan, "I'd like you to come forward."

"How can I help if I'm frozen?" he argued.

"Don't worry about that now. I need to see if she's capable of defending us. That's the issue at hand," Star replied.

There were no arguments from my mother as my father strolled towards Megan. He stopped several inches away from her before gazing again at Star.

"Alright, that's close enough. Megan you'll need to use your anger to paralyze him. I'd like it to be brief. Concentrate on something he did in the past that made you furious."

"Okay, but with The Shadows?"

"Once you see them trying to assault us, will that be adequate?"

"Yeah, you bet!" Megan exclaimed.

"Gavin and Gladiator will be targeted. We brought them to make sure they'd materialize. If Starla and Cal are not able to deflect The Shadows you and Jenson are to start the sequence freezing them," Star advised.

"Megan, you got this!" I said, giving her my best smile. I had to be brave for her.

She grinned at me nervously, turned to my father, and held up her hand. Did she see that on Charmed? I couldn't remember anyone on Buffy doing that.

A clap of thunder echoed in the background. I couldn't tell if she was retrieving a memory or in a meditative trance. She flicked her hand at him, then again. Nothing happened. No one said a word.

"Maybe you could use some help," Maine added pulling out a bundle of salt from her pocket throwing it to her. Megan caught it with her right hand.

"What am I going to do with this?" asked Megan observing it.

"Take a pinch of it, throw it at him as you project your anger," she stated.

I closed my eyes and prayed to the gods, higher power, one and only. Minutes later, I heard cheering followed by clapping. When I opened my eyes, Megan had a huge smile on her face. Star trotted up to her nuzzling her hand. Nayla joined them.

"Congratulations. We'll have to be careful as you need items to assist in your abilities. Maine, thank you. Everyone I need you to prepare. Cal and Starla connect. When linked, please blink twice at me. Maine, can you chant a protection mantra?" inquired Nayla.

"Yes, I'll whisper it as not to disturb Cal and Starla's concentration."

"Good, good."

"Cal, we can't hold hands, remember? I'll pull out a memory. Then you'll draw me in. Afterward, we'll radiate outward the pulse. We have to keep it around Hunter's Park. Then see if we can reflect whatever nightmares they start hashing out at us onto them," I suggested.

Cal let go of my hands but didn't answer me. I could hear the raccoons, and rabbits as they scurried about in the forest around us. Lance tapped his foot impatiently on the ground while Jenson's eyes caught mine. I turned away. I had to be in sync with her and ready because there was a chance I wouldn't hear Star, and Nayla, tell the goddess to depart. A feeling of intensity consumed me. Without any warning, I recalled our training with Minder. I'd almost gotten sick with her speed demon running. I tried not to laugh, then felt a tug. Cal, I let her connect, then pressed go. The fire between us lite up, well, not fire exactly, but the pulse radiated out of us.

"Goddess, Igaehindivo retire!" Star ordered. Thank goodness I could still perceive sound!

A coolness spread throughout the forest before anything arrived. Gladiator and Gavin shivered at the sudden change in the temperature. Jones and his crew leaned from side to side, peering every which way geared up to defend us. Jenson and Owl who'd bragged about protecting Megan shook in fear as the first shadow floated out of the woods. Fight it, Jenson. Don't let it steal your soul!

"Concentrate, focus, hold our link," Cal mind spoke to me. All we could do is blast our pulse, exude heat, and pray we'd sense the nightmares produced. Then use it to destroy them.

Chapter 15

Maine and Molly chanted in unison, "Our amulets protect against evil, shield us from harm. These amulets do not allow demons or negative entities to thrive in our world. This earth is our domain, and we alone determine who will exceed. No dark entities will overtake this region. As we will it so mote it be."

At least it was keeping them safe from the madness, I reasoned. I wasn't sure what it was doing for the rest of us. Gavin and Gladiator stayed close to Minder. A rush of wind hit me from behind practically taking me out. Remaining persistent, I held my place. Trigger materialized dodging in and out of the forest chasing shadows. They moved swiftly in route to us. I scanned the area, my people... Tri and Dan were off to the side near Jones. Dad was able to move his upper torso. He turned to see a shadow whiz over his head. Megan had her hand in the bag of salt ready to paralyze it. Jenson and Owl had positioned themselves on each side of her. The rest of them spread out around us. The first shadow, I had to focus on it, see if I could somehow determine what it was pondering!

"Starla! I'm going to drive it over to you then, once it faces you invade its mind."

Trigger, there are so many of them! I thought.

"I know, one at a time my dear. Keep it together. Look at Megan, but make it quick!"

She and Jenson had a few of them cornered. They'd frozen about four of them. Two remained, the one in front of us now, and another near Jones and his crew. It followed them as they circled the perimeter. I tried not to let my fear overcome me. If I did it would be used against me, and this wasn't a court of law. I laughed, and Cal gave me an angry look. Taking a deep breath, I cleared my head.

I could feel the coldness radiating off of the dark creature. Cal and I continued our pulse backing up to where Megan, Jenson, and Owl stood. It stalked us but made no effort to break our barrier. None of them were trying to touch us. Would it Kill them if they did?

"I'm going to attempt to gain access to the fears they've compiled. When I do, I'll warn you," Tri mentality spoke to me.

"Mom, are you saying I cannot do this on my own? I thought.

"We're a team," she replied, out loud answering me.

Trigger stopped behind my mother. She drew closer to the Shadow held by paralysis next to Megan. It had begun to twitch. She put up her hand like she was trying to sense an aura or something. My shoulders slumped while my strength waned. We hadn't been using our powers for long, but they were fading. It was tricky deciphering one Shadow from another. They were various hues of gray, white, and black. How many had the scientists created? Could we remove them all? The thing in front of us rushed Jenson, and my heart lurched into my stomach. The terror in his eyes was unrecognizable. Who was I supposed to have mom save? Jenson, or Megan?! She couldn't paralyze it twice! Minder shouted at Gavin and Gladiator to do something as they paced around the area hesitant to help us.

Lance and Nayla sprinted towards them. It was all I could do not to sever my bond with Cal. What were they going to do? None of them had ESP, but Tri could allocate information to every one of us. After that possibly take them out?

Starla, you know Megan, Think! What's she scared of? When that thing breaks free, it will attack! I scolded myself allowing my mind to roam..

Teddy bears, Giant Spiders, the boogie man? It had been a while since she'd slipped into my bedroom due to nightmares, not since L.A.

Don't give in, don't give up! I reflected.

Gremlins, hadn't we seen that film together? Mom warned us not to watch it. The eighties flick, one of our cousins had popped into the VCR one night at Christmas, I'd never forgotten. When it was time for bed, Megan wouldn't shut her eyes, and afterward, she woke up screaming they were after her. I'd run to her room, and soon mom had joined us.

"Megan, use it against them, use your imagination!" I shouted. She shrunk back in fright behind Owl.

Cal grabbed my hands, the walls around us fell. What? Wouldn't that make us stronger?

"What the hell happened? Lance, your fireballs! Will they work? You have to try," I shouted. Then ran in-between Megan and Jenson. Cal trailed behind me, but Lance pushed us aside. He drew his wolf-like paw into a fist, pulled it back, and threw the fire directly at the grayish blob Jenson was dodging. On impact, it began to smoke, and bit by bit dissolved. It looked like we'd won till the blackish globule next to my sister drove itself into it. They combined back together as one, then separated

"Shiznit, fireworks are out of the question!" Lance exclaimed.

They regenerate off of each other using fire! What the heck, I thought seizing Megan's hand in mine. I'd never mentally spoken to her before, but why not?

"Gremlins, they're everywhere!" Megan shouted.

Her terror traveled up my arm, emotions flowed into my body, and I combined mine with hers. "No, no, it's only an illusion, you're safe, I've got you. Use the hallucination against them! Get mad! They're trying to kill us. It's the only way," I mentality spoke. Perhaps I could draw her soul, merge it with mine, unit. Screw fear!

Megan's eye lit up, as our energy united. We lifted our right hands at the foe expunging our mojo through our fingertips. It gave off a red glow and hit the target. The instant the thing tried to enter another shadow, it exploded into tiny particles. The force flung us back, but somehow we both ended up eating dirt face first. I hoped Cal didn't feel too awful. Here she and I were supposed to guard our clan. And my sister The Key, combined with me, could kill these jerks! Together we pushed ourselves up off of the ground. Megan shivered as she sat up, and twisted around to face Nayla.

"We've got six left to destroy. Can we get some backup, please?"

Had the situation been different I would have chuckled. Nayla turned and motioned for Dan and Tri to join us while I searched for the additional shadows. Had they hightailed it out of here? What about the ones we'd frozen? Had they found a way to thaw themselves? Jenson was safe, Owl, everyone still breathing, alive, secure. The weight on my shoulders lifted. The problem, these things were still out there!

Trigger, where are they? We've finally discovered how to blast these suckers, and they withdraw!

"Afraid so, but they'll be back. I'll stand guard. It was a test, Starla."

"This was an exercise Starla, you passed. Megan, I never expected you to come this far so fast," Nayla rejoiced.

"Exercise? It's not as if I did any jumping jacks. Cal, our connection, me being the guardian. Is the entire thing a lie?" I asked devastated.

"It's not a lie. You're both connected, but your sister is blood. She's the key, and together you're able to do extraordinary things. If we combine it with the link, I'm not sure what will ensue. Dan, will you see that Starla and Molly move into the apartment you keep hassling her about?" urged Nayla.

"What about the rest of us?" questioned Cal.

"Yeah, and where's Star?" Maine wondered, scouring the vicinity.

"She left once the attack established our security," she answered. Then turned to speak with Minder. "Take Gavin and Gladiator back to their cell. Some help they were, If anything they drew in The Shadows."

"Will do," Minder replied, saluting her. She grabbed ahold of them both by the sides, dragging them away.

"Maine and Molly, thank you for staying, not running, and keeping your distance," Nayla noted.

Molly bowed respectfully then stood. "It was mostly Maine. She discovered the amulets to use as a safeguard."

"I got the chant online, then modified it. My mom gave me two red amulets. She told me to use them for protection if I ever needed them. I'd almost forgotten until this," Maine confessed.

"Does your mother practice dear?"

"No, not currently, but my aunt did. She handed them down to my mother before she passed. It was about two years ago now. She was considered quite eccentric, but lots of fun!"

"Alright, well that was lucky for us, I suppose. Thank the goddess everyone is still in one piece. Lance, that was some fine work; Shellena, I've never seen you so frightened! What happened?"

"Panic seized me filled with despair, guilt, and uselessness. I've never had this transpire." She shook her head in shame.

Lance placed his paw on her hairy shoulder, "Next time we'll use manipulation to draw them to Starla. I wasn't thinking clearly either. If I had been they'd all be dead," he told her.

"Please do not be troubled. We're in safe hands, and have what we need to eradicate them. Star will aid us in setting another trap, and this better be the last one. Cavin is at his wit's end. He retreated to the dining hall at some stage in this fiasco. He isn't as brave as the rest of us. Oh, and Owl. Has Ranger, Mike talked to you about Hunter's Park?" asked Nayla.

"He hasn't brought it up in days. I'll get on it. Mike's retiring this fall?" Owl inquired.

"That's his plan. Star told me you should start holding your pow-wows and Spring Markets here, but I'm getting off track. Let's sit, bring back our shield, then we'll disperse," Nayla added.

"Everyone's safe presently. Starla, I'm going to go. Amare will watch out for you, and so will I. Be safe," Trigger mind spoke to me.

I flopped to the ground while Jenson ambled over to me. Without a word, I took his hand. Megan, Molly, Maine, Tri, all of us sat near one another. I rolled my shoulders back, then forward. Jenson inched closer to me leaning in for a kiss. Our lips barely touched, and I pulled back.

"What's wrong?" he whispered.

"Nothing, I'd just rather be alone with you. Privacy, ya know?"

He nodded.

Megan smiled at me. Maine and Molly sat holding hands. My mom and dad were practically on each others lap. Young love, what about, old love? I thought, glancing at Nayla. My eyes wandered towards the huts as I spotted Star trotting out of the dining hall to us.

"Is everything alright? We're about to call the Sun goddess back," said Nayla as Star skidded to a halt beside me and sat down.

"Kaya's with Cavin. He had some kind of episode. Mango says it's stress related. She was arguing with him when I left. You know, telling him to let her take over. He's not having any of it, but he needs to rest," Star confirmed.

"Agreed, but Cavin is bullheaded. Can you join us? After, I'll go talk some sense into him."

"Good," she replied. Then took a deep breath before sighing.

Nayla closed her eyes, letting the silence fill the woods. We bowed in respect to Igaehindivo, the sun goddess. In synchronization, we lifted our heads to look at the sky. "Come back Sun, make us one! Come back Sun, make us one!"

The clouds parted, and the rays from the golden globe shone upon on us.

Chapter 16

Maine and Molly were certainly on their way home by now. I'd lingered discussing our circumstances with Nayla while Jenson waited outside. She assured me it would be safe for Molly and me to stay at the apartment. If needed, we could move in as soon as tomorrow. We stopped in the middle of the pathway leading to Hunter's Park. Jenson pulled me into him, and I pressed my body against his unable to get close enough. "I wasn't sure who to save, you or Megan. What happened back there? Did you panic? You know the paralysis spell. You didn't use it, and I thought you were going to die," I whispered in his ear.

He rubbed my back, afterward pulling back a bit to look at me. "I tried to there must have been something blocking me. And then I saw you take the lead, freak out, and it all turned out okay."

My heart beat rapidly as I pushed myself deeper into him. We'd never allowed this kind of closeness. He massaged my back, holding me for a few more minutes before he slid his hands away from my torso stepping back. My stomach fluttered with a desire I hadn't experienced before. Was this real love? I shivered while he touched my cheek with the tip of his finger. I kissed his lower lip, then top. Afterward, leaning my forehead against his while, we searched each other's eyes. It was a movie moment until he broke the silence.

"I love you, but we should wait."

"I love you to Jenson. I.. You could have been," I stuttered. Not even floored by the I love you I'd received.

"But I wasn't, and we're fine. Please, you've got what three more years of school? Me, we haven't talked about.."

"What you want to do?" I asked, reaching out to take his hand as I checked out our surroundings. It was strange seeing the forest lit up in the middle of the evening.

"Yeah," he answered, as we strolled on.

"Well, what is it?" I pressed.

"You'll find it silly, nuts, or unrealistic," he laughed. It was almost a giggle.

"You can tell me you love me, but can't tell me what you want to do for the rest of your life? Will it include me?" I tugged on his arm a smidgen pushing him to reveal his secret.

"That's putting on the pressure pretty lady," he chided.

I sighed. "I guess it is, so spill!"

"Owl asked me if I would take his place for the Ranger position. He's not sure if he wants it anymore. I'm considering it. Another idea he pondered was sharing the duties. I'd have to take a few more college classes," he explained.

"That seems sudden. I mean he was Du-Vance's best friend. You'd think he'd fancy it."

"Starla, you do realize you're using more girlie terms every day," he teased.

"All because I'm falling. No more trial basis," I said, gulping back tears.

"I should think so. After all, we've already spent a night together," he joked.

I pushed him aside spotting my family waiting for me a few feet ahead of us.

"Really!" I said, throwing up my hands while they sat at the picnic table.

"Be nice. They're worried about you. I'm surprised Tri, and Dan let us wander in the woods together after that event. At least we had some us time."

"True," I replied. As we walked towards them, Jenson let go of my hand.

"I'll see you later, tomorrow maybe?" he asked, then kissed my cheek.

I nodded, "Sure, I have to pack, converse with the parental units, and..." I stopped staring at Megan.

"Go ahead, if you need anything call."

"I will," I answered.

Jenson smiled at me and headed to his car. I sauntered over to the picnic table ready to leave.

"We should get going it's almost nine. We'll eat something when we get home," Tri said.

"Yeah, and I should pack. Maybe Megan could be of assistance? Dad, are you going to talk to Mrs. Fretner? You know, lay on the butter thick!"

Dan laughed, "Yeah, I can do that," he said standing.

"Alright, Megan, are you game?"

"Sure, I'd love to help. Plus, maybe I could decorate it a bit? Cal should stay with you too, don't you think?"

"I'll have to talk to Nuria about it, but we'll see. It is a good plan," I answered, then winked at her.

Megan and I sat on the floor in my room. We'd taken all of my clothes out of the closet and were trying to decide what to give to goodwill and what to keep. I held up an old pair of worn out jeans. Then my grayish T-shirt with Snoopy on it.

114

"Um, if you get rid of that, I'll take it," said Megan, eyeing the shirt.

"You can have it if you want. It's one of my fav's, but you deserve it after what you did today." I smiled at her, then folded the shirt setting it down. She sighed but didn't smile back. "What's wrong? Wasn't it incredible? I never expected we'd be fighting side by side."

"What about Cal? You two barely spoke after you left with Jenson."

"Cal's Okay. She's probably just happy these Shadows are getting vaporized." I professed, rolling my eyes.

"I don't want her to assume I'm taking her place. Nayla took me aside to tell me we'd discuss my powers when I visit next. Can I tag along when you drop off your things at the apartment?"

"Dad has to call the landlord first, but if everything is ready to be signed, yes. He's so sure he'll rent to us. But I have like no credit. Dad better be willing to vouch for me."

"Well, he got mom to let you into the clan, solve a mystery, and date Jenson. It's something, I mean look how far she's come. Mom's undeniably opened up more since he's come home."

"Right," I replied, standing and turned towards a box I'd hauled upstairs. Dad had given me quite a few. They were just lying around from when he'd moved in. I nudged it over with my foot to the pile of clothes next to us then bent down to pick them up. I had a handful of clothing when I heard my mom.

"Starla, Megan, the pizza's here."

"Come on Sis! I can see our pizza's now yours is filled with mega amounts of pepperoni and cheese. Mine has lots of banana peppers!"

"Me too," I added, jamming the garments into the box.

We skidded into the kitchen nearly knocking each other over.

"Sorry Sis, my stomachs grumbling," Megan announced as she moved past me brushing my shoulder. Then took the open seat next to my mom.

"I ordered everyone's favorite toppings," said Tri, placing a large piece of pizza on each of our plates. It looked like they had already eaten half of their pie.

"Hungry much?" I asked, taking a seat next to Megan.

"All of us need refueling. I can't say it was painless seeing both of you out there today. You're growing up at maximum speed. Isn't that what you say?" asked Dan.

I took a bite of my pepperoni pie, so I didn't have to respond. Then afterward washed it down with orange soda.

"Starla?" asked Tri.

"Yeah," I said, setting down my glass.

"I'm proud you've reacted positively towards Megan's abilities."

"Why wouldn't I mom? We're all in this together. Megan mentioned she's concerned that Cal may be upset because she and I were supposed to defeat these shadows. Did you get a chance to talk with Eva? Is Cal okay?"

Tri wiped her hand on a napkin beside her. Then took a long drink of her soda, setting it down before looking back up at me. "Cal's fine. Eva, I'm not so sure about. She got a message from Cal's father. He wants back in, to help us." Mom stared at the half-eaten slice on her plate.

"Isn't that a good thing? I mean, if she wants him back. Otherwise, maybe for Cal. She can have a relationship with her father again. Um, Can I see her tomorrow?"

"Once I get you settled. Chuck, the landlord gave me the okay. I'll need to sign under you on the lease. I'll pay for the first two months, plus deposit and after that, you'll take over. By then you should be back at Denny's. I pray to the gods we're all back on track by then," Dan said.

"What about Molly?" asked Megan.

"Molly's mother is a piece of work. I'm not convinced she'll let go of the reins. Starla, you should talk to her! Invite Molly to come with us to see the place," he suggested.

I nodded at him, then turned to Megan. "How are you feeling? Are you pumped, freaked out, or excited you've found a part of yourself now?"

Megan smiled, shivered, and sat up straight before responding. "I'm happy to get to be a part of the clan. I don't feel like an outsider anymore."

"I'm glad Megs, but you're still going to school tomorrow. Dad will drop you off.".

"School's good. I'll hang out with Tasha, and Chaz. Can I buy my lunch?"

"I'll make you a healthy lunch, but Thursday I'll give you money to go Ala Carte. Friday you'll be going to Grandville with us. You'll need to get your assignments that day for the weekend."

"Aw, mom. I have to wait till Thursday." Megan whined, grabbing another piece of pizza.

I shook my head at her pushing my chair back. "I'm finished, can I jet?"

"Go ahead, finish packing what you need. I can get you the rest later. After school tomorrow I'll take Megan to the apartment," said Dan.

"Mom, Dad, thank you. I can wait on getting a car. I'll be close to college and insurance is a ton anyway," I admitted.

My mom laughed, then touched my father's arm. He stood up from his seat and started gathering the plates. Tri took two of the half-empty pizza boxes off of the table and got up placing them on the counter. Megan still looked mad about lunch. She'd get over it. I thought, turning to leave.

"Sis, I'll be up in a minute to help you finish packing," she said, sliding her chair back from the table.

"It's cool. You should get some sleep. Aren't you tired from draining your magical energy?"

"Nah, let me help," she pressed.

"Jez. You've never been so obliging," I joked.

"Just let me, Okay. Then you can call Jenson, Molly, or whoever before you crash," she acknowledged.

"Fine," I replied. Then turned, heading out of the kitchen to my room.

Chapter 17

(Monday, April 12)

Beep, beep! "Darn alarm," I hollered, sitting up in bed to review the mess left from frenzied packing. I turned to hit the snooze button almost knocking my alarm clock on the floor. After I'd silenced the monster, I leaned against the headboard staring at the fox poster on my wall, close to the one of Buffy. I pushed the covers off of me to the end of the bed. Then willed my feet to the floor, stood up and began fixing the sheets and adjusting my pillows. Last night there was no time to call anyone. Megan and I stayed awake till one a.m. getting my things together for the move. I'd made piles of clothes for donations. Those had yet to be taken care of. Afterward, we'd filled three large boxes with items I would need. One of summer clothes. The other fall, and winter. Randomly, I'd selected essential novels and spell books, plus my compilation of Buffy episodes. I'd even let Megan borrow a book. Then made her promise not to tell Chaz or Tasha.

"Starla, are you up?" asked Megan, loitering in the hallway near my room.

"Yeah, I'm making the bed. Do you foresee mom changing this to a guest room?" I asked her as I finished.

"Nah, but she might add some books to that shelf. I saw a ton by her bed the other day. Want me to take down a few boxes for you?"

I grinned at her, then walked over to the boxes sitting near the doorway. I noticed her cute form-fitting jeans and an adorable peasant top with flowers on it. "Yeah, you can take two. I'll grab the largest of them. We'll set them on the landing. I've got to eat before we leave."

"Yeah, I wish mom would make us pancakes," she added. Then picked up the smaller of the two boxes. I laughed while I stacked the bigger two on top of each other, lifting them up as I carefully walked into the hallway.

"Can you see okay?" asked Megan.

"Yeah, I just look to my left around the boxes. We'll set em near the front door downstairs. If mom hasn't made pancakes, I will. If we have time," I stated.

"Can't I skip school today?" Megan begged as we headed downstairs.

"No way, mom would have a fit. I never skipped school, not even for a case," I reminded her setting my boxes aside.

"Little goody two shoes," she stated, giving me the evil eye. I held out my arms and took the box from her setting it down on top of the larger ones.

"There, now let's see what we can conjure up for breakfast," I said, turning towards the kitchen. Megan grabbed her coat off the rack in the hallway. Then followed behind me. The table was bare of any breakfasty items. No mom, or dad. Had something come up?

"I guess we're on our own. It's almost seven. I'll walk you to school, then head over to chat with Cal. I have to grab my cell and purse I left them upstairs. Can you manage?"

"I can make cereal. I'm not helpless," Megan scoffed.

"Good, I'll be back down in a minute."

"Hey, I'll get you a bowl of cornflakes. Do you want juice?" asked Megan.

"Do we have coffee?"

"Oh, alright, I'll make some," Megan groaned.

I half laughed, half smiled, as I headed upstairs.

When I reached my room, I saw my cell on the floor. It must have gotten bumped off when I turned off the alarm. I picked it up putting it in my pocket, hoping it was charged. Where oh where did my purse go? Glancing around the room, I realized it wasn't in the chair near my dresser, or sitting on the floor under the window by the bed. What about under it? I dropped down, pulled up the comforter, and discovered it in the farthest corner. I crawled to it avoiding the dust bunnies, and reached out, pulling it towards me. Odd how had it gotten there? I sneezed pushing myself backward, out into the open air. Dang, I'd have to move my bed, and sweep under it. That was nasty! As I turned, Trigger materialized before me.

I scrunched up my face in annoyance. "Hey, what are you doing here? I have to get Megan to school."

"I know, I'm going to keep an eye on her. Don't mind me. I'll make certain I'm not visible. You've got three days."

"For what?" I demanded, throwing my hands into the air.

"You and Megan have six shadows to disintegrate. I've spoken with Nayla. Cavin, he's resting. Everyone, including me, believes he needs to lay low. We can't have him dying on us."

"Good plan," I said, standing up. Then hurried into the hallway. I trotted down the stairs and practically leapt into the kitchen.

"Come on, let's go," I ordered.

"What about your breakfast?"

"I'll grab something on the way, throw the cereal in the disposal. There wasn't a note on the fridge from mom and dad was there?"

"No note, unusual," Megan observed.

"Yep," I responded, while I strolled towards the back door, eyeing the washroom where our dog liked to hide. "Did you feed Fritz?"

"He scarfed down his food, then ran to hide in the laundry room. I don't know what's up with him," she stated, shaking her head. Then got up from the table and threw the cereal away. I saw her grab a thermos out of the closet. "You'll need your coffee, get the creamer."

"Yeah, you're right," I answered. Then meandered back to the counter. I reached up and flipped open the cupboard above it rummaging around to search for the plastic packets mom kept in case of emergencies. After I'd moved a couple of items, I found them and shut the cupboard door as Megan handed me the container. I added in the cream and stirred leaning against the counter. Before I knew it, Megan had opened the back door and was standing with her backpack on her shoulder prepared to go. I held the thermos in my hand occasionally taking sips from it. A black outline slunk into the room. *Trigger?* He gradually faded into the background in a vapor like mist.

Megan gave me a weird look. "What did you see? Who was it?" she asked.

I capped the Thermos. "Nothing," I answered, adjusting my purse on my arm. I held the container in one hand, leaving the other free. "Let's go. I'd take a car, but with mom and dad, both gone. I'm sure there isn't one," I added. Thank goodness it had warmed up a bit. There were still some patches of snow lingering here and there. My cell rang as Megan locked and shut the door behind us. I pulled it out of my pocket, then picked it up. It had to be mom.

"Yes, I'm taking her to school now. Is everything okay?" I asked.

"Of course, dad had to go to a meeting for work. He couldn't give me details. I left for the library early this morning at six. Could you get Jenson to come over later so you can take your things to the apartment?"

"Mom, I don't have keys to the place. Dad hasn't even gotten them. Did he think about that before last night?"

"Probably not, sometimes he doesn't."

"Yeah. Anyway, after this, I'm heading to Cals. I'll call Jenson after I drop Megan off at school. I know I said I'd wait to get a car, but it would have come in handy this morning," I reminded her.

"We'll talk about it later. Are you watching traffic as you talk and walk?"

"Yes, mom. We're at a crosswalk now. I'll talk to you later tonight. Bye," I said. Then hung up, and pushed the phone into my jeans pocket.

"What happened?" asked Megan adjusting her backpack on her shoulder while we waited for the light to change.

"Dad got summoned to work this morning. Mom left earlier. I'm sure he just forgot to leave us a note. How's Chaz? You didn't say a lot about him last night. Friendzone still?"

Megan's eyes lit up as the sign changed to walk. We hightailed it a crossed the street, then turned to head to the school.

"I don't know if I'm comfortable with this."

"With what?" I asked as we walked down the sidewalk.

"Telling you about my love life," she answered.

I laughed, then placed my hand on her shoulder. We forged ahead while I held tightly onto the thermos of coffee in my other hand hoping my purse wouldn't fall off my shoulder.

"You never had a problem before. What's up?"

"Kissing is magical," she whispered. Then turned away from me quickly, as she blushed, power-walking in front of me.

"Kissing better be all your doing," I warned her.

"It is! I'm not dumb, and you're not my mom," she spat.

I rolled my eyes quickening my pace beside her. I didn't try to engage her in conversation. Once we'd reached the school, we stopped near the busing area.

"You don't have to walk me in. Tasha and Chaz are waiting for me," she said, pointing to them. They were milling about by the big statues.

"Okay, be safe. And I know I'm not, mom," I hollered.

Megan didn't respond. Instead, she waved to me and ran off to join her friends. Megan's sass was back. I hoped to see it on the battlefield in the next round of vaporizing The Shadows.

Chapter 18

As I trotted down the street, I finished the last of the coffee. Megan was right; I'd needed it. I took a deep breath of the fresh air and stopped to put the thermos into my purse fumbling with it before it unzipped.

"Hey, are you going somewhere?"

I looked up as Maine pulled up to the curb in her pink car. Then placed the empty container into my purse.

"Oh hey. I was heading to Hunter's Park. I'm supposed to see Cal. That, though, would be a foxtrot."

Maine laughed. "Hop in, and I'll take you. I'm on my way to pick up Molly. I imagine you know the way to Cal's?"

"Yes, it's a ways out. Have you heard of Outlook Point?" I asked as I strolled over. Then paused for oncoming traffic. Once it was clear, I sprinted to the car, flung open the door and climbed into the passenger's seat.

"Put on your safety belt , please. You really must get some wheels." She gloated turning the key in the ignition to start the car.

"Yeah, don't I know it," I responded, grabbing the seat belt. I fastened it and took my phone out of my jeans pocket. "Um, I have to make a phone call."

"It's fine. First, we'll stop by Molly's. You should invite Jenson. We'll get the whole gang together," Maine suggested.

I flipped open my phone to dial. "It's funny you should mention it. I told him I'd call last night. Megan and I stayed up way too late. Then mom and dad both had work emergencies. So, of course, I had to walk Megan to school. She probably could have made it there alone. You know parents, so overprotective."

"Not mine, I've been my own guide for a while. Molly's teaching me a few things, though. Keeping me in line, that is." Maine smiled, turning onto the street that led to Molly's house. I stared at my phone.

"Call him. I'm sure he'll be happy to hear from you," Maine coaxed.

I retrieved his number from my contact list, hit call, and dialed. It rang a few times before he answered.

"Hi, how's everything? Did you finish packing?" he asked.

"I got some of it done. Dad and Mom are at work. Dan had some kind of emergency. Maine and I are on our way to Molly's. Where are you?"

"Hunter's Park. Owl pulled me over here to chat with Ranger, Mike. Could we meet up later?"

"Maybe, the girls and I are heading over to Cal's. We're going to chill out, discuss current events if you get my drift."

"What direction are you drifting in?" he asked.

"Come on, be serious," I said as we passed several houses. "We've only got three days to pull this off. Then it's Grandville."

"Yeah, but take some time for yourself today. After that focus on our defense. Girl time?"

"Sure, but we'll in all probability be discussing Wicca, spells, and yesterday," I stressed.

"Okay, so either I'll see you later here, or I can take you to dinner?"

"Dinner is good, anywhere but Denny's," I added. Maine pulled up to Molly's house and rolled down the car window. I wasn't sure if it was to get air or yell for her.

"Okay, call me. Let me know where you're at, and I'll pick you up."

"Thanks, Jenson. Love you."

"You too," he replied.

I ended the call, then pushed the phone into my pocket.

"Are we going in, or are you going to holler for her?" I asked.

"Mrs. Fretner would never agree to that. Mol will be out in a Sec. She's probably throwing together some last minute items. I told her to bring our tarot cards, a few magic books, and supplies should we need them."

I wanted to tell her she was leaving out the Ouija board when Molly came bouncing out of the house onto the porch. She turned to wave goodbye to her mom. Afterward, Mrs. Fretner waved to us, then called out, "You girls be safe! Have fun, but not too much." Then closed the door.

Molly meandered to the car lingering beside the driver side door. "Maine, you brought Starla. So you're hanging out with us at the shop today?"

"There's been a change of plans. We're heading to Cal's. She needed a lift, and I thought it might be fun for us to hang. Are you disappointed?"

"No, that's a great idea! Do you like my outfit?"

Molly spun around letting her long flowing skirt spread out. She had on a blue hippie shirt with a red heart on it.

"It's far out!

"You two are becoming so retro! I'll hop in back," I commented. This would be an out of the ordinary day. I wondered if Nuria would be there or at Rascals? I missed him.

"Thanks," said Molly as I crawled into the back seat.

"I take it Jenson boy can't make it?" Maine asked.

"He's in a meeting with Ranger, Mike. Owls supposed to take his position in the park. He's not certain it's the best choice with all of the responsibilities he has to his tribe. He thought Jenson would be better," I acknowledged.

"Well, way to go Jenson!" Maine exclaimed.

"You Okay, back there?" asked Molly.

"Yeah, I was just thinking about Nuria and Rascal. I haven't seen them lately. You'd think they dropped off the face of the earth."

"Don't be so mellow dramatic, they're in love," Molly commented batting her eyes for effect.

"Even so, Minder has been left with the details of teaching Cal. I wish they'd just let her take the GED."

"Less than 5% of people with a GED ever get a bachelor's degree. It's a fact. So, I can see why they are homeschooling her the way they are," Molly explained.

"Huh, where did you get that? The internet?" I rebuked.

"Yeah, I did," she smirked.

"Good to know. Thanks, Mol," I answered, staring out the window. My stomach grumbled at me. If I was lucky Minder, or Nuria would have cookies or muffins.

Chapter 19

"Hey, Starla. Wake up, we're here," said Molly.

Groggily, I opened my eyes, shielding them from the sun, and peered out the window. Cal sat outside on the porch at a table. They must have set it up after the snow started disappearing.

"You found it Okay. Sorry, I fell asleep."

"It's alright. Molly helped me. I took a wrong turn back there, but we figured it out. Didn't we hun?"

"Yep, one wrong turn isn't bad," Molly replied, opening the passenger side door. A blast of fresh air blew in my face. It was startling, but just what I needed to wake up. I stretched out my arms, yawned and brought them back to my sides.

"I haven't spoken to Cal since yesterday. Have you discussed what happened regarding The Shadows amongst yourselves yet?" I wondered.

"Not extensively. We weren't a lot of use to you. Had we more time to prepare we could have been extra supportive. Send them to Hades perhaps?" Maine quipped.

I scoffed as I opened the back door. Then got out of the car shutting it behind me. I started up the walk, but Cal made no effort to hurry to us. She sat at the table eating her toast and drinking Orange Juice. Then smiled as I climbed the steps to the porch. Molly and Maine rushed to catch up.

"Hey, sit down. There is plenty of toast, fruit, and juice for everyone. Minder, Eva, Nuria, and Rascal are inside. They should come out soon to join us. They're discussing the situation with Cavin," Cal explained.

"He's still okay, isn't he?" I asked, sitting down next to her.

"Yeah, as far as I know. The elders are remaining cautious. Who can blame them? We have three days until the departure to Grandville."

"That we do," I emphasized, helping myself to a piece of toast off of a large tray already buttered. All right! I took a large bite, pulled out a chair and sat down. Molly and Maine proceeded to do the same.

"I'm still recovering from yesterday's events. How's Megan, holding up?" Cal asked, then took a sip of her juice.

"She's taking it well. It freaked her out at first, but she's on board. Last night while I was packing to move she seemed worried you might feel she was taking your place," I rambled.

Cal grabbed a jar of jam, then spread some of it with her knife onto another piece of toast. She looked into the window behind her. Minder, Nuria, Eva, and Rascal sat in an in-depth discussion. Cal winced as if in pain, and turned back to the group.

"Yeah, I'm more anxious about Dad, being back. He hasn't come to visit me yet. I guess he's been talking about going to Grandville with us. Mom thinks it's peculiar. Why come back if our life frazzled him so in the first place?"

Molly shrugged her shoulders, "He may have been overwhelmed. Did he even know about your kidnapping?"

"Apparently mom filled him in. He stopped by last night after I'd gone to sleep. I've been staying in Nuria's room. Minder doesn't seem to mind. Before that, I was on the couch, but she's been spending a lot of evenings at Rascals. She may even move in," Cal added.

"When did your dad contact Eva? Tri mentioned he'd gotten in touch with her just last night. Its sudden, plus out of place," I noted.

130

"They kept everything quiet. After the Bandits trial, he contacted my mother. I don't know who told him about it. Cavin's seen him, but no one was to give out information he was back. She hasn't discussed it with anyone til now. They spoke with me regarding it this morning. I should be angry, but I'm not. I was never close with my father," Cal answered calmly.

"Do you want to see him?" asked Maine.

"If he's permitted to assist our clan I won't have a choice. It's not like I hate him. I'm indifferent."

The door to the cabin swung open. I expected everyone to come traipsing out at once. Instead, Rascal and Nuria sat down with us. Afterward, Nuria turned to speak with Cal.

"Your mom's making coffee. She'll bring it out when it's ready. Minder went to grab your test results for your final midterms. The sixth-grade levels in Math, Science, and English. We're not worrying about the rest till later on."

"How long will it take for me to surf through seventh grade? I might not be able to start til after Grandville. Dang Bandits pushed me back in life. I'm trying to forge ahead," Cal muttered.

I patted her back, giving her a sympathetic smile. Then saw Molly hand Maine, a deck of tarot cards. I hoped Mr. Frenter didn't know about them. I could picture Tabitha having to defend Maine and Molly all over again.

"How are cards going to educate me?" Cal snorted.

Maine shrugged while she shuffled them. "They're not for that. I brought them to see what lies in our next conflict. It might give us a clue to the type of combat needed. It's not fixed, but when are they ever?"

"That's good to know," Cal proclaimed.

Maine spread out the cards, using the past, present, and future. She turned one over revealing the **Two of rods**. A smile emerged on her lips. "While it represents a boy, this card refers to communication, and experience gained in our pasts. It concerns new choices we'll have to make and our options. We have to trust our leaders in the clan. This card also represents a change.

"Go on," Cal pressed.

Maine nodded as she turned over the 2nd card the **Ace of cups**. "Strange, new love, lovers. Hmm, so someone here has found their love or some other emotional reason to celebrate. It's not explainable at this time, but it will be," she added. Then turned over the last card before we could answer her. **Four of rods**, Maine stood up speechless. "Someone in our group of family or friends will get engaged! Wowsers."

I laughed, "Now, these cards are only a guide. Let's not get too excited yet, it may or may not happen," I added.

Rascal kept silent and filled his plate with grapes, toast, and bacon. Then nibbled a bit as he observed us. I watched him wipe his hands on his napkin. He lifted his head nodding to Cal. "I'm not sure about those cards predictions. What I do know Cal is what you're due will return to you. Stick with your mates! They've got your back. You'll finish school. It might take longer, but eh. I didn't graduate until twenty-one. En, my father used to call me dumb. Now he's the one who's locked up. He couldn't put down the whiskey bottle," he grumbled.

"Where did that come from?" Minder challenged. She'd been eased dropping at the front door. I could see a green folder in her hands at her side.

"Life lessons need to be taught. I'm reminding Cal to keep at it. The tarot reading wasn't much help for Grandville. Thanks for trying Maine. The cards must have been picking up vibes from someone else. Anyway, Cal about your dad, he's going to assist us. Perhaps we shouldn't trust em,' but Cavin says everyone deserves a second chance. Your mom feels the same way," Rascal added as Eva came up behind Minder with the pot of coffee. She tapped her on the shoulder, and Eva moved aside. They sashayed to the table, and the door swung shut behind them.

"Starla, coffee?" Eva asked.

"Yes, thank you," I replied.

Eva picked up the mug beside my plate filling it up. "Cream?" she asked, pulling out a plastic container from her apron pocket. Then set it down beside me.

"Thanks," I answered, adding it to my cup. Maine gathered up the cards to put them away. After everyone had their coffee that wanted it, minus Maine and Molly. Eva sat down joining us. Minder had already chosen her spot next to Rascal. She flipped open the green folder and brought out a single sheet of paper.

"I'm pleased to say you've passed Math with an A! English, and Science you've maintained a B average. Nuria should work with you on your hypothesis skills, and grammar," she announced setting the paper aside. Cal jumped up and reached over the table giving Minder a high five, then Nuria, and last Eva. Afterward, plopping back down in her seat.

"Hey, I helped you the most," Nuria complained.

"Sorry, great news though, right?" she asked.

"Agreed. We'll wait to begin your lessons for seventh grade til after Grandville. Starla, Maine, and Molly, I'm pleased you stopped by. You came prepared. I wasn't planning on a tarot reading, though. What were you hoping to find out?" asked Nuria.

"What type of defense to use. I did a short reading, but they were picking up signals from someone else. It wasn't an accurate reading relevant to our mission. Megan and Starla still have shadows to defeat. We've got to come up with a better spell than a protection chant," Maine grumbled.

Nuria lifted her cup of coffee to her lips, took a sip, then set it down. "The book of spells next to you may be useful. We'll need to anticipate what the scientists might be planning. The real dilemma lies there. That is unless Triggers able to tip us off. Has he told you anything, Starla?"

"No, he's protecting Megan currently. It's crucial The Shadows recognize we have the power to eliminate them," I acknowledged.

Rascal sighed, reached over, and pulled the spell book across the table. He began to leaf through it.

"Do you have any experience with these things?" asked Minder, giving him a confused look.

"Nah, no experience. I'm a curious guy. Minder here, have a look. See if you can find anything to give us an advantage over evil scientists. One's who turn humans into Wolf Hybrids."

Minder snickered, glancing at the book, and looked directly at Rascal. She leaned towards him with her hand resting on her chin, "I am one of them you know. It's insane what they did, filled us up with all kinds of animal genetics, and chemicals. After that, we were fed raw meat. I threw up every time they forced it on us."

Cal shivered, pushing aside her leftover plate of food.

"Yeah, it would make me lose my appetite too," Minder commented to Cal.

I ran my fingers along the smooth surface of the coffee mug. Afterward, glancing at Eva. I cleared my throat before addressing her.

"Dan has it worked out that I'll be staying at his old apartment. He's signing the lease for me. Cal could stay there too. Not permanently, not unless you'd like her too."

Eva nodded and turned to Nuria, who shrugged. Minder said nothing. "I was considering staying in the dining hut to help with the planning for the journey. Nuria, you'll be at Rascals, and Minder, if you wouldn't mind keeping up the cabin. That is til we need you?"

"It would be useful having the place to myself. I've been meditating, asking my heart for guidance recently. Star believes I'm missing important details of my torture. If I can get them to return, I could determine our enemy's weakness. I haven't felt comfortable speaking of it. After you get Cal settled, and yourself it might expose itself to me," she answered.

"It's worth looking into I'm all for it. Cavin would graciously thank you," Rascal remarked, setting aside the magic book.

"Thank her? He'd ask her to move into the clan territory," Eva chuckled.

I placed my empty coffee cup off to the side. "Dad and I want Mrs. Fretner to let Molly move in permanently. We'd be close to the college, and Hunters Park," I blurted.

"Mom's reluctant to let go. She's afraid Maine and I will hook up. I.. I.. didn't mean to," Molly stuttered.

Maine covered her mouth, trying not to react. I wasn't sure if she was surprised at Molly's outburst or embarrassed by it.

"It's human nature, to desire another human being. I'm not sure why parents get so worked up about it," Rascal chimed-in.

"Because they can," I added, raising an eyebrow.

Maine nodded her head in agreement.

"What bites is they don't trust me they'll never be able to accept when I'm prepared to be intimate with someone either," Molly groaned.

"I'm afraid you're right. There is the fear of becoming a grandparent to quickly. One's inability to care for the children themselves I suppose. In your case, though, no kiddies. I don't mean to be rude, only truthful," Rascal explained.

"No offense taken. I'm grateful we can't procreate. Kids aren't my thing. What about you and Jenson?" asked Maine.

I studied Molly's reaction, and she seemed unaffected by Maine's remark. "Let's not go there. Especially given I'd have children with one-fourth of the Kitsune fox gene. Let's talk magic, healing, anything but procreation. I'm young. I want to live," I exaggerated.

Molly laughed, "We'd all like to live a full life. For me, it would mean being brave enough to leave home." Maine took Molly's hand in hers. Rascal smiled as Minder stood up from her seat. She started clearing the breakfast plates. Then reached over to grab my empty mug and bolted upright.

"Oh, Hey Shellena. We weren't expecting you. It's been a day of surprise visitors. Did you come with news? Where's Lance?"

"At the Park with Mike. Owl and Jenson are there also. Everything's good. Star is with Mango and Nayla. Dinner's at six this evening. The kits are fixing it, but it's self-serve. A brief meeting will follow, or not so concise. Nayla's edgy concerning the final elimination of The Shadows."

"Can we do anything to help?" asked Molly.

"Be there tonight, seven at the latest. I've got to run! I promised Lance I'd make it speedy. We're working on new strategies to share with everyone," she clarified leaving the porch. Then turned back to add, "Megan's at school right?"

"Yeah, mom wouldn't let her skip classes til Friday. Grandville," I stated as Shellena got down on all fours taking a runner's stance. She nodded to us then raced into the forest. I was memorized by her movements as I'd never seen her use her legs, arms, paws like that before.

"Shellena sure seemed like she was in a hurry," I stated, wiping off the last dish. I placed it underneath the small makeshift sink. Cal reached for the plug and took it out, allowing the water to drain. She nudged me, and I glanced at Maine and Molly. They were taking notes out of the spell book. Maine had tried to do another tarot reading earlier. It was a jumbled mess. Minder told her to put them up. She'd assist us if her meditations panned out. Had they found anything useful Rascal had missed? I set aside the damp towel and sat down. Cal pulled out a chair beside me.

"You found something?" she asked, leaning over to see what was written in the notebook.

"I wish. All the spells in here are rituals. They don't resemble chants, Lance's fireballs or the power shared between a group to banish or contain an entity. We're dealing with human monsters; human-made whom created themselves. Why were they messing with humans in the first place? We know they hate Starla's clan because of their diversity granting halfzies, and other creatures sanctuary into their society. They too in a way are modified, humans. They hate what we are since it reminds them of what they hate inside of themselves. Why though did the scientists create them? What was their purpose? If Minder can figure that out, at least we'd have another answer. I'm not sure if it would help us annihilate them." Maine slumped back in her chair appearing defeated.

"And those are your notes, what you've told me?" I asked.

"Pretty much. I jotted down a few items that may aid us. Molly and I will wear the amulets we have. I've got some money saved. I could purchase charms for the clan, or suggest they do so themselves before the mission," Maine admitted.

Minder stepped into the room and leaned in the doorway of the kitchen. "They would have to be specific to the individual for protection for it to work accurately. It's a good idea. I'd also suggest you have Star infuse them with inner strength, self-power. You'll need to propose it at the meeting this evening. I've got some bombs to drop there myself," she smirked, crossing her arms nearly hugging herself. "Cal, I want you to remember what occurred. I'm going now to ask Star if she'll lead us in meditation together. There's a chance it will reveal why the Bandits and I were engendered. I've nothing to hide; everyone needs to be present during the intervention. I'll do whatever I can to end this. Cal forgive me for being a coward when it comes to the scientists?" she pleaded. Her head hung low. I'd never seen Minder so upset or humble. Did she remember something? Eva came up behind Minder. She moved her arm out of the way and walked past her to sit beside Cal.

"How did we go from wanting to destroy the scientists to needing to understand why they've done what they've done?" I asked.

"There are reasons behind every action, causes, and consequences. Good intentions can lead to evil outcomes. Perhaps to justify our actions we need to know why they choose theirs," Eva affirmed.

"How did you? Are you psychic like my mother?" I asked.

"No, the walls are thin, and the living room is next door. A mother uses her tools to guard her children."

She must have discovered something before Cal started sleeping in Nuria's room. What I didn't know. My mind wandered to another dilemma.

"Hey, Mol how's Jinx? We've been so caught up in The Shadows. Is anybody on that?" I inquired out of the blue.

Maine gave Molly an alarmed look before getting up to push in her chair.

"What's going on? Is something wrong?"

"No. I'm glad you rattled my brain. I'd almost forgotten. Molly and I are supposed to meditate with him. If you want to come, you can. If not I'll drop you off at home so you can finish packing."

Molly picked up the book and Tarot cards cradling them in her hands, she pushed her chair back and stood up.

"Sorry, we have to run. A promise is a promise," Molly stated.

"Thanks for breakfast and letting us evaluate our circumstances. Gah, I sound like Jones!" I blurted. Minder and Eva grinned at my realization, as we turned to go Cal stood up from her seat and reached out to hug me. I accepted her embrace. Then let go, turning to leave with Molly and Maine.

"We'll see you later in the dining hall. Maine and I will fill you in on Jinx. Hopefully, we're able to ease his pain," Molly remarked.

"I hope so when it rains, it pours, and oh look at the rain," Eva commented.

"At least it isn't snow," I retaliated.

Chapter 20

Maine drove up to the back of the apartment near the rear exit, then parked.

"Are you sure you don't want to come?" asked Molly.

"Nah, I've got plenty of cray-cray in my life. I trust you can handle this, consider it part of your training. Good luck with Jinx," I said, closing the car door and waved as they left. I inhaled the clean air as the rain subsided. I'd finish packing, then call dad if mom wasn't home shortly. I searched inside my purse for my keys meandering to our stoop as I kept an eye on the parking lot. By the time I got there, the keys were in my hands. I glanced at the apartment to the right of ours shoving it in the door. I hadn't seen Fern or Earl in a while. A good neighbor would bring them cookies, but I didn't have time for that. I turned the key pushing the door open. Before stepping inside Fritz came bolting out of the laundry room barking frantically. He headed to the door in my direction. I leaned down as he rushed towards me and gently pushed him aside while I closed the door behind me.

"Fritz, it's okay. Mom and Dad will be home soon. Come upstairs while I finish packing," I said. Then unzipped my purse taking out the coffee container. I maneuvered around the corner of the counter and put it in the sink. Then turned back to the door, locked it, and headed out into the hallway. Fritz followed at my heels. Strange? He doesn't typically obey me. I bent down and gave him several pats on the head while listening for any intruders. Nothing. I tiptoed to our landing near the entrance, then turned right up to the stairs. Fritz raced ahead of me, and I followed him into my room. Nayla laid curled up on my bed. When Fritz spotted her, he began to growl.

"Fritz! Stop, it's only Nayla. Chill out!"

Nayla stirred, then stood, stretching out her body. She gave me a playful grin.

"What are you doing here? Jenson and Owl are at the park with the Ranger. Is there anything urgent happening?" I demanded. Then started picking up the clothes I'd left in neat piles on the floor. I reached over to where I'd left a few boxes and pulled them towards me.

"I needed to see you before tonight. How are you holding up?" she asked, jumping off of the bed onto the floor. Fritz backed out of my room and into the hall. I heard him clomp down the stairs. He was most likely heading to the laundry room his preferred spot in the house.

"I'm good. I mean, alright. Oh heck, I'm not certain at times," I said frazzled, closing the third box I'd stuffed full of clothes. Megan and I'd already taken three downstairs this morning. I picked up the shirts she'd requested setting them aside. My books I'd be bringing were in boxes next to my bookshelf.

"Following the gathering, I would like to meet with you, Megan, and Cal. Star will take Maine and Molly to practice their magic and Wicca skills," she said, pacing.

"Sounds like a plan. Will Cavin be there? I was just at Nuria's and Cal's. They said something about Kaya taking over?"

"She'd like to, Cavins rough around the edges. Unless he's unable to trot out to the meeting, he'll be there. I can't say I blame her for wanting to keep him on a leash. He's got some ugly internal scars. Not as fierce as Lance's," she stated, stopping next to my pile of stuffed toys.

"I haven't gotten to know Kaya well. And you're leaving me soon," I murmured, sitting down beside her.

"Not without the right tools I won't. I'll be staying till you, Megan and Cal have perfected connecting."

"Megan and I can vaporize The Shadows just fine. How does Cal fit in?"

"There is a way you can stay connected with Megan, and still protect yourselves inside the circle. Magic and knowledge are in a perpetual evolution with the users. As you've learned rules and responsibility accompany this."

"Nayla have you any idea why the Scientists turned humans into hybrid wolves? Who they were before this happened to them? Minder said she's struggling to recover memories.

"Our focus has always been on the Bandits. The goal was to stay in hiding until you came to us. You've changed our perspective since the recovery of Cal and Nuria. Minder, uniting with us was never expected. Only a few of the humans experimented on survived. The others, they didn't make it past the trial stage," she revealed.

"What? You never said anything about more of them? Now you tell me!"

"Because my child they no longer exist. They didn't make it past the process."

"How do you know this! Where is this news coming from?" I shouted.

Trigger materialized in front of us, "Because I told her. I've been observing them, attempting to get Intel for the showdown. I have your back. Amare's been with you since her last visit. You can't see her. I wasn't going to tell you either. We need you to believe in the power within. If you lose faith in it, we're toast.

She's here in case you slip or panic. She'll only step in to defend you. It's part of the learning sequence."

"Yeah, she said she'd be around. I haven't seen her recently. And now you're claiming she's been with me all along?" I asked, turning away from her in anger. I bent down and gathered the stuffed animals I planned on keeping shoving them into the carton beside me. When I stood up, I noticed Teddy on my shelf. I'd get him later. Nayla nudged my hand with her head and nuzzled up beside me. Trigger moved next to her as Amare emerged gradually til fully visible.

"Starla, Araina! You are bound to have questions about the scientists, what we kept hidden. All of it has been not only for our benefit but yours. Tri and Dan wanted to shield you. And so when we needed your aid, your father, let down his guard. You are a fine, trustworthy, beautiful women. Becoming one anyway, I realize you feel betrayed."

"So you know everything about the scientists! You've been hiding it since the beginning of this! You wanted to see for yourselves how smart I was. If I could figure it out? Could you have rescued Cal too?" I spat. Then stood up in a huff. I grabbed my stuffed bear off of my shelf hugging it tightly. "If you want my help, you'd better tell me everything you know," I snapped, backing into the wall behind me. "Was it truly the scientists that wanted to get rid of us? Or were the Bandits meant to lure us in so they could do experiments on us also? See if we could be of any use to them? All we want to do is co-exist with the world. I mean they used to burn witches at the stack. Does my dad know you're here?"

A door slammed downstairs, and Nayla jumped about a foot in the air before landing on her feet.

"It's only mom. She gets home first. Megan will be here soon as well," I commented, glancing at the clock that read five minutes to three. I dropped Mr. Bear on the floor, letting him fall near the window.

"We don't know everything. That's why we needed you. We were trying to respect your mother's wishes. She wanted us to wait till after you graduated college for you to discover your origin. Then Martin Du-Vance was killed. When that happened, we couldn't wait any longer. Your dad said you had gifts. The first step was getting Cal back. When we learned you shared a link it gave us the incentive to seek justice for Martin's death. We thought we had the whole thing under control until The Shadows showed up. Which leads us to the source that created the problem. The scientists. I never expected your sister to be The Key. Everything happens for a reason as absurd as it sounds."

"Please, what do you know? If you trust me, you can tell me," I pleaded wiping the tears from my cheeks.

"Very well then. Nayla, your permission?" Amare asked.

"None needed, you're her spirit guide. Trigger anything that might be helpful to Starla Araina, reveal it."

"Their intent was never to use The Bandits against us. They were prospective weapons in warfare. Minder hasn't been able to recall that. She said she remembers escaping their captors and the rage that developed after. The scientists used to pit them against one another. Then they banded together to break out from the unit they were held within. It's how they came up with their silly name. I always think of a raccoon when I hear it. The Bandits would have made them pay if they hadn't feared their creator. Minder's only been with us a few weeks. I couldn't expect her to lay it all out for us on one occasion."

"So, the anger is what they used against us. The Bandits were upset we exist because we are a natural chosen creation while they're human-made?" I questioned.

"Pretty much. Anger and hate do evil things to living beings. Minder said overtime Sika started to support the oppressors. I asked her their real names, human ones. She broke down in tears, said she couldn't recover them. They'd deliver electric shocks every time they said their true names."

I shuddered at the thought. "Now, I'm sorry I asked," I admitted.

"We'll discuss it further at the assembly after we've reviewed the battle plan for round 2 with The Shadows. I don't see us having to revisit this. Megan will be more prepared for what's coming," said Nayla.

"So we meet in the dining hall first with everyone. Then Megan, Cal, and I convene with you while Maine and Molly gather with Star?"

"Correct," Nayla replied.

"I should get back to your sister before she leaves school. It's where she's most susceptible to The Shadows."

I nodded to Trigger. "You should say hi to Dan. He usually picks her up."

"You call your dad Dan?" asked Trigger, cocking his head to the side.

"Sometimes. I better finish packing. I want to be ready to go when he gets home. This is it! I'm finally moving out on my own. Adulting, they call it," I added, grinning. Man mood swings, I'm such a girl. I shook my head at my inner thoughts.

"Ariana, I'll be with you," Amare said as Trigger evaporated.

"Beam me up, Scotty!" I exclaimed, lifting my arms towards the sky. Afterward allowing them to fall to my sides.

"What?" asked Amare.

"Oh, just Trigger and his tricks. He fades out and remains invisible. Kind of like being beamed up, disappearing and then ending up where you need to be. Like in Star Trek," I snickered.

Amare rolled her eyes at Nayla.

"At least it's a different pop culture reference. It sounds like something Dan would watch," Nayla acknowledged.

"One of Dad's favorites. Um, so you riled me up today, made me cry, even gave me data. Ha! I said Data!" I laughed.

"Another Star Trek ref, I take it?" Amare probed.

"Yep," said Nayla.

"Are you going to use the stairs, leave the ordinary way?"

"Nope, conventionality is out of the question. You better brush up on Buffy."

"Why?"

"You sound akin to Zander," Nayla retaliated, fading.

"Do you two always banter like that?" Amare asked.

"Not always," I added gathering up the boxes I meant to keep and placed them near the door. I'd put the others on my bed for dad take to goodwill.

"I'll be here if you need me."

I turned to face her. "So if I call out to you, you'll show up?"

"That's how it works. I encourage you to be self-sufficient, but should you discover yourself in danger..."

"I'll contact you, last resort. Nayla's got my back for now, and Trigger," I stated.

"Okay," she answered, not pushing it further.

Chapter 21

I sat on the floor next to the doorway of my room, leaning against the wall. Gah, it had been quite the day. Too bad it wasn't over yet. I needed to get my lazy butt up to collect the clothes I'd left on the floor near the last empty box. I'd put them in Megan's room for her. Then go downstairs and fix a late lunch, grilled cheese maybe? As I stood up, my cell phone rang. I reached into my purse still around my torso, pulled it out and answered.

"Hello?" I asked, resting against the door frame.

"Hey, is everything Okay?" asked Jenson.

"A bit overprotective are we?" I scolded. "Yeah, I'm fine. Nayla, Amare, and Trigger thought they'd visit me. Do they have plans for you at the meeting too?"

Jenson laughed, "They do. So maybe dinner is out?"

"Ah, I thought we'd grab something at the little pizza place in the convenience store, then head over. It will have to be fast. Mom's downstairs and I haven't gotten the chance to touch base with her. She showed up when Nayla and everyone came to deliberate over the scientists. They know more about them then I thought."

"More secrets, anything that will be able to advance us further?" he asked.

"Maybe. It explains why they're doing what they do, but not who they were before. After the trial, I realized The Bandits must detest themselves an awful lot to hate others. It's true. They were created for warfare. Whose war I'm not sure. I'm guessing the scientists were going to get a lot of money out of it. You know government stuff," I added.

"Is that what Nayla said?"

"She only said warfare, but what else would explain it?" I asked him shrugging my shoulders even though he couldn't see me.

"Right, but let's not jump to conclusions."

"Okay. Can you pick me up at five? Please."

"Um, Megan. Will you meet her there, or should she tag along?"

I felt my heart drop a bit, then cleared my throat.

"Starla, I understand you want us time. The other day our moment it meant indescribable things..."

"Yeah, but our focus should be on these shadows, Megan, and I's connection, blah blah blah," I complained.

"Ask her if she wants to join us. If not, it's cool. We all need someone to push us to be better people. "

"Mm-hmm. Sorry, I got sidetracked and didn't call. I'll still see you at five?"

"Okay, hearts," he replied, then I heard him hang up.

Hearts boys say that? I ended the call, then shrugged before heading to Megan's room.

"Hey, mom? Tri? Do we have any soda in that fridge?' I asked her as she stood staring into it.

"I don't usually buy it, but we might have a can or two left. It's been a long week. Is orange, okay?" Tri asked, taking out two of them. Then shut the door handing one to me before I could refuse.

"It's good, thanks," I replied, taking a seat at the table. Mom sat beside me leaning back in her chair as I glanced at the books and notebooks strewn about it.

"Lots of work. Aren't they letting up yet?" I popped the top on my can of soda. Then took a few sips and set it down.

"Well, we finished re-shelving books on the seventh. I wanted to research spells and psychic powers. I've tried using them on the neighbors."

"Mom! That isn't allowed. What if Nayla found out?" I gasped.

Tri snickered. "She told me I should practice. When we go to Grandville, it may come in handy."

I played with the condensation on my soda can, then took another sip.

"Everything alright?"

"Roger that. Nayla came to see me. She informed me the Bandits were initially produced for warfare, let me in on a few of the missing pieces no one has told me about," I added in a calm tone. Then stared at the can of soda in front of me.

"And you're handling it?"

"Yes, at first I was upset she kept it from me. Have you talked to Megan at all? Besides the other night at dinner?"

"No, the meetings tonight at six," said Tri.

"I'll be there," I answered, looking up at her. "Can you bring Megan? Jenson offered, but I'd like some time with him."

My mom put her arm around my shoulder, giving me a quick hug. I let myself lean in a bit, then pulled away, but she took hold of my arm tenderly.

"You and Jenson make a good team. As your mom, I have to advise you not to let him come between the bond you share with your sister."

"I won't. You should have heard him nagging on the phone about bringing Megan to the gathering. I need space. My own from all this. I love my clan and know it's my duty to look after them. That without all of us, we cannot get through this."

"I get it. Perhaps your dad knew better than I. He often has spoken the same way," she admitted. My mom drank the rest of her soda, then got up and put the can in the sink as the back door opened. Megan bounced in with my father behind her.

"I can't wait till I get my license. None of this bus or parental unit pick-up. It's not that I don't love you, dad," she stressed.

"Megan you sound more like me every day. You and sarcasm, it's scary! How was school? Grab a can of soda and sit down. We've got a gathering tonight."

Dan strolled over to my mother and kissed her sweetly on the lips while Megan ran to the refrigerator, and took out a cold orange drink. She walked over as I pulled out a seat for her.

"How's it going? Have you been keeping mom company since she got home?" asked Dan. He took a seat at the table while Tri lingered against the sink periodically glancing out the window.

"Nope, Nayla came to visit, then Trigger, afterward Amare. My day's been electrifying. Oh, and I hung out with Cal, Molly, Minder, and Eva. Rascal was there too. It was action-packed."

"Ah learn anything?"

"What I told mom, the Bandits were designed for warfare, government stuff presumably, but I don't want to rehash it."

"Alright then, at the assembly. Sorry about the emergency at work, did you pack?"

"Yeah, I'm set. Can you load it into your car? I have the boxes marked for donations. Jenson said he'd pick me up tonight for dinner. We've got a date."

"I wish I had one with Chaz, so you're ditching me?" Megan asked, lifting an eyebrow.

"No, I'll see you at the assembly. Apparently, there is going to be a spread of food there also. So we'll eat light. After the initial discussion, we'll be working with Nayla. Cal's joining us.

"So I get to learn new magic?" Megan trilled.

"Not sure, she said all three of us should be able to work together. Cal and I will shield the clan, while you and I unite to vaporize the bad guys. It sounds complicated."

"Cool!"

"And you agree to this?" Dan asked, turning to Tri. She stood near the sink biting her lower lip deep in thought.

"Why not? I left the clan due to my fear. Now that we're facing it together, and we've grown as a family I'm choosing not to run anymore."

Dan smiled, tearing up a bit.

"Oh, no tears, be strong. Okay? Starla, It's almost five."

"True."

"Help your dad, fill the car with your things."

"Alright, will do. And Megan?"

"Start your homework, in case we don't get home until late tonight," Tri ordered.

"That's everything going with me unless we rent a Uhaul," I commented as my dad shut the car door. I leaned against it scanning the small yard behind our complex. I could see spots of green grass growing. Megan and mom could plant the garden they talked about.

"I'll see about getting your bed there eventually. The one there isn't in bad shape. We'll purchase some new sheets for it."

"I'll manage. I can use my sleeping bag. Where will Cal sleep? It's one room, isn't it? One bed?"

"It has a room I used for an office. It's small, but it will suffice. Molly could room with you. It's not a huge space, but we could fit in a twin bed," he suggested.

I scoffed, "Yeah, maybe it would make Mrs. Fretner feel better. It's less likely that Jenson and I, or Maine and Molly will be getting it on if we share a room."

Dad laughed. Then shook his head.

"I'm just being honest," I answered, glancing at the passing cars beyond the parking lot. One that looked a lot like Jenson's pulled in trying to find a place to park. I smiled when I saw it was him. He seemed so serious. Hopefully, nothing was wrong.

"It looks like your ride is here. Can I say hi, or?"

"Um, Yeah. It's cool dad," I replied.

Jenson pulled into the parking space beside my dad's car, turned off the engine, and rolled down the window.

"Hey, how's it going?"

"Not bad. Are you prepared for the meeting tonight?" Dan retorted.

"Yeah," he answered, drumming his fingers on the steering wheel. "Mike has an announcement to make. I'm pretty excited about it," Jenson admitted.

"Well, I have to wait, don't I?" asked Dan.

My father, the impatient one, I thought, then nudged him with my elbow. I remained quiet, allowing them to chat.

"Mum's the word til later. I met with the tribe today. Rascal was at Nuria's I presume. One of my elders mentioned a mixture of certain herbs would draw in The Shadows. This way we don't have to involve the Bandits til Grandville."

"One less problem on our plate," I noted inching to the passenger door.

"I'll see you later dad?"

"Yeah, you and Jenson enjoy your twenty minutes, be there on time!"

"We will," he answered while I got in the car, and buckled up. My dad ambled back to the house, gazing back at us occasionally. Then waved before he shut the apartment door behind him.

Chapter 22

Jenson and I relaxed outside the convenience store at a picnic table. It had cooled down quite rapidly, and he'd given me his jacket to wear to ward off the chill. I pulled it around myself leaning into him. He draped one arm around me, and the held a slice of pie in the other.

"How's the pizza?" he asked.

"Fantastic," I mumbled between bites. Then reached for my cherry frozen, and took a drink. I nuzzled closer to him, but he edged away a tad. My heart fell, and I gazed out at the traffic on the street. "Is everything good... with us?"

He pulled me back closer but didn't answer right away.

"We haven't been dating long. I'm nervous about moving too hastily. I know guys are not supposed to think like that, but I'm not a typical guy."

I finished the slice I'd been eating, then turned to face him, taking his free hand in mine. "Just so we're clear. I'm not pressuring you into more intimacy than you can handle or want. Molly's been through this with Maine if you say no, I'll accept it. Any situation with us."

"Promise?"

"Yes, silly boy," I answered, leaning my forehead against his. I let go of his hand, drew back, and picked up my drink polishing it off. Without falling over Jenson, I got up and pulled my cell out of my purse. I flipped it open to gaze at the screen. "We'd better get trucking. It's five after seven. We're late. I don't want Kaya or Cavin to worry," I said. Then tucked it back

154

into my purse. Jenson maneuvered his legs out from under the table and jolted upright.

"Speed dating," he joked.

"Not exactly, but Momentarily yes," I acknowledged retrieving our trash. I tossed it in a bin alongside the end of the picnic table. Jenson linked his arm with mine, and we shuffled passed the entrance of the store, and into the parking lot

"Thanks for doing the dishes," he teased, moving to the passenger side door. He reached for the handle tugging it open. I slid into the car settling into the seat.

"Your welcome, now let's roll!" I exclaimed.

Jenson grinned mischievously at me, then shut the door. After buckling up I leaned over to push the door open for him returning the favor, and he climbed in.

"Crap!"

"Don't curse. What is it?"

"My birthmark is doing that glowy vibrating thing."

"Call them, if you're freaked out. It's not urgent, or Nayla would be here," he explained.

"Amare, tell them I'm Okay. We're on our way," I said out loud.

Jenson gave me a funny look as we pulled out of the convenience store parking lot.

"It's my spirit guide, you know her. She owes me one," I griped.

Quickly I ran down the path to the huts while Jenson struggled to keep up with me. I could hear him huffing and puffing. I tried not to let it bother me. He'd catch up.

"Starla, slow down. Earlier you were convinced Amare heard you."

I trotted at a slower pace glaring back at him. Once he caught up with me, I turned to him. "Do you see the sky? Those are rain clouds. I don't want to get stuck in a downpour," I hollered. Moving ahead, I gazed at the trees in front of me. Out of the corner of my eye, three rabbits scurried away while I picked up speed sprinting towards the huts. A loud rumble echoed in the distance as we approached clan-territory. I stopped to catch my breath when the first lightning bolt illuminated the horizon. Jenson stood beside me and placed a hand on my shoulder. We watched the light show for several minutes in anticipation of a downpour. From the right side of the forest, Nayla came prancing up to us.

"Amazing, isn't it?

"Yeah, but what are you doing out here? I thought you'd be in there." I pointed to the hut taking a step forward. Jenson and I shuffled closer to the door while she spoke.

"Cavin had me do a perimeter check of the woods. Jones can't make it tonight. Neither could the Trinity or the Crusaders."

"Oh, who the heck buzzed me? I don't see anything earth-shattering happening," I groaned.

"Cavin asked me to find you," she replied.

The wind picked up along with a crack of thunder that shook the forest. I reached for the door handle, then turned to Nayla. "Well, let's get inside before it pours buckets," I said, irritated and yanked the door open. We scrambled inside when it began to pour.

Jenson and I followed her down the hallway passed the reflection room. I sniffed the air as we went catching a whiff of stew and biscuits. As inviting as it smelled my mind wasn't focused on food. How had Molly and Maine faired with Jinx? Did they recover the lost part of his soul affected by his loss? Had they discussed Maine's initiation into Wicca? I hit something soft yet boney, then stumbled to the floor. Jenson bent down and reached for my hand helping me up. Once I was standing, I observed Nayla, blocking my way from moving further down the hall. I had almost passed the dining area.

"Why did you do that?"

"I asked you to stop, but you wouldn't respond! You left me no choice. Apparently, you were debating an intellectual dilemma. What's more imperative, than the meeting?" Nayla asked.

"Jinx healing, and Maine's Wicca initiation," I answered, twisting around to face the dining area. I took Jenson's hand in mine and walked right in.

Nayla trotted behind us chatting away. "I'm glad to hear you've been preparing yourself. Please take a moment to mingle, then be seated." With that Nayla swished her tail back and forth annoyed as she pranced ahead to Cavin and Kaya at the head of the table. Cal sat between Eva, and a man I presumed was her father at the far end on the right. She waved at us enthusiastically, then jumped up and hurried over to us. We met her half-way.

"It's so good to see you," Cal gushed. Afterward, giving Jenson and me each a hug. She pulled away, then glanced back at Eva. Then again at us, "I've been sitting with mom and Patrick. Um, my dad. It's awkward listening to them hash out issues I'd rather not hear about. Maine and Molly are sitting with Star. Jinx's not here. He left with Minder. Lance stayed, though."

"Did everything go as planned? Has Maine, or Molly, spoken to you?" I asked eagerly.

"They greeted me as soon as they showed up with Star. Later, we filled our plates with food and chose our seats. Have you eaten?"

"A slice of the best pepperoni in town. Thanks though," I answered. Then scanned the room for my folks. Gotcha! I spotted them on the left side of the table near Lance. Megan was almost sitting in his lap! I stifled a chuckle.

"I'd say Megan has a crush," Jenson blurted. Cal nodded in agreement.

I glanced at him annoyed, then let out a sigh, as I moved my shoulders back, reaching for the sky. Afterward, I let them fall to my sides trying to ground myself.

"Relax for now, but we better hurry. Cavin's about to use the gavel," said Owl, as he walked up to us.

Cavin's gavel swung down hard on the table. Wham! Wham! "Please take your seats, if you don't have one, find one."

I shuddered at his sternness as Jenson thoughtfully rubbed my back directing me to sit where Lance and my parents had made room for us.

"Now that I have your attention, Star will give us an update on Jinx's condition." Cavin sat back down while Star stood motioning for Maine and Molly to join her. A faint smile spread across her lips.

"Thank you, Cavin. I'm rather impressed with how this is evolving. I held a unique ritual mixing Shamen and Wiccan healing elements. We took Jinx to a nearby river where we formed a circle to bond with him. Once we helped him center himself into a position of peace, I burned sage. Maine and Cal spoke a healing blessing prayer. We stayed silent while he entered into a deep reflection."

Star stopped to look over at Maine who continued.

"He stated he spoke with Du-Vance. There he requested forgiveness, in which he claims he delivered. The catch is Du-Vance told him to rectify the wrong; he must go with us to Grandville."

"Why isn't he here then?" I demanded, standing up.

"Starla, this is the first step. The girls, Cavin, and the clan are stunned. As soon as we finished, I rushed Maine and Molly into Cavin and Kaya's chambers. I asked Jinx to go back to the Trinity, but to keep his silence. He, of course, is hard-pressed to unite with us," Star explained.

"Is there anything else Star?" questioned Cavin.

"Not at this time. I'm awaiting your decision regarding his attendance at Grandville," Star replied.

"Granted, but keep him out of the line of fire. We'll have Shellena and Lance use their venom if they need to. At present, let's focus our attention on these shadows."

My father stood clearing his throat, "Cavin, I spoke with elders from Rascal's tribe today. We won't need to use the Bandits to draw in The Shadows. They are putting together a bundle of herbs for us to use for that purpose. We'll still need to call off the Sun goddess. I don't want to hold off on this."

"Nayla, we've spoken and agreed you'll have the girls ready for tomorrow. There's one more concern to discuss before I give you leave to prepare. Am I correct?"

"Yes, I've already disclosed a portion of this to Starla," she said, nodding to me. "It's critical we distinguish the bandit's original role. The Scientists concept was to design a type of animal hybrid to use against foreign threats. They raced against time to develop a high bred animal killing machine and desired to be the first to achieve it. Minder said they were pumping them full of chemicals. She's been trying to recall who she was before the incident." Nayla paused, making eye contact with Tri, then Dan, and glimpsed at Cal's family. "I suspect they used humans due to their elevated intelligence, but I'm biased when it comes to animals. None of the other Bandits seem interested in discovering their past, and Minder hasn't confronted Sika. I spoke with her today after Jinx's healing. She's willing to grill Gavin and the Gladiator but refuses to talk to Sika. It isn't surprising given their history. Out of the blue, she confessed to me that the night we brought her and Cal to the park after their rescue, she'd felt at ease, in tune with the area. Almost as if she'd been here before." A sly smile formed on her fox lips, then she licked them and continued. "Of course, the Bandits would've had to know the layout to be stealthy enough to take our people and others. We can't rule out Minder having been a part of the kidnappings before Cal," she said. Then focused on Cavin with the gavel still resting in his hand. "We'll need to have multiple strategies. The Scientists may see themselves as innocent bystanders, targeting us simply to gain their weapons back or as Gladiator said during the trial, they could be after us as well. We cannot afford to let our guard down."

"Hear, hear!" Cavin agreed, raising the mallet above his head.

"I haven't seen you this animated in ages. You must be feeling better," Lance smirked.

Cavin lowered the gavel in his hand slowly, cleared his throat, then rolled back his shoulders settling into his seat. Afterward, handing it to Kaya. "It's a start. My sweet wife offered to take on a variety of my duties. I've granted her request. Nayla will return to her home in the arctic region when The Shadows are defeated."

I felt a slight change in room temperature as Patrick got up from his chair. Cavin motioned for him to speak.

"I want to apologize and ask for your amnesty. It was cowardly for me to leave without saying goodbye, giving a reason, or... - My life's been fairly unbearable. I've carried around a lot of guilt related to the choices I've made. I'll do my best to make them up to everybody including my family. Kaya, I'm determined to assist preparing the Bandits for Grandville. Cavin gave me the Okay, today. Lance, you'll permit to start A.S.A.P.?"

"Why not. I have gear for you. You don't want to get near Sika without it. He wasn't too bad when he first came here, but now he's highly uncooperative," Lance confirmed.

Cavin nodded in agreement, "I need to cut this meeting short. I'm heading back to my chambers. Nayla, Star, take those individuals and work with them. Tri, and Dan you may accompany Nayla. Eva and Patrick may also if you wish. Otherwise, you can help clean up the dinner plates."

Cavin moved off of his chair with Kaya's guidance. I stood up from my seat to turn to Nayla. Then let my hand graze her soft fur as she nuzzled my leg.

"Let's go. It could be a long night my sweet girl."

Chapter 23

I pushed the door to the reflection room opened peering inside as I held it for my friends and family to enter. A table had been set up against the back wall containing bottled water, granola, and fruit. To the right of that, an extra table was arranged with bags of different herbs, a bundle of candles and bottles of oils. I noticed a pile of books off to one side. Nayla nudged me inside, and I let the door close behind me. She gestured with her paw for me to sit in the center of the room where I joined Megan and Cal. As soon as I sat down, Owl slipped in, nodded to Dan and Tri, and then plopped down alongside Jenson.

"Where have you been? You missed the meeting, and Mike wasn't there. I thought you were going to make an announcement tonight," he blurted.

"Mike called me out since you'd already left with Starla. We had a situation in the forest. Three of The Shadows came upon our recently graduated kits now Juveniles. The ones we recently had a party for, Bitsy, Kern, and Glen. It was three against three. I found them first and used a foul herb to remove The Shadows. It's only a temporary solution. I stopped by Cavin's chambers to fill him in. He had Jones send out Trax and Sina to canvas the area for any unresolved issues. So my news will have to wait. Disappointing I know."

"Why didn't he contact me?" asked Dan.

"Cavin didn't want to disrupt the meeting. I'm sure Nayla would like to pull this together so we can move forward."

"Owl, thank you for the update. We're all playing for the same team," she reminded him.

I looked up and saw Star standing in the doorway of the reflection room. She sashayed over to Nayla in human form and sat down. Nayla continued, "I've set up a table with bottled water, and snacks. For Starla, Megan, and Cal, this will be emotionally and physically draining. Jenson, I've got a computer set up for you. It's on a desk behind you to the right of the doorway against the wall. In the past you've claimed yourself a super sleuth, prove it. Dig up dirt on the scientists using the clues you have. Maine and Molly will work with Star to create a healing ointment to use if needed during our battles. Tri, your psychic abilities need enhancing. When was the last time you used them?"

Tri laughed. "To spy on my neighbors, but it was mind-numbing," she admitted.

"You'll pair up with Eva. Please concentrate on the thoughts of those outside your own. Anyone in the room," she said. A sly smirk formed on her lips. " Patrick, join Jenson. If you desire to fight alongside us at Grandville it's best you recognize what you're in for. Dan, do you mind lending them a hand?"

"I'm on it!" he replied geeked to be included.

My eyes shifted to Owl, who looked annoyed that no one had asked him if he could help yet. Before anyone else spoke up, he blurted.

"What about me? How can I help?"

"Until Megan gains the full use of her abilities, I'll need you to continue shielding her."

Owl chuckled, "That I can do! I'll have the herbs on hand to draw them away, and back in. If only I could blast them as the girls demonstrated. I don't have a lot of talent in the magic arena. Apothecary, using herbs, natural ways to cure pain, and spirit quests. Those I'm more familiar with. Oh, and Kali sticks."

"These evil transparencies were created with one wicked imagination. Pun intended," I added, standing up.

"Wait, after we've worked on our goals this evening we'll come together to discuss our progress. It will be late when we're through. I'd like for everyone to remain near. I've got blankets and rolls to sleep on, and in the morning we'll have breakfast in the dining hall. Starla Araina, you and Cal will then be free for the remainder of the day. At dusk, we'll set up for the attack.

While Eva and my mother choose a private spot to practice their psychic abilities, Nayla led us over to the left side of the room. Space was cleared and a dense mat placed on the wood floor. Jenson and his gang were already deeply engaged in their internet search. I could hear them debating over what clues should be entered into the search engine as I attempted to rid myself of any anxiety.

"How exactly do we combine our abilities? Is it possible for all three of us to remain connected as we eliminate The Shadows?" I asked.

"Quite, it will take a considerable amount of concentration. As you're aware, you cannot always rely on fear to hold you up. It will often knock you down, if you don't stand up to it," Nayla advised.

"That's obvious, but I get your stance," Owl retorted.

"I'm glad you understand. Ultimately, you are to guard Megan. Don't hesitate to use any of your experiences in your native culture to fend them off. Keep those herbs with you to remove The Shadows just in case things get out of hand. Cal, if Megan and Starla break off the connection for any reason try to reunite. If you're unable to do so, seek refuge behind Lance and Shellena. I've spoken to them. They should compel The Shadows into submission before the removal takes place. That is our last resort due to the effects it has on those two. I don't want them to become hooked on persuasion."

"Okay, we get it. How are we going to practice without any shadows to wipe out?" Megan questioned.

"Star will create holograms mimicking The Shadows. It won't be precise, but it will have to do. It looks like she's almost finished setting Molly, and Maine up with the instructions for creating the ointment. Let's get into our positions. Megan, don't forget to use your salt on them. Do you have some with you?"

Megan reached into her pocket, pulling out a small purple satchel.

"Good, keep it with you at all times." Megan nodded to her pushing it back into her pocket while Nayla continued. " I want to make note that at Grandville Cal and Starla will both need to be able to morph in and out of fox form. Due to this need for mobility Kaya is working on outfits, so you shift without needing new clothes. I'm getting ahead of myself, though. Let's get started."

"Can we meditate first?" asked Cal.

I snorted, shaking my head at her.

"What?"

"This coming from the girl who thought, meditation was hokey!" I teased.

"I clear my mind of all negative thoughts, visualize my objective, and afterward invoke it," she replied.

"I'm impressed. When have you had time to work on this? You've only been meditating for a short time." I assumed, taken back by her choice of wording.

"In between studying, but mostly before bed. Minder and my mother encouraged it. Last night I slipped into sleep before ending my reflection. Nothing happened," Cal replied, gloomily.

I laid a comforting hand on her shoulder. "It will come. If not maybe the guys will find something on the net," I said reassuring her.

"Boo-yah!" Jenson hollered from the other side of the room. I chuckled at him as I removed my hand from Cal's shoulder glancing his way. He jumped up from his seat while Patrick and Dan got up to fiddle with the printer. It looked ancient.

Star turned her body towards them, "I'm glad to hear you're finding useful material, clues?"

Patrick gave Cal a thumbs up as Dan loaded the paper. "Yes, if we can repair the printer. If not I'll e-mail them to myself," Jenson replied.

"Good, keep it to a minimum. I'll need to concentrate on creating the hologram for the girls training." Star turned her attention back to Molly and Maine. "Are you all set? Instructions, spell work, and afterward, please advance with the meditation." They nodded to her as Cal, Megan and I took our positions. We stood to form a sort of triangle, Megan up front and Cal and I beside one another. "Alright then," Star called, briskly trotting over. She stopped next to Nayla only a few paws away from us.

"This is how it's going to work. Cal and Starla, you will merge to create the barrier. Then after you've united, and this is the trickiest part. Megan must recreate the terror experienced in the presence of The Shadows. It was your panic that grabbed hold of Starla combining your powers. In fright, you unified to eliminate the enemy. If you're not capable of re-enacting this it could cost us our lives," she sternly stated.

Nayla cleared her throat, "While Star is preparing, you'll meditate as Cal requested. Unclutter your brain of any unnecessary idea's leaving an open entrance for each other. Starla, you'll have to split your soul and energy between Cal and Megan. Begin!"

"How? What?" Megan blurted.

"Bow your heads, focus clear your mind, and when I reach out to you follow me," I instructed her.

Nayla nodded in approval. My feet were a bit sore as we'd been standing for nearly a half hour. I lowered my head, closed my eyes, and let go. I couldn't read minds but had felt Megan's emotions during the raid of The Shadows. I reached out to her and Cal. They both appeared in a state of calm. Good, that's what Nayla had asked of us. After several minutes, I nudged Cal wondering if there would be an ambush. She opened her mind to mine. An unexpected flood of scenery entered my consciousness. Cal and I were back at the dining table with Nayla. The speech was inaudible, but I met her halfway adding to the memory allowing her inside. The pulse beat quickly, my eyes fluttered open as shadows surrounded us. I counted six of them dancing in front of us.

"Megan! They're here!" I shouted. My heart pounded in my ears, I pressed the pulse outward, and Cal drew it back a bit.

"We don't want to burn Megan!" Cal blurted.

Owl stood behind her, not sure what to do. He didn't have his tools with him yet. Plus, I don't believe the illusions could be dismantled using them.

"Monkeys! The witches rats are here," Megan cried ducking to the ground. She pushed her hand into her pocket searching for the salt, pulled it and got ready to aim.

Oh great, *The Wizard of Oz* thing, here we go! I focused a part of myself on Cal, our mission, the bond we shared and promptly snatched Megan's hand. She must have a greater fear of monkeys than gremlins because I felt a spark as soon as our palms met. I had to pull back to leave a part of myself with Cal. Once I'd stabilized both presences of my soul, I shot out my right hand. Megan flung the salt in her left in the direction of The Shadows. They scurried, then drew near again.

"Hurry up! We don't have much time! They're after us!" I screamed.

She nodded, and we lifted our hands, aiming at them. First, we took out the one in front of us together, and then I turned to the side near Cal. Bam, Bam, One two three four! I hoped it would be this effortless in the field. Two more were left lingering beside Cal. I would have to turn away from Megan. I broke out in a cold sweat. Come on get it together Starla. "You've got this," I muttered.

"No, we've got it, let's use our joined hands. I'll twist the opposite way to the side. We'll blast the one headed for Owl together. Let me get the one behind Star. Hit it!" Megan cried.

We'd still need to blend our powers. I hoped she realized that. Together we stretched out so we could pull a Spiderman. Instead of webs a red light, either signifying blood, or our hearts would slay it. In unison, we raised our hands. I felt her push, and I joined in til the red light flared out towards The Shadows. I struggled to maintain my link to Cal as it struck it. Pain seared through me, but I stayed standing. Megan took out the last Shadow alone. My hand fell from hers while I stumbled over my feet onto the ground. I lay sprawled out, breathing, and stared at the ceiling.

"Now that was intense. And here I imagined it would be simple. Given that they were holograms," I announced to whoever would listen.

Chapter 24

My whole body ached something awful as I leaned against Jenson. He'd helped me up to stretch earlier before everyone had gathered around the snack table. We stood off to the side as I held my bottled water in my hand.

"Hey, come sit with us. There are empty seats you two. Please at least try to eat something," Megan pleaded, holding a half-eaten carrot stick in her hand.

I sighed, as Jenson eased me towards the table. Eva and my mother sat discussing their ability at the farthest end next to Star and Nayla. I picked up bits and pieces here and there. I set my water down, then pulled out a chair between Cal and Megan. Patrick slumped next to her while my dad munched on a handful of peanuts. They kept their eyes on me as I sat. What did they think I was going to do faint dead away? I'm exhausted, not overheated. Jenson planted a kiss on my head, then hugged me from behind. Owl glanced at us from the left corner.

"I'm going to sit with Owl," Jenson murmured in my ear.

"Alright," I answered, as his hands slide off my shoulders.

Megan grabbed some crackers, and cheese placing them on a plate for me. Usually, I would demand to do it myself, but I let her.

"Thanks," I said, and began to nibble. Then took several slow sips of water. It was strange how my sister hadn't even seemed to break a sweat. I put the water bottle down and capped it.

"Megan how come you're not affected by this?" I asked.

"I wish I had an answer," she responded, diverting her eyes to her plate.

"Starla, everyone's affected differently. Look at what happened the last time," Nayla commented.

My father nodded in agreement while I played with the leftover crackers on my plate.

"Enough whoa is me! Can I tell them? We could all use some uplifting news," Jenson suggested, grabbing a handful of grapes out of a bowl. He began to gulp them down.

"About the scientists, or our new positions as Rangers?" Owl asked, lifting an eyebrow.

I smiled, "So you're both going to patrol the park?"

"Not at the same time. One of us will be on night duty, the other during the day. Neither of us will have the gig full time. We'll need to work it out with class schedules," Owl revealed.

"It's not all planned out currently, but for now it will ease up on Mike. He'll take a few days off. Jones will be on high alert until tomorrow night when we annihilate these Shadows!" Jenson stated.

"Who's watching the park now," Star piped up.

"Jones and the immortals. Mike went out on a date this evening, some blonde chick. I'd never met her before," Owl admitted.

I rolled my eyes, men, boys, males on occasion they could be remarkably sexist. I laid my head on the cold wood table ready for a nap. The silence was music to my ears. Everyone had stopped talking. A few moments later, my ears perked up at the sound of rustling papers.

"You can't fall asleep, we haven't even told you about the scientists yet," Dan stressed.

I sat up as my dad leafed through a small pile of papers. All eyes were on him as he placed them in order.

"What did you find? Is it going to help us?" I demanded.

171

Tri smiled at him knowingly, and Eva elbowed her.

"You two, know something, don't you?" asked Star with a glint in her eyes.

"We overheard them discussing it using our psychic ability. You said to practice," Tri smirked.

"That I did, but let's let Dan reveal what he discovered. You can fill us in on any missing details if you deem them important," Nayla suggested.

"Okay. Honey, tell them what we're in for," Tri remarked.

"Since we're relatively sure they're hiding in Grandville, Illinois. I scoured the newspapers for any stories connecting them to that region. Jenson specifically searched for individuals with degrees in genetic engineering. A lot of them popped up, but only five stood out beyond the rest."

"Was I correct? There were two women and three men?" Cal questioned.

"Yes, but only two of the men are left. One died in an explosion a week ago in a warehouse used as a short-term animal shelter. The paper's said he volunteered there. It's probably a cover for what they're doing," Dan answered.

"Did you get his name? Were any others mentioned in the paper?" Nayla asked, twitching her tail back and forth.

"Jed Burg. It said the other volunteers were shaken. My guess is they were moving animals out of there. Perhaps attempting similar experiments on them as the Bandits? Why else would they be involved?" Dan questioned.

"I'm not certain. We'll want to look into the motive behind why they'd be in such a rush to generate new versions. Especially if they were going to come after us to get the Bandits back? Although they would have to alter them to function properly." Patrick shook his head in disbelief.

"Sika's the only one I could see rejoining their charade. Gladiator and Gavin are cooperative and even go against their leader at times," I added.

"It seems that way. We have to be on high alert in spite of what they appear to be. I don't want to chance them turning on us," Dan confirmed.

"No one wants that. At least we have an idea of what the scientists are up to," Star acknowledged.

"Also an address, I highlighted it. It's possible they're located close to where the shelter was. I'll ask Trigger, see if he can get us any dirt on it," Dan stated. He quickly scribbled something onto the paper.

I cleared my throat as a mist-like vapor dispersed into the room. He'd been watching over Megan, so I wasn't surprised when Trigger materialized beside Megan's chair.

"So you're aware of the situation. They haven't been able to replicate anything. The explosion ruined their plan. As for names, I can give you first, but not last," he explained.

"How did you get them?" I demand, pushing my plate aside.

"Starla I cannot disclose that, I'm being held by one of them. I've been unable to decipher which of them it is. It's too bad, Jed wasn't holding me captive. I'd be free. These names should help, but they're only first names: Zane, Rob, Bonnie, and Mara. I'll have more for you soon. Now get rid of The Shadows. The one holding me is controlling them. Once they're gone, she's no threat to me. If I were to detach from her now, she would use them against me. Good luck," he replied. Then bowed his head low to the ground and vanished.

Megan trembled in her seat next to me. I laid my hand on her shoulder, drawing her into a hug. "It will be okay. He hasn't let us down yet. We've got to trust him," I reminded her.

Megan pulled away, then turned to Nayla. "Can this be over, for tonight, at least I'm pretty spent. I'm not sure even Starla will want to move into the apartment now."

"Mango took care of it. Of course, your things are not all there. She just made up the bed, and put some items in the refrigerator for you."

"Okay, what about Molly and Maine?" I asked, looking over at them. "If they'd like to stay I could grab those sleeping bags you said you had handy. Did you guys finish the ointment? And what about new spells?"

"The ointments complete. We prepared several small jars for each member to keep with them. I'll hand them out before the journey. It heals most injuries, but cannot be used for gunshot wounds or large gashes. Those Molly will need to attend to, and I'm hoping it won't come to that. Maine, why don't you both explain what you've found," Star suggested, nodding to them.

Maine pulled the notebook on the table towards her, opening it to the first page and began to read. "When a practicing Wiccan reaches out to the goddess of the earth for the first time she's often gifted with one specific powerful ability. While there is light and dark within the practice, you must use your power responsibly." Maine paused as her hand lingered on the page. It lifted slightly, then fell back into place.

Did she do that? Could she move things? I glanced at Tri, and Eva, who did not seem shocked one ounce. The rest of us sat waiting for her to react.

"Tell them... You know when you talked to her," Molly pressed.

"Last night I set out to embark on my usual path of meditation before falling asleep. I relaxed on my bed with my legs crossed, allowing my hands to rest on my thighs. It's something I've always done, and it's used in numerous practices. I wasn't trying to call out to anyone in particular. As I sat, I focused on a picture of my aunt. The one who used Wicca. Something inside of me told me to move it, guide it towards me. A voice. It had to have been the goddess. I'm not sure how long I concentrated, but after several minutes it began to shake. Then levitated up off my shelf, floating towards me little by little. All of a sudden it flew into my lap. It totally, made sense after Star shared this information with me," she explained.

"And?" I added.

"Starla, that's it. I'm sure if I tried again, it would work. Star said it might be useful in a tough spot or situation. It's not as if it's as cool as transporting from one place to another in seconds, but it will do," Maine added.

Star laid a hand softly on her arm, "It will. Molly spoke to me regarding the amulets you mentioned us getting. I have the list and pictures from the website. Tomorrow at breakfast, I'll pass it around. Please pick one that calls out to you, write your name next to it. Once I get them, I'll place them on your neck; then we'll infuse them together with strength drawing from one another. Now go, get some rest. We've got a great deal to accomplish in the morning. Starla Ariana, Dan, Tri, Patrick, and Eva, thank you. Megan, Molly, and Maine if you could remain close it would be pleasing to us." Star allowed her hand drop off of Maine's shoulder. Instantly I stood up from my seat to help, but Nayla shooed me away.

"You need your sleep. I'll see everybody in the dining hall for breakfast, say ten-ish. Star, help me clean up," she ordered.

Star nodded to her as we collected our things, and left the room.

Chapter 25

Even with the Sun goddess protecting the park, the moon stood out in the sky above. I shuddered against Jenson as the cold wind blew through the forest. He held my hand in his, and we leisurely strolled down the pathway to the public area of the park. Molly, Maine, Cal, and Megan ambled on ahead of us. My sister had wanted to hear all about Maine's new ability. I couldn't blame her since it would be valuable to the final mission. It could be used to levitate an item in the enemy's possession or from a distance when they weren't looking. I'm sure Lance would capitalize on that. Heck, I was super surprised Owl hadn't brought it up.

"Owl left in a hurry. He didn't even stay to help Nayla and Star clean up. Where do you think he was going?" I asked.

"Home, he's hardly ever there. He told me the other day his folks have hit a rough patch. It's not something he discusses much."

"Oh," I answered, pulling his arm closer to me nearly hugging it. I saw Mom and Dad join Patrick and Eva up ahead. My eyes shifted to Megan, who kept walking as Molly and Maine slowed down. Were they waiting for us to catch up to them?

"We should go walk with them. I hope Molly's mom lets her stay. Do you suppose she's called her yet?" I asked.

"You know Molly. I love her, but she needs to stand up for herself. She's twenty-one."

"Your right Jenson. She does," I replied, as we drew closer to the parking lot. We were about to power walk over when Maine grinned at Molly, grabbed her hand, and skipped to us. Cal jogged along behind them. I smiled, as a short giggly snort erupted out of my mouth.

"Hey, I've convinced Molly to stay. It's going to be packed in your new place. Because everyone is staying there for the evening it should put Tabitha at ease," Maine added.

"That's a plus. Are you feeling confident about everything?" I stopped to scan the area for Megan spotting her beside Mom and Tri. Dan and Patrick spoke in hushed voices beside them. I relaxed knowing she was safe and felt Jenson drop my hand and ease his arm around my shoulders. We continued walking.

"Sort of, I'm not used to being able to move things with my mind. I'm more familiar with spellcasting, and chants."

"And you're a good teacher," Molly grinned.

"Thanks," Maine replied.

Cal yawned, turning to Jenson unexpectedly. "I'm kidnapping my best friend," she blurted.

"Is that alright with you?" he asked me raising an eyebrow for effect.

I shrugged, then lightly removed his hand from my shoulder. "Cal, did you remember something from your capture? Are you going to be okay?"

Without speaking, she placed her hand on my back guiding me away from the others leaving Jenson with Maine. After we'd walked a few feet, we stopped outside the entrance of the trail to the park. I took a few steps back and leaned against a tree crossing my arms.

"So what's up? Spill" I demanded.

"The names Trigger gave us sparked something inside of me." Cal shivered, almost shrinking back from the scenery in front of us.

"Are you sure you're all right?" I grabbed her hand, then squeezed it reassuringly. My eyes wandered to my family and friends as they hurried to the parking area. I watched them crowd around Ranger, Mike. Cavin's van sat parked in the lot. He must have left it for us to use in the morning.

"Yes, I'm safe here. I know that, but I need to.... I want you to be the first to know, and then I'll tell the others."

"Have you had any crazy dreams, illusions?" I asked, standing up straight. Then moved away from the tree.

Cal came closer to me, leaned in and whispered, "No, but I've met with them. No one knows, not even Nayla."

"Who?" I shivered, backing away from her speechless.

"The Bandits," she hissed.

"What does that have to do with the names Cal?"

"I heard them before. Sika would repeat them over and over again. Until tonight I didn't remember! I couldn't sleep most nights at the campsite and spent a lot of them tossing and turning due to weird noises. The Bandits made us move periodically so we couldn't be found. They lived in fear of the scientists discovering us. Every so often I would imagine I was somewhere else, at home in bed, warm and safe. If I was lucky, sleep would come. It didn't always work though." Cal paused and ran her hands up and down her arms, trying to get warm searching the trees for an unknown adversary. I wasn't sure what or who she was looking for. Before I could ask her anything else she sprinted to the van passed Mike and the others. I watched as she opened the door, scrambling inside.

What had spooked her? Did she see something in the forest I hadn't? Was it flashbacks from the past? I stood there stunned by her words. What else was buried within her? There had to be more to the story than this. If she was keeping secrets, it wasn't cool. We were supposed to be best friends. Then again, she'd been missing for years.

"Starla, is everything legit?" asked Jenson. He'd come up behind me while I was deep in thought.

"I'm not sure." I put my hands up to my temples and rubbed them. I hoped I wasn't starting to get a headache. Jenson went to put his arms around me, but I grabbed his hand instead. "Let's go. It looks like everyone's waiting,"

"Okay," he said, nuzzling my hair.

The van lurched forward as I snuggled up to Jenson. Cal sat in the midsection near the front with Maine and Molly. We'd chosen a seat in the back. I didn't feel like dealing with Cal or her vague messages. I closed my eyes ready to drift away when I heard them discussing a new spellbook Star had given them.

"Are you worried about Cal?" Jenson inquired.

Pain in my heart lingered. Why did I have to feel so close to so many people? I pushed myself closer to him wishing I could hide. I didn't want to be myself anymore. I sighed, not sure where my emotions were taking me.

"Starla, talk to me."

I shook my head no, and closed my eyes, waiting for sleep to come. I didn't want to deal, was this me? Was I a girl who ran away from my problems? As I drifted in and out of consciousness, I dreamed.

"Amare, Trigger? Where am I? " I asked, looking around. My eyes focused and I could see the beautiful golden wheat all

around me. It was my field, my sanctuary. Had I come here to seek inner peace? Guidance? I stood there for a moment, then sat down in the middle of it all. The cool breeze blew back the wheat as Amare stepped out. She pranced up to me, bent down, and sniffed my hair before sitting next to me.

"Sweet girl, trust Cal. She's struggling with what they did to her. Forgiveness is the key even concerning our worst enemies."

"They killed our kind Amare! How can you excuse something like that? Vengeance out of hatred, anger, pain, and.... And..".

"What is it, we hold for the Bandits? Is it not the same?"

"It's not the same as taking away life. They may have had their lives altered by changing who they appear to be, but their lives weren't stolen from them."

Amare's eyes brimmed with tears and as they dropped flowers sprung up out of the ground.

"From pain comes beauty, growth in the aches we suffer. It's difficult to see while we are passing through the phases in life as the moon itself changes."

"I can't accept it, I can't," I hollered, pounding my fists into the seat. Then stiffened when a hand touched my back. Whoever held it there hastily pulled away when I'd tensed up. Opening my eyes, I realized I was still in the van. Everyone had left except for Cal merely inches away from me.

"I was waiting for you to wake up. That must have been some dream! Jenson and everyone, are inside. It's late, almost one a.m.," she said, rubbing her arms to keep warm.

I sat up, pushing my hair away from my face, and leaned against the seat. I didn't want to go inside yet.

"I don't understand why you ran. What's going on with you?" I demanded, keeping my eyes on the floor.

"Please, I trust you. Don't shut me out. You saved my life, you've been here for me, I've been there for you, at least recently. I wouldn't put the clan in harm's way. I needed to face the Bandits. They have me on edge, all right, I've lived with terror for years. That's why I didn't want to face it. But I had to do it, take control. I.. I.. Really gave it to Sika. He put Minder through so much! He'd better leave her alone," she grumbled.

I lifted my head up, and Cal's eyes met mine. Streaks of tears glistened on her cheeks. I leaned forward and pulled her down to sit next to me. "What did you do to him?"

"At first, nothing. He kept badgering me imagining I'd leave. It made me want to hang around more. Maybe he'd blurt out a clue to me in a rage. When he didn't, I asked him about the scientists."

"And?"

Cal ran her hands along her thighs, rolled her shoulders back, and her head from side to side. I could tell she was trying to loosen up. Had she made them promises for information? I couldn't think of a whole lot we could permit them to do by law, considering Amare wanted me to forgive them.

"You didn't agree to let them kill the scientists did you!" I shouted.

"What, do you think I'm nuts! No way, I told them if they helped us, we'd find a way to get Mara, and the others locked up for life. The explosion of a facility that didn't belong to them. I'm sure they'll be penalized for that. I'm waiting for their response."

The door to the van flew open, and we both dropped to the floor as though we were about to be dive bombed.

"It's only me," Jenson yawned. "The bedrolls are all laid out. You both should get in, get some rest. Nearly everyone is asleep. Maine and Molly are, well, cuddling. It's kind of, cute but.."

"Are you envious?" I asked as Cal, and I helped each other up. I leaned on her til I was able to stand. I'd felt a bit dizzy.

"Just come on. You two better, fill me in on the top secret stuff in the morning. We can't keep things from each other," he added still holding the door open for us.

Cal and I stumbled outside while Jenson closed the door. Once it was closed, I took his hand, and Cal followed us to the small building. It stood among several others with trees in between each unit giving the area a more secluded look than it accurately was.

"I got the key. When we're inside, go directly to the empty sleeping bags and hunker down for the night."

Cal and I nodded in unison. I was too exhausted to argue as Jenson pulled out a key to unlock the door.

Chapter 26

(April 13th, Early Morning.)

I awakened to Jenson snuggled up alongside me. He must have shifted closer to me in the middle of the night. Instead of pulling away, I lay there savoring the intimacy. When I'd had enough, I glanced over the room. It was stripped of furniture, but full of people. This must be the living room. I'd been so tired when I came in last night I'd just crashed. Kind of obvious duh! I scolded myself. Carefully, I removed Jenson's arms from my torso to sit up. I'd explore before anyone else woke up. I wiggled out of my sleeping bag and stood, stretching a bit before silently inching towards the opening of a corridor on the left. I strolled down the mini hallway to peek inside. I ogled the kitchen, then wandered in. To the left was the counter a blue hard, almost ceramic looking space, above it cabinets. I touched it, smooth and clean. Next, I inspected the objects on it. A microwave, next to that a coffee maker, and beside it an empty sink. I reached up opening a cabinet. Inside were a few plastic cups, so I took one out, turned on the faucet and filled it with water. Then downed it before setting it in the sink.

"I see you've found the kitchen," said my dad.

"I didn't mean to wake you up. I thought I'd check out my new place. It's a lot bigger than what I anticipated. My stuff is still out in the car?" I asked.

"Yes, I'll bring it in for you later. All of it will fit in the bedroom for now."

"Thanks, dad," I said, sauntering over to him. He held out his arms to me, and I gave him a bear hug.

"So this is where you'll probably cook our meals," announced Jenson, standing in the entryway. I smirked at him before responding.

"Me, cook? I'd order pizza," I joked.

After my friends and I had gotten up, taken showers, and prepared we were ready to head to the dining hall for breakfast. My dad, Jenson, and Cal helped me put my things in the small bedroom. There was enough room for me, and it would accommodate an extra bed for Molly. I was amazed there were two closets. I wasn't sure where Cal would sleep if she joined us. Oh yeah, dad said something about an office room. Hmm, I hadn't seen that yet. I turned to leave and bumped into Megs.

"Um, so no school today? Mom's letting you skip?" I asked, raising an eyebrow.

"Yeah, right. I wish. I'm getting ready now. We stopped by the apartment to pick up my backpack last night. You were sound asleep by then," Megan replied, holding it up for me to see.

"How are you getting there? We've only got the van," I commented as mom poked her head into the room.

"Come on. We're dropping off Megan at school before we head to the park. Everyone else is in the van and ready to go."

"Okay, Mom. Just let me get my stuff," I answered.

"Sure, but hurry, please. It's chilly out there," she warned us turning away. Then rushed to the front door. I heard it slam shut a few seconds later.

"Hurry Sis! The day at school will fly by. Plus you'll get to see Chaz, and Tasha," I said. Megan nodded, grabbing one of my extra sweatshirts out of a box. She quickly put it on.

"I guess you can borrow that. I totally forgot I'd packed stuff for the apartment. I could have worn something clean," I groaned.

"Mom said to get going, don't forget your purse," Megan reminded me.

"Thanks," I replied, picking it up off the bed. I threw it over my shoulder as we headed out into the living room. Megan pulled open the front door for us, locked it, and twisted around closing it.

"I haven't seen you with Carol lately, what's up with that?" I asked heading to the van.

"Busy with Volleyball. Some girls started a team. They want Tasha and me to try out. I suck at it," she confessed as we approached the vehicle.

"Don't say sucks. Mom hates that," I scolded, pulling open the side door. I squeezed inside sitting down beside Cal. Then put on my safety belt, and leaned back into my seat. Megs slammed the door shut, then hollered for someone to make room so she could sit down. I patted the spot next to me. Then nodded to Jenson sitting across from us between Patrick and Dan. Molly and Maine were in the back seat. Maine had pulled out a magic book, and they were studying a few spells. I looked forward to the front, then grabbed my mom's headrest in front of me watching them. Eva struggled to get her seatbelt on but managed as Tri turned the key in the ignition. Grr, it hiccupped, and after a few more attempts the engine purred to life.

"Cavin needs to schedule a tune-up," Eva complained, sitting in the passenger's seat."

"You've got that right" Tri grumbled.

Megan reached for her safety belt to the left of her. She struggled but was able to get it fastened before mom lurched out of the parking space.

"Owl's going to be there right?" I inquired, turning to Jenson.

"Yeah, he's at the park with Mike. Jones is there also."

"I see. Mom, how are you and Eva? I didn't get to catch up with you last night,"

"Good. Our ability could assist us in attaining valuable data. I'm considering..." she raised an eyebrow. "No Eva and I are brooding over spying on the Bandits."

I nodded, keeping my mouth shut regarding the details Cal had shared with me in confidence. I was glad that Jenson hadn't pried it out of me.

"It's a grand idea. I'd love to be able to get inside their heads. Particularly to see what Sika may be contemplating. If anything, it could help us formulate a plan to ambush the scientists. They want them gone too..." Cal trailed off, leaning against her seat, and shut her eyes.

"Well, at the trial they claimed the plan was to eliminate them, then us. We'll help the Bandits seek justice. However, killing isn't something we do. We'll have to make sure we can hijack them within the regulations. Play the game in a way that gives the authority's grounds to arrest them. The problem is how?" Tri questioned, keeping her eyes on the road.

I rubbed my hands on the armrest next to me wiping the sweat off of my palms while I glanced outside at the neighborhoods whizzing by. We were almost to the school. Megan fidgeted in her seat.

"Those Bandits freak me out. They won't be with us tonight, will they?" she stuttered.

I laid a reassuring hand on her shoulder, then turned to face her. "Unless we're trying to scare them, or rile them up I don't see the point in it. We won't need to use them as bait. We've got herbs to attract The Shadows to us."

"The less confusion, the better," my dad added.

"Isn't that the truth. Once this is over, we can all rest easy." Patrick cut in.

Eva tapped her fingers nervously on the dashboard. "Rest, that isn't going to happen until the Bandits are reprimanded, and the scientist's imprisoned."

Tri pulled up to the school, put the car in park and let it idle. Several teens loitered outside as others were just being dropped off.

"Right, but we're using the Bandits as bait for Grandville. If they're destroyed during combat that's one thing. If not, what do we do with them? Amare came to me pleading we should forgive them. I can do that, but shouldn't they be punished?" I pondered.

"We'll cross that bridge when we come to it," Tri added, glancing back at Megan. "Hon, have a good day, and be careful."

"Yes, Mom," she groaned, unbuckling her safety belt. Then reached down to grab the backpack off the floor beside her. I leaned over and gave her a quick hug smiling when she didn't pull away.

After I let go, she stood up, getting ready to leave. "Clue me in on everything later. I hate being left out," she reminded me.

"Have a good day," mom called as my dad opened the door to let her out.

"Love you guys. Text me," she shouted. Then, quickly slammed the door shut.

Mom sighed, pulling out of the drop off area. "That girl, she's growing up. Text me, what's that?" Tri quipped.

"She probably meant, if something big happens, or text her before we pick her up. You know it's a teenage thing," Dan acknowledged.

I smirked, leaned over and gave my dad a high-five. What the heck did Nayla have planned for us so early this morning? It couldn't be just to pick out necklaces.

Entering the dining hall, I expected everyone to gather around the large rectangular table. I spotted Nayla alone on one side. Star sat to the right at what I thought was the head of the table. I observed from the sidelines as each individual choose their seat. As happy as I was that Megan was at school, I felt she should have been with us. Still, if she'd missed her classes, it would have annoyed me. Mom had never allowed me to play hooky. I saw Cal sit down between her parents on the opposite end of the table where Nayla sat. Maine pulled out a chair for Molly, and they settled in next to Star. They probably figured they could discuss the spells they'd been reviewing. Dan mingled near Nayla as they exchanged a few words. I couldn't make them out, and Jenson had taken a seat near Patrick. I stepped forward, trying to decide where I should sit, then turned back to glimpse at the entryway.

"Mom?"

"I'm right here, beside you waiting for you to choose our seats. Is there anything you want to talk about?"

I couldn't think of anything. What was I suppose to chat about? We hadn't, actually had any heart to hearts lately. We'd been distant since the trial. I'd felt closer to Megan, and my friends than anyone. I'd gotten information from Trigger, Amare, learned new things from Nayla, even Star, but mom and I hadn't spent a lot of time together.

"It's going to sound cheesy. I'm supposed to rebel, eat all this up, and I was. I dig kicking shadow butt, being a hero, sort of," I said, rolling my eyes at the ceiling. When I looked back at my mom, she had a confused look on her face. "Mom, I have the clan, but I still need you," I admitted.

"You and Jenson, you're not..."

"Mom, no. Have some faith in me. Can we ditch this meeting? I haven't had any fun since the trial," I groaned.

She held out her arms to me, and I snuggled into them holding back tears A few leaked out anyway. I wanted to stay there like that with her, safe. Gah! Being a girl was tough. I let go of my mom's arms, dried my tears, and sniffled.

"Where did all this come from? I'm proud of you. I never wanted this for you, but I admire you. Let's see what Nayla has planned. Maybe she'll surprise us."

I laughed as we moved to the table, stopping to pull out a chair beside Jenson. My mom sat down on the other side of me. She waved at my father, and picked up the glass of orange juice in front of her, then took a drink.

"Is everything okay?" Jenson asked

"Yes," I answered, brushing back a strand of my hair. I looked down at my plate of toast, eggs, bacon, and a side of fancy Jellie packets. In front of that was a glass of OJ. Nayla or the kits had outdone themselves. I guess she hadn't wanted us to bother with choices today. Nayla cleared her throat, which was an indication for us to pay attention to her. I sat up straight in my chair then began to eat. My stomach had been rumbling since the ride over.

"Star why don't you take the floor regarding the amulets."

"I'm going to pass around the packet Molly and Maine put together. Don't look at the prices. Go with your gut, take your time, and bear in mind this is a part of your protective cover. I'll be invoking them with you. Kaya's doing some paperwork for Cavin but will be here shortly. In the meantime, enjoy your meal," she stated. Then bent down and began to eat.

I picked up my fork and finished the eggs. They weren't my favorite, but the protein was essential, not that I couldn't get it from the bacon. I lifted it to my mouth and chewed savoring it. Nayla trotted over to me bumping my arm, which caused my plate to slide down towards my lap. I caught it, then pushed it further onto the table.

"Nayla what?" I snapped. My mouth still half full of the meaty goodness.

She peered up at me with a smirk on her muzzle. "Shellena and Lance told me Cal has been visiting the Bandits. Did you know about this?" she demanded.

Cal was only a few feet from us. Why didn't she ask her herself? I tried to swallow the rest of my food, then coughed. It caught in my throat, and I reached for my juice. It helped the bacon go down a bit smoother. I placed my drink back down on the table before turning towards her.

"Only since last night. Why aren't you talking to Cal? She's right over there," I added, pointing to her.

"I figured she'd give you the scoop. Shellena and Lance just happened to see her the other night. I guess she was hanging out near their cage. Sika was scoffing and carrying on. She refused to leave. Lance pulled Shellena aside, and they came to tell me about it. I wanted to clear this up before Cavin's back from his break."

"No one has wanted to deal with them since the trial. Shellena and Lance were supposed to be training them for Grandville, I argued.

"Well, that's why they were there. When they saw Cal, they thought they'd better let me know," Nayla barked.

I moved back a bit, then replied. "Cal was trying to get Sika on board. Gavin and Gladiator previously admitted they would support our battle against the scientists during their interrogation at the hearing. Sika, he's the troublemaker," I challenged, picking up a strawberry jam packet. I opened it and spread it on my toast. "No one has dealt with him yet. Cal didn't want to face her captures before the trial. Afterward, we weren't even able to take the stand," I argued. Then took a large bite of my toast, chewed, and drank some juice, before continuing. "I told her she should let them have it when I was training as the guardian. I'm glad she took matters into her own hands. I don't blame her. I'd have a few choice words for them myself. Although, she was nicer than I would be," I retorted.

"Tri, what do you think?" asked Nayla.

"Cal had a right to face them. Maybe she should have told someone. Then again, here you are talking behind her back. It's not like you Nayla. What's up?" inquired Tri, wiping her hands with the napkin on her lap.

Nayla let out a few geekering sounds, then sat down on her hind legs. I was wondering when she would sit, chill, and stop fidgeting. I glanced at Jenson, who'd been eavesdropping on our conversation. He patted me on the back, then handed me the necklace list. Nayla stayed silent until Shellena, Lance, and Owl walked in. Kaya still hadn't shown up. I wondered what was taking her so long.

"Hey there Cal," Lance greeted her. He sat down next to Eva nodding to us while Shellena pulled out a chair beside him.

"Owl, you made it," Jenson blurted.

"Yeah, the Ranger had me doing some last minute updates to his computer system. What's up?" he asked, taking a seat next to Nayla's empty chair.

"Star's passing around a paper with amulets. We're supposed to pick one for ourselves to protect us at Grandville. Then there's the..."

I put my hand over Jenson's mouth. Nayla needed to address it to everyone, the last thing we needed was more gossip.

I'd chosen my amulet. It had an intense red ruby in the middle of a trinity design. The same design used in charmed. They didn't have anything close to what Buffy wore. Plus, crosses aren't my thing. Although if I needed to ward off vampires, it might work. I'd never tried it with Shellena or Lance. My mom sat beside me debating over two choices. I got up from my chair to stretch needing to move around a bit. Nayla hadn't made an announcement or addressed any other issues. As I rolled my shoulders back, and stood on my toes, stretching my legs, I glanced at Lance leaning over Eva to speak to Cal. I could hear them chatting in low voices. I'd better see what those two were up to. They bolted upright as I approached.

"Hey, Nayla's been alerted of your visits to the Bandits," I declared.

"What a way to ruin my confessions," Lance admitted glowering at me.

"Well, has she gotten more out of them than you have?" I asked, pulling out the empty chair next to Shellena.

"Cal's ability to negotiate is either stronger than mine, or she's learned how to compel Sika. We'll never fully be able to trust them."

Cal nodded in agreement and stood up gazing at Nayla. She must have trotted to her seat without us noticing.

"Cal, did you want to say something?" she asked, standing up on her chair.

"I've been hassling Sika, as you know Gladiator and Gavin have been on board with us since the trial. Sika's ruthless!" Cal slammed her hand on the table for effect. Everyone jumped back including Kaya who'd just stepped in. She stood frozen in astonishment, watching as the scene played out. I'd never seen this side of Cal before.

"And what have you come up with?" questioned Star.

"Sika's determined to convince us to promise them not only freedom but that we reprimand the scientists who experimented on them by sentencing them to life imprisonment."

"And if we can't, and the authorities ever let them walk, then what?" asked Star

"We break our rules," said Kaya.

Molly and Maine gasped in shock as Tri's mouth dropped open.

"Eliminate them?" I asked.

"If that's what it takes," she answered.

Chapter 27

I unlocked the door to the apartment, shimmied inside and shut it behind me. I'd walked back on my own trying not to imagine what would happen if we couldn't provide the Bandits with their request. Nayla had begged me to stay a bit longer. I told her I needed some time to set up my new place. After Amare spoke with me about forgiveness, I was surprised that the clan would ever consider repealing the rule of the death penalty. I looked around at the sleeping bags littering the floor of my living room. Then turned to lock the door.

"Don't focus on the negative. It's the worst case scenario."

"What is?" I asked, turning around to see Amare curled up on my purple sleeping bag like she'd been waiting for me.

"The death penalty. It's never been used, but Cavin he can't take much more of this. Neither can we as a clan."

I bent down, and began to roll up a blue bag, then tied the strings together afterward setting it against the wall. I started another, yellow this time. "So you're telling me not to worry until it happens?"

"Exactly."

I nodded, not entirely convinced of anything. Then looked up at her from the bag I'd been rolling up. "What about forgiveness, that speech. Was it all a lie?"

"No, I see your point. I just cannot visualize the Bandits ever learning how to forgive. Maybe that makes me a bitter old fool."

"Can you tell if Cal's forgiven them yet?"

"She's made peace with what happened to her mostly since she's here with you, her family, and Minder."

"Do you know where Minder was today? Neither she nor Nuria, were at the gathering," I commented.

"At Rascal's tribal meeting. Minder volunteered to help out since Owl had this assembly. Rascal, he's been visiting Jinx."

I finished rolling the last sleeping bag placing it beside the others. Then turned back to Amare, but she'd vanished. I got up and wandered into my room. I might as well get it organized before Molly came back.

Ding-dong Ding dong! I jolted out of my sitting position scattering several empty boxes to the right of me. "Man! Really?" I shouted to no one in particular. Either the doorbell was haunted, or someone was here. Crap, I almost had my book collection lined up on the shelf in the closet. I bent down slightly to move the rest of my novels out of the way, then got up to see who it was. I traipsed into the living area and peered out the window. My father stood on the small stoop. I stepped over to the door to open it for him.

"Hey, Dad. What's up," I asked, moving aside so he could enter.

"I see you picked up all the bedrolls. I'll take them to the dining hall tonight when we go. Have you gotten a lot of unpacking done?"

I shrugged, "My books fit on the top shelf in the closet. I have a few more to add but have been standing on my tip toes to do it. My clothes all seem to fit into the one closet. Then I have my shampoo, conditioner, and girlie things. I'm not sure what to do about the living room. Currently, there's nothing to sit on."

My dad nodded as he pointed to his car parked at the curb. "I brought you an old T.V., a DVD player, and some bunny ears. It should work for now. Granted, I don't see you watching a lot of the tube."

I chuckled, "Did you bring a T.V stand too?"

"Of course. Why don't you help me bring it in? I've got two camping chairs you can use for now."

"Sure," I replied, following him outside to his car. I kept an eye on the door while Dad handed me the small 13-inch television. He grabbed the DVD player, and the stand had wheels thank goodness. He set the player on the stand, and we made our way back to my new place.

"I thought Jack. He's the landlord would have left you the old gray couch. It was here when I was the tenant. He must have thought it wasn't worth keeping," he added as we hauled the stuff inside through the front door.

"Well, it would have been nice. Thank you for this. Will Megan and mom be back? You know, coming over before this evening?"

"If you want I'll help you finish setting everything up. Afterward, we'll go out to stock you up on groceries. You have the essentials, eggs, butter, milk, bread. It was Mango. If we're going to make dinner this evening here before the smackdown, we'll need more than toast and eggs," Dad joked.

"That would be fantastic. Could you cook though? I told Jenson I didn't cook. I'd order pizza, and I don't want him to start expecting me to make a meal every time he's here."

My dad laughed, then pushed the television cart against the wall away from the door to the right. I grabbed the camping chairs and set them up several feet apart from it.

"If you're lucky Jenson will cook for you."

I stood up after adjusting the chairs to their positions. "Okay, have you ever cooked a meal for mom?" I asked, standing with my hands on my hips.

"I know, it's been ages since I prepared dinner for us. I'll chip in making it here. We can cook anything you'd like. How about it?"

"Sure, but first I'll lend a hand with the cords on the movie player thing, and the antenna. Then you'll take me shopping?"

"Sounds like a plan. One more thing though, I need you to decide what's on the menu for tonight."

I nodded, then began to help him set up the player. After we'd finished, he switched on the tube. I got in four channels: PBS, CBS, NBC, and ABC. It was better than nothing.

"So let me have it! Is it spaghetti, burritos, baked potatoes, with green beans, and chicken?"

"Dad," I said, pushing him aside.

"Come on. We should surprise the whole family. In fact, you should invite the gang!"

"I love it! I guess, then it will be baked potatoes, with green beans, and BBQ chicken off of the grill. Oh, and corn on the cob! For dessert vanilla ice cream."

"Yeah, on the way to the market I'll call Jenson and everyone. Then grab the grill before I return. Lance will let me borrow it."

"Cool," I replied.

I unpacked the groceries while dad fired up the grill in the small backyard. I couldn't wait to drink the ice-cold Rootbeer in the fridge. I'd also picked up lunch meat, apples, graham crackers, marshmallows, chocolate bars and vanilla ice cream.

I looked out the window above the sink watching as my dad bent down to light the charcoal inside the grill. He struggled with the wand lighter for a second before a flame caught. I smiled, then leaned over the sink to wash the potatoes. I'd have to slit holes in them before putting them on the grill. The chicken was marinating in a saucepan in the refrigerator. After I had the potatoes, washed and slit I placed them in a bowl and rushed out the back door.

"I've got the potatoes. Did you want them whole or cut in half?" I asked as the door swung shut behind me.

"Whole is okay. I'll put the potatoes on now since it takes an hour for them to cook.

"Alright, " I answered, handing them to him. He placed them on the barbecue rack, then put the top on. I found an old camping chair and pulled it over to sit down. The deck was small, but the yard was wide open for neighbors to share. An old swing set sat a ways back. My dad grabbed a wooden chair, dragging it over beside me. He slowly lowered himself into it, then leaned back, laying his arms on the armrests.

"Do kids ever come out to play on that old thing?" I asked him.

"I haven't seen any yet. How are you and Tri? I mean your mom?"

"Good, I think. We're both doing our own things," I replied.

He nodded as the doorbell rang. I got up to get it, motioning for him to stay. Then pulled open the back door, letting it swing shut behind me. I headed into the kitchen, then to the living area. Mom and Megan were most likely here. Owl and Jenson would arrive later. It wasn't even five yet. I opened the front door, letting them inside.

"Dad's out back. The potatoes are on the grill. I was just relaxing, come in and join us. Megs you can bring your homework."

"Okay, do you have any soda?" she said, shutting the door behind them.

"There's Rootbeer in the fridge. It might not be cold yet, but the ice is in the freezer. I'll meet you two out back." I turned to leave as mom stopped me taking hold of my shoulder.

"Starla, Eva's worried about Cal. Has she told you anything?" asked Tri.

"Nothing more than you already know," I replied, shrugging as she removed her hand from my shoulder.

"Alright then, where's the kitchen?"

Without a word, I strolled from the living room to the hall, and into the kitchen while they followed behind me. Once we were there, I went to the fridge, opened it and took out sodas for Meg and Tri.

"Mom. I wish I had all the answers regarding Cal," I explained, shutting the refrigerator door. I handed them their drinks as my cell in my pocket rang. Then reached in, took it out and flipped it open.

"It's Molly, give me a Sec," I said.

Tri nodded, to me. Megs opened the back door, and they headed out to the yard. I waited till the door had shut behind them to speak.

"Hey, are you two coming?" I asked.

"We're on our way now. Cal and Eva are with us," Molly replied.

"And Patrick?" I questioned, glancing outside at my folks.

"He's with Cavin, Kaya, and Nayla. They're working with Jones and his immortals."

"I hope Shellena and Lance show. Any new info?"

"No, Maine's been practicing moving things with her mind. I've been studying some additional healing spells, and oh.. We're almost here. I'll see you in a bit."

"Okay," I replied, ending the call. I turned to head back out when my dad pushed open the back door.

"Hey, can you hand me the chicken? Oh, and a plate also. I'll have to have something to put it on when it's cooked."

"Yeah," I answered, stepping over to the refrigerator. I pulled it open, grabbed the chicken, and shoved it closed. "Here, I'm going to set up the dining room table. You guys man the food," I added then handed him the chicken.

"A plate?"

I rolled my eyes, then went to the cupboard above the counter. I began opening them in search of one. In the last one to the right, I found some plastic plates, grabbed one and handed it to him.

"There, now let me set up all this," I said, gesturing to the table.

Molly and Maine finished putting the last plate on the table. I could smell the chicken grilling outside as my mouth watered. I touched the corner of the new tablecloth Minder had brought me as a housewarming gift. She and Lance were outdoors, talking with Eva and Tri. They'd dove into shop talk as soon as they'd arrived. Cal sat on the deck. It had gotten quite warm, almost fifty-five degrees. She held a notebook on her lap. Megan sat on the other side of her busy with her math homework. She'd have it finished by dinner I bet. I stood back to admire the daisies Maine had brought. I'd found an old blue, cream vase to place them in for our centerpiece.

"It's perfect, well close. Jenson and Owl better show," Maine stated agitated. She turned to head out back to join the others. I waited until the back door shut.

"So how are you guys doing?" I whispered.

"Not bad. Maine and I've had a few heated discussions. You and Jenson?"

I felt put on the spot. We'd been good, but something inside me led me to believe I wanted more from our relationship. Was it the physical thing? In my mind, I thought I was cool with not being intimate. We'd only been dating what? Almost two months. Hadn't I accused Maine of not knowing Molly that long?

"Spill, what's up?" she demanded, standing with her arms crossed. Molly gave me a bold look.

"Nothing. No flare-ups, fights, or miscommunications," I blurted, raising my arms high in the air. Then let them fall to my side. A knock on the front door startled me. No one knocked, they rang the bell.

"And that is?" asked Molly.

"How should I know? It could be Jenson. He had a key the other day. My Dad probably gave it to him in case I ever locked myself out," I acknowledged.

"Is anyone home? It's Rascal. Jenson and Owl are with me! Where's the grub?"

"We're in the kitchen, please shut the door behind you," I hollered.

"Starla, you could at least go greet them," Molly scolded me.

Before I could take two steps forward, Rascal hobbled into the kitchen. I pulled three soda's out of the fridge and set them down on the table.

"Hey, I've missed you! How are you holding up?" I asked, patting him on the back.

"Hanging in there, laying low, and getting ready for the market. Everything is ready to go thanks to Jenson and Owl. Where, where'd they go?"

"We're right here," Jenson answered, sauntering in with Owl at his side. "I wanted to give my bro the tour. I see your dad hooked you up with some old school decor. I'll have to bring over the Nintendo. We could play duck hunt or something?"

"Jenson, do you even have a Nintendo?"

"Yeah, Owl gave it to me after the trial."

"I told him he needed something to get his mind off all the hoopla. We've had fun with it when we're not busy fighting bad guys or dealing with tribe stuff.

"You kids and your game systems," Rascal commented, shaking his head. "Where's Tri and the gang?"

"Outside. Let's see if the food's ready. We'll need to eat fast. Nayla didn't tell us when to be back. Try not to overeat, just enough to increase our energy levels," I added. "Now you're talking like a gamer," Jenson teased.

Chapter 28

I stared at my empty plate, then pushed it aside, letting out a loud burp. It had been challenging resisting a second helping of everything. Jenson laughed, and I elbowed him. Boys, why did I like them?

"What was that for?" Jenson asked.

"Being a guy," I answered.

Owl shook his head, then added some more green beans to his plate. He shoved them into his mouth and chewed. Shellena and Lance chuckled.

"Sis, you should at least say excuse me," Megan piped up. Then went back to eating her ice cream.

It was kind of embarrassing, but I couldn't help it. People burped all the time. Gah! Guys even had contests concerning burps. I smiled at my father as my eyes spotted Cal, studying her notebook again relentlessly. I might as well get dishes started since everyone else seemed busy. It was my apartment now, and there was no dishwasher but me. I pushed back my chair and stood up to collect the plates off of the table.

"Do you want some help?" asked Tri.

"No, I've got it," I replied. Then gathered the plates and put them in the sink. I turned back to grab the empty pop cans off the table. My arm was halfway to them when Tri grabbed my hand pulling me near.

"Secret meeting tonight, girls only," she whispered. Then released my hand from her grasp.

"Okay."

What was that? I thought, reaching for the cans as Minder got up to help me. After we'd collected them, I swiped a garbage bag off of the counter, pulling it open while she dropped them inside.

"Don't worry about Sika. Lance and I will keep him on a tight leash. If he acts out, it will be on our behalf. I've made sure of that," she assured me.

"Are you mad at Cal?" I asked, glancing back at her. She and Maine were at the table fooling around with playing cards. Maine was trying to teach her how to shuffle them all fancy-like. Molly demonstrated how to accomplish it with her set.

"No, not at all. She's the one who gave me the courage to face Sika. Nayla gets worked up over these things."

I nodded in agreement setting the bag of cans aside.

"Jenson, Lance, could you help me clean up the grill?" Dan asked, standing up from the table.

"Yes, of course. I'll be there, in a minute.," Jenson replied.

"Megan, are you done with your ice cream? I need to get everything cleaned up."

"I'll get it," Lance offered, picking up her bowl. He started to take off the dirty tablecloth.

"Please, stop! I don't have a washer and dryer. It will have to stay there till I can get it home," I explained.

"Alrighty."

He let go of the end, and it fell back down. After they left to take care of the grill, I turned back to Minder. "Should I pack a bag for tonight? How late will we be there?"

"That will depend on how well, everyone works together. If we're in sync an hour, if not maybe two," she hinted.

"Nayla, she's leaving us right after?"

"Probably, she's got to get back to her home. Don't look so sullen. She's never stayed this long before which proves you're important to her."

"And Megan," I added. "It's going to be weird. I want it all to be over, but once it's finished. And it's not just The Shadows." My shoulders slumped a bit.

"Are you scared? Grandville, I mean. These baddies are minuscule compared to them."

"True, but they did kill Du-Vance. Did you notice how quiet Rascal was at dinner? He's usually talkative. At least he was when he first came in," I shrugged, leaning against the counter.

"He's going to pop the question to Nuria. He wanted to ask your dad for advice," she whispered.

"What?" I asked jolting upright.

"Yeah, mum's the word. Okay?"

"For now," I replied, unable to stop grinning. I tried to contain my excitement, but the giddy girl part of me wanted to jump up and down for joy. It felt like only yesterday Rascal was telling Jenson and me how he thought he'd lost her.

"Now, we'd better assemble everyone and jet. Rascal will want to head out alone," she admitted patting me on the arm. "Girls, wrap up your card thingy. Eva, Tri, see if the guys need any help with the grill.

"Yeah, sure," Eva replied, pushing in her chair. Tri got up, and as she walked past me lightly touched my shoulder. I smiled at her as Minder hollered, "Starla and I will meet everyone in the van."

The ride to the park was a bit bumpy. I hoped we'd be renting out an SUV for Grandville. After all the BBQ I ate, I thought I would be sick. And that was even after avoiding a second helping. It was too bad I hadn't taken my advice on not overindulging. I held on to the left side of the van as it lurched forward. It felt like I would hurl. Molly had her hand on my back, and Maine gave me a worried look as Minder pulled into a parking space. I breathed a sigh of relief once she'd stopped. Then sat up, taking a few deep breaths. Tri got up from her seat and opened the van door in the front letting in the cool breeze. She hopped out into the parking lot, then hollered at us, "Girls, I'd like you to walk with Eva and me."

I nodded at her from the back of the van. Then saw Lance step down out of the front passenger's seat. He closed the door, then motioned for us to get out.

"Are you going to be Okay to fight?" asked Maine.

"Yeah, this van is something else. I know I ate a lot of food, but the lurching, jerking, and inability to give us a smooth ride," I griped holding my stomach.

"I'll have Cavin take a look at it," Lance assured me, standing outside of the door. My dad gave me a sympathetic look, then moved to stand by Lance, who appeared ready for action.

"Everybody out. Let's get to the hut area," Dan ordered.

Owl and Megan got out of the van lingering near Lance. I wasn't sure I'd be able to make it out on my own. I needed to let my stomach settle for a minute. Jenson moved from the front of the van to the back to help me up.

"Thanks," I said, taking his hand.

"Yeah, no problem. You looked pretty bad back there," he admitted.

I stood up, then let go of his hand. He placed it on my back as we moved to the door. I took baby steps up to the edge of the van and cautiously stepped down.

"Thanks, I should go. Something about a girls-only meeting?"

"Funny, Dan was saying the same thing about the guys. I wonder what's up?" Jenson asked.

Bachelor party? He'd find out soon enough. Instead of giving him an answer I pulled him close to me. Then kissed him softly on the mouth. I pulled back slowly to gaze at his sweet face, then leaned my chin on his shoulder. I could see the sun beginning to set outside of the park. Cal crawled out of the van holding her notebook as Maine followed close to her. I watched Molly as she rolled her notebook up and tucked it into her back pocket before walking up to us.

"Hey lovebirds," she joked.

I shook my head. She and Maine were two peas in a pod. I wasn't sure who was getting sassier. I let go of Jenson and stood alongside him.

"What's up with the notebook?"

"Important observations to share, at the girl only meeting," she smirked.

"Does it have anything to do with our talk the other night? You know concerning the big bads?" I asked, linking her arm in mine.

"No, but I'm working on that. Shellena and Lance are assisting me. We're pretty close to finding out..."

Ranger, Mike bolted out of the station towards us shouting as he waved his arms. He held a radio talkie in one of his hands. "Everyone back in the vehicle! It's an emergency! Cavin radioed me! One of our kits, Kern is in critical condition. Don't ask me what happened to the sun goddess," he shouted, flinging the van doors open.

Everyone scrambled inside and buckled up. Mike sat in the driver's seat, then gunned it! I held on tight as we barreled across the park towards the huts. If I hurled now, I was going into battle wearing it! Shiznit was going down!

"Megan, Cal, we have to be prepared to take our positions immediately! There's no getting ready. We act on our gut instincts."

"You got it, Starla!"

"Owl, are you carrying? I want them gone. Dead, gone, but if it's going to cost us our lives, we might as well head out Grandville tonight!"

"Starla!" Tri hollered.

"Mom, she has a point," Megan remarked.

"I have the herb to remove them if it comes to that. I'm right behind you and Megan. Jenson, we'll distract them while they shot em' down. These aren't holograms. "

The van skidded to a halt in the middle of the huts. Mike radioed Cavin, while I scanned the forests for activity. I didn't see a shadow in sight. Maybe they were hiding, but they'd be back. I knew it! Anger flared inside my soul.

Calm Starla, please stay calm. Amare reminded me.

"Shouldn't we be out there. What's with this staling? Let's go," I pressed, unbuckling my safety belt. I went to stand, then stopped as I caught a glimpse of a mist-like vapor lingering near Megan. It must be Trigger.

"Mike we should get out there. It isn't doing us any good to sit here and wait," Dan stressed. Shellena, Minder, and Lance nodded in agreement. Tri hastily stood up and pushed the back door open. They hopped down, and Megan, Cal, and I did the same. Mike and Jenson dropped onto the ground, shuffling over to us. Without any warning, the door to the dining hut flew open. Nayla and Kaya bolted out of the building towards us. When they stopped, Kaya bent down trying to catch her breath.

I glanced at Maine and Molly at the entrance of the vehicle. When they saw Kaya, they rushed to console her. I hurried over to them as they each put an arm around her shoulders. Nayla stayed close to her side while I tried not to stare at Kaya's messy hair, or her fox ears, peeking out. She must be a nervous wreck. Everyone drew nearer, but at the same time gave them some space.

"I'm an untidy heap, yes. My concern is with Kern. Sina and Trax are with him now. He's's lost a lot of blood. Cavin called in Jinx to stay with him. Mango and Star are there presently."

"Where are The Shadows now? I don't see them anywhere," I observed.

"Hiding. Kern fought hard. He did everything he could to keep them from invading his body," Nayla remarked.

"How! I mean, didn't he freak out over an illusion they formed in his mind? How did he fight them?" I demanded.

"Sina witnessed it. She told me he was sporadically dodging them. She heard him, saying, no this isn't real, you're shadows. I can see you; then he kept moving until one hit him. After that, he aimed his body at a tree. He just started attacking it!

Eventually, the shadow took off! No one knows why maybe it could sense we were preparing for combat? If not that, was it called back to its lair? We don't have any clues. Right now the best thing to do is get them back here!" Kaya blurted.

"And the Sun goddess, is she Awall?" asked Molly.

"Yeah, everything turned dark. I can't tell if it's a spell or interference of some kind. I should be able to tell," Kaya stated, shaking her head in shame. Molly and Maine patted her on the back, then moved aside, allowing Nayla to come nearer.

She bumped Kaya's right hand with her nose, "It's not your fault go back to Kern. Molly, see if you can heal him using the ointment. Maine, you as well. Placing additional members in jeopardy is unnecessary. You'll be needed at Grandville."

Molly hurried to Maine taking hold of her hand and looked at me. "Stay safe, you and Jenson both. I.. I.. Mean everyone."

"You also. I'll do my best to keep The Shadows from entering any buildings," I assured her.

"Thank you, Starla. Nayla when it's over bring everybody to the reflection room. It's where we are praying to the Igaehindivo. I'm hoping to find out what happened to our sun. Lance and Shellena, assist Nayla. I expect to see you soon," she acknowledged. Then turned to the huts while Maine and Molly trotted beside her trying to keep up.

Chapter 29

This time there were no immortals to guard us. My heart pounded in my chest while I rubbed my sweaty palms against my jeans. My purse still hung around my shoulders swinging back and forth as I moved to stand beside Megan. I hadn't had any time to stash it in the van. Minder had insisted on using it to take Nuria back to the cabin. I shook off my fear as we took our places. Cal stood in front of me, but close enough for us to react to each other. We hadn't had much time to talk about what would happen. We just knew what we had to do. I glanced at Jenson behind us. He winked at me, and Owl smiled as he gripped the herbs in his hands. Lance held the lighter ready to ignite it. Dan and Mike would give the signal once the three of us had successfully unified. My mom and Eva sat beside Nayla. It wasn't safe, but they had requested it. I took a deep breath, then exhaled out. The tension in the forest sat in the pit of my stomach. The birds had stopped chirping. Something was coming. My eyes darted back and forth surveying the trees beyond.

"Let go, connect, use your memories," Amare whispered inside of my head.

"Yes," I thought. Then slowed my breathing down even more. As a slight tug pulled me to Megan, I took several steps forward, and Cal moved closer to me.

"They're almost here. I can feel them," Amare warned me.

A cold tremor traveled up my back. Mentally, I grappled for a correlation amongst the three of us. Cal shocked my consciousness with a surge of snapshots. Flashes of us defeating the holograms played out like a flip book inside my brain. I pushed them out towards *Megan. Please... Please...* I prayed to the goddess. *Let her accept this, let us....*

A slow warmth spread and I could sense the power connecting us. We must have been glowing. Had Dan given the signal?

"Starla watch out!" Jenson screamed.

A silhouette sprung towards us! I went to crouch down, but Megan dove for my hand. She grabbed it, then aimed it at the outline of the Shadow rushing us! Panic shot through me, I hesitated while Megan 'pushed me to the ground. The rhythmic thumping of Cal and I's link created vibrations. I drove it outward up at the shadow hovering above us. It knocked it off to the side, as another shot out from behind me. My eyes focused on Jenson squinting and flicking his hands rapidly at it. The shadow twitched in agony, fighting the freeze. The other three taunted Nayla as they circled her. Tri and Dan shuffled on their hands and knees advancing to Shellena and Lance. I spotted Eva bending down to take my mother's hand while Megan and I leapt up off of the ground. Cal pressed her energy into us.

Easy not too much Cal, I thought. I couldn't lose the balance of our power. None of them had yet attempted to issue our fears. Strange, were they aware of our game? Nayla crouched down low, digging into the ground, and burrowed inside of the hole. What was she doing? Wouldn't it make her an easier target?

"It's not the time to think! Zero in on it!" Megan yelled. Instinctively our hands shot out taking aim. I let my fury flow throughout my veins meeting Megs. The red light flickered shaking unsteadily, then hit the shadow behind us. The darkness burst into particles. The lights piercing glow bent, twisting, moving akin to a living thing reaching for the gray-white hue in front of us. It dodged our beam, but we kept our hands in motion until it hit. By now Jenson had frozen all but one of the baddies surrounding

Nayla. He kept flicking his hand but seemed to be out of mojo. We'd hit two of them. I bent down and panted out of breath. I'd have to rest... Only for a minute.

"You can't relax! Keep fighting. The Fear, it's coming! Starla, you have to listen, unlock your mind further, expand it, or I'll have to light the emergency herb!" Owl screeched

I could smell the dampness of death as I sniffed the air. Where was it? The last Shadow that I couldn't see. One drifted near Nayla. Shellena drove it to us. I lifted our hands anticipating the kill. Megan and I quivered. Cal shivered, and my insides began to freeze. I couldn't move my hand! We were stuck. Something swung out from the trees. I heard them rustling, leaves that had barely begun to bloom. At first, I thought it was an Owl. All black, but then it changed form, a ghoulish face stared down at me snickering.

"Ha ha ha, you cannot destroy us so easily. You nothings, little peasants playing tricks," it shouted. "Hmm, I feel your heart in sync with that one," he taunted eyeing Jenson. "What if I entered him, took all his life, and made him into one of me," it sneered.

"No! Lance, help." I croaked. But I remembered his fireballs wouldn't help me. They'd only create two of them. The mass shifted dawdling near Jenson. My mind reached out trying to grab hold of him. I couldn't physically, but mentally I yearned to be with him. I saw Eva and Tri, as they held one another for comfort. My dad nearby, with his head in his hands as if all this was his fault.

"Daddy, it's not, it's not," I mumbled. A few tears trickled down my cheeks. How could these things exist? Jenson wildly began to flick his hand at the enemy.

"See, your empathy only disables your power clarifying your weakness," it challenged. Then leapt in and out of Jenson's body. He gasped each time holding his stomach in pain.

"Stop! What do you want from us!" Tri shouted.

The corners of its mouth curled while it hovered above Jenson forming an evil grin. "To see your terror. Pain is our pleasure," it cooed.

Jenson flailed as he fell to the ground. Cuts and sores surfaced on his skin. My desire to hold him overcame me. Was it real, had they got to him? My love. Torn up, blood everywhere. I tried to pull my hand out of Megs, but she held on tight. I had to go to him. I had too.

"Jenson!" I cried.

Lance charged in my direction gripping the soil with his large wolf-feet.

"Jenson that's his name... it would be so effortless, I could use him to slaughter every one of you. Frighten you, breed terror into the things you thought he never was. I could wipe out your love."

Lance sprung himself onto the black mass as Shellena stalked it from behind. I could feel her pursing it, persuading it. Cavin and the others had told them not to.. Unless.

But they loved me and didn't want me to lose him. My heartbeat pounded as I listened to theirs, pulling them to me, towards me, connecting, uniting, into what all feared and intertwined as one whole. I pushed myself up, bringing Megan with me. Cal took hold of our wrists, and I aimed our hands at that sucker! Then pulled the trigger!

A red light burst out of them, but I couldn't stop trembling. It wasn't going to go down without a fight. It continued darting in and out of trees. Cal managed to steady our hands by that time

Shellena had him pinned with her compulsion. Mr. Baddie hovered a few inches from us. The shadow took a direct hit, and tiny particles fluttered to the ground. Megan positioned her body closer to mine, while I searched for the baby shadow. The Runt. I found Lance, laying off to the side injured, but not dead, thank the gods! Jenson where was he?

"Jenson, are you Okay?" I yelled.

"Yeah, yeah, a bit bruised, but I'll live," he replied, trying to stand. Owl bent down to help him.

I let out a sigh of relief, then looked for Nayla. When I couldn't see her I panicked, "Nayla, are you alive? Do you see it? The last one, we have to get rid of it to free Trigger!" I screamed, turning around. Megan let go of my wrist but wrapped her arm around my torso. She gripped the bag of salt in her other hand.

"I'm fine. It's hovering beside me, shaking in fear. Darn thing thinks I'll protect it!" Nayla hissed, peering out of the hole. She leapt up out of the burrow, stuck her tongue out mocking it, and rushed to me for protection. I pushed her behind us as Megan threw the salt freezing it. I didn't hesitate, just aimed at it using every ounce of anger to blast it.

"Wasted!" I hollered, dropping to the ground. I let go of Cal who leaned her chin on my shoulder. Megan squeezed me close refusing to release me as Jenson, hobbled in my direction. I watched Tri and Eva let go of each other, as my dad stood beside them.

"Lance, Mike are you injured? Owl what happened? I saw you help Jenson up, but before that, you disappeared."

Mike stepped out of the forest with him.

"I hid, I could have used the herb, I could have helped," Owl stammered.

"It would have come back. You did the right thing. I'm glad you're both okay don't do that in Grandville." A slight tug on my hand made me turn. Megan gradually pulled away, allowing me to stand. I squeezed her arm, then turned towards Jenson. Before he could say anything, I pulled him close, burying my face in his chest. I breathed him in, then ran my face up towards his shoulders so I could try to find Trigger. Wasn't he supposed to be here by now?

"Starla, hiding may have saved our lives. I'm glad everyone is safe," Mike stuttered inspecting the forest.

I attempted to nod at him. I didn't feel like challenging anyone. I was out of spunk, and ready to head to the reflection room. I let out a sigh of relief while Jenson leaned his forehead against mine. I didn't care who was watching.

"Thank you for saving me. I couldn't freeze it, couldn't do anything. It makes me feel worthless, defeated. I'm supposed to protect you," Jenson murmured into my hair.

"We're here to protect each other. It's not about guys protecting the girls. Didn't you learn anything from Buffy?" I stopped, realizing I sounded kind of harsh. "Sorry, I.. It's just me, being all…

Jenson pulled back a bit, gazing into my eyes. "Don't apologize for being a strong woman. I admire that. Although, next time it's my turn to save you," he chuckled.

I didn't want to let him let me go, but everyone was waiting. I heard Nayla loudly clear her throat. It was then that I turned to face the others huddled in a circle. Mike and Owl lingered near Lance and Shellena. Lance was pretty beat up. He had a black eye, and his knees were covered in several cuts from the branches he fell into when he'd plunged through the shadow. It looked like he'd be fine. I glanced at Eva and Cal as they stood together. My Mom and Dad were holding each other close. Trigger sat near Megan as she held her hand inches from his fur without noticing it.

"Now that the threat of The Shadows is extinct. I'll return to my home in the Arctic. Star and Trigger will take over any initial training required before Grandville. I'll stay until the morning sun rises. Let's join Kaya, and the others in the reflection room. I want to see how Kern is holding up.

"Jenson, I..."

"Go ahead, walk with her," he said.

I smiled, then quickly kissed him before running to Nayla.

When I reached her, I placed my hand on her back. She looked up at me as we trotted to the hut. I felt the chicken bone rise in my throat. I knew deep down I could make it without her. She'd taught me well. Still, I had a lot more to learn. Much more.

"I'm going to miss you, ya know. It won't be the same, fighting baddies." I clenched my bottom lip as it trembled. My hand lightly stroked her back.

"You'll do just fine. I'll have Kaya report the outcome to me once Grandville's dealt with. Trigger and Amare will guide you."

I glimpsed back at the others ambling towards the huts. A few of them were ahead of us. Nayla licked my hand. It tickled, and I pulled it back.

"Can I write you? At least let me know you got home safely," I pressed.

"Of course, my dear one. I'm sorry I wasn't much help back there. Even with my magic, I don't have the tools to defeat shadows. Others I can pull off, but those." She shook her head, stopping beside the door to the hut. I opened it waiting for her to go in.

"Come along. The others will catch up. Molly and Maine will be waiting to hear what happened."

I nodded and trailed after her.

Chapter 30

Nayla and I snuck into the reflection room without making a sound. I could hear my parents and friends behind us, but it sounded like they were being diverted to the dining hall.

"Nayla, are the others not coming?" I inquired, gazing back at the hallway. I'd left the door ajar, letting a small portion of light filter into the room. A few candles were lit on the mantle.

"Lance and Shellena thought it best if only you and I joined them here. Kern can't handle a lot of excitement," she whispered. Then trotted over to Star lying near the fireplace, close to several pillows and blankets scattered about. I caught a glimpse of Maine and Molly's silhouettes while I moved but continued until I stopped near Kern.

I sat down observing his slow, steady breaths as his chest moved up and down while he slept. There were numerous scars on his head, and his left front leg was bandaged including his back right. I could tell Molly had used her healing power on him. Sina and Trax must have sacrificed a part of themselves to stop the bleeding. If not they'd applied a tourniquet. We were in for a hell of a ride with these scientists. Lance was supposed to set up the formation for our infiltration of Grandville. Trigger better have some tricks to share with us in our defense. We hadn't had time to determine how to capture them, kill them, or at least get the authorities to inspect the neighborhood where they'd been before they tried to attack us if and when we reached their hideout. I took a deep breath, trying to calm myself. Then rummaged through my purse around my torso for my phone. When I'd found it, I immediately turned off the ringer so it wouldn't wake Kern and stuffed it in my bag. There he'd need his rest after today. As I looked up, Molly motioned for me to sit with them. She and Maine were both wrapped up in blankets. Cautiously, I scooted myself over in-between them. Maine handed me one, and I wrapped it around myself. My ears perked up, as I listened to Star and Nayla whisper concerning Kern's current condition. I glanced their way for a moment before turning back to Molly.

"Are you hanging in there?" she whispered.

"Everyone's breathing, but the last shadow terrified me. If Kern had met him alone, he'd have been a goner. It took everything within me to identify a way to eliminate him. If it was a he? I don't suppose shadows have genders," I shrugged, and my shoulders slumped somewhat. "It had me convinced it would seize Jenson. It toyed with me passing right through his solid form, put images in my head that I cannot unsee. Thank the goddess he's safe. Not only that three smaller shadows terrorized Nayla, Mom, Eva, and Dad," I stammered, staring at the floor.Molly and Maine laid their hands soothingly on my shoulders. "Cal, Megan, and I we were the only ones able to defend them. I'm not sure what happened to our mother's telepathy. It's possible The Shadows could have blocked their abilities as tenacious as they were. What's suspicious, is they didn't even attempt to fill our heads with nightmares. They managed to freeze us, though. And Jenson's paralysis spell wouldn't work," I rambled on.

"Everyone is safe, and that's what matters. Lance, Cavin, and Patrick are forming a sketch of our positions for Grandville. We sent Jones to investigate the area. He left this evening, but I didn't want to worry anyone," said Star.

"Did my dad know?" I asked, pulling my blanket closer.

"Yes, Dan knew. Jones should be back in time for brunch tomorrow. Has Trigger contacted you yet?"

"No, Where's Kaya?" I asked, tugging off my shoes. Then set them down beside me.

"She helped us stabilize Kern then left to stay with Cavin. They're sleeping in their quarters. Sina and Trax are in the dining hall. I had to have someone meet the group there. I'm going to get some shut-eye. You should at least try," she advised. Then crawled closer to the fireplace. She snuggled down into a blanket lying on the floor and closed her eyes.

Maine and Molly let their hands slide off my shoulder as I reached for a pillow beside me. I hugged it to my chest, wishing Jenson was with me then yawned. Nalya pulled over an extra blanket dropping it beside me.

"In case you wake up chilled. The one you have is rather thin. Now go to sleep. I'll be here when you wake up. At dawn, Sina, Trax and I are taking Kern back to join the kits. I'll be at the meeting later in the day. We'll catch up," she assured me.

"I nodded, then took the 2nd blanket, wrapped it around myself, and laid down. Molly was on one side of me, and Maine on the other. I closed my eyes to meditate. After that, I felt Nayla squeeze in between Molly and me.

The heat of the sun-beat, down on my back as I looked around at the field of golden wheat surrounding me. Amare had to be here somewhere? I stood up from where I sat moving towards the cool breeze. I wasn't even sure if I was going forward or back. I followed the air, smelled it, then felt one or two drops of rain on my shoulders. I looked down at my hands, but they were not there.

My fox paws. I was on all fours. I leapt up and took off running towards the scent of rain. I hadn't gone far when I arrived at a small lake. It was only misting as I lay down beside it and stared into the water. Amare's image reflected back at me.

"Starla? I'd hoped you'd come. You've almost reached the end of your journey."

"The end, my life isn't over yet. I hope."

"No, no darling only the disasters initiated through hatred. Some folks create it themselves. They don't see the truth inside the reason."

I looked over my left shoulder and saw she was standing behind me. Then gave her a puzzled look.

"People, animals, entities, any living being, holds reasons behind doing things. One is to gain something for themselves or help others to obtain needs for survival."

"What does that have to do with the Bandits? Why did the sun goddess leave us?"

"I can't tell you about the Sun goddess. The Bandits did what they had to survive. The scientists, they are the true-evil. Good intentions are not always as they seem. Granted, I'm still contemplating if Sika will learn to forgive the scientists. You haven't had any problems with them recently?"

I shook my head, no. "I haven't had any contact with them. We'll be tossed together on the trip. Lance and Shellena are dealing with it. Patrick too, I guess."

"They should be successful in helping you attain your goal. Why did you call me?"

Why had I called her? I'd defeated The Shadows... Jenson could have died. I'd tried not to think about it, but my heart had just found him. I'd only just discovered love... I buried my fox nose in my paws.

"*Starla, be at ease. He didn't die. He's still here. Your spirits restless, juggling love, intimacy, knowledge. You can handle this. Listen to your heart. It hasn't let you down before. You know it was guiding you this evening. It helped you save your friends.*"

"*I didn't do it alone.*"

"*You weren't supposed to,*" she answered nuzzling me. "*You're one with your clan. The three musketeers, or some other cliche you'd use. Right?*"

"*Pretty much.*"

"*I am a spirit guide. I can offer advice, be there, but you have to use it to enhance who you are, grow.*"

"*And?*"

"*Buffy didn't get by without help from her friends. Remember that Starla.*"

"*I know.*"

"*Then, have a little faith... You've got this.*"

Chapter 31

(April 14th, Morning.)

I was rolling, being shaken. What was going on? I wasn't having a seizure. I didn't have those like ever. Was I in fox form, or human form?

"Starla, wake up," said Nayla.

I pushed her away, and sat up, rubbing my eyes. Human form. I hadn't switched over in my meditation. I looked around to see it was only she and I in the room. The others must have left for breakfast. I remembered she was staying till then.

"I've left my contact information with Cavin for you. I'm sorry to wake you so early, but I didn't want to leave without saying goodbye."

"You said, you'd stay for brunch. What happened?" I asked.

"I'm needed back home to help train the kits. It's long overdue. I've stayed much longer than planned. I'll be returning. It's not forever.

I nodded, trying not to let the tears that filled my eyes touch my cheeks then reached for her. Nayla moved towards me, and I crouched down, pulling her into a close hug.

"Write to me. I can read, and there are a few Kitsunes, who will aid me in conversing back. I could send a message to Amare even."

"Thank you, Nayla. For... for everything you've done." I buried myself-then in her fur allowing my tears to fall. We stayed there like that for several minutes until she pulled away.

"I must go, child. Please tell Megan, Maine, and Molly goodbye."

"I will," I answered, wiping the tears from my eyes.

I walked to the dining hall telling myself to be strong. Nayla was on her way back to the Arctic, and we had scientists to slay. My girlie emotions needed to stand aside! I rushed to the door when someone bumped into me.

"Ah, sorry about that. I didn't see ya there."

"Rascal! Did you propose yet?" I whispered.

"I tried, but with the fiasco going on... I thought I'd better put it on hold. Who's talking this morning, at this thing? Do ya know?"

"No clue," I added shrugging my shoulders. "Nayla just left to go back to the Arctic. Have you seen Mango?"

"Ah, that feisty character is certainly in there stirring the pot. Kern, he's doing much better. Thank the gods for Molly, and Maine. You're good kids," he said, punching my arm.

"I'm 19. Not really, a kid anymore," I pressed. Then pushed open the door to the dining hall. Almost everyone was seated by now eating breakfast. I noticed Kaya with Cavin at the large table. There was enough room for everyone to sit together.

"Let's get some grub! You're hungry, aren't you?" asked Rascal as he strolled to the main table.

"Famished," I replied, moving along with him. I stopped at the table, taking a plate off of the pile. Whoever prepared the meal had outdone themselves. There were waffles, fruit, maple syrup, cherries, eggs, bacon, and toast. I piled on a few waffles, adding maple syrup and strawberries. I had to have a slice of bacon too! When I looked up from my plate, Nuria was sitting near Tri and Dan. Minder must have stayed behind to hold down the cabin. She didn't seem to be getting out as much these days. My eyes wandered to Megan. She had a mouthful of waffles she was trying to chew. The cherries and whip barely had made it into her mouth. Owl played with his food next to her. I'm not sure he liked the fruit and berries. I bet Mango picked them. Cal sat next to Eva. She waved to me, and I smiled at her, then turned to Rascal.

"Nuria's here, but she isn't coming to Grandville is she?"

"No, no. I can't lose her like I lost my boy," he mumbled. Then picked up some bacon, and reached for some waffles. He kept piling food on his plate as he spoke. "I'm keeping that one safe. She's pretty grounded. Of course, she has her rituals during the full moon. She has to go on her midnight runs, or she goes stir crazy." He stopped filling his plate to grab a few napkins.

"Right, I haven't been able to take the edge off in a while," I said, picking up my plate to head to the table.

"No fox trots, huh?" he remarked as we walked.

"No, not recently. Nayla said or was it Star that I would be more mobile in my fox form for Grandville. Jinx is coming, plus Patrick. I'm confident Trigger will aid us in our defense. We should have people, eh clan members on the front lines, then those most vulnerable in the back." I paused to look around, "Jones isn't back yet. Where are they?"

"Apparently he hasn't returned from the top secret mission. Cavin's probably experiencing a nerve-racking internal fight with himself for sending him out there alone. The immortals are with Kern and the kits. Someone has to watch them. I'm going to join your folks over yonder. Be prepared for a lecture from Cavin. I'm convinced he'll have one for us regarding what's coming. You did good, with The Shadows," he grinned. Then winked at me while he took a seat next to Nuria.

I stood near the table observing my family. What would happen to them, to me? Cal chatted with Eva, but I couldn't make out what she was saying. Patrick and my dad were currently engaged in a theoretical conversation. Everybody seemed relieved, excluding me. I wouldn't feel secure until we had the scientists behind bars. Last night was a blur. Thank the gods we were all safe. Some of us injured, but not dead, at least.

"Starla, over here!"

I snapped myself out of my trance and saw Jenson waving me over to sit with him. Megan, Owl, Molly, and Maine, gathered close to one another. Cautiously, I balanced my plate while he pulled out a seat for me.

"Yum, you know how to pick out food," he said, taking my plate to set it down for me.

I pulled out the chair beside him, plopped down, and rested my chin in my hand. "Thanks, are you going back for more?"

"I'm full up. Owl? What about you?"

"Nah, I'd better not ruin lunch," he joked. I watched him grab the glass of juice in front of him. He downed it too quickly, which caused him to cough. I sat up startled as Jenson leaned over striking him hard on the back.

"What's that for, man? I'm not dying," he assured him.

"Guys, stop. Where's Nayla?" Megan wondered.

"She wanted me to tell you goodbye. What's the empty seat beside you for?" I inquired, tearing off a piece of waffle, then swirled it in the syrup and berries.

"Trigger, in case he shows up. I thought he was tailing me. I haven't sensed him with me since last night? In any case, why would she leave without telling me goodbye? She was my friend too. And she told you to tell me?" she drawled.

"Megs, she had to go. She has a clan in the Arctic." I reached over to grab her hand, but she pulled it away.

"Cal won't be happy either," she snapped.

"Look she came here to help us. Cavin says she comes once a year. She'll be back next winter. She's left Cavin with an address so we can write to her."

"Fine," Megan shouted.

Cavin sat straight up in his seat, glaring at us from the head of the table. "Attention! Everyone, sit back and listen."

That was my cue to eat and stay quiet. Shellena and Lance rushed up to us holding their meals. Lance nodded to Maine who moved over to make room for them. She and Molly had been focusing on eating their breakfast. Cavin waited till they were seated to proceed while Kaya fidgeted beside him.

"I sent Jones out to see if he could locate the hideout last night. Unfortunately, I haven't heard back from him yet. We'll need to execute a plan of attack. It has to be stealthy."

"I barely made it through the shadow battle, and we nearly lost Jinx, Kern, and Jenson. How do you propose we prepare ourselves for this infiltration? Our abilities are not unlimited," I interrupted him.

"Sis, are you saying you want to quit? When did you start giving in so easily?"

"No, I'm not giving up. We need a new way to ensure our protection. I don't want to lose any of you," I stressed. My eyes wandered around the table, taking them all in. "Nayla left us and while I understand she had to, what I don't get is why Trigger hasn't shown up either? Where is he!?" I picked my fork up stabbing the rest of my waffle in anger, then raised it to my mouth and chewed.

Shellena and Lance abruptly stood up, pushing their seats back.

Kaya lifted her head up from her notes to address them. "Yes, go ahead. What do you have to add?"

"Shellena and I've been working with the Bandits for a short period. Gavin and the Gladiator are all geared up. They're eager to seek vengeance. Sika, he's another matter. Cal had him pinned for a bit. We may require her to be of assistance on that," he remarked nodding towards her.

"I'm game," she smirked.

Eva gave her daughter a fleeting look as Lance continued.

"Manipulation is the key to acquire what we desire. We'd like authorization to use our gift of persuasion. It's risky, but Starla has pinpointed the main issue. If we go into this as we are without a shield of protection other than what we have, we'll be in trouble."

"You didn't get permission last night when you used it on the shadow," Cavin challenged.

"That was an emergency!" he growled. "I wasn't going to let Jenson die, or that shadow kill everyone! You didn't see what he did!" Lance shouted as he shook his fists in disgust.

Cavin pushed his seat back, then sighed. "In this case, what would you use manipulation for? Would it be during combat when encountering circumstances deemed worthy? Or to get the Bandits to give us an accurate site where they're hiding? That is if Jones hasn't discovered it. Keep in mind Grandville is immense on the park-side. Frankly, I don't believe they even know where they are." Cavin took his paws and ran them over his ears in distress. "He better show up soon," he grumbled.

"Jones hasn't let us down before," stated Kaya, setting her hand on Cavin's shoulder.

He turned to look at her, "yes?"

"Let Lance decide. Our safety is more crucial than the aftermath."

Cavin laid his fox head on her shoulder and whispered in her ear, "You're correct."

"Can you say that again?" Kaya murmured.

"Lance, she's right. But"

"It's only to be utilized in extreme positions. I get it," he snarled.

Cavin grumbled something under his breath.

"Trigger would be beneficial if he's released. He should be capable of telling us if they're still in the Grandville area. Dan the animal shelter that exploded, where's it located?" inquired Lance.

"Conveniently in the residential area. It sits by itself at the end of the block. The warehouse was there before the subdivision went in. They had it converted into a shelter."

"Dad! When did you uncover this? You were with us last night weren't you?" I demanded angrily.

"Yes, then after everyone fell asleep, I met with Patrick. Cavin permitted us to access his computer in the study. We printed off photos of the warehouse used to advertise the shelter before the explosion. Grandville park is on the left-hand side, in between that is a road, then on the right-hand side houses. It was as clear as the vision-dream, I had had."

"Can we see them?" I asked.

"We'll hand them around," Kaya answered, giving them to Mango. She'd been repulsively calm, which was unlike her. I hadn't heard a peep since we'd walked in.

"Mango is everything alright?" asked Nuria.

"I can't wrap my head around how crazy this has gotten. Every part of it makes me nervous. Not the funny kind where I usually laugh or joke to ease the tension, but scared." She acknowledged leafing quickly through the papers. Afterward, handing them to Lance.

"I understand, it's frightening for all of us," said Trigger materializing beside Megan. She reached out a hand patting him on the back. It wasn't unusual, but this time her hand didn't go through him. I gasped, he was supposed to be a spirit.

"My soul has rejoined a body. One that wasn't currently, taken. No, I didn't kill it or anyone for it. I've taken the physical form you've experienced me in. It's temporary until the missions accomplished. Later on, I'll relocate to another who needs a guide."

Cavin nodded his head in understanding. Maine and Molly set down their forks. Their plates now empty while Jenson took my hand in his.

"Is everyone still in?" asked Kaya, glancing around the table.

I looked over at my mom. She'd appeared alright when I'd come in. Now she sat with her head on my dad's shoulder. Eva reached over and patted her hand reassuringly. What was this doing to her? She'd seen me last night, then Jenson practically killed.

"We've made it this far. I don't want to chicken out currently. However, Starla, if you or Jenson die. I'll never forgive you," Tri warned us.

"I'll do my best mom," I gulped. Then attempted a weak smile.

Lance cleared his throat to speak. "This is how I see our journey to Grandville playing out. When we get there, the Bandits will lead the way. Shellena and I will follow behind them. Sika's the only one who'll need to be cuffed. If necessary, I'll apply manipulation on Gavin and the Gladiator. I'm more concerned about having to use it on the scientists. Patrick and Dan, you'll be upfront with us. We can decide where Jones will fit in when he returns. Tri, you and Eva will remain behind us. I'll need you to listen in on any conversations they might be having. Can you do that?"

"Yes, I've been practicing tuning out unwanted voices and honing in on the crucial ones. Eva has been exceptionally supportive of me," she affirmed.

"Good. Starla, last night your quick actions saved us."

"No, we rescued each other. It's sappy, nevertheless our need to keep each other alive. That's what saved us, not me alone. Even Buffy knows that Zander and Willow hold an imperative position as sidekicks. That's what the writers portrayed them as. Not that you are. Everyone here's turned into a family. We fight for each other, stand by each other. Gah, I promised myself I wouldn't get girlie emotional," I quipped.

"You don't constantly have to be strong. Let down your guard now and again. Take some time to recharge," Lance suggested.

"I will when this is over. When are we leaving?"

"Soon," Shellena added.

"And the rest of us? Where will we be?" asked Molly.

"You'll follow close behind us. I want your trio near Eva and Tri. Jinx mentioned wanting to creep into the enemy hideout and has this wild scheme planned. Sensi is a part of it. Cavin, can you get them here?"

"I'm on it," he sputtered, jumping down from his seat. "Wait here, and discuss things amongst yourselves. Trigger if you have any fresh data, be prepared to disclose it when I return!"

"How long?" asked Patrick.

Cavin paused, "Give me a half hour, hopefully, he's not snoozing!" he hollered, trotting out of the dining hall.

Chapter 32

As soon as Cavin left, I pushed my chair backward, got up, and took the plates off of the table. Maybe Kaya would help me wash them. When I turned to go to the kitchen, Lance and Shellena were in the process of putting away the leftover food. What he'd proposed made sense to me. It was a relief not to have to worry about being the primary target for these monsters. I trusted Shellena and Lance's ability to defend us.

"Hey, I got this," said Kaya resting a gentle hand on my shoulder.

"For being a Kitsune you stay in human form regularly," I observed, passing her the dirty dishes.

"True, it's what I prefer. Even Cavin says it's pleasing to him. I know I'm supposed to be new age, feminist. While I support that view, I love being human."

"Don't you miss running in your wild fox form?" I asked collecting the juice glasses.

"At times, I help Mango with the kits occasionally. Then I use my fox form. It's fun teaching them how to hunt. Kern's going to be a tad on edge. Thank goodness mating is on hold. Plus, we don't have enough pairs presently." She sighed, reaching for a tray on the table with her free hand.

"Are you sure I can't help you with anything?" I pressed.

"I've got this. Lance and Shellena will put the leftovers in the fridge. You should be chatting with your friends. Especially Megan."

I nodded, setting the glasses down in a bunch, then turned towards them. Megan laughed at the goofy faces Trigger was making. She even at her age was commanding him to do tricks. I shook my head at the silliness of it all and strolled over to them.

"Kaya wouldn't let you do dishes would she?" jested Owl.

"Nah, told me I should hang out with you nerds," I retaliated, pulling out the seat beside Jenson. I sat down and placed my elbows on the table.

"I sort of feel like we're going to be the sidekicks on this mission," Molly declared.

"It's better than being dead meat," I rebuked.

"You've got that right," Jenson interjected.

"Come on now. It's as Starla said. We're a team. Megan, are you freaked about the scientists? How's everyone doing?" Trigger pleaded.

"Holding up, and growing up," Megan replied.

"Maine, and Molly, the Wiccan faith. Are you serious about it? Have you been using the gift your ancestors gave you?"

Maine held Molly's hand in a tight grip. She bit her bottom lip, then answered. "I've been practicing proficiency in maneuvering and moving objects using my mind. I trust it would be valuable. If someone from the clan can produce tranquilizing darts to make them sleep, I could aim, and fire from a distance. It would give us an advantage. Even if we don't use them, it's a safeguard. It would give us time to call the authorities before they wake up. I'm not sure they'd believe us when we told them they're evil though."

"Good. Molly?" he asked.

"There's nothing Wiccany about me. I've only been efficient at healing. Maine's helping me with a few protection spells. I'm pretty solid there. She's taught me chants, mantra's, things like that."

"Great!" he exclaimed, swishing his tail.

Cal shimmied to us out of the kitchen and pulled out a seat beside me. I repositioned my chair to face her.

"Please don't ask me if I'm Okay. Nuria keeps pestering me," she commented, glowering in her direction. Cal slowly ran her hands through her hair. I could tell she needed a good shower, maybe some sleep too. She rubbed her eyes, then leaned back in the chair.

"Kaya must have thought you needed a distraction. She wouldn't let me help her with the dishes," I complained.

"What do you suppose, I'm doing out here?" she muttered, picking up a napkin. Then began to rip it into tiny pieces.

"Well, any thoughts on Lance's plan?" I asked, drumming my fingers on the table.

"It's admirable. I'm not cranky about this being a team effort. Rascal's somewhere around here." Cal paused to hunt for him. We all scanned the room, then spotted him speaking with Eva and Tri.

"Nah, I don't expect I'll be going to Grandville," he said rather loudly. "We've got the Spring Market scheduled for the day you leave, plus it would be too much for me. What they did to my boy is unforgivable! I'd pound em myself, worse than the Bandits," he bellowed sitting down next to them.

Cal turned back to us, "It doesn't sound like he'll be coming."

"It's probably for the best. You heard him. If he were to see them, he'd aim to kill them himself. We can't have that hanging over our heads. Elimination is a probability, but only if they threaten our lives," Trigger commented.

"Only if Shellena and Lance can't compel them. We have to hope they haven't yet created a new distraction to assault us with." I lectured.

"It's a good thing we're using The Bandits as bait then. We won't be the first course on the menu." Cal blurted, shoving aside the pile of napkins she'd shredded.

"Darn Tootin," I chimed in as Megan cleared her throat pointing to the doorway. We looked up to see Cavin nudging Jinx into the hall. Jones limped slowly in front of them holding his arm against his chest. He was banged up, but still intact.

"There's no need to be alarmed. I fell on some branches on the way here. I was running away. I'll own up to that. The scientists have an operation going on not too far from where the explosion took place. It's about a mile from where the warehouse was on the opposite side of the residential area heading east. There we discovered an old hunting shack, pretty cramped if you ask me," he acknowledged.

Patrick got up out of his seat to help Jones.

"Are you sure you're not injured, nothing is broken?" he asked, strolling over to him.

"Nah, I can move it. See," he emphasized, swinging his arm back and forth. "Ouch, crap. It's going to be sore for a while."

"Molly and Maine can fix you up. Let's sit you over next to them. Kaya's either taking a long time loading the dishwasher or baking," he said, carefully taking his arm.

"I hope she's baking cookies. I'm going to need some after attempting to heal that arm. Did you see how bruised it is?" asked Molly.

I nodded to her then got up to gather a few chairs. I wasn't sure if Cavin would be sitting with us, or if he and Jones would add a seat near Kaya. I stood waiting for them to reach us while Jones hobbled all the way. Patrick let go of his arm, then lowered him into the seat sit between Molly and me.

"There, I'll let Molly look you over when you've settled. I'm going to go see what Kaya is up to in that kitchen."

"Thanks," he replied, adjusting himself in the chair.

I caught a glimpse of Dan as he pulled out an extra chair for Jinx. Cavin nodded for him to sit down in between himself and Kaya's. Then headed into the kitchen. I turned back to address Jones. "I'm glad you made it back. Cavin was worried something awful had happened to you," I confided, sitting down.

Molly pushed her chair closer to his. "May I have a look at your arm professor?"

"Of course, just call me Jones," he demanded, pulling up his sleeve. He observed her intently concentrating on the scratches and blemishes that went from his elbow all the way to his shoulder bone.

"I don't think I could do that," she stuttered running her fingers over his wounds. She closed her eyes to focus. Molly breathed deeply in, then exhaled. "Oh great goddess mother of mercy, heal this man. Protect him, look after him, and allow my touch to repair his wound." She released his arm. "Did it work?" she asked, raising an eyebrow.

He moved his arm up halfway raising it above his shoulders, then afterward gradually lowered it onto his lap.

Jone's face lit up like Christmas morning. "I don't feel any pain, at all. Glorious, thank you. Now when Patrick gets Kaya out here, I'm telling you everything!"

"I'd hope so. Molly that was brilliant! I'm glad the chant I taught you, worked. Does anyone here know if Star put a rush on those amulets?" inquired Maine, searching the room with her eyes.

"I haven't a clue on that one," Mango sang out.

Tri chuckled in her direction, "You could ask her yourself. She's on her way in just in time for dessert."

Star trotted to the table and came to an abrupt stop beside Maine and Molly. "Sorry, I'm a tad late. I left Sina and Trax with the kits. Maybe it's my paranoia, but I don't trust leaving them unattended after what occurred."

"Can't say I blame ya!" Mango hollered.

"Mango, why don't you go see if the amulets have shipped. They should be here tomorrow. I'd like to have them ASAP," Star ordered.

"Alright, I'm going." She groaned, hoping down from her seat. "I'm too sassy for ya! Aren't I?" she chuckled, prancing to the door.

"It's a beautiful day out! Oh, and on your way check to see if Sina and Trax need anything. You'll be staying with the Kits when we go to Grandville," Star informed her.

"I figured that," she replied, rolling her eyes.

"You can place mirages around the park. It's for everyone's safety. Thank you!" Star shouted.

"You're welcome," she grumbled, trotting out the door.

Jones had been correct about Kaya preparing food. Several minutes after Cavin and Patrick had gone into the kitchen, she came out carrying a tray of homemade sliced bread, cheese, ham, tomatoes, and pickles. Shellena and Lance followed her with glasses and a gallon of milk. Patrick ambled along behind her with a plate of homemade chocolate chip cookies. They carefully made their way to the table.

"Cavin will be out in Sec. He insisted on having a few moments to himself before hearing what Jones has to say," she remarked. Then sashayed over setting the tray down in the middle of the table.

"Someone has to go get the plates," Cal blurted.

"I've got them under the cookies. It's nearly two p.m. so we should eat while Jones fills us in. Cavin wants us to be geared up to leave tomorrow at daybreak. He's persistent about it. Minder is on her way here. She's going to see if the van can be fixed," Patrick informed them.

"Good. I can't take riding around in that shaky box," I winced as Patrick sat down the plate of cookies. I picked them up, took one, and a plate. Then sent them down the line. Jones nodded to me as I passed a dish to Molly. She took one, then gave them to Maine and so on.

"What's there to drink? You can't have cookies without milk," Rascal complained.

"I've got them right here," said Lance, placing them on the table. Shellena began to pour milk into the glasses and handed one to each of us.

"Isn't it a little early for lunch?" I asked Shellena, taking the glass from her.

"It's almost two O'clock. As disheveled as most of us look. I'm hoping after this; Cavin gives us a time-out. You need to change into some new duds."

I sniffed my shirt, then looked up at her. "Yeah. Sort-of gross I guess, with everything I didn't notice," I grumbled. My purse still hung against me. I'd slept with everything on from the previous evening. I'd been wearing these clothes for two days, sickening!

"We all smell cruddy," Jenson acknowledged. Then began to fill his plate with fixing for a sandwich.

I stuck with a cheese and tomato with pickle sandwich. After I finished my masterpiece, I cut it down the middle, then began to eat while the others chatted near me. Jones was discussing how Star might have a few gypsy spells she'd been concealing. Perhaps, they might benefit us in our operation. I set down my glass of milk as Star trotted into the room. Cavin was exiting the kitchen when she entered. I put down my sandwich to observe their interaction. I perked up my ears, to hone in using my fox abilities. I had to concentrate. It had been a while since I'd accessed them.

"Hey, Kern is resting. She's in good spirits, and the others are watching over her. Sina and Trax wish to stay with her," Star whispered.

"It's fine. Lance discussed with us how he'd like this to play out. I agree with him on the setup, but I'm not sure I want so many clan members in the field. Patrick wants to prove himself, Jinx feels he needs to be there, and everyone else is deep in this. We should have Sensi check the area before we enter their territory. We'll have to get on that. Rascal, bowed out, thinks he'd slash em. I'm not sure he'd have it in him."

"I wouldn't nix it. I see Jones made it back," Star replied and caught me staring. She waved while she and Cavin made their way to the table. He took his seat next to Kaya, and Star claimed an empty seat Eva had placed next to her.

"Jones it's good to see you made it back in one piece! Lance has a plan to infiltrate the scientists. I'm hoping you'll fill us in on what you've found."

He put his hand up indicating he'd speak in a bit. Jones finished chewing the last of his cookie and drank some milk to help it go down.

"Yes, I told the others when I came in. They've got a shack set up about a mile from the explosion. It's tight, one large living area that's separated into sections, then a closet containing a toilet and slanted shower. It looks like the women are still working with them as it's been kept up. I broke in rather easily. I tried not to leave any prints, didn't touch a thing. There were three cages. One held a few rabbits, another held several mice, and one." He paused, shivered, then clenched and unclenched his fists.

"Yes, go on Jones," Kaya said, waving her hand in anticipation.

"One was a young fox. It backed away when I tried to touch it. A shy tiny thing, it made geekering noises at me, conceivably in fear. Evidently, I can't read the language as you're able Cavin. It seemed ordinary and left me frightened. Perhaps they're considering experimenting on the clan next. Originally, I had no notion as to why they'd be holding mice and rabbits. Unless they believed they could inject them with the chemicals needed to change us. It's a scary possibility," he admitted, shaking his head.

I took a deep breath, reaching for Jenson's hand. Megan dropped her unfinished sandwich on her plate, pushed it aside, and commented to Owl.

"I think, I'm gonna be sick. I can't even eat. That poor little fox. We've got to save him. Sis," she pleaded.

I nodded at her, then saw my mother's face had turned a pale white. Eva spoke before I could get a word out.

"I'll give em' this. The devious suckers aren't getting my pity. I"m with Rascal. Lance we can't let them live."

"Genetic engineering and modifying beings are a controversial subject. There are restrictions and regulations in the good ole' USA. If it's not approved, they're in deep Doo Doo," Dan confirmed.

"And who knows if it was permitted by the military," Rascal cut in. "If so the Bandits would have had to volunteer. It doesn't appear to be the case with their wrath towards the captures. How the heck did they let them get away?"

"Renegades or military-militia that takes matters into their own hands. They would also be contemplating terms of compensation for their good deeds." Patrick cut in.

"If your accurate Rascal the authorities will be all over this! We have to make sure when they show up, only those who can project themselves as humans are present. We don't need anyone on our tails," Cavin advised us.

"That's definite. I'm not convinced you need me," Trigger added as Minder and Mango pushed the dining hall door open. It closed loudly behind them.

"Cavin, that van is a piece of junk. It's a relic that needs replacing, and I can't assure you it will last. It's a temporary fix. Mango, go ahead and tell Star about the charms. I'm starving, and those sandwiches look delish!" She gushed, grabbing a chair and squeezed in between Rascal and Trigger.

Owl smirked at her eagerness. As she packed her plate, Mango filled us in.

"They should be here tonight. I changed the order since you sounded adamant about them arriving rapidly. I hope you don't mind paying an extra ten bucks," Mango pressed.

"No, it's fine. Jones, you'll be with us this evening. Everyone needs to change, refresh, and be back here by six; eat something light. We'll be training, seeking counsel from the gods, and establishing a more specific strategy," Cavin remarked.

I wasn't going to argue, my hair, clothes, and body felt rank. Owl stood up from his chair, stretching out his arms.

"I'm heading to my folks. Things are rocky with them, so I need to make sure no landslides fall. I should be here this evening. Jenson, let Mike know where I'm at if he calls," Owl said.

"Right, I'll let him know," Jenson replied, fidgeting with his shirt.

Chapter 33

I let the shower flow over my body imagining myself under a beautiful waterfall. I needed the illusion of fantasy an element outside of our current dilemma. The potent scent of soothing lavender filled the room. I breathed it in, exhaled, and finished washing my hair. Everyone had pretty much gone their separate ways excluding my family. Maine and Molly had left to go back to her folks. They figured they'd better make an appearance before they disappeared again. I wasn't sure what line they'd fed Mrs. Fretner. She'd never let Mol hang with me again if she knew who we really were. I shuddered a bit, then allowed the warm water to calm me. I took the conditioner off of the shelf applying it to my hair. I'd better leave it in, or I'd be dealing with major frizz issues. While I worked it in, I thought about Jenson. He'd headed home to see Sage. I wondered if he was telling her about our adventures in a more elementary way. After I washed the conditioner out of my hair, I turned off the shower, pulling the curtain open to grab the towel on the toilet seat. After I dried off, I put on my undergarments and jeans. Then my clean, green sweatshirt, socks and a pair of sneakers. I almost felt like a new person. I gathered up the pile of dirty clothes as I pushed the door to the small hallway opened using my other hand. I'd drop them off in my room, then went to see what Megan and Trigger were up to.

First, I heard the music coming from the television. It sounded like Mario were they playing video games? I thought they'd be strategizing ways to kick scientist butt. I strolled out of the bedroom, turned the corner, and saw my dad with the controller in his hand. Megan and Trigger sat next to him watching in awe.

"Hey, where's mom?" I asked.

"Checking in at the library with one of the girls covering her shift for the week. She'll be back. I wanted to unwind, why don't you play for a bit?"

I shrugged and sat on the floor next to Megan as he handed me the controller.

"I'm going to call Tri and see what's keeping her. How long of a shower did you need?"

"Dad, this is your oasis. The shower was mine," I scolded.

"That's fair. I'll be in the backyard. I get better reception on my phone there," he replied, heading out the front door.

I set down the controller letting Mario die from a mushroom guy. Trigger wandered closer to me, while Megan picked up the controller. When had Jenson dropped this off anyway? Huh, Odd, I pondered.

"You don't want to play? It's kinda fun, even if it's old school," she commented beginning a new game.

"I'm afraid I wouldn't be able to focus on fun. Trigger, you said you'd lead us through Grandville. Is there anything we should know about besides what Jones has revealed?"

He circled his choice spot three times, then sat down on his hind legs. "No, I'm quite impressed with his breakthrough today. There is one thing I've been mulling over. I'm not certain how the spirits will react to it. I'm considering seeking their permission to become a permanent spirit guide for Megan. That's if it's okay with you. In the beginning, I was sent to aid you, Starla. Now that we know Megan's the key she'll need me."

Megan's eyes grew wide as the controller dropped to the ground. A few seconds later Mario plummeted into the abyss.

"I have Amare, and it isn't fair for me to have more than one spirit guide. It makes sense, and it isn't like I'd never see you," I replied.

A sly smile played upon Tiggers face in acceptance.

"Would they let you do that? Is it possible?" Megan asked, leaning forward towards him.

"I won't know until I request it. I'd like to keep this body, but I'll have to inquire about consent for that as well."

"As the key can I learn other spells, magic? I don't want to go to Grandville helpless. I'd like to be able to shield myself if Starla, Cal and I become separated."

"I don't suppose Star would object to me teaching you a distraction spell. We'll have to ask the goddess for approval tonight. It's quite simple and would give you time to break away from an enemy," he added. Then stood up on all fours stretching. "I'm not used to having this body. What time is it anyway? I'm ravenous."

I pushed myself up off of the floor to glance down the hallway into the kitchen. A clock hung above the refrigerator.

"Well?" asked Trigger.

I turned to face him as Megan got up. "If that clock's correct, it's almost five. Mom should be on her way home soon. If you guys follow me to the kitchen, I'll see what I've got left in the fridge. I think I have some fruit left, eggs, bacon, toast, and juice. It's not much, but Star said to eat light. Come on," I offered.

As we entered the kitchen, the back door swung shut behind my dad.

"Hey, so your mom will be home soon. Have you come up with anything for dinner?" he asked, heading to the fridge.

"Yeah, actually breakfast. It's filling, but if we each have one egg, a piece of toast, and two slices of bacon we should be excellent. I'll get started on the coffee. That's if we have any," I added. Then moved to the cupboards searching them.

"Here, let me look. You can get out the stuff we need from the fridge. Megan, please find a pan for the eggs, and Starla the toaster should be on the counter. You can make that. If Jenson's planning on meeting you before we leave make extra."

"Yes, sir. I'm not sure I need to call him, but I left my cell in my purse, and that's in my room."

"Use mine," he offered, digging it out of his pocket. He laid it on the counter, and reached up, to pull out a bag of ungrounded beans.

"Drat, you didn't bring a grinder did you?" he asked as I dialed Jenson's number.

"No, dad. We'll have to live with juice."

"Live with juice Starla are you sick?" he asked, throwing up his hands.

I shrugged at him, juggling the phone to my ear. Then opened the fridge and took out the items we needed one by one as the phone rang. I placed them on the side of the counter attempting not to be in the way.

"Starla?"

"Hey Jenson, how fast can you be here?"

"Why, what's up?"

"Impromptu dinner. Eh breakfast before the smackdown. Well, training errr. You know!"

"You sound agitated."

"Yeah, we have coffee, but no grinder. Can you help with that?"

"I'm on it. I bet Megan's loving the Nintendo?"

"Yeah, when did you drop it off?" I asked.

"I gave it to your dad at the meeting. He must have set it up when you got home."

"Oh, Okay. Thanks," I added.

"Oh, and Molly and Maine called me. They're meeting us there. I guess Mr. and Mrs. Frenter are taking them out to eat first then to the park. Molly's mom insisted on it. Anyway, I should jet. I'll see you in 15? Mom should have a coffee grinder I can borrow around here somewhere."

"Cool, love ya J."

"J?"

"Yeah, as in Jenson. Byeee." I hung up the phone and sighed, realizing my heart had taken over my brain.

I opened the door, letting Jenson inside. Mom had arrived just in time to set the table. My ears twitched while someone or something smacked its lips in the kitchen. It sounded like Trigger was tasting bacon for the first time. I heard him call our Eureka! Then shut the door behind Jenson.

"I guess he likes it," I commented.

"What?" asked Jenson as I went to take his coat. He held it tightly around himself.

"Trigger's tasting bacon for the first time. Why won't you let me take your coat?" I stood there surprised he hadn't tried to hug or kiss me already.

"It's chilly in here. Anything new happen? Crop up, occur?" he asked, surveying the messy living area.

"Megan wants to become skilled at additional spells. We'll discuss it with Star and are considering a distraction spell. That way, if she gets separated from us, she can keep herself out of harm's way."

He nodded, then took the coffee grinder out of his coat and handed it to me.

"Thanks. We'll need this, anyway Trigger would like to stay here, as Megan's permanent spirit guide. He's getting used to having a solid form, wants to keep that also," I grinned. Then reached for his hand, leading him into the kitchen.

"Smells great, did you cook it yourself?" he asked, taking a seat.

"She made the toast, and dad cooked the eggs and bacon. We'll have coffee now that you bought the grinder."

"Megs you don't drink coffee," I said, handing it to my dad. Then pulled out a seat between Jenson and my mother. She laid a hand on my shoulder, and I smiled at her.

"How was the library? Any thrilling new adventures?" I challenged.

Mom handed me the pile of toast, and I took a piece before she set it aside. She glanced at my father clearing her throat while he began to grind the beans for the brew.

"My shifts covered til this coming Monday, all the books that needed stacking have been restocked. I did have to fill her in on the new computer filing program. Other than that I didn't see much else that needed to be taken care of."

Dad nodded to her as he added the coffee to the pot. Then grabbed a piece of bacon off a plate on the table and nibbled. I sniffed the aroma of fresh coffee brewing, and when it had finished, he handed a cup to me. Trigger chocked down his toast, and Jenson ate eggs on his toast. Where was my witty humor when I needed it? I reached for the jam, spread it on my toast, then snagged some bacon. Eggs, I'd skip those. I hoped that training this evening was more exciting than this meal and Jenson's lack of affection. It troubled me. I took a bite of my toast gazing at him while he ate.

"So mom. I'm going to ask Star about distraction spells. Trigger and I discussed it, dad you were on your phone calling her at the time. I realize being the key is a crucial aspect of protecting our clan. But I must also be able to look after myself if I become separated from Cal and Starla."

"I agree, it's a good plan. Let's finish up. We're going to be late," Dan added, eyeing his watch.

"Okay, um can I ride with Jenson? I'll meet you guys there."

"Sure, just help me with the dishes. We may be leaving in the morning, and I don't think you want to come back to a sink full of them," Dan added.

"Not really. Jenson, Megs, will you chip in?" I asked. Then stuffed the last wedge of toast into my mouth. After I'd chewed, I figured I'd better down the rest of my caffeine.

"I'll dry the dishes if Megan washes them," Jenson offered.

"Nah, I'm not washing dishes tonight. Trigger and I have a spell to research on the net," Megan rejoiced.

"You'll have to help your sister first. We'll discuss the spell with Star at the meeting," Dan warned.

Trigger eased back in his chair he'd sat on. He didn't look like he wanted to get involved in this argument. I set down my empty cup of coffee. "It's good, let them investigate." I insisted.

Megan pushed her chair away from the table, "Thanks, Sis! You won't regret it."

"Dad, you'll have to drive them to Hunter's Park. I don't have internet access yet." I reminded him, as Tri got up collecting the empty serving dishes. She gathered my dad's plate, Jenson's and then Megan's. I was still chewing on my last piece of bacon.

"Be careful, and mindful of Star's suggestions," Tri commented, stepping alongside my father. She pulled him close, kissed him, and affectionately pushed him aside setting the plates she'd collected on the counter. "I'm going to head out to meet Eva, Cal, and Patrick."

"Alright, I guess that leaves Starla to lock up."

"Dad, it is my place," I reminded him.

"Right, let's go guys. Megan, get your coat. It's cold this evening."

Trigger hopped down off of his seat, and Megan followed him out into the hallway with my dad tagging along.

I filled the sink with watery suds looking into the backyard and noticed the sun had nearly set. Summer would be here soon; warm, pleasant weather less than two months away. I reached for the plates beside me, then took the cups, placing them into the warm water. I turned back to face Jenson while I cleaned them.

"How's everything at the home front? Sage is she good?"

"As silly as ever. The other night she was skulking around, then trotting, and afterward acting like an undercover agent. When I asked her what she was doing, she told me she was a spy. Get this a fox spy," he chuckled.

"Hmm, sounds like she has her suspicions about us unless she's come across a new TV show. I'm always behind on current pop culture," I added quickly setting a few dishes in the drainer. Then started on the plastic cups. I'd almost finished when Jenson came up beside me. I smiled at him and grabbed a towel laying off to the side.

"Here, you can dry them, after that put them away."

"Sure, so Megan seemed geeked about new spells. It wouldn't hurt for us to learn a few of them."

"You've got that right. I don't know if the ability Cal, Megan and I share will work for us the same way with the scientists as it did The Shadows. I mean we can't zap and kill em! Omitting our buzz to keep them away would work to guard the clan, but we need to draw them in, capture them, detain them, and get the authorities to arrive. We can't guarantee Maine will be able to target them with tranquilizer-darts, or even if they have something else following us. If we could uncover their profiles, it would be fantastic! What are their backgrounds or specialties? I'm amped up to go in and kick major booty, but is it planned out well enough that we'll succeed?"

"Lance wouldn't lead us into death's arms. What about Cal's visions? They must be as yours are since she never ran into the scientists themselves. She only overheard the Bandits speak of them."

"True, unless she's hiding something else. My mom questioned me concerning it. I guess Eva is worried," I confided.

"Moms do that," Jenson added, placing the last mug into the cupboard. As I turned to leave the room, Jenson grabbed me from behind, pulling me into a hug. I tried to hug him back, and he released me, placing his hands on my shoulders. Then affectionately began to massage them. I leaned back, allowing myself to relax as the tension diminished. "Hmm, it feels great, but what if we're late? It has got to be close to six, or after by now," I reminded him.

"No one's buzzed you yet," he murmured.

I turned to face him but first raised my shirt sleeve to inspect my birthmark. No glowing, buzzing, or other weird indicators. It must not be six yet. I pulled the cloth over it and peered up at Jenson.

"See, I told you. No one is apprehensive yet."

"Yet," I repeated touching his face. I leaned my forehead against his our lips only inches from one another. I thought he was going to kiss me when he pulled me into a tight embrace. I nuzzled into his chest while I ran my hands up and down his back. Was Jenson scared? Was this his way of saying I love you, don't leave me? He gradually let go of me holding me at arm's length.

"Are you ready for this?" I whispered.

"No one can ever be fully equipped for something like this. Anythings possible, but I have faith in us and the clan."

"Okay. I hate to ruin the moment, but I have to get my purse and coat. My cell is in there also. I've got to have it on me."

He lightly touched my cheek, then nodded to me. "I'll meet you out front."

"Alright," I replied, then hurried out of the kitchen towards my room.

Chapter 34

I sat beside Jenson in the passenger's seat while he drove with one hand on the wheel and the other resting on my leg as I leaned back to shut my eyes for a minute. Earlier I'd called Tri to let her know we were on our way. She sounded relieved and told me that Kaya had finished making our outfits for Grandville. It was nice to find out that I wouldn't be losing my clothes out there. I could hear Molly, Maine, and Jinx discussing spells in the background. It also sounded like Sensi was among them. Lance and Owl were bashing Kali sticks against each other. I'd heard them clanking. Then Owl dropped his on the floor before mom had ended the call.

"Starla, wake up. We're at the huts."

"What?" I asked, rubbing my sleepy eyes. I sat up, unbuckled my belt, and noticed Jenson had parked next to the dining hall hut. The other van was parked alongside us.

"You just drove up, down the path, and here? I sure hope Cavin doesn't blow a gasket," I huffed.

"Considering that both of your parent's cars are parked over there near the entryway, I doubt he'll care. Plus, if the van goes haywire, we'll need a backup," he added pushing the car door open.

I couldn't argue with that; I thought while I waited until he came over to the passenger side door. He opened it for me, and I got out. As Jenson closed the door, a streak of lightning flashed across the sky.

"Come on, it looks like it's going to rain," he commented, taking my hand.

As we grew closer to the dining hall, I tugged Jenson forward. "Come on we've seen these pictures on the walls before. I should get Star to update our history as soon as this shiznits settled." I rolled my eyes at him

"Yeah, but what if someone added one? What if there's a clue right under our noises about the scientists?"

"Jenson get real! This place is like Fort Knox. You saw the setup when we came in. I couldn't find my way the last time and am surprised even I'm getting used to this new entryway. Why would someone want to give themselves away? If anything, it would be a trap," I argued.

"Give me a Sec, if you want to go ahead, go! I'm trying to figure something out."

I sighed, staring up at the photos. The first one I glanced at was of Mom, Dad, Star, Eva, and Patrick. They were much younger in the picture. Next to it was another of Cavin and Kaya nuzzling one another. The last photograph I checked was the notorious girl-fox, but nothing unusual jumped out at me. I stood there annoyed when a clip clomp sound advanced towards us from down the hall, heading our way. I turned around as Minder came towards us.

"Star asked me to come fetch you two. She wants to start invoking the amulets with your internal strength for our journey. What are you doing out here anyway?"

"Jenson has it in his head there's some amazing clue about the scientists in these photos. Or that perhaps someone decided to add one. The elders have this place spellbound, so who in their right mind would dare to break in?"

"Come on, don't be so dramatic," Jenson added.

"Okay, let's take a look at them. Maybe I'll see something you both missed."

Minder scanned the six photos in slow mode. She ran her finger along each one, her eyes analyzing the prints. Then took down the snapshot of the young girl fox/human.

"Who is this?" she asked.

"That's the same question I had when I first entered this hall. Apparently, she's pretty famous around here. Nayla told me that, but nothing else regarding her. The photo is rather old but in color. Mom didn't know her or else she would have told me," I added.

"Come along you two. Jenson, I have to side with Starla on this one. There's nothing back there in those prints that are going to help us.

Minder pushed open the dining hall door, and immediately I spotted Sensi near Owl practicing Kali stick moves. Lance was with them. Everyone else had lined up to receive the amulets Star had ordered. Cal waved to us as Molly was busy helping Star. Hurriedly I kissed Jenson and rushed over to see her.

"Hey, sorry I'm late. We had to do dishes then Jenson had it in his head there was a grand clue in the hallway," I groaned.

"You should get in line, stand by me. Mom and Patrick are near the front of it. I thought Star would have made this an all-out affair, but with the ceremony, we keep putting off for Maine…"

"Where is she?" I asked, searching the room. Jenson had joined Owl and the others. He was guiding Sensi in some moves. I'd wanted to see Cal so I wasn't hurt, he'd taken off. I turned back to her.

"Looks like Jenson discovered where he's needed. At any rate, Kaya had a special ceremony cape made for her. She's putting it on now, along with some makeup I guess." Cal admitted, then turned watching Star attach the clasp to Eva's necklace. Molly stood adjacent to her, chanting along with them. A wisp of white light emanated all around her, then was sucked into the amulet.

"Hmm, not all of us are getting charms?" I questioned eyeing those in line.

"Um, yeah, most of us are, but not everyone felt they required them."

"It's odd, I assumed everyone would be involved, we'd call upon the goddess as a group for one person similar to when Molly received her gift."

"Things change, plus it's a more efficient use of our time," she explained.

I nodded in agreement fidgeting in my spot as Star began her invoking with Patrick. Cal gently touched my back.

"Anything new with you?"

"Nah, you? New visions, visits with The Bandits?" I asked.

Cal's slid her hand off my back, and we sat down on the floor. She started to pull a few papers out of her pocket as Megan and Trigger got out of line to sit beside us.

"Minder and I took notes on the details today. Sika grumbled, hit Gavin and Gladiator, plus was a complete jerk the entire time. These are profiles on each of them," Cal whispered.

"Who?"

"The scientists, duh!" Megan blurted.

Minder bolted over to us, kneeled down, and hissed, "Put them away till we've finished our rituals. Those documents are priceless, besides my memory isn't photographic!"

"Sorry," Cal mumbled carefully folding them up, then pushed them into her pocket.

"Jones, Seni, and Trax will be stopping by after the ceremony for Maine. Afterward, we'll share what we've discovered together. Till then I expect everyone to keep what you know to yourselves."

"Minder, we get it. No distractions til the rest of our agendas settled. Cal, Star is waving you over," I reported.

Cal glared at Minder while she stomped over to Star to obtain her amulet.

"I understand those documents are imperative, but did you have to be so harsh," Trigger commented.

"I saw her pull them out and reacted. It wasn't the best thing to do. Megan, I apologize if I frightened you," she said, sitting down with us.

"I'll survive. You're a teddy bear compared to the wolves on nature shows."

"Thanks, kid I'm rough around the edges. I've been through some stuff," she mumbled.

"Haven't we all? Starla pulled the death card on me. I thought it meant I'd die physically, but instead, here I am."

"Tarot I take it?" asked Minder.

"Yeah, can you not hold that against me? I told you it meant growth, change, and I was right wasn't I?"

Minder chuckled as Cal hurried back to us rubbing the amulet that hung from her neck.

"Can I see? I didn't get an opportunity to check out the symbol you selected," I said while she scooted in next to me.

She held it up so I could get a closer look. The tree made of copper sat on top of a dark blue stone. It was a beautiful choice, well suited for her.

"It's breathtaking. Mine's the trinity with a ruby accent in the middle. Megan, what did you decide on?"

"You'll have to wait and see, I'm being summoned."

"Oh, how do you know that?" I questioned.

"Star's waving at me. I'll tell her to let Jenson and Owl go next. You'll be last, that way when Maine gets here…"

"Megan, I'm waiting," Star hollered, tapping her feet.

Trigger gave her a modest nudge urging her forward. She looked back at me for a Sec."I'll show you when I get back," she gushed.

I smiled as she skipped all the way to Star and Molly.

"Such ambition," Minder commented.

"Megan's pretty happy about being a part of this. She does freak out easily at times, but she's loyal," I acknowledged.

"I've noticed," Minder replied.

"Cal, should we meditate for a bit before Maine's ceremony? You know to find our center and maybe call Amare?" I asked.

"Sure, I'm not sure who my spirit guide is. I honestly don't believe I have one," she admitted.

We'd almost bowed our heads when I heard the door swing open. Both of us looked up to see Maine and Kaya entering the dining hall. She wore a beautiful purple cape over her black yoga pants and a soft long sleeve black T-shirt. My eyes fell on her Tiger-eye amulet. The one her aunt must have given her, um, mom. She wore half-moon earrings, along with subtle makeup. Dark red lips, with a hint of sparkle on her eyelids.

"Astonishing," I murmured. If she threw me for a loop, Molly would flip. Gracefully she seemed to float passed.

"She is quite dazzling in her beauty. It's surprising what makeup and an outfit can do to transform a person," Cal remarked.

Maine waited patiently beside Star and Molly while they summoned protection into Megan's emblem. The light emitting from it burned a vibrant greenish purple, then dove into the butterfly.

"Open your eyes, it's complete," Star clarified.

Megan placed her hand on the butterfly as she gazed up at Star. Then glanced at Molly and Maine. "It's still warm as if I were burning?"

"Yes, that's the strength inside of you, pieces that will bring light during dark times. It will guard you almost as well as Trigger has," she clarified.

"May I go?"

"Yes, but listen. Maine will stand aside as we implore Owl and Jenson's medallions. Being guys they don't care for the term amulets. I guess it's too girly," Star clarified.

Maine stifled a laugh, and I put my hand over my mouth to keep from snorting myself.

"Starla's last?"

"Yes, then we'll start the ceremony."

I'd closed my eyes only moments ago, hoping to catch a glimpse of Amare before I'd be called on to invoke protection. I sat in the silence of my mind tuning out all the noises around me. Unexpectedly, I felt a nudge on my leg.

Amare?

Child, remember all I've told you. This ending is a beginning of the release of past wrongs made right. Some will choose to forgive, grieve, let go. Don't be afraid of love, healing, hope, or defiance. All exist as I said from pain a flower will grow. Be yourself, but at the same time, share it, and once in a while… In your near future let go.

Is that all?

Yes, dear. Now go!

"Starla, Starla, Star is calling you. It's your turn!" Megan hollered, shaking me.

My eyes fluttered open startled by being brought out of my sudden trance. I shook my body out, rolled my shoulders back and got up feeling as if all eyes were on me. My Mom and Dad stood near Patrick and Eva. Owl and Jenson seemed to fixate on me. What? I wasn't the pop star here. Maine was receiving her acceptance into the Wiccan world. I turned and walked up to Molly.

"Hey, sorry about the audience. I guess it's because you're the last in line. Star has your amulet. I'll just take it from her. It may burn, be icy, or at the worst nothing will occur. It's never happened yet, but you never know."

"Mm-hmm," I added, bowing my head down to accept the necklace. It softly touched the nape of my neck, sending tingles down my chest. A warm rush rose up to my cheeks, then back into my heart. It fluttered rotating in a circle, an everlasting current as if caressed by regenerating love. What was happening? I wasn't faultless so why did I feel such a persistent tug from my heart to the rest of me? My face flushed a bright red, but I couldn't release my eyes. No one spoke, suddenly I jolted upright, my eyes automatically opening as I gasped for breath.

"It's been a generation or two since I've seen such a strong heart base. It takes a lot to rattle you girl," Sensi hooted.

I blushed, embarrassed by the remark not certain where to turn. Jenson came up, wrapped his arm around me, and I just stood there frozen.

Jenson kissed my cheek and turned to go.

"Where are you taking off to?" I demanded.

"Lance and I have to do some exercises with Sensi before Maine's initiation. There's nothing to set up since we're using Kali sticks again. We have to step up our game." He winked at me sauntering off as Shellena jogged over to me.

"Hey, are you cool? You froze after that reflection of warmth. Frankly, I'm surprised Star didn't speak with you after that. She just took Molly over to help Maine prepare."

"It's peculiar. Why do I feel singled out? Yeah, I'm the guardian, but others are as important as me."

"We each have our gifts. This simply proves we've several advantages over our adversaries. It's nothing to be ashamed of. That's why you are who you are. You see good, and truth in others, believe in yourself, but still retain doubt. Hang on. I have to assist Star with Maine."

"Sure." I ran my shoe along the carpeted floor, glancing up to see Jenson hanging with Owl and Lance. Sensi flew above them catching and releasing Kali sticks back to them. I chuckled to myself, shaking my head. Then touched the red stone in the middle of my trinity amulet. A slow warmth filled my body, curious as to where it was coming from I looked down to discover it glowing a brilliant crimson. My hand dropped to my sides.

"I saw that."

"Hmm, what?" I asked, twisting around to see who it was.

"It's just me. You'll receive your 2nd tail soon. It's too bad Nayla isn't here to see it," Trigger reminded me.

"Is that what the glow means?"

"It's part of it," he answered.

"Where's Megan? I thought she was with you."

"No worries, she's setting up chairs for the meeting after Maine's initiation. Usually, Wiccan ceremonies are performed with only those in your coven. A witch alone typically keeps it between themselves and the goddess."

"We're the closest thing to a coven she has. Our magic, beliefs, and ideals differ a bit, but not by much. What do we worship anyway?" I added, squinting in confusion.

"The earth, a universal god, one that is everlastingly forgiving, accepting, and refuses to denounce us."

"My Mom and Dad didn't make a big deal out of my necklace. Are they aware of a gift, I'm not?"

"Most likely they're as clueless as you are. We all evolve at some point in our lives. The Trinity is united in perfect formation. Come on! The ceremonies about to start."

"But they were just setting up," I complained.

"Look, the chairs are in a circular pattern. Maine is there in the middle where she'll call on the goddess, dedicating herself to the craft. Now come," Trigger order.

I accompanied him across the room to our seats. Shellena nodded to me as she strolled over to find hers.

I plopped down as quietly as possible next to Cal. Patrick and Eva sat on the other side of her. I nodded, acknowledging them, twisting to look to the left. Trigger sat beside me, Megan beside him, and then Owl, Jenson, and Lance. My dad held mom's hand in anticipation. Eva, Kaya, and Shellena were on the edge of their seats. The lights in the hall dimmed as I looked around the circle for Sensi. She was nowhere to be found. Maybe she'd decided to take an evening flight back to her abode.

Maine was in the center of the circle with Star on one side of her, and Molly on the other. She'd bowed her head as if she were praying. In front of her were three white candles placed in a triangle. Within that lye a red candle on a pentagram. A goblet stood on the left side of the triangle. It must have been water or a type of drink for the ritual. I noticed a stick of incense to the right.

"Friends we have gathered here tonight so that Maine can dedicate her life to the study of Wicca. She's informed me she's prepared to accept the responsibility that comes with the craft.

Molly and I will be assisting her during the ceremony. Please stay silent while she begins with her meditation. Thank you," Star whispered.

Molly handed Maine a lighter, and she reached over lighting a white tipped candle. A few minutes later she ignited the remaining white candles, then spoke her name, "Maine."

Molly nodded at her to carry on. I watched as the incense was lit. It gave off a sweet yet woodsy scent with a mixture of roses. I felt my body relax. There was a calmness of peace in the air. An elegance I couldn't identify. Maine slowly removed the hood of her cape, then nodded to Molly and Star. She picked up the incense and as she spoke rotated it around the candles.

"On this evening I come before the elements asking for the guardian to arise. Open the path, open the entry, open the way, I am here."

Maine put the incense back in the holder, grabbed the lighter and lit the red candle. Afterward, standing up she stretched out her arms as if talking to the goddess.

"I desire to be a part of the world with each element clearly in balance within me. I shall hold myself to high standards when in practice. Each spell cast, prayer, and moment of truth will be to assist, honor, and protect those around me. I shall be accountable for my actions. Earth Mother I invoke you!"

My eyes followed Maine while she kneeled before the altar in front of her. Radiating off of her was the dedication she felt to use this practice for good. She picked up the goblet passing it over the candles. "Bless me earth mother, with this water indict your energies within," she chanted, placing the cup of water down with her palms now above it. "As to the earth, as to me, may this water purify me." She cupped the goblet holding it high over her head, "Open the path, open the entry, open the way, I am here."

Maine lifted the water to her mouth and drank. She touched her fingers to her tongue, then used them to put out the red candle before her. "Great earth mother, blessed be. I'm charged, so mote it be."

We sat in silence until the white candles burned out. I wasn't sure how long had passed when Star sat a burlap purple canvas bag beside Maine. Molly began to help her pick up the remaining contents left.

"Lance, will you get the lights? Cavin will be here in five minutes. He wanted to be present while we organize the rest of the procedure for Grandville."

"Of course," he replied, standing up from his seat.

Chapter 35

After the dining hall had been re-established everyone sat down to discuss what needed to happen before we left Springville.

"Instead of me restating what we've discussed does anyone have any suggestions or questions concerning the current plan?" asked Lance.

"Why have Cal and I in our animal forms. How will we be able to enter combat? We can't omit our power to keep people away if we want to draw the enemy in. While we have established our positions, I need to know what our tasks will be. If we stay in human form, we can use Kali sticks. With me in fox form, and Cal in her mixed form, we could fight. Naturally, I've not yet been trained, but if it is inside me, instinctual then we're set. Megan wants to learn a displacement spell. It's smart, now what do you suggest we do?" I demanded.

"That's my Starla, tough girl your back," Jenson commented.

"Yeah, she comes and goes," I admitted.

Lance smirked, shaking his head, but before he could answer Kaya cut in.

"That is why we've created clothing in which you can shift back and forth. I understand you haven't practiced transforming frequently. Therefore, it won't be effortless," she acknowledged.

"It will be useful since it will provide us access to battle with the Kali sticks if needed. Megan though, the spell?" I pressed.

"We'll get to it soon. Star what is it you were mumbling to me regarding Maine?"

"Lance has darts primed for you to carry in the canvas bag. You'll deposit them in the pocket within it. I've created a strap to fasten to it so it can be carried like a messenger bag. I considered making you a tool belt, but if an enemy got too close, he could get a hold of the darts and use them against us. It's not much safer, but better," Star addressed.

"That I do," he said, laying them on the table in front of us. Maine nodded to him, afterward carefully reaching for the weapons. Star took the strap out of her satchel sitting near her and placed it on the table.

The door to the dining hall scraped against the floor while it opened. Kaya's face lit up, and everyone turned to see who it was. Cavin trotted into the room as Jones, Sina, and Trax followed close behind him.

"I take it the ceremony went accordingly. I see you've been handing out weapons," he added approaching us. Kaya got up and pulled out a chair so he could sit next to her. Jones, Sina, and Trax remained standing near.

"Yes, there are only a few more things to do before we depart on this final mission. Megan must learn a displacement spell for protection. The goddess should grant it to her instantaneously due to our circumstances. I'm flustered because we're blindly plunging into enemy territory with little knowledge of who they are," Star stammered.

I looked at Minder then asked the question weighing on my mind, but not spoken ever since the Sun goddess vanished. "The goddess! It was never resolved. Will she answer us?"

Kaya sighed, shifted, and made loud Ra Ra noises into the air, sounding an alarm. Time passed while we anxiously waited. Slowly but surely a bright light illuminated the entire dining hall.

"I couldn't shield you any longer, returning wasn't an option, till presently. I'd been called to another predicament I'm unable to disclose. I'll gift Megan with displacement. I'd lower myself lower into the room, but I would blind you."

"It is understood. Before you move forward with that, have you any words of advice for our journey?" Cavin muttered shielding his eyes with his right paw.

"There's one among you with information to disclose. I advise them to share it when I've gone. Megan, come-forth. It will be quick, but you must remain open to acquire it. To use it you must picture yourself one step in front of the enemy. It's comparable to morphing from one place to another. Do not use it for fun, or you'll not have it accessible when desired. It will create an illusion protecting your current location for up to three minutes. In those, you must find a way to protect yourself. Now kneel down as I relinquish this gift."

Megan stood up from her seat and bent down to partake of the ability. A single ray of light danced upon her shoulders. It flickered on and off as the beam of the goddess bounced off of her. One second she was kneeling before the goddess and the next she grinned sheepishly at the door to the hall. When the displacement had faded, she brought her head back up gazing above at the light.

"Thank you. I will use it wisely only with the intent of shielding myself. May I use it on others? If they're in trouble?"

"It's questionable if it will work in that manner. I can't promise it will, but in a pinch do not hesitate to try. Good Luck my friends. I must now depart.

And her light went out.

"What does she mean someone is withholding information," Cavin bellowed. Sina, Trax, and Jones immediately exchanged glances amongst each other. I trembled as Jenson pulled me close to him, then laid my head against his chest. Megan, who'd been bouncing around earlier happy about her new ability shrank back into her seat slumping down. I caught a glimpse of Owl playing with his key ring. He ran his fingers over the metal feather in his hand while Maine and Molly whispered to one another. I could barely hear them as Maine promised to keep her safe.

"Dear, settle down. Maybe if you address everyone, someone will come forth. Did you consider they might be holding it back for a reason?" Kaya asked, laying a paw on his shoulder.

Minder waved frantically at Cal. Quickly she reached into her pocket and pulled out the papers, tossing them haphazardly onto the table before us.

"There, Minder and I have been grilling the Bandits for profiles regarding the scientists. It's all there. What we need to know to face them properly. Would someone please read them briefly out loud."

Lance picked up the papers and unfolded them clearing his throat.

"Zane: Male, blonde hair, tallish with a medium build, it says here he studied DNA modification. This included taking cells from the wolves' bodies, and injecting them into humans to create weapons. Hmm, sounds like our prisoners." He lifted his head up, rolled his shoulders back, then went on…"It says here they were going to sell them to the government as weapons. Talk about human trafficking," he mumbled.

"Is there anything else?" Star wondered.

"Oh, he's got brown eyes. Cal noted he's jittery, wears a lot of black, constantly is paranoid watching his back, nervous, a worrier," he added, setting the paper down. He held three more in his hands.

"How pissed was Sika when you pulled this data out of Gavin and Gladiator?" Dan inquired.

Minder smirked at the remark. "So livid; I had to pull him off of them. Cal helped, but they remained cuffed. Therefore it was rather painless."

Cavin rolled his eyes, "Keep reading!"

"Rob: Male, hair color rustic red, short and slender. He has brown eyes. This guy developed the chemicals to mix with the wolf DNA."

"Yeah, the one that forced us to eat that raw meat," Minder mumbled.

Jones pulled out chairs, then motioned for Sina and Trax to sit. Star sighed, snatching the papers out of Lance's hands.

"This one is upbeat, listens to pop music?" She lifted her eyes in astonishment. "Oh, he also likes oldies, hmm says, he bosses Zane around. Was that their reference or yours Minder?"

"There, I told you I only recall snippets! Aren't you impressed that Cal and I've retrieved this information? There are two more, both are women," she spat.

Star seemed amused, almost happy she'd brought out the anger in Minder. Was she playing games, or attempting to get us hyped for the hunt?

"Bonnie: female, has brown hair, height 5'4, green eyes, body type average. This one's specialty was genetic coding, probably helped that guy make the chemical," she noted. "Crap, this one's got a photographic memory, be careful if you run into her! Do not let any secrets slip, and she's obsessed with wolves. Cal, be careful since you are part wolf." She let the paper fall from her hands to the table.

"There's one more, it's not good," Cal admitted.

"Here you do the honors then seeing as you and Minder uncovered this," she stated, handing the papers over to her.

"Mara: female of course. She has black hair, is 5'6 a bit larger, and has blue eyes. This is the chilling part not only did she study genetic engineering, but she spent four years in the army. It's where Sika finally admitted something. He said she'd come up with the idea for wolf hybrids there. This girl is gothic, but with rainbow colors."

Cal sat the paper on top of the others. "I wish we had photographs, all I can do is imagine what they look like in my head.

"It's alright," said Minder, laying a furry paw on top of Cal's hand. Cavin jumped down from his chair, and Kaya got up to go after him.

"Where is he off to? It's not the time for him to wimp out on us!" Tri exclaimed.

"Cavin! What are you thinking?" Kaya shrieked.

He turned back to face her, "Tomorrow evening I want the group to depart. Owl will have to miss the Spring Market. I'll send someone to aid them. I'm not sure who, but this. It's time."

Chapter 36

The gang sat in the middle of my living room floor minus Cal. She'd stayed behind with Minder. Mom and Dad headed back to their apartment for a bit of R, and R., but Megan had begged to stay here with me, and they gave in. I smiled, standing at the window while they drove away. Then let the curtain fall back into place.

"It's late. Molly, Maine you've spoken with your folks about staying?" I asked, turning towards them.

"Yes, it's fine. Were you sad that Owl and Jenson took off?" Molly asked as Maine pulled something out of her canvas bag. She held a dark burlap cloth over it.

"Nah, they had stuff to do, plus it's nearly one am. I'm about to drop into Zombieville. What's up?" I asked, walking over to them.

"I didn't want to give this to you till we were here. It isn't much, but Molly and I picked it out at the mall. We noticed you didn't have a clock in the living room. This way you don't have to keep eyeing your cell phone," she added, handing me the item.

Megan set down the controller for the game she'd been playing. She got up, and Trigger followed her over afterward sniffing the item in my hands.

"It isn't chow" he observed sitting down beside Megan, who'd popped a squat next to Maine. I chuckled, un-wrapping the clock. It was nostalgic, the outside a see-through tube around the clock containing water and glitter. I turned it over to see a package of batteries attached to it.

"When you put those in it lights up. We weren't sure how retro you are, but we thought it was cool."

"I could go all ninja turtles on you, but that's rather 90's," I added, opening the batteries. "I'll hang this right above where the television is. I'm not sure if the bedrolls are still here. If not, there are blankets in my closet. Heads up, cuz I'm grabbing some hot cocoa, then after heading to bed. I'm spun after the...."

I stopped, listening to something outside. A flutter of wings wrapped against the window near the entrance. An Owl was it Sensi? I scrambled to the door, opening it, and the bird flew inside. Quickly, I slammed the door shut locking it behind her.

"Are you Okay? Is someone after you?" I stammered as we huddled around her.

"I'm unharmed. Please, I need solitude to transform, do you have clothes I could borrow?"

"Yes, everyone, let's give her some privacy. We'll find something for you to wear. Then you can tell us what happened."

Sensi sat with a cup of hot cocoa in her hands. I figured something warm would calm her. I thumbed my mug of CoCo as it was still somewhat hot, then blew on it allowing it to cool. Sensi sipped from her cup silently as I glanced at the full moon shining through the kitchen window.

"Starla, I'm alright just rattled. Sika tried to get a hold of me tonight. He wanted me to lead him to the scientists. I told him I'd only been to a few meetings. I had no clue how to get to Grandville from here. We're leaving soon, but I wish it were tonight," she stuttered, lowering her head, allowing the vapors from the drink to fill her nose.

"Well, you can stay here until morning. Megan, get my cell out of my purse and call Ranger, Mike. Tell him to let the clan know she's here and safe."

"It's in your room on the bed, right?" she asked, pushing her chair back.

"Yes, just go grab it, call him on the way back. That way your cocoa will stay warm. Also, if he needs to speak with me..."

"Yeah, Yeah, I know," she mocked heading to the living area.

"Why would Sika want to go after them himself?" I asked, turning back to my friends. I ran my right hand along the mug, cupped it, brought it to my lips and drank.

"That is what I was curious about unless he believes he'll be able to kill them himself. Nothing like your own weapons you created turning against you. With Sika that seems to be the point, getting his vengeance on those that did him wrong. Cal only promised him part of what he wanted. I don't suppose he was very truthful with Minder," Sensi added.

"Was this the first time he's ever approached you about this?" Molly questioned.

"Genuinely yes, I was flying by their enclosure, chamber, cage, whatever, and saw his paw reach out for me. He couldn't break the barrier and fell back on his bum, but next shook his fists at it, calling out to me. That's when I decided to fly straight here to tell you. I figured there wasn't much anyone could do. They aren't going anywhere. It's excellent that you're informing the clan. It just worked me up a million times over. I wanted to feel safe, and you are the guardian," Sensi rambled, turning towards me.

A weak smile spread a crossed my face as I set down the cocoa I'd been sipping. "Thanks for having faith in me. I'm sure Mike will let the Crusaders know you're safe," I added.

"I feel like a fool. I've been flying surveying the park for Mike, keeping a close eye on everything. He was fairly worried those Scientists might come after us until Cavin told him what your father had found. He and Patrick, I mean."

"Yeah, the computer thing, the shelter explosion," Maine said, sitting her empty cup down on the table.

I almost stood up to gather the mugs when I heard Megan enter the room. She set my cell down beside me, then sat.

"Starla, Mike says not to fret. He's contacting the Crusaders, then Cavin. Minder will keep a close eye on Sika till dawn. Later he'll have Lance take over so she can get some sleep before we leave."

"That's a relief. How's Chaz?" I asked, changing the subject.

"I wish I knew since I haven't been in school in a few days. I have no clue," Megan replied.

"He hasn't called you?" I inquired, finally standing to gather the cups. Molly and Maine both handed me theirs. Sensi was still sipping.

"We kissed, he told me I was beautiful then mentioned, we should see a movie. After that, nada. It was, magic just like I said." Megan smiled and picked up her drink to sip.

"Do you still have mom's old cell? I thought she gave you one for emergencies. It's not fantabulous, but it works. Call him tomorrow, or Tasha, see if you can find anything out before you leave. If it's important to you, don't give up."

"I agree with Starla," Trigger added. He nudged Megan to hurry her along. When she finished her drink, she handed me her cup.

"Guys, we all need sleep. I'll set these in the sink. Then unless you need blankets or anything, I'm heading to bed."

"How about we camp out with you," Sensi suggested.

"My room's not large, but if you want to hunker down on the floor your welcome to," I replied, setting the cups in the sink.

Chapter 37

(April 15, Thursday)

I laid in bed listening to my friends snore as I tossed and turned attempting to sleep. I'd been so spent earlier, and now I couldn't shut my mind off. I didn't understand why Sika would want Sensi to lead them to the scientists this evening. It didn't make sense, but at the same time had Sika ever made sense? Well, except for the revenge thing, of course. I pulled my legs up towards my chest and sat up. Afterward, pushing the covers off of myself. Then got up tiptoeing carefully around my friends out into the living room. I stretched my arms out wide turning to the window that faced the outer door. The moon was a beautiful crescent orb hanging in the sky. I let my arms fall to my sides and decided to get a glass of water. As I twisted back towards the hallway, I caught sight of a black tail. Maybe Trigger was having a tough time sleeping too. Cautiously I crept down the hall into the kitchen. Had he moved? Where was he?

"Trigger?" I crept further into the kitchen, then caught a glimpse of him alongside the back door. "Is everything okay?"

"I got an uneasy feeling earlier, so I wanted to keep watch. It seemed to me that if someone were to try to break in, they'd come through this doorway. I'm presumably paranoid ever since Sensi told me about Sika," he stated, standing up.

"I can't sleep either," I confessed walking over to him. I laid my hand on his back, then began to pet him calming my nerves. He turned towards me, licking my hand, then nuzzled my leg. I scratched behind his ears, and he backed up a bit.

"I was going to grab a glass of water, would you like a bowl?"

A sly grin spread on his lips. "Sure, then what?"

I shrugged. Then made my way over to the cupboard and opened it. I grabbed myself a glass and him a bowl then filled them both. Afterward, I set the dish down next to him, and he lapped it up hurriedly.

"After I drink this water, I'm heading back to try and get some sleep." I shivered, then took a sip.

He nodded to me, "Meditation might induce slumber You'll need it for our journey."

"I know, I wish we could have left for Grandville tonight," I admitted, downing the rest of the liquid. I set the glass in the sink and turned to leave. "Then again the timing would be off. Sika's cooling down, I sense one of the clan members is with him now. I'm probably positively suspicious but better safe than sorry," I sighed.

"True, now seek peace. I'll see you in the morning, and I'd like to try that black stuff you call coffee."

I laughed, nodding as I headed back to the bedroom.

A slow, calm overcame me when I snuggled into bed. I let go of any thoughts stuck in my head, allowing them to drift I pictured them dancing in the clouds. Then sniffed at the air as I sat in the field of golden wheat swaying back and forth in the gentle breeze. Sleep began to overtake me, but before I could fall, I was lucid.

"Starla, be careful. Trigger's got your back."

"What about you? Can't you protect me?" I mind-spoke to her.

"I'm only here to guide you plus he has a physical form now. Hopefully, the elders will let him keep it. If things get ugly, I'll ask to be allowed to step in. I have faith in your ambition, wit, and keen sense. You'll be fine, now that you've found your peace. Slumber."

A blast of soft sand delicately fell upon my eyelids sinking me into a profound state of REM. When I opened my eyes, I guessed it was morning. I sat up and noticed all the blankets had been folded and placed near the closet. The smell of coffee drifted into the room. I reached down to the crate I'd set my phone in retrieving it to check the time, 11 a.m.! It was enough to get me out of bed, dressed, and into the kitchen.

Megan and the others had made coffee, toast, and what was left of the bacon. I sat sipping coffee while Trigger lapped up his. He wore a sour expression on his face each time he took a gulp.

"Are you sure you don't want some cream and sugar? It helps it go down easier," I suggested.

"Nah, I'll manage," he added looking up from his bowl. Megan smirked at his statement, and I shook my head.

"I won't even touch coffee without it, or a hot cocoa packet," Molly remarked reaching for a slice of toast. Maine had already eaten two, plus the bacon on her plate.

"Thanks for cleaning up the blankets. Did Sensi leave to go back to the park this morning?" I asked, adding more coffee to my mug.

"She left to check in with Shellena and Lance. They're packing the tools needed for this evening. Kaya wants you and Cal to meet with her to try on your outfits. You'll practice shifting in them. Owl and Jenson should be there already," Trigger explained.

"How long will it take to get to Grandville?" Maine asked, picking up her plate she headed towards the sink.

"We'll leave at sundown. It's four and a half hours away from here which means a long car ride with one break."

"And you've discussed this with Lance?" I asked.

"Yes, everyone is on board. There's not a lot for anyone to do right now but wait. Molly and Maine, you have the healing ointment? Also the packets of herbs from your lists. The one Star gave you ages ago?" Trigger inquired.

"Yes, it's all ready to go. We've each got some, plus I issued some ointment to Megan. She can carry it with her just in case we're unable to contact you. I doubt we'll get separated, but it helps to be prepared," Molly stated while Maine sat back down.

"Good, now after we've cleaned up we'll head over to the huts."

Maine appeared irritated since she'd just sat back down. I got up clearing the table of the plates. I was glad there were not any leftovers to put away. I'd have to go shopping after all this was over. I put the dishes in the sink, turned off the coffee pot, and placed the pan on the counter that was left on the stove. I'd deal with it later. I turned back to face my friends.

"Come on. Collect anything you'll need for this trip. I don't plan to come back to the apartment today. I'll call Mom and Dad on the way. I take it we're walking?"

"It looks that way unless you want to wait for Jenson and Owl. My mom needed the car so yesterday she dropped us off at the park," Maine declared.

"Alright then, I'll lock the back door, get my things, and you guys get yours then meet me out front. Whoever is last, please lock the door. Not that I have anything exciting to steal anyway," I added.

Chapter 38

I breathed in the fresh air as we hiked on the path to the clan area. Maine and Molly were pointing out wildlife as we went. We'd seen several squirrels, chipmunks, and a few robins. I shivered pulling my coat closer to my body. A few days ago, it had felt like spring, but when we'd ventured out, I'd had to go back for my hat and gloves. Molly and Maine had been prepared.

"Sis, I watched the weatherman this morning on channel ten. It's supposed to warm up soon," Megan noted as we entered the hut area. Cal, Lance, and Shellena were throwing around Kali sticks. They stopped when they saw us.

"It looks like you're equipped to head out right now,'" Lance called out to us.

"Yeah, we've got everything we'll need," I shouted hurrying over to them. I felt for my purse inside my jacket. It was there, with my cell, and other necessities

"Good, Trigger gave you the update. Oh, I see him behind Megan. Anyway, Sika's been taken care of. We've discussed with Gavin and Gladiator how to handle him. Now, I'm supposed to take you to the gym."

"Are Jenson and Owl, there?" I asked, trying to keep up with them.

"Yes, Kaya, Sensi, Patrick, everyone who's coming with us tonight. We're taking two vans." I nodded to him swallowing the frog in my throat. He opened the door of the gym and right away I saw Kaya with Jinx. Megan rushed passed me, and I caught sight of Cal standing off to the side. Kaya motioned both of us over to her. I didn't even have time to glance Jenson's way. Cal and I rushed over to see what she had concocted for us.

"I've taken into consideration your styles, comfort, and color choices. I laid out two outfits for each of you. Starla, your's are on the right side of the table and Cals are on the left. You may choose one outfit for this mission."

I nodded eyeing the long sleeve lightweight green shirt along with the black yoga stretchy pants. They would be perfect, hold up well, and appeared extremely comfortable. It would be easy to move in them, and switching should be effortless. They could be a bit loose-fitting if they didn't conform to my fox body versus human. I picked them up while Cal chose hers.

"Good, now go to the back bathroom, try them on, see how they fit. Then come out to join us. I'll need you to shift in them a few times to make sure the elasticity holds up under pressure. I'm keeping my fingers crossed." She winked at us then trotted to where Star stood with Maine and Molly.

I smirked at Cal, elbowing her towards the gym changing rooms. We started to power walk there. One was set up for the girls, and another for the guys.

"I hope once we get these on I'll remember how to shift. It feels like forever!" Cal commented, walking with a bounce in her step.

I grinned, "Yeah, it sure feels that way. My favorite part of being in fox form is the knack to run super fast! Plus, I can't recall if we've used our powers in this form," I contemplated.

"Nayla said it would be the same, it was easier to be in human form for The Shadows," she admitted as we entered the changing area. I grabbed a locker and began to undress. After putting on my new garments, I shoved my old ones into it.

"Shouldn't we take them with us? We're going to be all hot and sweaty after this operation. I'd hate to have to wear these all the way back to Springville," Cal stressed.

"Ugh, you're right," I replied. Then took my clothes back out of the locker. I opened up my purse stuffing them inside. Cal took a round object out of her pocket, unraveled it, and I did the same.

"Ah, a satchel bag, sort of like mine," I said while we headed back to the gym.

"Yeah, it's Minders. She was adamant we take it, that it would hold most of the items we'd need.

"Cool," I stated, catching a glimpse of Molly as she jogged up to us.

I chuckled observing the purse hanging like a messenger bag. "Everyone's getting these? " I asked.

"No, Maine thought it would be great for the journey. It holds a lot of stuff! I made her hang on to her ointment though. In case we are divided during battle."

"Good. How are things at home? We've been so wrapped up in this." I spread out my arms indicating everything while we walked back to Kaya.

"Mom and Dad are working things out. I'm proud of him. It's not easy, they still fight, but dad's getting better about Maine and me," she confided.

In spite of all the crazy things were looking up. I pulled Molly into a side hug. "I'm glad. Mr. Fretner if nothing else is allowing your happiness and attempting to understand."

"Starla's right," Cal chimed-in.

"He is step by step. Has been I mean. Kicking him out is off the chopping block. She came close a few times. Mom says she's having him talk with our new minister."

I released Molly from my embrace as we stopped near Kaya. Maine was waiting there for Molly.

"Those fit you both exactly as I'd planned," Kaya gushed, clasping her hands in front of her. "Cal, how do you like yours?"

Cal bent down to touch the smooth black leggings, then stood up straight examining her blue top. "The leggings are form-fitting, as well as the shirt. When I alter my shape if it stretches it will work," she reasoned. Afterward, looking back at us.

"Good, now. Maine and Molly if you wish to stay, fine. Please give us a bit of room so the girls can begin the conversion."

Cal and I playfully ran alongside each other circling the gym, then crashed in a heap in front of Kaya. She shook her head at us and sighed.

"Well, the outfits work, extend, plus flex. You could practice pushing away enemies, blasting them, err burning. That's what Minder said you accidentally did to her. It might come in handy with the scientists if one gets too close."

"The ultimate goal is to capture them. I don't suppose I'll be too involved in that. We might corner the scientists to keep them from harming the others in tandem as Maine shoots them down with tranqs. That is unless Lance gets to them first. They could all attack us at once, or send out one individual at a time. It's hard to tell what we're getting into," I advised.

"Be ready for anything," Shellena suggested, as she strolled up to us. Then nodded towards Megan working on her displacement spell with Trigger.

"They seemed to be getting the hang of it," I commented.

"She will be of great help, and as you put recently, we'll all need to work together to create a barrier they cannot surpass. Sure, Lance can use his will to control them, but he'll grow weak fast with four of them. I can assist but will only be capable of holding them for so long."

"Okay, we're playing it by ear, or do we have a permanent plan?" asked Cal.

"A bit of both, but we're not altering the order in which Lance has instructed you. I spoke with Tri. She'll attempt to provide instructions via her psychic ability. It will confirm any changes, locations of the scientists, etc.

"Brilliant. Why don't we fetch everyone and head to the dining hall? We'll have a quick mid-meal there," Kaya stated.

"Lance! Everyone, please gather for a moment." Minder hollered clapping her hands to get our attention.

Kaya rolled her eyes at her, "I could have done that."

It worked because the guys stopped sparring. Sensi shifted into human form. The clothes flexed with her conversion, and she hurried to stand beside us. Lightly she patted me on the head, then gave Cal a quick grin.

"Can I change back? It's going to be awkward eating with paws," I complained.

"She's right," Cal said, standing up.

"Yes, quickly. Oh, and get your purses, you'll have to attach them to your torso somehow, or they'll get lost when you shift," Kaya noted.

"I'll see you guys in the dining hall. Oh, Megan's coming over," she added, quickly moving towards the door.

"Hey, I'm going to wait for you while you shift. Mom said it's okay. Maine and Molly are saving us seats. I overheard Lance saying, Rascal and Nuria will be there. I wonder what that's about?" she pondered.

"We were going to have a secret girls meeting. That never happened, maybe it has something to do with that," Cal remarked.

"Right, before The Shadows attacked Kern," I clarified. My eyes scanned the gym noticing almost everyone had left. Star lingered, then slipped out into the hallway. I looked back at Meg's. "Has mom said anything about me? The mission, or anything? I'm curious because she didn't even approach me after the switch."

"She's focusing on her ability to read minds, listen for voices, and all. She's pretty on edge about it. This is her first mission since she's been back in the clan. It's only my 2nd. It makes sense that she's nervous about it. Look at what happened with The Shadows."

"Yeah, um. Cal, should we just poof we're humans out here, or?" I asked

"Here I guess if Megan doesn't mind watching. It's slightly eerie and gross," she added.

"I can handle it. I'm in eighth grade and will be a high schooler next year. I'd like it if you'd treat me with some dignity and respect," she demanded, folding her arms.

"Alright, chill out, and give us some space," I chuckled amusedly at her request.

Cal and I took our stances. A shiver raced up my backbone, while I breathed in, let it out, then felt my body flipping, my fur and whiskers retracted as my body regained its original shape. Cal was still shifting when I became acclimated to my human structure.

"Man, why does it always have to be so wicked! It seemed to drain me more than the last time," I complained. Then tried not to stumble while I lifted upper body to stand from my four-legged position. Megan gathered our purses clutching them to her chest, her eyes wide with disbelief.

"Are you Okay, there?" Cal asked, rubbing the back of her head. She must have bumped it during her switch.

"What you just did, it was repulsive. I could never see that again and be better," she added.

"Well, too bad. I love you Sis, but I hate to tell you during the mission it might transpire. We have to be on our toes, ready to rumble, and it may mean poof I'm a fox!

Megan shook her head in annoyance. "Whatever," she drawled, wandering to the door. She held it open for us as we departed.

Sina and Trax welcomed us into the dining area. I was hugging them both at once when I noticed Jones chatting with Patrick and my father. Tri waved to us as she sat with Eva at the big wooden table. Later, we walked with them over to a large pot of chili. It was a mixture of vegetables, meat, and beans. A big bowl of garden salad sat beside it along with garlic bread on a large platter. I picked up bowls handing them to Megan and Cal. Molly and Maine came skipping over to us.

"Maine, do you eat meat?" I asked, not recalling if she was a vegetarian.

"On occasions, but not frequently. I'll give it a go this time, small portion though. The salad looks delightful," she added, grabbing a plate. "So Sina, are you and Trax planning to tag along tonight?"

"It's critical we're there. Sina and I plan to monitor everything as we would have done with The Shadows if we hadn't needed to stay with Kern. Being we're semi-immortal, we can step in if things get heated."

"Can you save the fox Jones found, the one those awful scientists captured?" Megan inquired. She paused, picked up a bowl filling it with chili, then topped it with a ton of cheese.

"Maybe, I keep telling Jones to let us take care of those jerks, but he says it's not our battle," Trax scoffed. Jenson and Owl ambled over. Then each filled their bowls with chili muttering to each other.

"Hey, boys, what's up?" asked Cal.

"Not a lot. We've practiced with the Kali sticks so much I could spin them in my sleep. I've been holding off on the paralysis spell saving my energy. It was Rascal's suggestion. Nuria and Mike will be at the Spring Market at noon. They decided to delay it till then. It shouldn't harm sales."

"That's good news for the tribe." I picked up a bowl, then filled it with chili. Then added cheese and stuck a slice of bread in it.

"Yep," Owl replied.

"I'm going to sit with Mom and Eva if you'd like to join us." I paused, "Is Cavin speaking tonight?"

"Shortly, but Rascal demanded to be first after we've eaten. If I'm correct, we're leaving around seven," Owl clarified.

I nodded in response as Jenson reached for my hand. I clasped it in mine, then all of us headed to the table.

"It will be dark by then. Is there a way we'll be able to sneak up on the enemy, and still see them?" Megan worried.

"Lance has that covered. He'll enlighten us following Rascal speech," Owl confirmed setting his food on the table.

Patrick stood up from his seat to take down some chairs that had been stacked up behind him. He placed them along the vacant portion of the table so we could sit.

"Thanks, has my dad spoken to you regarding connections?" I asked, letting go of Jenson's hand. Then carefully placed my food on the table. Jenson set down his to grab the pitcher of lemonade while Molly and Maine choose their seats. He began to pour himself a drink.

"Rascal and I've discussed this. I have a few contacts from the department that owe me favors. They're not thrilled about involving themselves in this sort of situation, but Rascal's got us covered if they fall through. He knows several federal agents," Dan revealed from across the table. Rascal nodded beside him, then took a large bite of his garlic bread.

"Wowsers!" Megan exclaimed accepting the lemonade Jenson had poured for her. Trigger lingered near not at all interested in food. I wondered if maybe the coffee had disagreed with him.

"Wowsers is right. Cavin and I are grateful to have these agents available." Kaya replied, setting down a plate of brownies for us. Trigger leapt up with his front paws on the table, sniffing.

Cavin stifled a laugh and took a brownie out of the pan. He set it beside Trigger who gladly wolfed it down.

"Didn't want any regular food I see, but you sure love Kaya's brownies," Cavin commented.

"Stomachs a bit upset. Coffee doesn't agree with me, but I'm not turning down dessert," he yapped.

"I never do. Now, I'd like to get this show on the road. Sensi should fly in any second. Rascal, take the floor.

Rascal cleared his throat, then stood, lifting his glass of lemonade. "I'd like to make a toast to everyone here. May the goddess protect you on your journey to justice. It's long overdue, not only in the name of my son, but all who have perished, or suffered at the hands of these assailants. Trust your instincts when it comes to apprehending them. Do not hesitate to injure them if necessary, but by no means eliminate them. They should suffer, and to do so must live. Nuria, would you like to add anything?"

She shuddered, then turned to him. "After all, they put me through, darn tootin I've got something to add," she sassed. Then twisted back to face us. "Cal, you've come a long way since returning home. Eva, your daughter is a fighter strong, remarkable. And Starla, Megan, your bond will shelter you during this last storm. Corny, I know. Upon your return, I hope we'll be celebrating. Maine, and Molly. I have yet to know you well, but there's something about you two," she added with a spark in her eye.

My heart warmed, and I looked down at my amulet to see it emitting a red glow. I took it pushing it into my shirt. Then finished my chili, and sipped my lemonade. Jenson reached over me, and it fell out of my hands onto the table. Tri grabbed some napkins sitting beside me helping me to clean up the spill.

"Sorry," I blurted.

"It's fine. Nuria any advice for Jenson, or Owl before I give the final orders?" asked Lance. Shellena drummed her fingers on the table beside him. I noticed Minder nibbling at her salad taking in the activity in the room.

"Never let the enemy steal your heart turning it cold. Always remember no matter how evil they are, someone turned them," she spoke sternly.

Minder nodded in agreement with the statement. She certainly understood it better than most of us, having been in that position herself. Without warning the door to the dining hall swung open. I turned to see Sensi and Jinx as they dashed in letting it slam behind them.

Lance got up from his seat, frowning. "The Bandits didn't get out of the holding chambers did they?"

"No, we were running late. Jinx and I thought we'd take a jaunt into Hunters park. We spoke with Mike, who wished us luck. There was a blonde chick there with him. Don't worry. Jinx stayed hidden when he saw her. I spoke with him in human form, of course," Sensi assured him.

"Oh, the one he's dating," Owl commented.

"Fair enough," Lance grumbled, sitting back down. "Now let's get back to our agenda. The Bandits will ride with Shellena, and me. Patrick and Dan, I'll need you in the van with us. No offense ladies, but I'd rather not have you deal with these brutes. Sika is the worst of them. Cal? Where's Minder?"

"I'm right here, just quiet. I'm not sure two vans are going to be enough. We'll have to cram into them."

"The Bandits will sit in back with the supplies. Patrick and I will keep an eye on them while Shellena drives, and Dan will sit up front with her. We'll have some passenger space left which means Sina, and Trax can ride with us. Jones, are you still coming with us?"

Jones seemed perplexed. He'd been planning on joining us in this mission and even had helped formulate some of it. I watched as he shook his head, letting out a long sigh. "I've done all I'm able. Looking back at everything I realize now the dean wouldn't be thrilled if he discovered I was involved in this type of scheme. Sina and Trax, you've got this covered?"

"We're on it!"

"Okay Jones, at least meet us afterward in the dining hall for a follow-up," Lance remarked.

"Certainly," he replied.

"Okay then, we'll park the vans along the roadside park entering from the left. We want to stay clear of the residential side to the right. I have glow sticks for everyone, but your eyes should adjust to the darkness. Most of us possess night vision that are halfzies or supernatural creatures. I'll equip the others with small flashlights, but don't use them unless you need to," Lance instructed.

"I'll drive the 2nd van then. In case one of them breaks down, I'll bring my gear. Are we using mind-speak, or should I bring the walkies for that?" Minder pressed.

"The walkies, I can't take the chance of taking my eyes off of the Bandits. Especially Sika.

"We should leave it's after five. Then later get something to eat on the way," Dan suggested.

"True, but we'll want to eat in the van. Starla, you and Megan will need to go in, place the order and deliver the food. We can't chance being seen or use our manipulative powers. We can't risk draining them," Shellena advised.

"We can do that, plus Maine and Molly will help. It's going to be a lot of grub!" I commented.

"Hey, I want to order my own food," Owl grunted.

"We'll figure it out on the way," Lance fumed.

Chapter 39

Everyone had been fighting over Mc Donald's or Arby's. Lance finally ended it over the walkies by suggesting we stop at Mc Donald's first, then Arby's. I sat next to Jenson eating fries glancing out at the trees to the left of me. We'd parked off to the side in St Louis Illinois. Thank god we were at the halfway point. Everyone was growing restless. I'd been hoping we'd find a rest area so we could stretch our legs, but we hadn't had any luck. Jenson tapped me on the shoulder to get my attention.

"What?" I asked, and he pointed to Maine and Molly. I noticed Megan in the back with them nibbling on some apples. They were her favorite. I guess she wanted to make them last. All three were hunched over peering out of the back of the van window. It appeared as if they were spying on Shellena and Lance behind us.

"Why don't you guys go ask them if they're behaving themselves," I suggested, getting up from my seat. I pushed the leftover French-fry container into the empty paper sack sitting in the consul between us. Then picked it up to give it to Jenson.

"Thanks, I'll take care of my trash while you go see if anything shady is going on," he said.

I patted him on the back while moving to the middle aisle of the van. He turned around giving me a cheesy grin. Owl had opted to ride with Shellena and Lance. His words were I can handle it.

"Hey, anything electrifying I should be tuned-into?" I inquired, moving to the back.

"The Bandits scarfed down their meals rather rapidly. Patrick and Dan, are on the walkies talking to somebody. Who?" Maine questioned.

"Cavin, he has one too. Star, or perhaps Kaya?" Megan offered.

"Shellena and Lance keep moving back and forth in the vehicle. Sina, Trax, and Owl are still eating. Jinx looks rather restless, he keeps pacing, and it reminds me of Nayla. Sika could be grumbling about being dragged out, but he looks calm," Molly reported. She turned suddenly to look at me.

"Great observations. I'm sure if the info is urgent, dad will contact us. I'm just irritated that I won't get the opportunity to stretch my legs before we leave," I complained, leaning on the seat to the right of me.

"True that," Jenson hollered.

I twisted around to ogle the front passenger's seats. My Mom, Eva, and Minder huddled together in a deep conversation. I strained to hear what they were saying, trying to hone in on my fox senses.

"We'll make certain to notify each clan member of their location, then move to the next, it has to be brief," Eva whispered.

"Yes, plus swift, nothing chatty," Minder cut in.

I cleared my throat loudly before interrupting them, "How much longer do we have?"

"A good hour. Didn't you bring any games along?" Tri asked.

"No, I can't say I was as prepared for that part of the trip," I quipped.

"Well, relax for now. No one is getting out of the van. Cavin was adamant about us staying clear of being seen. Thank goodness this park has a scenic entry. When we get there, it's going to get sketchy," she declared.

"Sensi, Cal how are you two holding up back there?" Minder asked, peering over her headrest.

"Bored like Starla," she answered.

"Well, we'll be off again once the guys radio us. Dan told me he was checking in on the station a few minutes ago. The one at Grandville. I'm not clear on how he got connections there," Tri added. She smirked, then got up heading to the middle part of the van to see what Megan and the girls were up to. I let her pass. Afterward, deciding I should check on Cal. She'd been quiet the whole way here except to order her food. I took a deep breath, then let it out little by little as I headed over. She was staring out the window in silence.

"Sensi, can I.."

Sensi nodded, getting up, so I could sit down in her spot. As Cal turned to me, I could tell she'd been crying.

"Sorry," she sniffled.

I put my arm around her, drawing her close into a comforting hug. "What are you apologizing for?"

"My emotions. I've never met the scientist jerks, and here I am overwhelmed. We're practically invading them with an army. Nevertheless, here I'm worried we'll get blasted," she babbled.

"It's perfectly normal. Inside I'm a jittery mess, but staying cool outside til I'm put in the pool." Cal's face brightened at my joke.

"See, I nearly had you laughing. Thanks for having our backs, you and Minder. Those profiles will aid us."

"I expect so. The description of that army girl Mara has me spooked something bad," Cal gulped.

"None of them sound friendly," I clarified, easing my arm off of her shoulders. If only, I could have made the big baddies go away by myself.

"Your strength is in numbers," Amare whispered.

"Of course," I answered her.

"Tri, Come in. We've got permission to fly," Dan affirmed through the walkie.

She picked it up to speak. "Right, I'll have everyone settle into their seats. Everyone on your ends accounted for, no mishaps with the prisoners?"

"None, Sikas getting on my last nerves. He won't shut up about how he's going to use his razor-sharp claws to scratch the scientist's eyes out. While that's cooperative, it's not relevant at the moment. Lance has threatened to tranq him if he doesn't put a sock in it. Owls with them now, hearing them out on their grand plan. It seems to be something that's just come up."

Minder chuckled under her breath. Then sat down in the driver's seat as I glanced back at Maine, Molly, and Megan. They'd situated themselves in the rear back seat.

"Right I'll take the lead. Trigger, can sit with us in case of an ambush."

"Coming, but I don't believe they'll cut us off or ensnare us while we're in the van. We stand a greater chance of being struck during battle," Trigger explained, moving past Cal and me.

Cal shivered beside me. "You should sit with Jenson. You'll be connected to Megs and me during the entire mission. If something happened…" She shook her head, then reached for my hand.

I squeezed it briefly. "Thanks," I replied, then got up switching seats with Sensi.

"Cal's good?" Jenson asked as I sat down.

"Yeah, she's fine. She just shows her anxiety on the outside," I added, laying my head on his shoulder. He placed his arm around me lightly. As I snuggled into Jenson, I watched Eva turn back to make sure we were all seated. I felt like I was on a high school field trip, but inside my stomach did flip-flops knowing what we were about to face.

"Stay seated, remain quiet, tranquil, and collective. I recommend attempting to get some sleep, maybe meditation. We may not return until late tomorrow," Minder advised.

Chapter 40

An hour later…

I gazed out the window at the endless trees. They went on and on! I gasped, leaning forward to get a better look through the front windshield. "Trigger are you sure this is the way?" I asked, sitting up straight beside Jenson. He'd dozed off, but I hadn't been able to wake him.

"It's a little further ahead. You'll see residential housing on one side, after that the park is on the left. It's your passenger's side Minder."

"Oh, look, there's a sign! Slow down," Tri ordered.

Minder took her foot off of the gas and pumped the brakes till we reached the turn-off and pulled into the subdivision. After passing several empty lots, the homes gradually emerged on the right.

"Okay, now where do I pull over? I don't see any signs for the park," she groaned.

"Be patient. I'm sure it'll turn up," Tri declared.

I kept my eyes on the left side of the road anticipating its appearance like a child going to an amusement park.

"The entry's on the left, pull off! " Cal blurted.

Minder quickly turned the wheel to the left swerving onto the dirt road. I glanced back at Megan, Maine, and Molly as they held onto their seats.

"Geez, I wasn't expecting that kind of entrance," Megan gasped.

"Hey kid, I've never been here before. I'll have to locate a secluded place to park this thing. Tri, radio Dan."

Megan rolled her eyes, leaning back against the seat.

"Everyone, simmer down. We're entering enemy territory," Trigger advised.

"Jenson, Jenson," I whispered, shaking him.

"What, this better be good," he grunted rubbing the sleep from his eyes as he turned to look out the window.

"See we're here, almost," I added, laying my hand on his shoulder. "Minder's finding a spot to hide the vans. Lance will proceed ahead of us with the Bandits. Eva and Tri will follow them. Then I'm pretty sure Cal, Megan, and I will have to find a way to connect. It'll have to be fast, so I'd better start thinking about what will link us instantaneously."

"Okay, take a few minutes, but promise me you'll say goodbye in case…" he stopped to look at the floor.

"Jenson, don't talk like that," I scolded him.

"The Shadows practically had me. I haven't wanted to discuss it, yet it replays in my dreams. Nightmares, though, are more like it," he mumbled.

"We'll get through this, kick scientist butt," I added, lifting his chin up, so his eyes met mine. I rested my hand on his face, stroking his cheek. "Everyone in the vans… maybe minus the Bandits, have our backs."

"I know," he whispered while I leaned my forehead against his. Slowly our lips met, and I shut out everything going on around me. I could have melted into him entirely and been warm, safe and… I pushed myself to disengage remembering why we were here in the first place, but before I pulled myself away, I heard someone clearing their throat.

"Ahem!"

Jenson and I jumped almost hitting our heads against one another. I turned to see my mom tapping her foot with irritation.

"You're mom's not mad? Is she?" asked Jenson as we climbed out of the van.

"It'll be all right," I answered, shutting the door. We passed Lance attempting to keep the Bandits in line. Sina and Trax faced Sika, and he growled staring them down. I stifled a laugh, then turned to see Gavin smirk like he was pleased to be here. Gladiator shook his fists glancing around the forest. I rolled my eyes at the scene. Then smiled at Jenson. He took hold of my hand in time for me to drag him over to where everybody had gathered haphazardly. We stopped next to Molly and Maine.

"Do you suppose Lance's posse will be able to keep them in check?" she asked.

"Yeah, he's pretty tough. I thought he was a goner when he leapt into that shadow," I confessed. Then grabbed a hair band from my wrist, putting it up. Maine held tightly onto Mol's hand. I ground my feet into the dirt a bit uneasy. Afterward, looking up as Owl jogged over. He bent down panting for a few seconds, then stood.

"You didn't take off to scope out the scientists digs already, did you? I mean we haven't even grouped up yet," Jenson observed.

"No, but Sensi and Jinx did with consent from Lance. Didn't you see her get out of the van?" he asked.

"We were kind of busy," I blushed.

"Ah, Oh," Owl commented not sure what to say.

"I find it funny that my mom wasn't too upset when you accidentally stayed over, but you should have seen her face after we kissed," I declared while Jenson laid a hand lightly on my back.

"Must have been some kiss," Shellena added, ambling up to us. I nodded scanning the area to see where Mom and Dad had gone. Tri hadn't said much about the kiss. Maybe I'd just startled her. She'd never seen me kiss anyone before. At least I didn't think she had? There! Eva, Patrick, Tri, and Dan were crouched together. Cal stood off to the side with Minder. I watched her pull Cal close, then whisper something to her. We'd needed to connect soon.

"Where's Megan?"

"I'm right here, and I heard you. The kiss? It was possibly just as magical as the one I got from Chaz," she blurted, stepping out from behind Shellena.

I snickered at the remark as Trigger emerged. He ran his paw through the dirt, leaned down, sniffed, then glanced around the wooded area. I felt a chill travel down my back, everyone stopped talking, and Lance turned to look at Trigger.

"We shouldn't linger here much longer. Megan, Cal, and Starla need to link. Sensi and Jinx will be back soon. Tri, and Eva focus! See if you can pick anything up occurring in the surrounding area," he ordered.

They nodded to him. At that instant, my mom turned to Dan, and Patrick to Eva. I tried not to watch as they kissed goodbye. I turned to look away, but a part of me remained connected. Mom and Dad. Their feelings mimicked Jenson and me. Still, it was weird watching my parents kiss.

"As weird for you as it is for them," Amare whispered.

I turned to look for her, but it was only her voice. "I get it, any advice before we go?"

"Be brave, keep them safe, listen to those around you... take care, Starla."

There was a slight tug on my hand. Megan had taken hold of it and was pulling me towards Cal and Minder.

"Give me a minute," I snapped.

She let go of my hand, then turned away in anger. I sighed, a bit mad at myself, but I couldn't go without consoling Jenson.

"You didn't have to be so rude," he pressed.

I eyed Megan beside Trigger appearing sullen, but not ready to punch me yet.

"I've got to go, promise you'll follow behind us with Maine, and Molly. I'll do my best to protect everyone, but I can't..."

"Yeah, me either. You should go, link, and remember she is the key if she needs to gain control trust her. I've got an uneasy feeling that if you don't things will turn sour," he warned me.

"Alright, but she is younger than me," I pressed.

"I heard that!" Megan exclaimed.

Jenson laughed, pulled me close quickly kissing me. I let go of his hands, then let Megan lead me over to Minder and Cal.

As we traipsed through the forest, I worked on keeping my mind focused on the bond Megan, and I shared. But my eyes fell on the amulet burning a bright red that hung from my neck. I'd thrown my coat back in the van, along with my purse. I'd left the handbag too. Everyone else had been equipped with weapons of some sort. I tried not to shiver as a flake of snow drifted out of the sky. Terrific, if it got cold fast, and I needed to switch, I'd freeze. I listened to the silence around us waiting for instructions from Tri, or Eva.

"Where do you suppose they are?" Cal muttered, trotting along the path Trigger claimed would lead us to the hideout.

"We can't be certain. It's a big forest, but we haven't run into anyone yet. It isn't good. Either they are hiding, or." I stopped listening to the movement of the Bandits up ahead. Lance and Shellena followed behind them. A branch snapped, and I did a 180.

"Keep going," Jenson hissed in a low voice.

I crept forward surveying everything without turning back around. A pocket of warm air brushed passed me. I swung back to see Trigger move closer to Megan.

"This is creeping me out Sis," she whispered.

"Stay focused on creating the shield, in case we have to burn one of them. Jenson has the Kali sticks. Sina and Trax can block them somehow," I added, trying not to freak myself out. I shook, then swiftly trotted forward to get closer to Shellena and Lance. He still looked upset that Jinx had chosen to scope out the scientist's shack. Sensi was circling it from above, the lookout. What the heck were they planning to do there?

"Do you see anything? All I've heard is complete silence except for Jenson stepping on a fallen branch," I admitted.

"Hush," Shellena spat. She turned to our right looking beyond the trees. Trigger sprinted away from Megan to investigate. The hair on his back stood straight up as he emitted a low growl.

"There, this way! Lance and Shellena make the bandit's head over here. We'll need to travel deeper into this region. Minder everyone, please stay together do not stray!" he warned.

Cautiously we inched into the woods without a path. Megan reached out, grabbing my fox fur. I shuddered. Fearful it would break our link, but nothing happened.

"Something's coming from the left. It's rushing rapidly at us, be careful," Tri mind spoke to us.

The amulet around my neck grew brighter frantically blinking on and off like a flashlight. My heart flew to my throat as I looked at the others who'd taken their positions equipped for battle. Maine grabbed her tranq darts while Molly stood behind her. Owl and the others each held Kali sticks in their hands.

"Mom, do you hear anything? The scientists speaking to each other?"… "*Please*," I pleaded, mind speaking to her.

"They're scattered, We're coming up behind Sina and Trax currently. Once they reveal themselves, we'll need protection. I can use Kali sticks, but I'm a bit rusty. I'm not sure about Eva."

"Get ready," I whispered to Cal and Megan. Hopeful they'd recall how to channel rage and anger.

I turned back towards Sina and Trax as Eva emerged.

"Hey!" she shouted. A figure brushed past her pushing her aside. It sped at us, but I couldn't make out whether it was a shadow or a human being? Had it seen the Bandits, taken the bait?

"Look what I have here! Where are they? The weapons, we want them back!" She spat, backing up as she saw Maine's tranquilizers rise. They were aimed right at her. This would be a cinch! It didn't appear this chick had any superpowers. I took note of her brown hair, weight, height, green eyes. It had to be Bonnie.

"Stop! Maine, how will we transport her?" I shouted.

"Do it!" Trax blurted.

Maine nodded at her and before anyone else could react the tranquilizer dart accelerated propelling itself at Bonnie. She rushed into the trees, but Sika, who'd been watching the whole time surged past Lance. Maine steadied the dart, waiting to see if her target would be captured. I held my breath while I watched him reach out with his cuffed hands grabbing hold of Bonnie. He pushed his body on top of her's pinning her to the ground. She fought kicking and scratching. Then grabbed Sika's hair, yanking him to the side of her.

"Let go of me!" he howled.

"Tranq her already!" Minder screamed.

"What about questioning her?" Dan shouted as he and Patrick approached the prey. Shellena stood next to Lance grinning at Sika as the rest of us stared at Bonnie.

"She's not too bright if you ask me," Molly remarked.

"Come on, she isn't going to tell us anything," Sika protested.

"He's right," Gavin agreed.

Gladiator covered his mouth, stifling a laugh.

"Alright, but Sika you're responsible for dragging her the rest of the way. I'll have to cuff her. It isn't what I'd envisioned," Dan muttered.

Maine let go, and the dart hit Bonnie directly in the arm. It only took a few seconds for her to stop fighting Sika.

The Bandits dragged Bonnie behind them. I shuddered, wondering what else was in store for us. She'd been an easy target, but I doubted the others would be. There have always been one or two dumb sidekicks in a group of villains. I'd seen it in movies, and so far this was playing out as such.

"You okay Cal?" I asked her.

She moved closer to me then motioned to the Bandits whispering in low voices amongst themselves.

"What about them?"

"Sika's on the prowl. He's enjoying the revenge kick, but we've got to keep a close eye on them. We've discussed setting them free, banishment, and forgiveness, but I don't see any of that working out in our favor," she acknowledged.

"What would Nuria suggest? There, isn't much else we can do. Unless anyone knows of a supernatural jail," I added, shaking my head. I observed Megan glimpsing back at Sina and Trax scouring the area as we moved.

"How are we going to confiscate the materials the scientists have been using. We can't let the feds get ahold of them. They could use them against us," Megan quavered.

"Let us take care of it," Sina trilled.

Trax snorted at her as they grew closer to us. I winced realizing my legs were beginning to ache from all the walking. How far had we gone since we'd captured Bonnie? I glanced at Jenson and Owl tossing Kali sticks. I sensed they were disappointed they weren't included in Bonnie's bust. I kept my eyes alert, ears up then quickened my pace. A faint melody drifted into the forest, and I caught sight of the moon casting a shadow in the trees revealing a human silhouette.

"Short, male, to your right, doesn't suspect a thing," Eva mind spoke.

I stiffened, then turned to the noise. Err, music and spotted the man bebopping to it. "I've got it, let me take him down," I responded in thought.

"Take Megan, and Cal with you, be careful. Oh, and don't let him see them, have them fall back," Tri added using her mind.

"Got it," I replied in thought.

"What did you just agree to," hissed Trigger.

He followed us tailing the accused. A sly smile played upon my fox lips. "You're going to get him to hunt you while we pursue you both from behind. We'll herd him towards Lance and the Bandits like cattle. If he tries to harm you Megan and I will burn him."

"Mom said for us to stay behind you," Megan whispered at my side.

"Yes, you and Cal run side by side in the darkness, but stay near," I warned her.

As they fell back, I maintained my speed. Trigger nodded to me. "I hope you know what you're doing," he grunted, taking off into the woods in front of our suspect.

Through the trees, I saw him stop, right in front of him. The man dropped his portable radio, then bent down to pick it back up. Red hair, which one had rustic red? My ears perked up as I heard him.

"Beautiful. You'd be a great asset to our collection," he mumbled, reaching for something in his pocket. Slowly he withdrew the item.

Crap! He had a vile of something. No, it was a syringe of fluid. "Red alert! Move in!" I hollered within myself to Cal and Megan. "We have to use our rage and anger as soon as we get near him. He's got a syringe of chemicals!"

"Fudge!" Megan grimaced.

She and Cal scampered up alongside me. Trigger must have realized it as well because he took off zigzagging. He'd stop, then go on as soon as the guy grew closer. I could see Lance, Shellena and the Bandits now. They were to my left, but Trigger had stopped to pant. The man held the syringe in his hand by his side staring at him.

"Come here. It will only hurt for a Sec. You'll hardly feel a thing. I promise," he assured him slithering closer.

"Shiznit! Come on," I whispered. Cal and I crouched down low on all fours inching towards him. Trigger would nearly be caught, then dash off again. I continued waiting for him to slip up, and then he'd be gone. Megan's spirit guide would be dead? Could he die? What would that vile do? Spirit Guide plus a dose of hybrid chemicals? I shook my head mulling it over. No! I didn't' want to find out. I grabbed Megan's hand, but she was the one who aimed it at him without warning. Warmth filled my body full of her fury. Consequently, the red light sprinted out of our palms hitting him in the back, and knocked him to the ground. The syringe fell from his hand onto the soil.

Trigger scurried up to me inspecting my body with his nose. I backed away, "What the heck are you doing! I saved your life, but I'm not your sniffing toy," I added irritated.

"Look behind you!"

I turned to take a peak. A long beautiful tail of deep red waved alongside my first one. "Okay, so I got my 2nd tail. Get Lance and Shellena. We have to tie this guy up or something before he comes to," I snarled.

Trigger took off howling to get their attention as Megan backed away in shock. She sprinted to where the red-haired man was sprawled out. I caught her leaning down to pick up the syringe off of the ground.

"Megan, stop!" I shouted.

"What?" she asked, glaring at me.

"It's got his prints on it, don't touch it or you'll compromise evidence! Let dad, bag it. The cops, feds, or whoever, are going to need it!"

She stood up with her hands in the air, "Okay, Okay, sorry," she added.

"Come back near me in case he wakes up." She unhappily ambled over as my father emerged with Lance and Shellena following him. Maine, Molly, and the rest of the gang came trudging through the branches scattered about the forest floor. Tri and Eva darted directly at us as if we were wounded. I twitched my tails hitting something behind me. "Cal is that you?"

I turned to see her disheveled and human. "I can't help it. I switched when I heard you scream at Megan."

Tri and Eva glared at me.

"It's all right. Dan is making some phone calls now. He's bringing in a team from an offshoot unit giving them directions to the shack. Lance is collecting the evidence in the bag, see there," Tri pointed at him.

Sika stood a few feet away from my dad who was chatting on the phone. Gladiator and Gavin were dealing with Bonnie.

"But there are still two scientists left out there! We can't just leave," Sika shouted over him.

"Calm down. The units will be our back up. That's why we have walkies," Shellena declared, rolling her eyes at him.

My gaze wandered back to the suspect as his arm shook. Unexpectedly the accused started to push himself up but collapsed. He lifted his head a few inches from the ground peering at us. "Where am I? What are all you people doing here? Where's that wolf! I need the wolf!"

"Someone better, cuff the suspect!" Megan shrieked.

Patrick swiped the restraints off of my father's belt and dove at him landing on his back. He pulled the man's arms behind him roughly.

"Can't you give me a break! I'm a scientist, a good guy," he grumbled.

"Not in my book you're not," added Patrick pulling the man to his feet.

"Minder, get over here! Can you identify this man!" Eva shrieked.

She moved past Owl and Jenson transfixed by the whole fiasco. Jenson hadn't even come over to check on me. Oh, well. It wasn't like I wasn't safe.

"Rob, the piece of trash that pumped chemicals into us. No wonder he was trying to shoot up Trigger," she fumed.

"You, You ran away! We had big plans for you! I can't believe that Mara let you get away!" he spat.

Dan closed his flip phone and turned to Patrick. "I've alerted the officers of our situation. As soon as we have the other suspects in custody, we're to call them."

"Call them, she's savvy," he sneered at Dan.

"What if we require a backup, then what?" Patrick demanded.

"I'll deal with it then. I can't expect them to send the team if we aren't able to locate their position. They could be hiding out anywhere. For all, we know Sensi and Jinx could have them cornered."

"Dan, come on! What would Jinx be able to do, and Sensi? They may be great at bringing us info, but it isn't likely they've got the other scientists in the bag," Patrick countered.

Rob laughed, and my dad ignored him.

"Well, let's get moving. You keep an eye on Rob here; Sika let Gladiator carry Bonnie for a while. We'll need your eyes and ears open for this Mara. You're familiar with her?" Dan asked.

Lance lifted an eyebrow, waiting for him to respond while Shellena tapped her foot against the earth.

315

"She's the one that turned him, she did! He's got it out for her," Gavin cackled.

An evil grin formed on Sika's lips while he rung his paws in anticipation. "It will be my finest hour when I put her in her place. Rob may have administered the drugs, but she was wicked!"

I trembled at his brutality as Jenson meandered towards me with Owl at his side. I turned towards him.

"Maybe we should stick close to you. In case anything comes up that you can't handle," he suggested laying a hand on my back.

I sighed, exasperated, but realized he was right. "Okay, but Cal, Megan and I will need to link again before we take off. Mara spent four years in the army. I sure hope Sika's got this. I have no experience with someone of that caliber," I confided.

Lance shuffled past the others taking us aside. He gestured for Molly and Maine to hurry over. "Keep an eye on Sika, and the Bandits. I've got Patrick and Dan on it, but it can't hurt. I'm heading out on my own to the shack. I want to check on Sensi and Jinx. Eva and Tri haven't been able to communicate with them via telepathy. Mara or Zane could be holding them captive, or they could be out of range. I'm not certain, but I'd rather check it out myself."

"Lance, that's crazy! How will you…?"

He placed his finger to his lips to shush me.

"I can manipulate people, so can Shellena. I'll warn Tri and Eva of any danger before everyone has arrived. Your dad has the officers on high alert.

"Right. Be safe and don't hesitate to use your abilities".

"Ditto. Maine great job with the tranqs! Megan, Starla, and Cal, way to put it to Rob," he winked.

"Hey, what about me?" asked Trigger waving his tail in the air annoyed.

Lance shook his head, then began ambling away, "You too, now I'll see you at the cabin. Be ready to act upon arrival," he warned.

Chapter 41

(April 16th, Friday)

12 a.m.

I sat against a tree in meditation, straining to ground myself. We'd caught two of the big baddies. I should be ecstatic with glee. Instead, a sense of overwhelming worry concerning Zane and Mara played with my mind. Minder had come up to hug me before returning to aid Patrick and my father with the Bandits and prisoners. It was then I'd begged to get a chance to recharge. Cal, Maine, and Molly sat near, and I felt hands on opposite sides grab my paws. Megan had chosen to sit this one out. She and Trigger decided to bond by practicing spells. I shifted my body till I got comfortable. It was odd being in fox form, but I hadn't wanted to transform twice. Tranquility spread throughout my being as I relaxed remembering Tri and Eva stood by guarding us.

"Starla Ariana?"

My body jolted forward, and I almost opened my eyes, then sensed them being held shut. I shuddered but kept listening.

"It's me Amare. Don't open your eyes, Maine, Molly welcome. Cal, stay strong The wheat field isn't present, and all you see is blackness. It's the hate and rage I'm picking up on in the surrounding area. The two you've captured were sent to toy with you. The real obstacle is ahead. Maine, you'll need to use tranqs one last time. Molly your power to heal will save lives previously affected by the evil. Cal facing your past is petrifying, but you've handled it well. Don't give up."

"What about Jinx and Sensi? Are they safe?" I mind-spoke.

"I can't disclose that to you. Trust Starla, trust! Oh, and faith in your clan."

"The cabin, do you know if they are there currently?" Maine inquired.

A shiver slithered up my tails, into my torso, and I held back the urge to disrupt our circle. Something was close, I sensed it, and my ears perked up attentive to the outside.

"I can't tell at this time," Amare responded to her.

"Nothing for me! I thought, No words of advice," I huffed still chilled by an outside presence.

"Starla, beware of remote doubts in yourself, go with your gut instincts. You've been tested since your journey began, proven your worthiness. Now you must accept that you are."

My eyelids fluttered open as I stood, shook, and tried to restrain my displeasure. Had I ever thought I wasn't worthy of being in the clan? That my life wasn't worth living? Or was it something in the back of my inner soul I'd denied. Yeah, parts of me contemplated if I'd been good enough, for Jenson. The clan, but I'd never vocalized it. Never shared it because I'd always overcome these feelings through my actions. Saving Cal was a big ego booster and The Shadows even if I'd needed a little assistance. Didn't everyone?

"I don't get it. I thought I've always been the strong one?" I confided blinking as my eyes adjusted to the night. It was possibly early morning by now.

"Just take the advice, use it to better yourself, don't look at it as criticism for who you are," Molly observed.

Cal and Maine stood up together as Eva stepped back. My Mom shuffled around them to kneel down eye to eye with me. She gave me a weak smile, patted my head, then finally pulled me close. As I accepted her embrace, I watched Maine and Molly drift in Megan's direction. Trigger sat loyally beside her. Eva and Cal spoke in whispers several feet away from us.

"My kit, all grown up. I'm so grateful for the women you've become," Tri confessed. She let go of me then sighed, pushing her long hair behind her ears.

"Mom, we've got to get going. I love you and all..."

"I know, I just needed a moment with you before we face them. I know we haven't been close lately. I hope after all this is dealt with that will change."

"Mom, I want.. I need to be with Jenson," I stuttered. Then turned away, embarrassed by my openness.

"Well, that puts a lump in my throat. Let's just get through this first. If you must though, but I am your Mom. That isn't easy to hear even if I remember your father and I's first. Just be prepared, be careful, take precautions, and don't end up like me. Your grandmother was so upset with your father and me! If only you could have met her." She sighed, then stood, turning to go. "Mom, I need to be myself. I'll forever be your daughter, but like Molly, I need to be true to me," I protested.

"I understand. Now go! Connect with Cal and the others. Eva and I will be corresponding with Lance. I need to take this in," she confirmed.

I couldn't believe I'd told my mom I wanted to be with Jenson! Why did I need or seek her approval? Especially, if I was my own person, I pondered.

"Starla, focus!" Cal snapped.

"Sorry, personal stuff," I admitted, taking my stance beside her and Megan. Instead of closing my eyes, I looked directly at them both, urging them to blend with me. I couldn't get the picture of Jenson and I together out of my head. I kicked my feet against the ground, snorted, shook, and pushed myself to let it go. I needed a recollection of them both at once, mixed.

"Let me try," Megan blurted. Trigger lingered beside her, and she bent down grabbing him by the nape of his neck.

"Go for it. I can't seem to bring us together." I opened my mind, listening to Megan, and Cal. At first, I didn't' recognize the reflection, but drew it in as it came.

The courtroom, all of us were there as the Bandits were questioned. I struggled to attach myself to my friends using emotions we'd experienced. My whiskers twitched, and I sensed Cal transform. Megan clung to us. As I let out a breath of relief, we combined.

Chapter 42

1 a.m.

"What bothered you so much that you couldn't concentrate on the task at hand," Megan pressed.

I glanced at her beside me while Cal trotted near the front. I didn't want to tell her, give her any idea's about Chaz. She was too young, and I was practically an adult. I was ready to make these decisions. She, in my opinion, wasn't yet. Besides, hadn't Amare said to trust my gut? That I needed to, not doubt myself?

"It has to do with Jenson. You know how you like Chaz. Did you call him, you know after we left?"

"Yeah, you were snuggled up with Jenson inhaling fries." She rolled her eyes, "Chaz's fine. I had to lie to him about why I wasn't in school. I hate lying. It's soo wrong," she drawled.

"What did you tell him? Fake sick?" I asked as we trotted along. I watched Patrick slow his pace a bit, Dan followed. Had they found something, someone?

"Family emergency, I didn't give him details," she responded.

"I get it," I answered.

My ears perked up at the sound of feet pounding on the earth behind us. I looked over my right shoulder to catch a glimpse of Sina and Trax streaking by so rapidly I could barely make out their profiles. Subsequently, Jenson and Owl passed us shielding their heads, and kicking out their legs like fools. I couldn't avert my eyes, seeing that Maine and Molly trailed after them. They squatted low to the ground steadily advancing while they assessed our environment. What was going on? I hadn't seen anything creep upon us. Bonnie and Rob were still out of sorts unless...

"Hey, uh guys. I think Patrick wants us to stop," Megan chimed in pointing towards him and Dan.

Before I could retreat, Tri and Eva sprang out from opposite ends of the forest, and roughly with urgency herded us to where they'd assembled.

I stumbled on my front paws into Jenson while he was bent down attempting to recuperate. He placed his hands on my back and lifted himself upright

"Ah, sorry," I explained, looking up at him.

"Yeah, trying to catch my breath, like out of the air," he joked.

I would have laughed, but Patrick started to address us. My dad stood in silence next to him. Sika, Gavin, and Gladiator held Bonnie and Rob. Lucky for us Bonnie hadn't woken up yet.

"Everyone, listen up! Sensi has just flown in and has an update. It's extremely imperative, therefore, be attentive!" Patrick affirmed.

Tri and Eva nodded in agreement. I spied Megan, and Trigger huddled up near Maine and Molly positioning themselves beside Sina and Trax.

Listen? I didn't see Sensi anywhere? Shellena and Minder appeared A-Wall too. Owl looked around curious as to where they were as well. He inched up beside Jenson and me.

"Okay, so where is Sensi?" he whispered to Jenson.

"There with Minder, and Shellena, off a-ways. Do you see them coming out of the woods now? There from the path we were supposed to be taking," he replied, motioning his hand in their direction.

Sensi fluttered alongside Minder and Shellena as they rushed into our circle. She seemed to be having difficulty flying as she kept fluctuating from high to low. Shellena reached out, and Sensi landed on her arm. She placed Sensi on the ground, then turned around covering her so she could shift. Minder bent down to hand her what was most likely a change of clothing.

"What's going on?" Megan demanded.

"Give her a minute," Dan advised.

Moments later Shellena and Minder moved aside, revealing a bruised and battered Sensi. Most of us gasped in fear.

"I met Lance on the way back to warn you concerning Jinx capture. We have to be careful. Zane left to track you. They're on to us. Let me clarify what occurred. Jinx was laying low, scouring the cabin while I flew about the perimeter. I didn't spot Mara slithering on her stomach towards him once I saw her it was too late. I dove several times, but she hit me with her pellet gun. Note the bruises, and I'm fortunate that's all they are. Zane came out of the Cabin to check on Mara. That's when I flew frantically barely escaping. When I hit Lance, he tried to shoo me away. After several attempts, he noticed who I was. Afterward, I told him what happened. He's headed there to access the situation."

"Why didn't he contact me?" Tri scolded, crossing her arms in annoyance.

"Lance, he said they might have abilities, pick up on it, endanger the clan, he… he said to come, notify you, send back up, send back up," she hooted.

I trembled frightened while Jenson put his hand on my back to soothe me. Megan drew Trigger close to her, and Molly embraced Maine.

"Enough! Let Sensi calm down. Lance sent her with orders, a plan. Dan, please get a hold of the unit. Tell them to prepare to arrive. We need them to surround the premises." Patrick ordered.

Dan frowned at him, placing his hands on his sides appearing defiant. "We need to get into that cabin. The fox that's being held prisoner; what if there are more of them? Plus, they have Jinx, and I don't want him, confiscated as evidence. Let's move out. Eyes opened, ears up, and if you even think you see Zane take Shellena with you! Damn, Jinx, damn!" he mumbled.

Chapter 43

We were supposed to stay spread out, but that's sort of sketchy when you're trudging along in terror of what's to come. I held my head down to inspect Zane's profile. It translated akin to someone in the business of immense insecurity. Cal and Megan power-walked beside me. Minder stood by waiting for me to return the paper. I'd had to convert back to human form and thanked the gods it was quicker than switching to a fox.

"What do you think?" she asked, coming up alongside me.

"Things don't always appear as they are. If so maybe it's his insecurity that gives him strength," I said, handing her the document. She took it and placed it in her shoulder bag.

"If it gives him a heads up on our actions then yes. It could only be then that watching over your shoulder due to doubt might help."

"If you're constantly in observation mode, you're ready for anything," Megan blurted.

Weakly I smiled at her then glanced ahead at my father and Patrick. He held his phone to his ear intently listening to whoever was talking to him while Sika sniffed the air scanning the area. Rob grumbled, fighting to get his cuffs off, then spun around knocking Gladiator down who'd been holding him. I stiffened as Minder laid a hand on my back. Megan and I watched Sika dive towards Rob. I gasped when he pulled a sharp stick out of his pocket pointing it at Sika's throat. Minder dropped her hand off my back, and we moved quickly towards my father, but a hand pulled me back.

"Starla and Megan stay right here," Tri instructed, pulling us tightly to her.

Sika backed off, and Dan dropped the phone he'd been holding. It crunched under Gavin's feet as he sneaked up to grab Rob from behind. Megan hid her face in my mother's chest, but I kept watching as Rob backed away, holding the knife with both hands still cuffed.

"Yes, I'm going to leave, join Zane, then we'll kill you all," he threatened.

"Minder! He's going to escape, come on we have to get him!" Cal shrieked. I positioned myself slightly and observed Sina drop down on all fours crawling towards them. Trax followed her from behind. Minder whispered something to Eva, then Trigger. They nodded to one another and spread out preparing to tackle him if needed. Sensi hid behind a tree out of sight. I heard her murmur a hoot of alarm. Then spotted Shellena's furry paw on her shoulder, holding her near. It wasn't like her to hide. Perhaps she felt she needed to guard Sensi after what happened. Cal trudged alongside Jenson while he pushed passed Molly and Maine with Kali sticks in his hands. Owl steadily came up behind him prepared for battle. My heart pounded nearly out of my throat in fear when I heard a scream. Then another coming from the forest.

"Bear, there's a bear after me! Help me, please!"

"Zane? Is that you?" Rob asked, glancing around the perimeter.

"Go, go," whispered Minder.

Trigger stealthily crept into the woods where Zane had been calling careful to keep Rob from seeing him exit. After he disappeared Jenson proceeded to get closer to our prisoner. Sina and Trax kept an eye on Rob. Maybe they were trying to come up with a way to take that knife. Now only inches away from Jenson, Rob thrust the stick at him missing. Jenson stumbled back several feet while he scrunched up his face concentrating.

"What's he doing, he looks like he's constipated. Zane get your butt out here!" Rob exclaimed, waving his pointy stick in the air. "This isn't funny," he shouted, turning to face the woods.

Jenson flicked his wrist at the assailant, and the knife clattered to the ground just as Rob froze. Owl ran up and gave him a high-five. I put my thumbs-up as I tried to wiggle free from my mother's arms. Megan clung to her but kept peeking out to see what had happened.

"Mom, please let go of me now. We're safe," I reassured her.

"Wait til Dad checks his pockets for any other weapons," she whispered loosening her hold on us. I listened for the sound of Trigger running, nothing. I hoped he'd catch Zane, and bring him back, so we could finally get Mara.

Warily Shellena and Sensi hobbled out of the woods. They hadn't made it all the way to us when Sika, Gladiator, and Gavin began to kick at Rob.

"Stop, let us handle this, or I'll have Jenson freeze you!" Dan threatened.

Sika glared at him but did as he said while Gavin and Gladiator milled-about. Patrick bent down, picked up the stick, broke it in two, and tossed it into the forest.

4a.m.

Currently, things were messy. My dad had no cell phone to call for backup, and I'd left mine inside my purse in the van. Mom? I hadn't yet asked her because after they'd tranqed Bonnie yet again and Rob, I had to comfort Megan. She was freaked that Trigger had left without her. I'd tried to convince her he'd be back. Someone had to go after Zane, but she'd stormed off to walk with Molly and Maine. I felt like she'd been spending more time with them on this journey than I had. Jenson held my hand as we headed for the scientist's shack.

"So if any big bads jump out at us will you freeze them for me?"

"Only if you want me to," he grinned pulling me near.

I smiled up at him, then glanced back at Tri. I wondered if she had her cell on her. If she did, she hadn't said anything. I sighed, afterward taking a long hard look at the wooded area, we were about to enter. I turned my head to gaze to the right when Mom jogged up to me with Minder beside her.

"Hey, Mom. What's up?" I asked, letting go of Jenson's hand.

"Lance made it to the shack and is monitoring the activity. He was able to sneak a peek inside. Jinx is locked in a cage, but it doesn't appear as if they've done any testing on him so far."

"Thank the gods!" I exclaimed, continuing to walk on at a steady pace.

"I've informed Dan and Patrick. Minder says we can tune the walkies to channels. Their police issued, so it has a CB built into them.

"Dan brought his, then?"

"Yes, your father, and Patrick. I guess he didn't think to give one to Lance. Then again contacting me via telepathically would be more efficient anyway. Unless the jerks can pick that up too," Minder added.

"That's a relief. What's the plan when we get there? Has he even confronted Mara! I mean we're close, aren't we?" I nagged.

"Ten Minutes give or take. Cal's with Eva, but might need to pair back up with you and Megan before we explore."

"Good idea, what else?"

"Shellena is presently guarding Sensi. Trigger better get his butt back here in time. He's stealthy, and could assist Lance if required."

"Why doesn't he bust in and vamp em!" I held my hand over my mouth realizing how loudly I'd spoken.

"Shh, that's not how we handle things. Not unless it gets out of control. Magic wise, it's best that Megan uses the displacement spell. Maine has three tranqs left on her which will need to use wisely. We don't want to call in backup til we've collected the infected foxes. Including whatever various animals they've captured. We're going to have to rehabilitate them. Minder has that covered, don't you?" Tri questioned.

"I've got a scheme going in my head on how to generate an antidote. It'll take me a day or two to produce it, but with Molly and Maine's aid I'm confident it will be successful!"

"You must have been mulling over this for a while," Maine commented, curiously darting our way. Megan and Molly chatted amongst themselves towards us.

"Yes, since we discovered they were holding a fox confined. I've nearly got every ingredient needed, written down. A few will be tricky to obtain, but I may be able to order them online."

"Good," Tri replied.

"Minder, has Cavin said anything about Nayla? Did she make it home safe," I stammered.

"She's fine and back with the kits in the Arctic. I'll have Cavin get the address for you after things have settled. Out of sight, out of mind, she's been with all this," Minder murmured.

"I almost feel as if we've neglected her," Megan sniffled hanging her head.

I put my hand on Megan's shoulder to comfort her as we slowed our pace. Sensi hiked beside Shellana and Owl as he too had apparently promised to guard her following the Rob debacle. I strained my eyes to see further ahead as we moved I could barely make out a small shack directly in front of us. I turned to say something to my mother when she yelled.

"Fall behind. There's something or someone approaching."

Cautiously we stepped back in unison crouching down low while Tri concentrated. I listened for any outside noise I might pick up but only heard Dan and Patrick shushing the Bandits. Megan nudged me, and I turned my head to see Tri motioning for Sina and Trax to move further into the brush. When they'd disappeared, I glanced at Maine. She held one of her tranqs in her hand prepared to fire, as Molly clutched the jar of healing salve in her right hand. Eva and Cal crawled on the ground, then laid low beside us. A low, deep guttural growl echoed throughout the woods as my ears perked up. Something or someone was being dragged on the ground moving towards us. We waited, anticipating what was to come.

Chapter 44

Trigger pulled Zane along, gripping the cuff of his shirt in his mouth. The foe appeared as if he'd put up a fight, but had received the worst of it. At first, I only noticed how badly bruised he was from being pulled through the brush that must have scraped against his skin. How far had Trigger dragged him? The man winced in pain turning his head, which only caused him to bite his lip more.

"Let me go you crazy wolf! That Sina chick isn't going to last against Mara!"

Trigger held him tighter gripping his throat. Then sunk his teeth into his flesh, just enough to pierce the skin.

"I didn't mean it, I didn't mean it," he begged.

"Is he gonna kill him?" Megan gasped, hiding her face in my shoulder.

"Let him," Shellena spat while Sensi shook next to her.

"No! Amare said killing isn't in our nature, although Trigger isn't hypothetically a part of our clan yet. Buffy would dust him."

"He's not a vamp Sis," Megan whined.

"Yeah, it's too bad, isn't it," I sighed.

Trax came up behind Zane and bent down, taking hold of him. It was then that Trigger released him and stepped aside. He spat a few times to get the taste of him out of his mouth. When Zane was upright, I saw the long gash on the side of his right face. Up along his leg, a piece of flesh was torn from his upper thigh. A trail of blood had dried, but it seemed to have stopped. Why was he wearing shorts? In this weather how dumb could you get? Zane struggled to break free of Trax grasp but refrained realizing if he kept it up he too would take him out.

"Dan, grab the extra cuffs from Patrick, and bring them here! I don't want to have to knock em out! The authorities will want to speak with him. Oh, and come to think of it, we'll need to leave the evidence. Minder you can save the animals but without proof of foul play, the chemicals they won't take them into custody. We can't have that happen, or we'll have to destroy them ourselves.

"Kill them! Kill them!" Sika began to chant.

Minders face turned an angry bright red as her paws squeezed into fists. I wondered if she was going to run over there to pound him. Impulsively, she lunged at Sika grabbing him harshly by the cuffs staring him in the face. "Shut up it isn't like you're innocent in all this. Your lucky we're saving your hides. Plus your bait. Maybe Mara will trade you for Jinx!"

Shellena chuckled at her comment as Sika clammed up mumbling like a fool. Minder pushed him, and he stumbled back, almost falling over Gavin. Gladiator kept his mouth shut. My dad rushed passed us with the handcuffs ignoring the chaos. He most likely figured Minder had it under control and Tri or Eva would step in if needed. Dan grabbed Zane's hands restraining them while Patrick kept him from trying to break free.

"There those ought to hold you for a while. Now, Trigger the shack is up ahead. Tell me how we should handle this. I assume you've been there."

"No, only on the outskirts. I made Zane take me there and Sina. She's waiting for us. All that he was confirming were lies attempting to get you to react. She's going to lead the Bandits out into view so Mara will see them. When she comes to claim them, we'll demand Jinx in return."

"No, we won't do it!" Sika snapped.

"It's settled you're cuffed, and if all you want is an exile, you'd better," Patrick butted-in.

"What about the infected animals!" Megan sniffled.

"Minder will see to it; they're released later once a cure is discovered. Til then they'll stay at the park. If all goes as intended, you'll take them along with Eva and Cal back to Hunter's Park," Trigger confirmed.

"Okay, but will everyone fit in the other van?"

"It shouldn't be a problem. We'll cram the Bandits in the back of it for the time being. Cavin's got a spot picked out for me to release them for banishment. He didn't want to disclose it till it's complete," Patrick replied.

"He trusts you?" Minder questioned.

"It's the least I could do after running off on Cal and Eva." He nodded in their direction. "I owe the clan that much. Now let's go. The sun is almost up, and I want this finished before the day sets in."

Dan, Patrick, and Trax hustled the Bandits along. I could hear them grumbling on about how they weren't going to succumb to them. Bonnie and Rob groggily stumbled beside Zane spitting out profanities I won't repeat. I shook my head at their lack of intelligence. Maybe they'd tear up Mara before the officers arrived. I sighed, then looked over my shoulder at Molly and Maine holding hands. Maine's other hand held a tranq, and Mol clutched a jar of ointment. Behind me Jenson chatted on with Owl concerning the use of the Kali sticks as Megan stroked Trigger's fur while we walked. A few more feet and we'd be in the vicinity of the shack. I shuddered falling back a bit, allowing Jenson to catch up to me. Minder, Tri, Eva, and Cal roamed on ahead rapidly.

"So when Sina leads the Bandits into view Mara should come running out. That's my chance to hit her with the tranquilizer before she sees me. Afterward, Minder will go in to rescue the foxes, wolves, etc. Megan and Starla will assist, meanwhile Owl and Jenson will patrol the grid. It'll have to be quick since Minder will need to get them to the van. That's all before Dan radio's backup on the walkies," Maine explained.

Molly nodded to her at the same time as Jenson fell in sync beside me. I reached out to take his hand. He accepted it in his drawing me near.

"They're going to be heroes," he added, smiling.

"Mmm hmm, if all goes as intended. Be primed to intervene with the Kalie sticks, or that bear kicking thing."

"Will do," he replied, then planted a kiss on my forehead.

Chapter 45

5 a.m.

Patrick and Dan motioned for us to stop near a large Oak tree. Sensi, who'd switched back into her owl form perched on the branch above us. Shellena stood underneath the tree scanning the area for Lance. I could see him and Sina as they circled the shack. When he saw us, he nodded to Sina, took hold of her shoulders, then pushed her our way. Minder held her finger to her lips indicating silence. Bonnie, Zane, and Rob appeared in a daze, loopy from the tranqs. Not a word was spoken as she sprinted toward us. I leaned into Jenson, and he held me close while Maine and Molly huddled near us. Cal appeared unsettled standing next to Eva and Tri. I watched Megan draw Trigger close to her side.

"Mara's been grilling Jinx on the Bandits for hours. He's ready to crack so we need you to hand them over immediately," Sina stammered.

"Let me at her! I tried to get Sensi to take me to her on Wednesday, but no! Look at me! I'm a freak, just like all of you!" Sika erupted moving his hands in cuffs about in a rage.

"Shut up you'll get us all killed!" Sina snarled, looking back to see if Mara had emerged.

"It couldn't hurt, at least not me," he replied.

Patrick hit him upside the head, then pushed him over to Sina. "Go, before we change our minds," he muttered.

Gavin and Gladiator chuckled as they shook their heads at Sika. They followed him to where Sina stood.

"Come on. You'll get your opportunity to settle the score. Remember, we want them alive when the officers arrive."

"What about us? I thought we were getting immunity," Gavin moaned.

"Not if your ring leader keeps up his antics. You better keep him in line, or we'll send you to be experimented on further. I'm sure the officers will want more specifics when they find the chemicals in the shack," Sina threatened.

Gavin shuddered at the remark, and they awkwardly bumbled en route to the shack. We stood there observing them as they went. Sika practically ran trying not to fall on his face with his cuffs in front of him. Gladiator followed close behind while Gavin had to be shoved by Sina to move. He looked petrified at what was to come.

"What now?" I whispered to Tri.

"Wait til Mara is outside in a frenzy. Once Sina lets him out of the cuffs, and they start fighting, run. Right now we'll crawl along the perimeter of the wooded area close to the shack. We'll angle ourselves, so we're across from it. Owl and Jenson, after the girls and Minder, get inside you'll dash out with Kali sticks," Dan instructed.

"What! Us, against them?" Owl choked.

"I'm afraid so. We'll need as many distractions as possible. Starla, take Megan's hand, prepare to link. If you need to use your displacement spell for safety, do so."

"Okay, dad."

"Get ready, One, two, three….."

Megan's hand gripped mine firmly. Gradually we crept discreetly along the west side of the wooded area. My free hand shook while the other sweated profusely. Jenson and Owl kept gazing at us as they inched further on. The goal was for us to get across to the shack before Mara discovered we were there. Minder slunk down low next to us. I caught Lance eyeing us from the east side, and I wondered how Shellean was feeling. She hadn't stepped in but had stood by Sensi protecting her. I guess you did what you had to under these circumstances.

"Don't worry. I've got your backs. At present we must rescue the innocents," Trigger whispered.

I gave him a thumbs up only he could see as he drew himself closer to Megan while we moved. Eva and Cal had gone back so they could meet us in the van after the rescue. Cal hadn't been happy about leaving me behind, but I'd reassured her I would be fine. She almost wouldn't let go of me when we'd hugged goodbye. I wasn't sure it was a good idea, but who was I to argue? Later we would take the animals to Hunters Park, where Cavin had a hut prepared for them. Dan and Patrick would be obliged to fill out paperwork at the local station. How would they hide the Bandits from the authorities? I hoped they had that one figured out. Maybe they'd have Owl and Jenson deal with it. I shivered just as Owl spotted Mara engaged with Sika in a wrestling match.

"Let's Go!" Minder pressed.

Megan and I bolted out in front of her accelerating rapidly upon the shack. My heart pounded as I tried not to look at Mara and the Bandits. I hoped they'd keep her busy! I heard them yelling, and hollering out at one another. Something about the army's orders, how it affected them all including Sika. What? He'd never been in the military? I scoffed, as Minder sprinted in front of Megan and me. We followed close behind her panting nearly out

338

of breath. Minder go-go! You're almost to the door. I thought, watching as she reached for it, ready to fling it open. Mara turned and her gaze met mine. Sika dove in her direction as she charged at me. He tried to grab hold of her, but wasn't quick enough! I scrambled backward, falling. Then got up and did a double take realizing Gavin and Gladiator were trying to run with cuffed hands to attack her. I let out a screech when Jenson leapt out of the woods with Owl at his side. They were throwing Kali sticks all over the place. It didn't matter because Mara crawled underneath them, then hurled herself at me. Immediately I curled myself into a ball, and rolled out of her way, jumped up on all fours and ran fast! Fox fast? Had I changed, I hadn't even felt it. Shiznit! I was trotting but didn't stop to inspect myself. "Open it now!" I yelped at Minder.

I didn't even look but went on faith launching myself where the door should have been.

Chapter 46

As the door slammed shut behind me, I heard Tri yelling at Maine to use the tranqs. I crashed on the floor in a heap exhausted, but I couldn't stay down for long. I lifted my head up slightly grimacing at Trigger beside me.

"It's okay, your safe now," he reassured me.

"For how long, unless Maine can tranq her, I bet she bursts in," I remarked.

"Megan's moving the cabinet in front of the door now," he added. I moved my eyes to the right of me and watched her pull it there. She crouched down low inching towards him, then sat down.

"It looks like Sika and his gang are giving them, hell out there. Minder's searching the place for Jinx. I thought I heard him whimper towards the back there," she commented.

I stood up, stretched, then closed my eyes to change back.

"Wait, Sis. Maybe you should stay a fox for your safety," she murmured laying a hand on my back.

"Why didn't you guys help me? Especially Minder," I snapped, irritated they'd assume I didn't need their help.

"I thought it would be better to let you fight your own battle. I knew you could handle yourself in the way you're growing as a Kitsune fox. Nayla would have done the same thing. Megan, on the other hand, needs our protection. She's just beginning her journey with our clan. Now, where did Minder take off too?"

"Let me switch quickly then we'll find out. Jones said this living area is separated into sections," I responded. Then stood up on my hindquarters to get a better look at our surroundings. I swung my body to the left away from any windows, shuddered at the noises outside and afterward it was like a light switch flickering. There were a few seconds in which I felt transparent, and my body morphed.

"Cool," Megan marveled. No longer grossed-out by my transformation.

"That was weird," I added, peering at a curtain hanging from the ceiling. It was right in front of us, and then off to the side stood a privacy screen. In between them, a small opening existed allowing one to enter either one. Wouldn't Trigger have seen Minder go in there? Cautiously I stepped in front of the curtain, then pulled it back jumping as I did.

"Nothing, but equipment in here, but what about to the left of it?"

"It's where they store them," Minder disclosed waving us into the small area.

"Jinx, did you find him? Is he here?" Megan pressed as she came up behind me, accompanied by Trigger.

My eyes grew wide at the immense amount of beakers and vials. They sat on a large metal table resembling a kitchen island. Some were full of strange fluids, but a few looked like they held blood samples. Along the bottom of it were several drawers.

"Don't touch anything. The two foxes in holding are sedated along with Jinx. Mara must have dosed them anticipating our arrival. She knew they'd cry out for help. I've been searching through their supplies. They'd use these adrenaline shots on us, to wake us up. Then sedate us when needed. They've got to be around here somewhere!" Minder exclaimed, bending down to search underneath the metal table I'd been eyeing.

"Ah ha! I found two. I'll wake up Jinx first, then one of the foxes. Starla, check on the other side and see if there are any more drawers," she ordered. Then meandered over to the cages covered with drop clothes to look like tables. One was by itself and the other two positioned side by side. All of them sat against the far wall to the right. Megan and I hustled to the other side of the table, bent down and discovered two more drawers adjacent to each other. I pulled it open at the same time as Megan did the other. There were clothes, bandages, tape, scissors, including aspirin in mine. I shut it turning to see what she'd found. Megan held up several syringes marked Adrenaline.

"I think I found their stash," she smirked.

"Yeah, but we only need one. Are there any sedatives? They could come in handy with Mara out there," I added, waving my thumb near the exit.

"We're leaving Mara to the others. Maine may even have her tranqued by now. If that's the case they'll head back with us," Trigger acknowledged nodding towards Jinx. He was blinking his eyes trying to adjust them to the light.

"Uh… what are you doing here? Is everyone Okay? Minder. Mara, she's been threatening to turn us over to the government. That… we're going to be utilized for some super warfare plot," he whimpered.

Minder stroked his head in slow movements to calm him. "No, no. We're here to free you and these foxes. We're going to take everyone back to Hunter's Park. Now, do you know if anyone gave them any chemicals? Have you been infected yet?"

"Not me, no. I'm not sure about the foxes. They bark alert signals trying to find their folks. They're just young ones. Mara's not especially patient with them," he stated.

"Hopefully the queen of evil is sedated now," I said rolling my eyes. Megan, Trigger and I moved closer to Jinx. Minder took her hand off of his head turning to face two cages that sat side by side.

"I need that syringe," she pressed.

Megan moved quickly handing it to her.

"Thanks," she replied, kneeling down to unlatch the cage with her free hand.

"Wait! What do we do when they wake up? Won't they freak out on us?" Megan asked.

"At first yes, but what choice do they have but to trust us? We're rescuing them," Minder hissed. Carefully, she reached in injecting the first fox. It jolted it's head up letting out a startled yelp. Then backed up against the cage staring straight at Trigger. After he'd barked several times at the fox, it came out of the pen and stood next to him.

"What did you do?" I asked.

"Her name is Swift, and that's her brother Fargo. They were in the woods when they were captured," he answered.

Swift nudged Trigger again, then barked something quietly into his ear. She still appeared pretty frightened.

"Well, wake him up now!" Trigger ordered, pointing his nose at Fargo.

"Jinx, I'm sure is alert enough to creep out of here with us. Aren't you Jinx?" asked Megan.

"Yeah, these scientists are nuts! You should have seen Zane tare out of here, and afterward Mara and her threats. Come on now, hurry!"

"Okay. Send Swift over so she can clarify, he's safe," Minder instructed, opening the cage.

Trigger relayed the message in a few short barks. Swift nodded to him, then trotted near the cage, leaving room for Minder to place her arm inside to administer the adrenaline. When she'd finished the first thing Fargo saw was Swift. He struggled to stand but wobbled somewhat before he was able to regain his balance. A few minutes later he bolted out of the cage nuzzling against her chest. She put her head down, whispering to him in muffled barks. I couldn't make it out but figured she was reassuring him.

"Now that everyone's awake shouldn't we make sure Mara's sedated before trying to get these guys to the van?" Megan questioned.

"No duh!" I blurted.

"Starla, come on. Let's go out into the living area. I'll peek out and see what's going on. If the coasts clear we'll check in with Dan and Patrick."

"Great, but grab a few of those sedatives just to be safe," I advised.

Minder let out an annoyed groan while standing to stretch. Trigger, Megan, Swift and I scrambled to the exit. I kept an eye on Minder to make sure she'd grab the loot. When I saw it in her paw, I stepped into the living area. I couldn't hear anything outside. Not a peep, and it had me on edge. I tiptoed to the window to look out. I felt Megan place her hand on my shoulder, leaning over me to see.

"What's going on?" Minder asked.

"Mara is in cuffs, not yet sedated and Sika is wailing on her. Oh, and now Sina is pulling him back!" I had to try to stop myself from dancing in place. Then glimpsed back at Minder, "That hybrid wolf is tough, even in handcuffs!" I exclaimed, turning away from the window.

"Let's jet!" Jinx pressed.

"No, it looks like Maine is tranqing her."

Minder came up beside me and lifted the curtain back further to get a better view. We stared through the window pane til the scientists were sedated, then she opened the door.

I shielded my eyes while I walked outside. Swift and Fargo stayed close to Trigger as we made our way to my dad. He and Patrick milled about with walkies in their hands appearing ready to make the call. Megan inched closer to me, and I took her hand. Afterward stopping to scan the area for Jenson. Where was he? I caught sight of Sika beating the ground with his fists in anger, while Gladiator tried to grab them with his free hand. Gavin sat quietly annoyed scowling at them both. I was considering asking my dad when Maine and Molly came running up to us with Tri alongside them. I glanced at Sina and Trax moving quickly towards the Bandits. My dad and Patrick held the walkie-talkies out in front of them. Zane, Rob, Bonnie, and Mara lay in a heap sedated.

"Mom! What's going on? Where are Jenson and Owl? Are the authorities coming to take the scientists in?" I babbled.

"Take a breath, relax, center yourself," she instructed.

I closed my eyes, breathed in, then out, and rolled my shoulders back. A soft hand settled around my torso, then pulled me near. I felt Megan's hand slip out of mine. Then turned to see Jenson beside me.

"It's going to be fine. Dan and Patrick are staying with the scientists until the officers get here. They'll escort them back to Springville shortly. Minder, Sina, and Trax offered to take the Bandits back in the other van. Shellena and Lance are hoofing it home. Sensi's flying there, plus they want to make sure she arrives unharmed. I'm not sure why they're walking. Maybe she's afraid of the Bandits," Jenson whispered.

I opened my eyes, turned, and exhaled the breath I'd been holding in.

"Owl and I were guarding the perimeter of the shack. Everyone else kept the Bandits in line while Maine and Molly were our back up," he added, nodding to them.

"So you were behind the shack, and just came out... of-of hiding?" I asked dumbfounded.

"Yeah, and we've got to get back. Cavin wants the foxes in the hut, and to talk with Jinx," he stressed.

"Alright, it sounds like another long day," I groaned.

Chapter 47

6 a.m.

I leaned on Jenson as we walked, wondering what Cal and Eva had done to pass the time while we kicked major butt. Sina and Trax had gathered up the Bandits and were hiking in front of us with Minder. I smiled at Owl who strolled close by at a steady pace. Then tried to tune out everyone around me for a moment nuzzling into Jenson. That is until I heard a rustling that caused me to look up. I placed my hand on my chest as the squirrel raced out of nowhere. Jenson patted my back, reassuring me, then nodded as it scrambled up a tree with a nut, it's mouth. Megan meandered along with Trigger, Swift, and Fargo. No one was attempting to be stealthy as they spoke back and forth to one another.

"How are you holding up?" asked Owl.

I shrugged, then peered back at Molly and Maine whispering to one another. We stopped to let them catch up.

"Hey, you two! Why so glum?" asked Maine.

"Yeah, almost everything went as planned! I didn't even need to heal anyone," Molly smirked.

"First, I've been up the entire night without any caffeine to speak of and chased down evil villains. I hope Cavin, Mike or someone has it on tap when we get there. I'll need it to stay awake during our revamp. Plus, screech and Jenson have the spring market thing, if you're still going. Then to top it all off my entire body aches from those maneuvers avoiding Mara. As exciting as it's been I'll be glad to snuggle under my covers this evening. I hope we don't have any more adventures for a while."

Jenson chuckled, " I can't say the same. Since I met you, Starla, I've had more excitement in my life than I've had in years."

"Really?" I asked, pulling him near. He leaned his face down towards mine.

"Absolutely, the total impact of romance and risk."

I blushed and slapped him playfully on the shoulder. He moved an arm's length away.

"No, I mean it!"

Minder turned around to face us as she marched backward. "We're nearly there. Come on, crew! Cal and Eva are waiting for us. I'm sure they're ready to get back to the dining hall. Sina and Trax are supposed to meet Cavin so he can give them the location to release these guys."

"And they better not give us any further problems, or we'll have no choice but to annihilate them," Trax grunted, pushing Sika forward. Sina grasped Gladiator and Gavin, who didn't appear as irritated.

I shivered at the remark but understood why Trax felt this way. I was super surprised the Bandits hadn't fought to stay to watch the scientists get reprimanded, but that would have meant they would've been taken in as well. Sika glowered at Trax, and we entered the path leading to the vans.

I expected Cal and Eva to jump out to greet us, but as the sun rose on the horizon and the birds began to chirp there was no sight of them. I guess they were sleeping inside. I took in a deep breath, shaking off the escapade of earlier this morning. Jenson squeezed my hand, then let go to open the van door. I waited while everyone clambered inside.

Where was my mom? Had she stayed behind to help? I put my hand up to my head, then turned to ask Jenson as Minder stepped up beside us.

"Tri, my mom. She stayed behind to meet with them too?"

"Yes, and Sensi's flying back presently with Shellena and Lance." Minder acknowledged.

"Sorry, I'm out of sorts. No caffeine, a tumble with a scientist and…"

"You and Jenson get inside the van. I'll radio Cavin to have some coffee ready for us. It shouldn't be an issue, and if it is, we'll stop for some. The goddess knows we deserve it after what we've been through."

I nodded to her while Jenson kindly helped me in. I didn't stop to see where anyone sat. Instead, I took the nearest seat beside him, shutting my eyes while he put my safety belt on for me. I laid my head against his shoulder and listened while Minder started up the van, and afterward slipped into what I thought was sleep.

The warm sun lifted my spirits as I sat in the field of wheat. I told myself that my only concern now was college, Jenson, my friends, oh and yeah my clan of course.

"Starla?"

I lifted my head up opening my eyes to see Amare trotting through the golden wheat towards me. I started to get up to stand, but she put her hand out to stop me.

"Wait, I'll come sit with you."

"Alright, it feels so serene being here now; After all that's happened recently," I replied.

"As I've meant it to be my dear one. Nayla wishes you to know she's proud of you. It's as she hoped it would be. Molly and Maine will help Minder with the recovery of Fargo and Swift."

"So they'll be alright?"

"Faith and our clan will be in perfect harmony. As-is with Maine and Molly in spite of the worlds detrimental judgments."

"Jenson and I.. We.."

"Yes, and that time has come. Growing up, getting your 2nd tail! I'm giddy for you girl!"

I smiled, then blushed.

"Remember, there is no rush but in your time."

I nodded to her as she laid down beside me.

"Now fall, sleep, dreamless, float free within your soul. And when you wake, you'll feel restored, and there will be coffee."

I was so spent I couldn't even giggle. I just drifted...

Chapter 48

10 a.m.

Minder ushered us out of the van and into the hut that led to the dining hall. She wouldn't even let us in on where the Bandits would be released. It was only for the elders and those involved to know. I sighed as we wandered through the hallway with pictures of the past. I thought about the girl in the photo. The one Jenson had pointed out to me and wished I'd been able to meet her. Still, I knew nothing of her except she was some kind of hero. Star, Kaya, Nayla, Cavin, all of them had entered my life unexpectedly. I'd fit in with my strange abilities unlike L.A. I reached out to take Molly and Maine's hands. They grasped mine in theirs pulling me aside as Jenson and Owl disappeared into the Dining hall.

"I wanted to tell you how sorry I am for how horrible; I was when Molly and I were fighting. You've supported me with being Wiccan. Mol and me being together, and we'll always be here for you," Maine assured me.

"I what's this about?" I asked.

"It's just we heard you talking to your mom about wanting to take the next step with Jenson," Molly beamed.

I blushed, embarrassed, "does everyone know?"

"If they do, it wasn't from us. You haven't asked him yet, have you?" Molly inquired.

"Heck no. I'm waiting for the right time, but it still feels rushed. You guys. I mean Mol you wanted to wait," I pressed.

"Things change. Anyway, we should get in there. You haven't spoken to Cal at all since we've been back. We should sit with her," Molly advised.

"Yeah, good idea. Plus Minder promised coffee," I grinned.

Pink and green streamers were strung up on the ceiling in addition to balloons floating in each corner of the room. A large sign that read congratulations hung on the far back wall. I smelled bacon, toast, eggs, and most importantly coffee! French Vanilla to be exact. I let go of Maine and Molly's hands, but they pulled me into a tight hug. Then let go.

"Let's get something to eat. I'm in need of sustenance," I gushed, spotting Cal next to Eva. My stomach grumbled while my friends followed me over.

"It's good to see you made it back unharmed," said Dan, wiping the sweat from his forehead. Mom sat next to him in silence, smiling at me. "I stayed busy helping Trigger and Minder with the kits. It kept me from agonizing over it too much."

"Is the banner for us?" I asked, sitting down. Molly and Maine pulled out chairs next to one another.

"Um, no. I'm told once everyone is here the secret will be revealed," Cal grinned joining us.

"Hmm, I wonder if it has anything to do with the secret girls meeting we were supposed to have," I jested.

"It could be," Eva commented.

My mom just nodded as she ate.

I reached over cramming my plate with food, then filled my cup with coffee. Megan raced up beside us with Trigger at her side.

"Good news, Trigger says he can stay with me for good, in this form!"

Trigger gave us a lopsided smile and hopped up on the chair next to Maine. Megan sat down on the other side of him. Then helped herself to provisions.

"I'd pat you on the back, but my arms don't reach that far," I told Trigger. Afterward, taking a sip of the excellent warm vanilla brew.

"Just do me a favor, don't ever let me drink coffee again," he exclaimed pointing his snout at my cup.

I chuckled, then watched while more friends and family appeared at the table.

A little later…

The room fell to a hush as soon as Rascal and Nuria came through the dining hall door. I was starting on my 2nd cup of Java when it happened. She was dressed in a beautiful rose print dress, and he wore black dress pants along with a matching jacket. Odd for Rascal because he never dressed up. They swaggered to the front of the table holding hands. He stopped, then bent down on a knee, pulling out a ring. Rascal's hand quivered as did his voice while he spoke.

"Nuria, my sweet friend. At this instant justice has reigned in the clan, our family, my native people." He paused and swallowed holding back tears. "Would you be my wife?"

A bright smile formed on Nuria's lips, and she bent down to gaze into his eyes. Then leaned in planting a soft, sweet kiss on his lips.

"I guess that's a yes!" he exclaimed, placing the ring on her finger.

"It's beautiful. A ruby, with small diamonds surrounding it. Oh, thank you so much for everything," she blurted.

"No, thank you. Let's celebrate with everyone. The girls have a special surprise for you before the wedding."

I looked at my mother who mouthed to me, bachelorette party. I smiled back, giving her thumbs up, Jenson pulled me close, kissed me, and then Maine and Molly started to cheer. I felt the warmth of my family and friends surrounding me. No one was left out of our celebration except well the Bandits of course.

Epilogue

Dear Diary

I can't believe all the joy that has come from Nuria and Rascal's union. It's only September, and they already have a little one on the way. I don't especially want my own little ones, but I can't wait to babysit for Nuria's! I'm not sure how to tell Jenson this. We've talked about marriage, but it's just too soon for us. He's great with dealing with my work shifts at Denny's alongside college, and then the clan. He even got me the last season of Buffy! Now that's what I call being a superhero. Mom and dad weren't thrilled when he moved in, but they're dealing. I guess just as I dealt with them, keeping secrets from me for so long. Megan's becoming more and more immersed in the clan, which kind of scares Tri. Oh, I mean Mom. Jez…

Mol is still living at home for now. My guess though is she and Maine will eventually get a place. That's in spite of the fact that she sleeps over here now and again. I still need my best friend. Cal's been hassling Eva about moving in with me.

Then yesterday I came upon Cavin in his study. It was after a shift at work, and I'd decided to stop by. It was nice not having to walk in the cold since Dad finally helped me pick out a used car. I started discussing Nayla and her kits, and when would she be coming to visit. Soon, soon, but first I think you've earned the right to know where the Bandits are located.

I mean, what! Where did that come from and what did I do? I asked him, and Cavin replied: saved us. Starla, you and your friends. I don't think we could have ever captured them if you hadn't joined us. It all had a domino effect on us. Each step you took: saving Cal, the trial for the Bandits, it all led to the scientists being assessed by the government. Now that they're in prison we're safe. That's until some other nut decides we're a threat.

My heart leaped then, and it was so right if anyone discovered us, people who couldn't handle us, our diverseness then we could all be eliminated. I'd seen the real world, people hurting people. It happened all the time. So then I asked him.

O'kay where are they? And he told me. Nope, I can't tell you, not even you-diary because if I did someone could read the words, even Megan. But this is the end of my story. The clan is safe, I've got Jenson, my family, and Maine and Molly are free to love each other. All is well, and maybe someday another's story will begin.

The End

Angela K. Crandall

Author's note:

I'd like to thank you for reading Seeking Justice. It isn't always easy to sit down and put my pen to paper. Starla and Jenson mean the world to me. I hope you've grown to love them as much as I do. Their hearts see more than black and white. My goal as a writer is to share our differences through my characters. While this is the last book in this series, I'm planning to release a poetry book soon. Until then you can find me on Facebook, Twitter, and Instagram.